Cat

R C Hilty

R C Hilty

NEWMAN SPRINGS PUBLISHING
320 Broad Street
Red Bank, NJ 07701

First originally published by Newman Springs Publishing 2020

ISBN 978-1-64801-511-3 (Paperback)
ISBN 978-1-64801-512-0 (Digital)

Printed in the United States of America

1

Cat looks through the lens of the SN-3 T-Pal, the best rifle scope US Optics had to offer, which is mounted on a Surgeon rifle, chambered in .338 Lapua Magnum. She starts to wonder, *How did I end up here? In four days I'm to be at the firing line of the largest long-range competition in the world, the Big Shoot.*

The Big Shoot, a competition like no other, is to start in four days. Never has so much prize money been made available to long-range rifle shooters. This will be to a shooter as Frontier Days is to a cowboy.

Next will be a turning point in Cat's life. This is not a competition where a miss will just mean a lower score. The next three rounds she fires from her rifle will be more important than any competition. Hiding behind a pile of firewood under a tree, she is all that stands between three terrorists and the hundreds of people trapped on the highway.

She looks down at the three cartridges that she had picked out. It reminds her of the biblical story, *David and Goliath*, when David picked up five smooth stones to fight the giant Goliath. She knew she will need the Lord's help just as much, if not more than David did. Her eyes wandered over to her brother, who is looking through the spotting scope-and-range finder, punching numbers into his laptop. She had always depended on him and his math skills, especially trigonometry. Now would be no different. This will be a tough shot, over 1,700 yards, uphill into the bright sunlight.

Cat is confident that they have picked out a good spot that will keep the sun from reflecting off their equipment and giving away their position to the terrorists. She looks over to her brother one more time. He looks up at her and nods. She puts a cartridge in the chamber and closes the bolt. She has less than three seconds to fire three accurate, well-placed shots. All three have to hit the mark, or hundreds of men, women, and children will perish, including her dad and brother. She puts herself in a bubble, slows her heart rate, and wishes she had not had the third cup of coffee this morning. She says a prayer, places her finger on the trigger, and slowly starts to squeeze...

*****

Catherine, who went by Cat, was born in upstate New York, the youngest of three children. In the early summer of 2009, her dad, Dave, had lost his job as a bank vice president due to downsizing. He researched the job market in the surrounding areas, traveling to Albany and New York City for interviews with a couple of the major banks. After searching all summer and no results and not wanting to go back to working all the time with no time for the family, he decided to do what he had always wanted to do but never had the guts to before. He called Greg Campbell in Kentucky. Greg had been taking care of a cabin that had been left to Dave by an uncle. He knew that his wife, Betty, would think he had taken too many pain killers, but what the hell—you only live once.

A few days after his call to Greg, Dave called a family meeting. It had been awhile since the whole family had been together at one time. After Betty and the children, Cat, Ben, and Liz, sat down around the kitchen table, he said as matter of fact, "We are selling everything we own and moving to Kentucky."

Betty's sarcasm cut like a knife, "What have you been smoking?"

Dave replied, "Nothing. I'm getting tired of the rat race. We have that cabin that Uncle Jeff left me."

"What will you do for income?"

"I'll find something."

"I'm not going to live out in the boondocks away from civilization or in some hick town where everybody knows your business.

No way am I going to carry water from the river or wash clothes on a rock."

"I said we're moving to Kentucky, not to some third world country. Believe it or not, they do have running water and indoor plumbing there."

"I don't care. I like it here."

"Hey, Dad, I think it's great. You know how much I love to hunt and fish. We can live off the land!" Cat chimed excitedly. It had always been her dream to live somewhere in the wild. She always knew that she had been born 150 years too late.

Betty shook her head and went into the kitchen. It didn't matter much what she said or did. Without Dave having a well-paying, job there was no way they could afford to stay where they were.

"I don't want to live where I can't get on the Internet," Ben said.

"There is more to life than the Internet and video games," Cat responded.

"Like what? Going off living in the wild, eating what you can shoot and catch?"

"That's a lot better than burning your eyes out staring at the computer."

Liz shook her head as she went to her room. It didn't matter much to her, because she would be going off to school soon anyway.

*****

The next month Dave had an auction, selling the house and everything else that they were not taking with them. With his severance pay and cashing in some of his 401(k)s, he was able to pay off everything he owed, including the vehicles.

Dave rented a trailer to pull behind his pickup. It took some doing, but they got everything they wanted to take to their new home loaded into the pickup, trailer, and van.

The family taking their time enjoying the trip they finally made it to a small town in Kentucky. The looks they got made Cat wonder if this was such a good idea. She had heard that little, close-knit towns, especially down South, didn't like outsiders moving in.

Dave stopped at the local gas station to fill up. Dave asked the attendant if he knew Greg Campbell. The attendant said, "That would be me. You must be Jeff Brewer's nephew."

"Yes, I am. Is the courthouse still open?" Dave replied.

"You look a little like him. You still have time to get to the courthouse before it closes. You can get a room at Harper's Motel. It's just outside of town. Stop back here at nine in the morning, and I'll show you the way to the cabin."

"I hope Uncle Jeff was right that this is a great place to live."

"It is, especially if you like a more laid-back lifestyle."

"I would sure like to give it a try."

"I like it."

*****

The next morning Dave woke up the family. They went to the local diner, ate breakfast, went over to pick up Greg, and headed for their new home. They drove about ten miles out of town and turned off the main road, if one could call it that. They drove up a winding road around five miles, and there, on a flat spot on the ridge, sat the cabin.

"Jeff had a new roof put on about a year before he died," said Greg.

"Great, looks like it is in good shape," replied Dave.

"I'd come up here every once in a while, cut the grass around the house, and make sure no critters had moved in."

"It looks like you have been taking good care of the place."

"Well, your uncle and I got along pretty good. I'd have hated to see the place go to hell."

"Thanks."

"My wife and daughter came up and cleaned it when we found out you were moving here."

Betty asked, "And just how long ago did he let you know we were moving down here?"

Greg figured it would be in his best interest to let Dave answer that question. It appeared as though Betty wasn't at all thrilled with move.

Dave said, "The day after we all talked about it."

Betty replied, "It was probably the day after you lost your job."

"Now, dear."

"Don't 'now dear' me!"

Dave knew there was no use arguing. She wouldn't believe him anyway. He was hoping his family would be able to blend in here. He knew one thing for certain: Cat would be able to.

"Dad," yelled Cat, "you won't believe what I saw!"

"What's that?" asked Dave.

"Three deer and about forty squirrels."

"Sounds like you will like it here."

"Oh yeah, I will! This is my dream! When's squirrel season come in?"

Greg replied, "Squirrel opens in two weeks. Opening day is a holiday in these parts, schools are even closed. The only places open are the diner and gas station."

Cat's eyes grew big as saucers when she heard that.

Betty walked into the cabin and started to check out the place. The appliances although older were in good shape. There was a woodstove, plus Uncle Jeff put in a new propane furnace. There wasn't any air-conditioning. Maybe they would be able to at least get a window unit by next summer. There were some big-shade trees close to the house that should help. The place wasn't quite as small as Betty thought it would be. He had built an addition this would be hers and Dave's bedroom. The other two would be divided between Ben and his sisters. Betty, Liz, and Ben knew to complain about moving down here would be useless. Dave liked it, and Cat loved it!

Dave and Greg unloaded the trailer first and started on the pickup. Dave said, "Amazing how those kids can disappear when there is work to do."

Greg replied, "Yeah, it is."

As Dave and Greg carried the stuff into the house, Betty said, "Just put the kitchen stuff by that wall. The rest of the boxes, you can pile in that corner by the closet."

"All right," said Dave.

While Dave and Greg finished unloading the vehicles, Betty walked through the house trying to figure out where to put what. She walked into the kitchen and opened some of the cupboards while thinking, *It looks like it has just been cleaned. That's good. One less thing I'll have to do.* She walked around, looking it over some more. *I guess this won't be too bad. Still I wonder what I was thinking when I said 'I do.' Mom was right when she said 'Love blinds.' That has to be the reason I married him."*

*****

Greg, Dave, and Cat went back to town while Betty, Ben, and Liz put the house in order. After they dropped Greg off at the station, Dave and Cat went to the store to buy some food and a few other supplies. Cat wandered over to the sporting goods like she always did. She went straight to the firearms section. A .17 rimfire Magnum rifle caught her eye. *Wow!* She thought. *I could hit a squirrel at one hundred yards with that!* She knew her parents couldn't afford one. She would have to make do with her single-shot .22 long rifle and her .410 shotgun for now.

"Cat," yelled Dave.

"Over here," answered Cat.

"Let me guess. A new rifle caught your attention."

"Yeah, a .17 rimfire Magnum, it's a beauty!"

"You know I can't afford anything except what we need."

"I know. I just like dreaming."

Dave smiled and laughed a little. "Let's get this stuff in the truck and get home before your mom sends a search party after us."

"Or heads back to New York."

Dave smiled a little. "I doubt she would be that extreme."

Cat smiled back. "You think the rest of the family will like it here?"

"Ben will probably do okay as long as he can find some way to get on the Internet. Liz will be going to school pretty soon, so she ain't really gonna care one way or the other."

"What about Mom?"

"Now, that could be another story."

Dave pulled up to the house. Cat said, "I hope it doesn't take Mom long to fix supper."

"The faster you get these groceries in the house, the faster Mom can get supper ready."

"We're home," yelled Cat as she brought the groceries into the house.

Ben said, "Should have known you would show up when the work was done."

Cat ignored him.

Betty had the kitchen stuff pretty much put away. Ben and Liz had moved everything to the rooms where they needed to be. Cat put the perishables in the refrigerator. The rest she put on the table.

While Betty fixed supper, Cat went outside to see what was in the area. Dave had inherited forty acres. Cat didn't know just how much that was. All she knew was that it was the biggest backyard she ever had. Three hundred yards from the house was a nice stream. This was Cat's dream come true. The area was filled with wild game, squirrels, rabbits, and deer.

"What a place! I can hunt, fish, camp, and trap within walking distance of the house." She thought she had died and gone to heaven.

"Cat," yelled Dad, "supper is ready."

"Coming," Cat answered as she walked back toward the house, passing the two car garage and a small barn.

"Where have you been?" Betty asked.

"Exploring!"

"Find anything?"

"You bet! There is a stream not too far from the house. I am going to get my fishing pole and catch tomorrow night's supper. You would not believe the wild game I saw. We won't go hungry!"

Great! Cat was serious about living off the land! Betty thought as they sat down to eat supper.

Dave said, "Greg told me that he could use some help at the station part-time a couple days a week. I told him that would be great. At least that will give us a little income till I find something better."

Betty replied, "I might as well give this a try. I've gone this far. I saw a 'Help Wanted' sign in the window at the diner. I'll stop in there the next time I am in town."

"That would be great."

"I have to go to town pretty soon anyway to register the kids for school."

"That's right, it is that time of the year."

"Uh, yeah, I am sure school starts here around the same time as it did in New York."

The family finished supper. Dave went out on the porch, sat down on the bench, and lit a cigar to enjoy the quiet evening. Ben and Liz cleared the table then went to their rooms. Cat went to the kitchen to help her mom with the dishes.

"Thanks," Mom said.

"No problem," replied Cat.

"Something on your mind?"

"Not really."

"Okay, what's on your mind?"

"Oh, Mom, it's just that I am so excited that we moved down here, and I didn't really think about how the rest of the family felt."

"I can honestly say that I am not as thrilled as you are, but who knows? It might grow on me."

Cat smiled. "I hope it does, because I don't want to move back to the city."

"We couldn't afford it now anyway. Thanks for helping with the dishes."

"You're welcome."

"You better get to bed. Your sheets and blankets are by the closet. Good night."

Cat kissed her mom. "Good night, love you."

Cat went to the door, opened it, and said, "Good night, Dad."

"Good night, honey, sweet dreams."

The next morning Cat ran into the kitchen and said, "Morning, Mom. That sure smells good."

"I thought bacon would bring you running. Do I have to ask if you want eggs?"

"No, you don't have to ask. Is the coffee done?"

"Yeah, the second pot, your dad finished off the first one."

"Great! I'll grab a cup and talk to Dad on the porch till breakfast is ready."

"Okay, I want you to help me with the dishes when we're done. Ben and Liz are going to town with Dad."

"Oh, all right."

After breakfast Dave and the two older children went into town to buy what they would need for the rest of the week. Dave also wanted to price freezers. For as much opportunity that Cat would have to hunt and fish, they would definitely need one.

As Betty and Cat finished up the dishes, Betty asked, "Help me arrange the stuff in the house."

Cat smiled and laughed a little. "Would this be considered quality time?"

Betty smiled back. "Yeah, we'll call it that."

That afternoon, Dave, Liz, and Ben came home. Cat, who was outside, came in and yelled to Betty, "Mom, you won't believe the size of the freezer Dad bought! Boy, it'll take me a month to fill it!"

Cat ran back outside and said to her dad, "I'll have to hunt and fish quite a bit to fill this."

Dave replied, "Fill this, one and I'll get another."

Betty went outside and looked in the truck, then said to Dave, "Where are we going to put it? It won't fit in the kitchen."

"If it won't fit, I can put it in the garage. I just couldn't pass up this deal."

"Then I'll have to go to the garage to get the food."

"Now, you know that you'll have me or one of the kids get the stuff out of the freezer."

"Well, yeah."

"This one was on sale. I can always get a smaller one for the kitchen later. Who knows, they might have another sale."

Betty shook her head and went back inside the house.

*****

11

Betty yelled from the kitchen, "Breakfast's ready, come and get it."

Dave came in from the porch; the three children from their rooms and sat down at the table. As the food was disappearing from the serving dishes and appearing on the plates, Betty commented, "I don't know if my cooking's that good or if you guys are just hungry."

Dave replied, "Both."

"Yeah, I guess. Ben, you and Cat need to go to town with me so that I can get you two registered for school. Liz, would you be a dear and clean up the kitchen this morning?"

"I suppose."

Dave said, "Greg needs me to work later. Liz, you can ride into town with me, and we'll have lunch at the diner. Your mom can stop by the station on the way home and pick you up."

Liz smiled. "Quality time?"

"You bet."

After breakfast Betty, Ben, and Cat got into the car and goes into town. Before Dave went out on to the porch to drink another cup of coffee, he asked, "Liz, why don't you get a cup and join me?"

"I need to get the kitchen cleaned up."

"A few minutes won't matter."

Liz filled her coffee cup then walked out to the porch. "Yeah, guess you're right... Won't be long, I'll be off to school."

"Hard to believe, seems like yesterday you were just learning to walk."

Dave and Liz finished their coffee. Dave helped with the dishes. Liz really enjoyed spending time with her dad. He was gone quite a bit when she was younger. She knew he tried his best to spend some with her. Even so, she felt she had missed out.

*****

Betty pulled into the parking lot of the high school. This school was different from any school that Cat had seen before. It wasn't a very large building. The main entrance was on the north side. To the east were the track and football field. The west side had a baseball diamond. What really impressed her was the sign that told about the wildlife habitat area that was behind the school. It was an area where students could study nature. It even had a small lake. Cat knew she would have to check this out before they went back home. The last line on the sign, she didn't much care for.

NO HUNTING OR FISHING IN WILDLIFE HABITAT AREA.

Cat said, "Hey, Mom, I'm gonna check out that wildlife area behind the school."

"All right, don't take too long. I'll register your brother first, should take about a half hour."

Cat walked back to the wildlife habitat area. Trails wound through the trees. Bird feeders and houses were set up throughout the trees. Signs by the feeders explained the type of birds which frequented each type of feeder and what type of feed each species ate. There were even areas with tables and chairs set up. She learned later that some of the science and biology classes are held out here, weather permitting.

The students had done most of the construction work on the habitat. It started out as a project to get the students interested in coming to school. It worked better than expected. Each year something new is added, such as new bird or squirrel feeders. This year's project would be setting up places for the water fowl to nest. Cat would definitely fit in at this school.

Cat thought she had better head back to the school. As she was walking out of the area, a fat squirrel sitting on a "no hunting" sign started chattering at her.

Cat said, "Yeah, you're pretty brave knowing I can't have you for dinner."

*****

As Betty was filling out the paperwork, Ben looked through the list of classes that were offered. Ben would be a junior this year. His majors were math and computer science. After he filled out his class preferences, he looked at the after-school clubs. The computer gaming club caught his eye. They even designed new games. There was a national contest every year sponsored by computer companies and software giants. The grand prize was a scholarship to a top college. The lesser prizes were new computers and equipment for the school. Ben thought to himself, *This school could sure use some new computers. I bet I can help them win some.*

Betty asked, "You have your class preferences filled out?"

Ben replied, "Yeah, and also my after-school clubs."

"I probably don't have to ask what they are."

"No, you don't. Computers one night and gaming another night."

"Should have known. Your sister back yet?"

"Don't know, I'll check."

"Thank you."

Cat walked in the door as Ben started out. "Hey, Cat, Mom's looking for you."

"Yeah. They have the neatest thing here. The wildlife area is great. Too bad I can't hunt there. I'm gonna like this place."

"I think I'll be able to tolerate it here. There are computer clubs and a video game designer club."

"You, your computers, and video games…"

"Makes more sense than trying to live 150 years ago," replied Ben.

"Whatever."

Betty said, "Come on, Cat, we ain't got all day. I have filled out your papers. You need to pick out your classes and anything you would like to do after school."

"All right."

Betty handed her the form and list of classes and after-school activities to choose from. It was pretty basic. She had to take at least one semester of home economics. *Great,* she thought, *some goofy teacher is gonna try and teach me how to cook. My mom can teach me all I need to know about cooking.*

The after-school activities caught Cat's eye. "Yes, rifle club!" she yelled.

Betty said, "I am so glad that you're able to control your excitement."

"No problem, Mom."

"Let's get in line to see the counselor. Your dad has absolutely no idea what he is missing out on."

Betty sat down with Cat. The counselor went over the classes Cat had signed up for. He went on to explain that some after-school activities were held off school grounds, such as the rifle club. An orientation meeting would be held in the gym next Monday at 7:30 PM. School would be starting the following Wednesday.

On the way home after picking up Liz, Cat said, "I think I am going to like this school."

Betty replied, "Why is that, the wildlife area or the rifle club?"

Cat smiled, "Yes."

Liz asked, "They have a rifle club?"

"Oh! You wouldn't believe it, a rifle club *and* a wildlife habitat area with a pond."

"Sounds like at least you fit in down here."

"You bet!"

Within a couple of weeks, the family started to feel at home. Dave was working two or three days per week at the station. Betty was now working at the diner. She had expected a day or two a week, but it ended up being four or five. She worked the breakfast shift. The hours fit their schedule great. Since Dave worked in the afternoon, he was able to make sure that the children were up ready and off to school.

*****

In the third week of school, one of the smart-aleck boys walked up to Cat, knocked her books out of her hand, and called her a "four-eyed, girly-girl from the city."

As Bob started to get up after receiving a black-eye and bloody nose, he thought to himself, *This ain't the smartest thing I ever done.* Cat picked up her books and went on to class as though nothing happened.

That afternoon Cat rode her bike home unaware that even before she had left school, the whole town had heard what happened.

When she arrived home, she parked her bike and walked up onto the porch. Dave was sitting in his chair drinking a cup of coffee and smoking a cigar.

"Anything exciting happen at school this morning?" asked Dave.

"Not really," answered Cat.

"Let me see your left hand."

"Why?" she said as she showed her hand to Dave.

"Leave a little of your knuckle on that boy today?"

Cat pulled her hand back. "Well, the last thing I need to hear is that I am a girly-girl."

"Diplomacy has never been a virtue of yours."

"How did you hear about it? I never got called to the office."

"News like that travels faster than a wildfire. I better go over and talk to Bob's dad."

"Oh, that's his name?"

Dave laughed as he put out his cigar and brought his coffee cup inside.

Betty walked into the house, saw Cat and Dave standing there, and said to Dave, "Did you hear what your daughter did today? It was the topic of conversation at the diner the entire day. The boy told the teacher that he tripped and fell." She turned to Cat and asked, "Well, what do you have to say for yourself?"

"He ain't gonna make fun of me again!"

Dave laughed. "Not if he has any smarts. I'm going over to Bob's house, talk to his dad, and see how he's doing."

Betty stared at Dave, not thinking any of this was funny.

Dave kissed Betty on the cheek. "I'll be home in time for supper honey."

It was all that Cat could do to keep from laughing. One of the unintended benefits of Mom getting mad was that she would calm herself down by cooking. There would be plenty of food for supper and lots of pies and cakes for the week. Dave and Cat had often been accused of getting Betty mad on purpose.

*****

Dave came home from work, grabbed a cigar, a cup of coffee, and walked out onto the porch to enjoy the evening while Betty was finishing supper. Betty filled a glass with lemonade, walked out to the porch, and sat down by Dave.

"What kind of enjoyment do you get out of smoking them stinky things?"

"Ah! A good cigar—one of the three finer things of life. I know you didn't come out here to complain about my cigars, so what's on your mind?"

"I'm kinda worried about Cat."

Dave set his coffee cup down, took a puff on his cigar, and set it in the ashtray, knowing this was going to be anything but a short conversation.

"You're worried about Cat? Grades falling, knocking another boy on his ass?"

"No, the teachers say her grades are good. Haven't heard anything about fights. I'm sure I would have at the diner."

"So what's the problem?"

"Cat went to the library to study while I was finishing up at the diner. When I picked her up, the librarian told me that Cat spent most of her time searching the web for information on long-range shooters, military snipers, and shooting matches both military and civilian. She showed me the book Cat had checked out, *93 Confirmed Kills*. It's about some sniper in Vietnam."

"Okay, what's the problem? You know she has always shown an interest in firearms."

"I know, but have you heard what she is going to write for extra credit in history?"

"No, but I am sure you're going to let me know."

"It's about some guy shooting an Indian off a horse at over 1,700 yards."

"That would have been Billy Dixon at Adobe Walls in Texas. Seven hundred Indians attacked the outpost. On the third day of the attack, Billy Dixon used a Big 50 Sharps and shot an Indian off his horse at a distance of almost a mile. The Indians called off their attack. I showed her that story on the web."

"Of course you did."

"She is doing fine in school. No longer than we have been here she has made quite a few friends. Almost everyone in the town knows her."

"Oh yeah, I don't know if that is a good thing or not. I am known as Cat's mom, not Betty. Still, she ain't normal. Most girls at her age are reading *Teen*, *Vogue*, or some other young-girl magazine. She is reading *Women and Guns* and *Outdoor Life*. She bookmarked a website called 'Girls Just Wanna Have Guns.'"

"Ain't normal? What is your first clue, when she made that cannon out of Pringle cans, knocked the flower pot off the porch, and broke the neighbor's window?"

"How can you be so calm? She hunts, fishes, and camps by herself. I heard her talking. She wants to take up trapping. She could get hurt."

"Yeah, I know. It ain't a good idea her going off by herself, but she has her cell phone."

"If she is in an area where there's service…"

"She will be fine. She has overcome a lot in her young age. In less than four years she sprained her ankle that took forever to heal, broke her leg, and broke her arm. Oh yeah, she also had that migraine that lasted over fourteen months, never letting up going to bed with it and waking up with it. We can't put her in a bubble."

"I guess you are right. I shouldn't worry. I am sure she will be fine. I'm gonna check on supper."

"What we having?"

"Squirrel. Cat has sure been bringing home some big ones."

"Where's she at now?"

"Hunting."

Dave got another cup of coffee and sat back down to finish his cigar. The phone rang.

Betty answered it, "Hello."

Cat said, "Mom?"

"Cat, you okay?"

"I'm not hurt if that's what you're concerned about."

"Okay, where you at?"

"In the county jail."

"Jail?" Betty turned her head and yelled, "Dave, Cat's in jail! You have to go get her!"

"What did she do?"

"What did you do?"

"I got caught squirrel hunting in the school's wildlife habitat area."

"You what?" yelled Betty. "Dave, you need to go get your daughter. She was hunting in that wildlife habitat area!"

"All right, calm down. I'll go get her."

"Calm down? That girl is going to be the death of me yet!"

*****

As Dave drove to town, a lot of things were going through his mind. He had pretty good kids. Liz was off to college. Ben was doing well in school, straight As. He never took a book home; math was a breeze to him. The top complaint from teachers was that he never wanted to show his work, and another was of him sleeping in class. There wasn't much that could be done because he always had the correct answer when the teacher woke him up. This would cause more embarrassment to the teacher than to Ben. Cat, on the other hand, had to work hard to keep her grades up studying every night. She knew she had to keep her grades up, or she wouldn't be able to stay in rifle club. She still found plenty of time to hunt and fish, maybe too much time.

Dave walked into the sheriff's office. It was stereotypical of the small town. The deputy behind the desk looked up.

"May I help you?"

Dave answered, "Yes, you're holding my daughter."

"Yes, have a seat. The game warden will be with you in a moment."

"Okay." Dave grabbed a magazine and sat down.

The game warden walked out and introduced himself to Dave. "I'm Officer Gene Conrad."

"I'm Dave, Cat's father. What did my youngest do to get a free ride here?"

"Well, I caught her coming out of the wildlife habit area with five squirrels. She did have her license, but hunting is prohibited in that area. I will keep her rifle till she has her court date."

"May I take her home?"

"I don't see why not. I called the judge. He should be returning my call pretty soon. I'll go back and get her." He left to let Cat out of the jail cell.

As she was brought up to the desk, Cat said, "Hi, Dad."

Dave replied, "Hello, Cat."

"What'd Mom say?"

"The usual…mad then worried if you're all right."

The deputy, after answering the phone, said to Officer Conrad, "Judge Bean is on the phone."

"I'll take it in my office."

After talking to the Judge Bean, Officer Conrad called Cat and Dave into his office. As they walked in, he said, "Have a seat."

Dave and Cat sat down. Cat watched as Officer Conrad filled out some papers.

Officer Conrad, as he handed Dave the release papers, said, "I talked to Judge Bean. He said, 'Since there is little chance of a flight risk, she can be released to her parents' custody.' Read the papers, sign, and date. You need to go in front of Judge Paul Bean nine Monday morning."

Cat asked, "Judge Paul Bean? Does his family tree go back to Judge Roy Bean, the hanging judge?"

Officer Conrad laughed a little. "Oh yeah, that's what got him interested in law."

"Great, first time in front of a judge, and I get a descendant of the famous hanging judge!"

Officer Conrad had a hard time not laughing. "Don't fret about it. The truth is Judge Roy Bean is known to have sentenced only two to hang, one escaped."

Dave and Cat, surprised, asked at the same time, "Really?"

Officer Conrad replied, "Yes, most of what you hear about Judge Roy Bean is Hollywood legend."

Cat replied, "'Hang 'em first, try 'em later' is Hollywood legend?"

"Oh, I'm sure he said that quite a bit. He did stage a few hangings, giving outlaws a second chance. After the *hanging*, they were never seen again in the area. He did fine a dead man $40, the amount he found on him. He used the money to buy a casket and pay the gravedigger. He kept the pistol and used it as a gavel in his courtroom."

Dave signed the release papers, handing them back to the warden. "Anything else?"

"No, that should do it till Monday morning. Hey, I'm supposed to destroy or give confiscated game to needy families. I'm kind of busy."

"We'll take care of it."

Officer Conrad smiled. "See you Monday morning."

Cat asked, "Will you wipe my rifle barrel down? I don't want it to rust."

"Sure, I'll do that."

*****

On the way home, Dave asked Cat, "Okay, why were you hunting in a no hunting area?"

"Lazy, I guess. I would see all those big, fat squirrels there every day when I went to school. They were a lot easier to get there than on state ground."

"Well, yeah, they're not used to getting shot at."

"Should have listen to my gut and quit after four. Just couldn't resist that last one on my way out. He was chewing on a nut and chattering at me."

"Did it ever occur to you that it may have been best not to hunt there? Chances are, this wasn't the first time the warden saw you. He knew you would be back. He just waited."

"How did you know this wasn't my first time?"

"The size of the squirrels your mom has been cooking. I was wondering where you were getting such big ones."

"I guess you know now. Think Mom waited supper on us?"

"Your guess is as good as mine."

Dave parked the truck in the driveway. As they get out, Dave said, "After supper I'll help you clean the squirrels."

"Thanks, Dad."

Mom had waited supper on them. Dave and Cat washed up before going to the kitchen table.

As they all sat down to the table, Ben said, "See ya made it home, jailbird."

Betty said, "Ben!"

"Well, she is."

Dave said, "All right, that's enough."

Betty asked, "So what's next?"

Dave answered, "I have to take Cat down to the courthouse Monday morning. We will find out then."

After supper, Ben helped Betty with clearing the table and washing the dishes. Dave and Cat went out to clean the squirrels. By the time they got back into the house, the rest of the family were in bed. Cat brushed her teeth and goes to bed. She was worried, hoping she would get her rifle back and not lose her hunting privileges. Eventually, she fell asleep.

2

Cat stood in front of the bench awaiting her fate.

The judge hit the bench hard with his gavel and yelled, "Who do you think you are, poaching wildlife in my county? You will spend thirty days in jail no visitors, and I'm going to keep your rifle. Bailiff, put the cuffs on her and get her out of here, NOW!"

Cat couldn't believe it. All this for just a few squirrels? As she was taken away, she could hear her mom yelling from the back of the courtroom, "Caaaat... Caaaat... CAT!"

All of a sudden, Cat sat straight up in bed, eyes wide open. She looked and saw Mom hovering over her.

"Honey, you okay? You need to get up and get ready. You and your dad need to be at the courthouse at nine."

Cat replied, "Uh, yeah. I'm fine. Coffee made?"

"Like every other morning. You sure you're okay?"

"Yeah, I am fine. I hope the hearing this morning goes better than the one last night."

"Bad dream?"

"You could say that."

"Go ahead and get a cup of coffee. Your dad's on the porch. Breakfast is about ready."

"Thanks, Mom."

*****

Dave and Cat walked into the courtroom. Cat signed in then sat down beside Dave. It looked as though hers was the first case of the morning.

Cat whispered to Dave, "I hope the judge had a good night's sleep."

"I'm sure you'll be fine."

The bailiff said, "All rise. The Honorable Judge Paul Bean, presiding."

Everyone stood up. The judge entered and sat down. The people sat down.

The bailiff said, "Court's in session."

The bailiff handed the Judge Bean some papers. He read them over than nodded to the bailiff.

Cat was called up to the bench.

Judge Bean said, "I see you're a minor. Is there a parent or guardian here with you?"

"Yes, Your Honor. My dad is here with me."

"Very well, let's get started. How do you plead?"

"Guilty, Your Honor."

"Let's see, Officer Conrad caught you coming out of the school's habitat area with a rifle and five squirrels."

"Yes, Your Honor."

"You have violated several laws, hunting in prohibitive area, firearm on school property, among other state, local, and federal laws. Why were you hunting there? There are plenty other areas that are legal for you to hunt."

"Your Honor, to be honest, I couldn't see any harm in it. The area is far enough away from the school. There were no other students in the area. Not only that, there are so many of them, plus they're so fat."

"So you figured why not, who's gonna notice?"

"Yes, Your Honor."

"That's all you have to say?"

"I really don't see the use of telling you that my family moved down here from New York because my dad lost his job. My parents don't have a lot of money, so I use my hunting and fishing skills to help my parents with the food costs. Like I said, the squirrels there were so plentiful and fat it didn't take long for me to get the next day's supper. I will accept whatever the court decides."

Dave was having a hard time keeping a straight face. Judge Bean just found out what Dave had learned a long time ago with Cat. Don't ask her to explain herself. Just give her the punishment you believe is fair. She'll take it in stride and move on.

In a way, Judge Bean was impressed with Cat. There had been plenty of juveniles that went through his courtroom. Most of the time they'd try to lie their way out of trouble. There was just something about Cat that he liked, the way that she accepted responsibility for her own actions. It was kind of refreshing to see a young person that was so honest and didn't try to blame others for her actions. He had heard the rumor that she had broken Bob's nose. Bob had been in court more than once. He was sure Bob had asked for it.

Judge Bean stroking his chin stared at Cat. He looked down at the papers on the bench. His stare then went over to Dave, then back to Cat, not saying a word. The silence was deafening to Cat. Her thoughts went to the dream she had last night.

After just a couple of minutes, but what seemed like hours to Cat, Judge Bean broke the silence.

"Young lady, I have several options on a case such as this. Like I said, you violated local, state, and federal laws. You seem to be a good kid. You also take responsibility for your actions. I checked with the school. The teachers say you are a hardworking student. You seem to do your best to help your parents. I am going to drop all the charges except hunting in an unauthorized area. You were caught with five squirrels. I see no sense in fining you, as your parents would end up paying the fine. Therefore, I'm sentencing you to eight hours of community service. I walk by the town park every day. The benches need a good coat of paint. You will show up at the courthouse at eight thirty Saturday morning wearing appropriate clothing. I'll take you down to the town garage where you will be given the tools and supplies you need." He looked at Dave. "It'll be your reasonability to make sure she is here."

Dave replied, "Yes, Your Honor."

"Are there any questions?"

Cat asked, "When may I have my rifle back?"

"When you have completed your service."

"Thank you."

"There are some papers for you and your dad to sign, and then you're free to go."

Dave and Cat walked over to the table, signed the papers, and left the courthouse. As they walked toward the truck, Dave asked, "You hungry?"

Cat smiled. "Yeah, a little."

"I don't like it when you say a little. That always means you're starving. We might as well stop over at the diner. I'm sure your mom will want to know how it turned out. After we eat, I'll drop you off at school."

"Okay."

*****

Betty knocked on Cat's door. "Honey, you need to get up. Breakfast will be ready pretty soon. You don't want to be late, might make the judge mad."

"Saturday morning already?" asked Cat.

"Yes, it is. It's supposed to be pretty nice today, sunny, around seventy degrees."

"Great day to paint park benches."

"I think you got off pretty easy."

"Yeah, you're right. Coffee ready?"

"Yes, you better get a cup pretty soon. Your dad is on his second one."

Cat rolled out of bed went to the kitchen and poured herself a cup of coffee. She walked out onto the porch.

"Morning, Dad."

"Good morning, Cat, ready to do some painting?"

"'Bout as ready as I'll ever be."

"It won't be too bad, nice day to paint."

"Yeah, you're right. I'm gonna finish getting ready. See ya at breakfast."

"Don't take too long."

"Yes, Dad."

*****

Judge Bean was looking over some paperwork when Dave and Cat walked into the courthouse. He looked up.

"Good morning, ready to get to work?"

Cat replied, "'Bout as ready as I'll ever be.

"That's the spirit." He looked at Dave. "Drive your pickup?"

"Yes, I did."

"Good, we can put the stuff she needs in that, and you can drive it over to the park. Meet me at the town garage. It is just down the street next to the fire house."

"Okay. See you there."

Dave drove his truck down to the garage. Judge Bean, Dave, and Cat loaded the paint and equipment into the truck.

After it was loaded, Judge Bean said, "Go ahead and drive over to the park, and park along the street by the benches. I'll be there shortly."

Dave replied, "All right."

Dave parked his truck by one of the groups of benches. It was a nice little park, plenty of shade trees, picnic tables, grills, and benches. People would bring their families for a cheap afternoon getaway.

Dave said, "Well, Cat, pick out the one you want to start on, and I'll help you carry the stuff over."

"Might as well start on the one that is in the shade, that way I can just follow the shade as the sun moves."

"That's my girl, always thinking."

Cat started scraping off the loose paint. One thing her dad taught her was that any job worth doing was worth doing well, even if it wasn't for herself. Not only that, she didn't want to do it over.

Judge walked up to Dave. "Let's go over to the diner and get a cup of coffee while she gets started. We can come back and check on her later."

Dave looked at Judge Bean a little hesitant. "Well, okay."

"She'll be all right. I asked the warden to keep an eye on her."

"Cat, I'm going with Judge Bean to get a cup of coffee. I'll be back. Your water jug is in the back of the truck."

"Okay, Dad, you know where I'll be."

*****

Judge Bean and Dave walked into the diner and sat down at a booth. The waitress came up to the table.

"Morning, Judge, the usual?"

"Yeah, no sense changing now."

The waitress turned to Dave. "And what can I get you?"

"I'll just have coffee."

"Okay, hon, I'll bring that right out. Cream, sugar?"

"No, black."

Judge Bean said, "I hope you like strong coffee."

"The stronger the better," Dave replied.

"So you lost your job in New York?"

"Yeah, I was the vice president of a big bank. I held on after 9-11, but when the housing bubble broke, that's all it took. They had to downsize."

"You inherited Jeff Brewer's place?"

"Yeah, he had wanted me to move down here before, but I had a steady job. He said this was like going back in time a hundred years, only with modern conveniences. He also said life was at a slower pace here. You could actually enjoy life."

"I bet your daughter is a handful."

"That she is."

"I have had a lot of people come through my court. I am semiretired now. I just take misdemeanor game violations, traffic, and juvenile cases. That helps free up the county courthouse. All the felony cases go there. The most we do for that is hold them overnight till they're transported. I'm enjoying my retirement. It gives me time to get involved with the people and hopefully keep some of the young people from getting into big trouble."

"How long you've been retired?"

"A little over five years, the county was going to close this court-house. We had a town meeting and came up with an idea to keep it open. We sent the plan in, and the state agreed to let us try it for a year to see how it worked out. The only full-time law officer here is the game warden, and he is paid by the state. All we have to do is keep an office here for him."

"Seems to be working."

The waitress brought Judge Bean his breakfast and refilled their coffee cups. "Can I get either of you anything else?"

"No, that should do it," Judge Bean replied.

Dave replied, "No thanks."

Judge Bean turned to Dave. "Like I said, I am a pretty good judge of character. I would say your daughter has strong convictions and will probably do about anything to help her family and anyone else that needs help."

"Oh yeah, she's a real good kid, although she has her moments. She'll help anyone that she can, even if it means bending the rules a bit."

"Noticed that. I talked to the school, they said that she does real well in class. Haven't had any problems with her. Although rumors have it that she knocked Bob on his ass."

"That was probably true."

"I am sure it was, but Bob's pride wasn't gonna let him say anything."

"I talked to his dad. That's what he figured. He said that maybe his son would watch his mouth from now on."

"I take it that Cat likes to hunt quite a bit."

"Yes, she also enjoys fishing, trapping, and camping anything that has to do with the outdoors and the wild. She is a very deter-mined child. Very confident and bullheaded...will take anything that is thrown at her in stride. I know her dream is to get into com-petitive shooting. She is reading everything she can get her hands on that pertains to long-range shooters. Whether it is military snipers, competing, or whatever, it doesn't matter as long as it has something to do with firearms. She is just fascinated with how a target can be hit from so far away."

"I heard she was doing well in rifle club, putting some of the seniors to shame. There's a local contest coming up pretty soon, entry fee isn't much. It is limited to rimfires."

"She'd love it."

"I'll give her rifle back to her today when she is done. Ya know, I have to say, I haven't seen many rifles like that with a scope."

"She would put a scope on a slingshot if she could. She'll be glad to hear she gets her rifle back. You'd thought she lost a family member when the warden kept it."

Judge Bean laughed. "Well, we'd better get back and see how she's doing."

"Yeah, I guess we'd better. Thanks for the coffee."

"You're welcome."

*****

The benches were in need of new paint. Cat scraped off the loose paint, sanded the rough spots, and put on a good primer coat. After she applied the finish coat, she stepped back admiring her work. Talking out loud, "That looks a lot better. I did a good job, if I do say so myself."

She looked at the other benches, which really looked terrible now. "I might as well start on the next one." She placed a *"WET PAINT"* sign by the bench she had just finished and moved all her stuff over to the next bench. There were a few clouds in bright sunny sky. She went to work on the second bench. The temperature was rising. It was definitely going to beat the seventy-degree mark forecast. Sweat kept getting in her eyes. A nice breeze would be welcomed about now.

An old man carrying a newspaper walked up to Cat and rudely asked, "What are you doing?"

Cat thought to herself, *You blind or what?* She turned toward him and asked, "What's it look like? I'm building a doghouse."

"No, you're not! You're painting the benches!"

"Then why ask?"

"Don't get smart with me, *girly*. I come to town every Saturday morning, buy a newspaper, sit on *this* bench, and read my paper.

Now you've painted it, and I can't sit there. You must be new here because everyone in town knows my routine on Saturdays."

Being called girly was one sure way to get Cat riled up. She really didn't want to be here in the first place. The bench looked real nice, and all he could do was complain about it. The thought of wishing she had not put the sign up crossed her mind. She also thought to herself, *Sometimes it is difficult to give respect to older people as I have been taught.*

She looked at the old man and replied, "It's not like that's the only bench in the park."

"I always sit on that one."

"Well, you'll just have to pick another." She held back calling him an old goat.

"Oh, *all right*, just remember, that's *my* bench."

"You want me to paint your name on it?"

"Just stay away from me."

"No problem, have a nice day."

The old man walked over to a bench as far away from Cat as he could get and still stay in the park.

Judge Bean and Dave walked up to Cat just as the old man was leaving.

Dave asked, "Well, Cat, how's it going?"

"Not too bad till that old man came up and started yelling at me for painting *his* bench. I wish I hadn't put up the 'wet paint' sign, then he would have really had something to complain about. Who is that old coot anyways?"

Judge Bean answered, "That would be grumpy Mike."

"I'll say."

"He lives not too far from your place. It is really a nice place, well kept, has a three-acre pond…has plenty of game there also. It is hard to see his house, the driveway is pretty well hidden. He used to let people hunt and fish on his place. After his wife died, he wouldn't let anybody on his place except his son. He wasn't always that way. After he retired, he and his wife used to come to town every Saturday morning. They would stop by the diner and get a newspaper, a couple of doughnuts, coffee, and sit on that bench. He really enjoyed that."

Cat was starting to feel bad.

Judge Bean continued, "He was a sniper in the Marine Corp, served three tours in Vietnam. After he was discharged, he built a gunsmith shop. He enjoyed long-range precision shooting. He would go to Camp Perry every year to compete. His son would make it a point to go with him every year after his wife died. He was the only family Mike had left. Five years ago, his son was killed by a drunk driver. That was the straw that broke the camel's back. He became very bitter. His son joined the service after the Towers got hit, served in Afghanistan and Iraq, then came home and got killed by a drunk driver."

Cat asked, "Did he still go to Camp Perry after that?"

"He competed the next year. The year after that he went, but didn't compete. After that, he quit going. He stays home now, only comes to town on Saturdays to get what he needs. He has a routine… He drops his grocery list off at the store, buys a paper, and reads it in the park. When he's done, he stops at the store, picks up his groceries, and goes home. Don't see him again till the next week."

"Does anybody ever visit him?"

"People have tried but given up. Some are scared of him. I go up and check on him once in a while. He just wants to be left alone till he can join his wife."

"That is so sad. Would he hurt anybody?"

"No, his bark is worse than his bite."

"So he is a good shot and knows a lot about long-range shooting?"

"When Mike was competing in the local shoots, the best anyone else could place was second."

As Cat was working on the second bench, she was beating herself up on how she had treated Mike. Not only did she make him even bitterer, but here was a guy that could probably teach her everything she would ever need to know about long-range shooting and then some. Again, her temper got in her way.

*****

Judge Bean stopped by in the afternoon. Cat had finished four benches.

He said, "I'll have to say, you did a fine job. These benches never looked better. It sure makes the rest of them look bad."

"Thank you."

As Cat was putting the stuff back into the truck, she started thinking to herself, *I probably did too good a job. I am sure they will find some reason for me to do community service till all the benches are done.*

Dave came back. "Well, Cat, ready to drop this stuff off at the garage and head home?"

"Yeah, this has been an eventful day."

"That it has. Want to stop and get some ice cream on the way home?"

"Aren't you afraid that will spoil my supper?"

Dave laughed. "No, I ain't seen anything to spoil your supper."

Cat grinned. "You know I kinda feel bad for that old guy."

"Well, you didn't know."

"Yeah, I know. I would sure like to get to know him."

"Your conscience bothering you, or is it because he knows a lot about shooting?"

Cat smiled, "A little of both."

"I see. If there's a way, I'm sure you'll find it."

By the time they got home and had supper, Cat was dead tired. She didn't have any trouble sleeping that night.

*****

A few weeks had passed since Cat's community service when she entered a local shooting competition. She took second place and won twenty dollars. That hooked her. There wasn't a contest within forty miles that didn't see Cat and her trusty .22. On a few occasions, she had been disqualified from a match. It took a bit for her to get used to following the rules and safety policies of the contests.

Cat liked and enjoyed shooting her .22 rimfire. Her dream was shooting center-fire rifles. Being able to hit a target at six hundred to one thousand yards, now, that would be some serious shooting. She knew that could only be a dream for now. It would take a lot of money for a good rifle and optics. Neither she nor her parents could afford that. Maybe if she could get to know Mike, he would teach her about long-range shooting.

3

After breakfast Cat and Ben went squirrel hunting in the woods behind their house. Ben liked to hunt once in a while but the computer used up most of his spare time. When he did go, Cat would always get the first squirrel. This irritated him a bit. Cat not only was a better shot than Ben but a little quicker and spotted the squirrels first. It was going to be different this time. Ben placed a piece of black tape over the lens of Cat's rifle scope then put the lens cap back on. He could barely keep from laughing because he knew he was going to get the first squirrel this time. It wasn't long until Cat spotted a squirrel sitting on a branch. Cat took aim, but she couldn't see anything through the tape over the end of the scope.

"What the…?"

Ben saw the squirrel and shot it. He started walking over to pick it up, laughing all the way. Cat removed the tape. She took careful aim and shot Ben's knife off his belt. She reloaded and put a bullet in the handle while it was on the ground.

Ben turned around. "What the hell are you doing? Trying to kill me?"

"Never mess with my rifle or anything else that is mine. I ain't trying to kill you, or you'd be dead. Besides that, ain't got time for a funeral."

"You ruined my knife. I just bought it. It's *brand-new!*"

"You can still use it, the blade's fine. Just sand the handle down. The bullet will give it character. Maybe when you use it from now on, you'll remember not to touch my stuff."

"*I guess.*" Ben picked up his knife and the squirrel.

Betty knew something was up when the kids came back so soon and with only one squirrel. She cornered Ben and asked him what was wrong. Betty was not at all happy when she found out what happened.

Betty yelled, "Catherine, get in here!"

Cat knew that tone, plus Mom called her Catherine. *I'm in big trouble!* "Yes, Mom."

"You sit there," pointing to a chair. "Ben, over there."

Betty walked over to the door and yelled at Dave, who was working on the lawn mower. "Dave, get in here!"

Dave walked into the house. "What's up?"

"Do you know what your daughter did?"

"My daughter?"

"Yes, your daughter. She almost killed Ben."

"Mom, if Cat was trying to kill me, you'd be making funeral arrangements instead of yelling at us."

Dave was doing his best to keep a straight and serious face. Ben was right, but it was a stupid stunt. It wasn't easy raising an "Annie Oakley." It didn't matter what punishment Dave came up with. It wouldn't be good enough for Betty. She was more scared than mad. The kids were her life. If anything would happen to them...well, Dave didn't want to think about it.

"All right, Cat. You know better."

"I do, but Ben made me mad."

"You're going to have to get your anger under control. If you don't, it's going to get the best of you."

Cat put her head down. "Yes, Dad."

"And, Ben, you know that Cat doesn't like anybody messing with her stuff."

"But, Dad, she is always trying to one-up me."

"Oh, the joy of sibling rivalry."

"Cat, you gonna do another stupid stunt like this again?"

Cat looked down at the floor. "No, Dad. I'm sorry."

"Ben, you gonna stay out of your sister's stuff?"

"Yes, Dad."

"All right then. Cat, bring me your rifle. Ben, get your laptop."

"Why?"

"Just do it."

Ben got his laptop and Cat her rifle. Dave took them. "You'll get them back in a week. That should give you time to think about how stupid you two were."

Cat and Ben both wailed, "Daaaad."

"You wanna try for two weeks?"

"No."

"Very well, now get out of here."

Betty said, "Is that all?"

"What you want me to do, give 'em twenty lashes?"

"I give up." Betty shook her head as she went back to the kitchen. It looked like there was going to be a lot of bake goods around.

Cat never pulled a stunt like that on her brother again. Ben thought it best to leave Cat's stuff alone.

*****

Cat found herself in front of Judge Bean again.

"Well, Cat, I see you decided to try fishing in the habitat area. I'm sure you have read your student handbook. You know that the only time fishing is allowed is during the parent-student picnic weekend or other days specified by the school, right?"

"Yes, Your Honor."

"So what did you take out of the pond?"

"Two bass and three catfish."

"You know, you did such a good job at the park, I think I will sentence you to eight more hours of community service. Keep this up, and all the benches should be painted before winter."

"Yes, Your Honor. Saturday morning, eight thirty?"

"That will be fine. Tell your dad it's his turn to buy coffee."

"Okay." She left the courthouse. *I knew I was doing too good of a job.*

*****

Mike came into town and dropped off his grocery list. He bought a paper and a cup of coffee. He walked over to the bench he always sat on. On the back of the bench painted in black letters was his name. The bench looked real nice, as did all the ones Cat had painted. As he went to sit down, he noticed a bag. He opened it. Inside were a doughnut and a note that read, "Sorry."

Cat was watching from a distance to see what the reaction would be. Mike just sat the bag back down and began reading the paper. Every time he took a sip of coffee, he would look at the bag. When he was just about done with his coffee, he opened up the bag, took out the doughnut, and ate it. He wadded up the bag and threw it in the trash.

As Mike walked toward the store, Cat met him.

"Good morning."

"That's what you think."

"How are you today?"

"Ain't none of your business."

*****

Cat was reading the community bulletin board to see if there were any rifle contests coming up. Judge Bean walked up.

"Good morning, Cat."

"Hi, Judge."

"Hey, I would like to talk to you, if you have a minute."

"I ain't in trouble, am I?"

"Should you be?"

"I'll plead the Fifth."

Judge Bean laughed. "I was wondering if you could do me a favor."

"What's that?"

"Widow Johnson's place is on your way home. Her husband was killed in a mining accident a couple of weeks ago. I have some food that I'm sure she can use. Would you drop it off to her?"

"Sure, that's fine with me, but I'll have to ask Dad."

"I've already talked to him. He said that'll be fine. I'll be over at the courthouse when you're ready to leave. If you have time, would you mind helping her around the house a little? She has three children. I'm sure she'd appreciate it."

"I can do that. Oh, Judge…"

"Yes?"

"I would like to get to know Mike. You have any suggestions on how I can do that?"

"Grumpy Mike?"

"Yeah, I painted his name on his bench and left a doughnut with a note that said I was sorry. I said good morning to him, but he was still rude to me."

"I hope you like a challenge. If you can get him to overcome his bitterness and start enjoying life again, well, that would be a Godsend."

"Any ideas?"

"Maybe, I don't know if it would work or not."

"I'm willing to give it a try."

"A few years ago a stray dog came up to my house. I didn't want him around, so I didn't feed him. I chased him away. He kept coming back no matter what I did. Every time I opened the door in the morning, he was there. I'd come home at night he was there. So I either had to let him stay or shoot him. I brought him in fed him, cleaned him up, and took him to the vet. You know, that's the most loyal dog I ever had."

"So I should keep trying till Mike opens up or shoots me?"

Judge Bean laughed. "I don't think he'll go that far, might threaten it though. The most he would do is file charges for stalking or trespassing. I doubt that would even happen. I think he stays in his shell because he doesn't want to get attached to anything for fear of losing it. He has lost everything he has ever cared for."

"Okay, thanks. Dad and I will be over to the court house in a bit."

*****

Widow Johnson answered Cat's knocking on the door. "Hello."

"Hi, I have some food that Judge Bean asked me to drop off for you and your kids."

"Oh, you must be Cat. The judge said you might be by."

"It's in my dad's truck. I'll go get it."

Dave and Cat brought the food into the house. "Just set it on the table. Thank you."

Cat asked, "Anything I can help you with?"

"Not really, but I wouldn't mind some company for a bit."

Dave asked Cat, "You want me to come back after ya?"

"No. I'll just cut through the back."

"Okay, I'll see you later. Be careful."

Cat waved at Dave as he drove away. Widow Johnson asked, "Care for a cup of coffee? I just made a fresh pot."

"That sounds good."

"Cream, sugar?"

"No, black is fine."

One of the boys walked up to Cat. "Who are you?"

Cat laughed. "I'm Cat. I brought some food from town for ya."

"Why they call you Cat? You ain't no cat. You're a people."

Cat laughed even harder. "That's my nickname, short for Catherine."

Widow Johnson shook her head. "Go play with your brother." She turned to Cat. "Don't have to wonder what's on his mind."

"Oh, that's okay. How old is he?"

"Seven, has to work on his grammar and manners. My oldest boy is eleven. I also have a daughter who just turned four."

"Looks like you have your hands full."

"Yes, I do. I sure appreciate what the town and church has done since my husband passed."

"If there is anything you'd like me to do, let me know."

"Thank you, I will keep that in mind."

"I'll help you put this stuff way."

"Thank you. There is something you could do. The town has been very generous with food, but the boys have been wanting some meat. My husband used to hunt a lot. The boys used to go with him.

I don't want them to go by themselves. Judge Bean says you like to hunt."

"You could say that's how we got to know each other."

Widow Johnson laughed. "Yeah, he told me you have been in front of his bench a couple times."

"Yeah, we'll go with a couple."

"Would you mind getting me a couple squirrels, rabbits, or whatever's in season?"

"No, I'd be glad to."

"That'd be great. Thank you. I know the boys will like it."

"I had better get going. Thanks for the coffee. I will see if I can get a couple squirrels for you tomorrow after school."

"You're welcome. Now, don't get them out of the wildlife area."

Cat laughed. "I take it Judge Bean told you quite a bit about me."

"A little."

"See ya tomorrow."

The next day after school, Cat took a couple of squirrels over to Widow Johnson's. While she was there, she helped the widow finish up the dishes. Widow Johnson poured Cat a cup of coffee.

"Can you stay and talk a little?"

"Sure."

"Good, it's nice to have a conversation with someone that isn't calling me mom. Don't get me wrong, I love my kids."

"That's not a problem. I like kids."

"They really miss their dad. Of course I do too. My boys especially, they miss the weekends he would take them camping, fishing, and hunting."

"I'm sure they do. Say, do you have a freezer?"

"Yes, I do, a small chest freezer. Why?"

"Oh, I was just having a thought."

"Now, don't get yourself in trouble for me."

"Nah, don't worry. Thanks for the coffee, I have to get going. I'll be back."

"You're welcome."

On the way home, Cat had a lot of things on her mind. It would be a lot easier to just get a deer and fill Widow Johnson's freezer. That would probably get her into more trouble than painting a few benches. Getting to know Mike and convincing him to teach her what he knew about long-range shooting was another thing that was on her mind. She didn't really know if the stray dog tactic would work or not.

Since Mike's place was on her way home, she decided to sneak in and check it out. The pond was about one-quarter of a mile from his house. It was a really nice and well kept. The pond was so clear you could see to the bottom in parts of it. He had trails throughout the woods and lots and lots of squirrels. *This place is great!* There was even a rifle range. It looked as though it had been a while since it had been used. *I will just have to find a way to get to know him.*

*****

Betty yelled, "Breakfast's ready. I have to work today. Anybody want a ride to town?"

Cat replied, "Yeah, I do."

Ben said, "Me too, I want to check if there are any new games at the library I can download."

Betty put the food on the table. "Check and see if Liz sent any e-mails."

"Oh, all right."

Betty turned toward Cat. "Gonna pester that old man again? You must be getting to him. Some of my customers said that he's been complaining about a girl that won't mind her own business and keeps bothering him."

"If he's talking about me, maybe it's working."

"What kind of doughnut you want this morning?

"The maple cream."

"Okay, I will put it in a bag for you, and you can stop at the diner and pick it up."

"Thanks, Mom."

Mike was getting used to the doughnut being on the bench. One day when Cat was running late, Mike stayed by the store until she put the doughnut on the bench.

As Cat was walking out of the library, Judge Bean stopped her.

"How's the plan of softening up Mike coming along?"

"I really don't know for sure."

"Well, you didn't hear it from me, but he does enjoy those doughnuts he finds on his bench. He also likes his name on the bench even if he won't admit it."

"How do you know?"

"'Cause he bitches about it every time he sees me."

Cat laughed. "I guess it's time for phase 2."

"Phase 2? Never mind, probably be better I didn't know."

"Probably not."

"I'm sure he'll tell me about it."

*****

For no longer than Cat had lived down here, she knew the backwoods pretty well. There were old logging roads as well as abandoned mines. Her first mission would be to get Widow Johnson some venison. Then she would work on phase 2 of getting to know Mike.

One evening, as Cat was leaving with her .410 shotgun, her mom asked, "Where you going at this time of the evening?"

"I thought I would do a little exploring. No school tomorrow, teachers' conference."

"I take it you plan on staying all night in the woods."

"Planned on it, I was going to let you know after I got my backpack packed."

"Yeah, your dad and I have given up on you asking."

"Mom, you know that if you tell me to stay home, I will. I always let you know where I'm going."

"Yeah, the woods."

"I have my cell phone that you make me take with me."

"I just worry about you."

"*Mom*, I'll be fine."

Cat kissed her mom and went out the back door. Betty was having a hard time getting used to the fact that her baby was growing up.

*****

Cat had found a trail that was overgrown with brush and vines. It was not too far from their property line that bordered on state ground. She had found it off an old logging road while she was hunting. It went down to a valley, which had plenty of grass for deer. This was what she called the back way into the valley. It was also accessible from a logging road that ran on the other side. She set up camp in a small cave, then she hiked over to the other side of the valley to a patch of pine trees that had been planted by the mining company.

She sat down by a big rock that was in between two tall pine trees. *This will be great. The deer will come down this trail.* This was the first time that she had taken a deer out of season or at night, convincing herself that just because it was illegal didn't mean that it was wrong. After all, Widow Johnson's family did need the meat. Surely, she was not the only one that had done this. It was also getting exciting for her. Would she be able pull this off? How great it would have been to live 150 years earlier. No game laws—very few laws, period—and to find a piece of ground and build a cabin. Live off the land. Of course, there were a lot of things that were taken for granted in modern times that wasn't around back then. Then again, you can't miss anything you've never had.

This was not the first time she had sat in this valley in the moonlight. There was always activity at night, coyotes howling and raccoons wandering around. It was very peaceful with the moon casting shadows in the valley from the tall pine trees. Her thoughts were interrupted when a buck walked out into the moonlight. He was huge. His antlers were so large it looked as if he had trees on his head. The moon reflected its light off of them. Cat's heart was racing. She had never seen anything that big. He walked with pride. He looked toward Cat, raised his head, and sniffed the air. Cat knew he had spotted her. For what seemed like an hour, they just stared at each other. Time seemed to stand still. She wanted to get a better look at him. She brought her shotgun up to her shoulder and looked through the scope. "Wow!"

Cat was after meat. This was not the time to be thinking of a wall hanger. Taking him at night would not be right. He should be taken in season during legal shooting hours. Still, she was in awe of how he just stood there. It was as though they were communicating with each other.

"I am going to call you *the monster*. You're safe tonight. Another time, another place it may be different." He looked at her for another minute, then nodded, as if saying, "Thank you." Then he walked away.

Within a couple minutes, a yearling walked in sight. *Could it be?* Cat raised her shotgun, lined the crosshairs up on the heart-lung area, and squeezed the trigger. The deer ran twenty yards and fell over. She took her gun apart put it in her carrying case and set the case by the tree. Taking her knife and backpack, she walked up to the deer. It was nice size, not too big. Then she carefully skinned the deer and cut the meat off the bone. The temperature was in the lower fifties. It would have been better if it were colder, but there was nothing she could do about that. She wrapped the meat in some old bedsheets that her mother had thrown away. Then she placed it in large plastic bags and put it in her backpack.

Cat put the backpack on, walked over, picked up her gun, and walked back to the cave. She left her gun in the cave with her other stuff and headed up the trail to Widow Johnson's house. *This is going to be more of a workout than I expected. I hope I don't scare Widow Johnson when I show up at this time of the night.*

As Cat walked up to Widow Johnson's house, she noticed a light on. She knocked on the door.

Widow Johnson answered, "Who is it?"

"It's Cat."

Widow Johnson opened the door. "My land girl, what are you doing here at this time of night?"

As Cat walked in, "I brought you something." She set her backpack on the kitchen floor and started putting the bags of meat on the table.

"Bless your heart, you're gonna get yourself in trouble, girl."

"I'll be okay."

Widow Johnson got some freezer bags and a cutting board and laid them on the table. "The kids are going to enjoy this."

"It's not as cold as I would like, but it should be all right. I'll help you cut it up and get it in the freezer."

"Bless your heart. What does your mother think, you being out this late?"

"I'm camping tonight, no school tomorrow."

They cut the meat up into steaks, a few roasts, and the rest into stew meat. After it was all put in the freezer, Cat said, "That should last you a little while. I had better get going."

"Okay, thank you. Leave those sheets here, and I'll wash them for you."

"Thanks, I'll see you later."

Cat hiked back to her campsite, fixed her something to eat, then went to sleep. The next morning she cleaned up the area and put her gear in her backpack. She spent the rest of the day hiking and enjoying nature; this was her home.

Cat made it home close to dark. As she walked into the house, Betty asked, "Have a good time?"

"Always have a good time camping and hiking."

"I don't understand how sleeping under the stars on the hard, cold ground can be fun. Don't make any sense when you have a fine bed here in the house."

"It's so relaxing and peaceful being out in nature."

"If you say so. There's some supper leftover if you're hungry. I just put it in the fridge. It should still be warm."

"Thanks, I think I will eat a bite and get ready for bed, have school tomorrow."

"Okay."

*****

Cat started helping other families in the area that needed it. She kept them supplied with meat, rabbits, squirrels, and sometimes venison. They would never ask questions, just said, "Thanks." It wasn't long until everyone in the county either knew Cat or had heard about her.

Cat found herself in front Judge Bean a few more times. It was usually for having more than the legal limit of either small game or fish. She had a sneaking suspicion that Judge Bean sent the game warden out to catch her when he wanted more work done in the park. It wasn't long until she was on a first-name basis with the judge and game warden. She never got caught taking a deer. Although one night, she had a funny feeling she was being watched. After that night, she quit poaching deer. There'd be more than community service if she got caught poaching a deer. So she stuck with small game and fish.

Almost everybody liked Cat. Even though she had a knack of getting into trouble, she had a heart of gold. The city park looked the best it had in years.

Whenever anyone would see her working in the park, they would ask, "What did she do this time?"

Someone would reply, "I don't know."

Then another would chime in, "I think Judge Bean just likes her work."

4

Cat had been scouting the woods behind her house. She found an area where the deer had been feeding. Gun season for deer was still a few weeks away, but this would be a good place on opening day. After that the deer would change their routine. She could hardly wait. Her family would love to have some venison. The deer she had poached, she gave away to the needy. The last thing she wanted was for her dad and mom to find out that she had been poaching.

Cat was pretty busy keeping her grades up and helping the people of the county. One day while she was at the diner visiting with her mom, Judge Bean walked up sat down beside her and asked, "How are you today?"

"Pretty good."

"I was talking to Widow Johnson. She said that you have been a great help."

"She is a nice woman. Her kids are great."

"I also heard that you have been pretty busy giving a hand to some of the other families that has fallen on hard times."

"Yeah, I really enjoy giving a hand to people that need it. They all seem to appreciate it."

"Oh, they do. Haven't heard a bad word about you. Except Grumpy Mike he said that you were like a stray dog that won't stay away."

"You think I'll be able to get him to come out of his shell?"

"If anyone can, it'll be you."

Betty walked up and said, "Hi, Judge, get you anything?"

"I'll just take a cup of coffee."

"My daughter ain't in trouble again, is she?"

"No, not today."

"I tell you what. If she had done as much work fixing up our place as she has had to do at the park, there would be a picture of it in *Better Homes and Gardens*."

"Aw, Mom."

"Next time I'll sentence her to do work at home. The park looks the best it has in a long time."

Judge Bean drank a cup of coffee, and as he got up to leave, he said, "Cat, you take it easy, and try to stay out of trouble."

"Always."

Cat was starting to wonder if she had been spotted killing those deer. One thing she had learned was never to volunteer any information. She finished her coffee.

Betty asked, "More coffee?"

"No, Mom. I want to get back home."

"You ain't doing anything to get yourself in trouble, are you?"

"Not me."

"And you all wonder why I have gray hair."

*****

Friday after school, Cat went home, grabbed her fishing pole and gear, and headed over to Mike's. Phase 2 was about to start. She had come up with a plan. Whether it was a good one or not would be seen. Hopefully, Judge Bean was right that Mike's bark was worse than his bite. Being arrested for trespassing would not make her parents happy.

Cat rode her bike past his house and went right back to the pond. She baited her hook and then cast the line into the water. It wasn't long until a nice-size catfish took the bait. She took the fish off the hook, put it into her basket, rebaited the hook, and threw the line back in the water. When she put the third fish in her basket, Mike walked up. Cat could practically see the steam coming from his ears.

"What the hell are you doing?"

Cat began thinking maybe this wasn't such a good plan, but oh well, no sense retreating now. "What, you blind? I'm building a doghouse."

That only managed to make Mike's blood pressure raise another twenty points. "No, you ain't! You are stealing my fish!"

Cat began putting her tackle away. "I ain't stealing your fish."

"Yes, you are! I'll have you arrested for trespassing!"

Cat got on her bike. "Go ahead. I am sure you know the number to the law."

"You get out of here, and don't come back, and stop leaving doughnuts on my bench!"

Cat rode up to Mike's house. She noticed a bucket by a water hydrant. She put some water in the bucket and dumped the fish in it. By the time Mike had walked up to his house, Cat had already found a board and was cleaning the first fish. Mike was out of breath by the time he got to the house.

"I told you to leave or I was going to call the law."

Cat continued to clean the fish. "Go ahead. I'm sure you know where your phone is."

Now Mike didn't know what to do. Cat was the stubbornest female he had ever run into. He could call the law; he had every legal right to do so. Why was this girl trying so hard to be nice to him? Mike went and got his phone and sat on the porch, all the while Cat was cleaning the fish. Cat finished then started to go into Mike's house to find a bowl to put the fillets in. Mike just looked at her in amazement.

"You want to get arrested for breaking and entering too?"

"You have the phone, forget the number?"

Cat found a bowl to put the fish in. She covered them with water added salt and put them in the refrigerator. Cat noticed he didn't have much as far as food goes a few potatoes, onions, and some canned goods. Probably just got enough stuff to last him a week.

"I didn't forget the number."

Cat walked out of the house. "I put the fish in salt water. Just let them alone, and I will be back tomorrow and fry them up for you."

"You leave and don't come back."

Mike's heart was starting to thaw a little. It had been a long time since he had home-fried fish. His wife used to fry fish for him every Sunday even though she didn't care for fish. Mike would catch a mess on Saturday clean them, and she would fry them after they got home from church.

Cat was doing a lot of thinking on her bike ride home. Would Mike call the law on her if she went back? She would find out tomorrow afternoon. She couldn't give up now. When she got home, she put her bike and fishing pole away and walked into the house.

Betty asked, "Catch anything?"

"Some small ones, I threw them back."

"Supper should be ready by the time you get cleaned up."

"That's good. I'm kinda hungry."

*****

Saturday morning, Mike left his list at the grocery store, bought a paper and coffee, then went over to his bench. There wasn't a doughnut sitting there like there usually was. Mike had gotten kind of used to it being there. As he sat down to read the paper, he began thinking, *Maybe I was a little hard on that girl. Now she probably won't come over and fry the fish.* In a way he was starting to like her even if she was stubborn as a mule. He finished reading his paper and drank the last of his coffee. He went back to the store to pick up his groceries.

As he walked in, the cashier said, "I've got everything ready for you. You have a pretty big order today, you expecting company this week?"

"Nah, I was just getting low on groceries."

"You all right, no smart-ass comment?"

"I'm fine, see you next week." Mike left the store feeling kind of down. He really missed that doughnut.

After he got home, he put his stuff away, looked in the refrigerator, saw the fish, and thought to himself, *I guess I can fry them tomorrow.* Mike grabbed a glass of ice water, went outside, and sat on the porch. He sat there for a while, looking at the trees blowing in the breeze. He looked up, and there came Cat, riding her bike up the lane. When she got to the house, she said "Hi," and walked right into the kitchen and started preparing the fish.

Mike came in right behind. "What are you doing here? I told you not to come back. Didn't you hear me?"

"Oh, I heard you. I just didn't listen. Now where are your skillets?"

"Get out of here. There in the drawer under the stove where they're supposed to be. Now leave!"

"I will as soon as I'm done." Cat kept right on working on the meal. She fried some potatoes and onions to go along with the fish.

Mike sat at the table. After Cat was done cooking, she put it on a plate and set it on the table with a fork and a glass of water. Mike looked at it. "I ain't hungry."

"Suit yourself. I'm gonna go out and see if I can get a couple of squirrels for your dinner tomorrow. I will stop by and fry them up for you tomorrow after church."

"Oh no, you don't. Get out of here!"

Cat went outside to her bike took her rifle out of its case and headed for Mike's woods. After Cat left, Mike wolfed down the fish and potatoes. He hadn't had a meal like that in a long time. Cat came back with two squirrels already cleaned. After she rinsed them off, she put them in a container of water and added some salt.

As she placed them in the refrigerator, she turned to Mike, "Changed your mind?"

"Couldn't see throwing it out, after all it was mine."

"Well, don't get used to it. I will see you tomorrow."

"I probably don't have a choice."

"Nope."

"So you're pretty good with that little rifle?"

"Not bad."

"There's a groundhog that's under my workshop that sticks his nose out about this time every day. Think you can hit him?"

"From your porch? Yeah, piece of cake."

Mike knew soon as the groundhog would hear the click when Cat cocked her rifle, he would be long gone. Cat got her rifle and sat on the porch and waited. Mike couldn't wait. He knew she wouldn't be able to get him. It wasn't long till the groundhog stuck his head out. Cat raised her rifle. She held the trigger back as she cocked the rifle so it wouldn't make the click. The groundhog was sitting there. Cat let out a shrill whistle. The groundhog stood up on his hind legs and looked around. When he did that, Cat squeezed the trigger. The groundhog fell over and started flopping on the ground.

"One dead groundhog!"

Mike couldn't believe it. Maybe she was a little smarter than he had given her credit. "I guess so. That wasn't bad."

"Well, I had better get going. I have some chores to do."

"Good, it's about time you're leaving."

"You know, I bet deep down, you have a heart probably real deep."

"Just go. I expect a doughnut on my bench next Saturday."

Cat would stop by two or three nights a week after school and visit with him. Mike would act like he didn't want her around, but he never actually kicked her off his place. He was starting to enjoy her company. There was no way he would let anyone know.

*****

Cat was walking toward the diner one day after school when Mike walked past her.

"What are you doing here? Today ain't Saturday?" asked Cat.

"None of your business, brat."

"Oh, you like me. Just don't know it yet."

"Whatever."

Cat walked into the diner and sat up at the counter.

Betty said, "Hi, Cat, what you doing?"

"Oh, thought I would just stop by and see how you're doing."

"AKA, buy me a cup of coffee?"

Cat smiled. "Sure, thanks for offering."

Judge Bean walked in and sat down beside Cat. Betty brought Cat a cup of coffee then turned to Judge Bean and asked, "What would you like?"

"Coffee will be fine." He turned to Cat. "I take it you have started 'phase 2' on getting to know Grumpy Mike?"

"You've heard?"

"Oh yeah, Mike has talked to me more in the last few days than he had for the last two years."

"I take it my stray-dog approach is starting to work?"

"I think so. He calls me every time you show up and complains about you. I always ask him, 'What do you want me to do about it? Put her in jail?'"

"What's he say?"

"Not much, he won't admit it, but I think he likes you being around."

Judge Bean laid a dollar on the counter. "See you later."

Betty replied, "Thanks, Judge."

"Mom, thanks for the coffee. I am going to stop by and see Mike on the way home. I'll be home in time for supper."

"Your dad is going to put something on the grill tonight. The last thing I want to do after cooking all day is to go home and make supper."

"Okay, see ya then."

*****

Cat knocked on Mike's door. Mike opened the door. "What do you want?"

"Good to see you too."

"Why you keep bothering me?"

"'Cause you like me."

Mike shook his head. He was starting to like Cat. There was just something about her. "Now, why would I like an annoying little brat like you?"

"Because you really don't like being mad at the world, it's just that after all these years, that's all you know."

"What, you taking psychology 101 in high school?"

"Very funny."

"I'm sure that there is something you want from me. Nobody tries this hard to be friends with a grumpy old man like me for no reason."

"Maybe I like a challenge."

"Now, cut the bullshit and tell me what you really want."

"You got me. Yes, there is something I'd like you to do."

"I knew it. What is it?

"I would like you to teach me how to shoot long-range, like a thousand yards or better."

Mike was quite for a little bit. *She has been going through all this just to get me to teach her how to shoot. This would take a little thinking. Will I be able to stand her being around all the time? Like she stays away now just like a stray dog always coming back.* Judge Bean had been telling him that Cat had been holding her own on the rifle team. It has been a long time since he had done any shooting. The most he had done in the last few years was take his rifles out, clean and oil them, then put them back in the safe.

Cat just looked at Mike for a while, wondering what he was thinking. "Well, you gonna teach me or not?"

"What makes you think I can teach you?"

"Well, according to the judge, you knocked a nut out of a squirrel's mouth at 200 yards and didn't hurt the squirrel."

"It was 250, but I did have a hundred dollar bet on that shot."

"Think I'd be able to do that?"

"I heard you shot a knife off your brother's belt."

Cat put her head down and with a sheepish grin said, "Yeah, he kind of made me mad."

"You know, that was pretty stupid."

"Oh yeah, Mom and Dad let me know that!"

"What about your brother?"

"He didn't say much. He never messed with my stuff after that."

"Smart boy. If you ever pull a stunt like that with me, I'll quit teaching you."

Cat smiled. "Is that a yes?"

"Might as well, don't look like I am gonna get rid of ya.

Cat gave Mike a big hug. "Thank you."

"Now, don't start getting mushy. Ruin my reputation."

"Okay, okay, when do we start?"

"I suppose a week from Saturday after I get back from town. There had better be a maple cream doughnut on my bench."

"You bet. I better get going. I'm gonna stop in and see Widow Johnson. See ya Saturday."

"Remember, maple cream on my bench every Saturday."

As Cat left, Mike was talking to himself, "Oh, Lord, what have I gotten myself into? I hope this is a blessing, not a test." He looked up. "Probably both."

He sat down in front of the TV. He was glad no one could see the little smile he had. Teaching Cat to shoot would give him a sense of purpose.

Cat knocked on Widow Johnson's door. She opened the door. "Hi, Cat, come on in. How have you been?"

"Doing great. Just thought I would stop by to see how you and the kids were doing. Do you need anything?"

"We are doing fine. I hate to ask, but the boys would sure like some more venison. We've been out for a bit. But now, don't do it if you'll get in trouble."

"No reason I can't, as long as you don't mind me showing up in the middle of the night."

"Bless your heart."

*****

Friday after Cat got home from school, she started packing her backpack. Betty came into her room.

"Going camping again this weekend?"

"Yeah, after I get my chores done and eat supper."

"I should be used to it by now. I can't help but worry about you when you're out there by yourself."

"As you have said, that's a mother's job to worry about her kids."

After supper Cat put on her backpack, picked up her shotgun, and hiked to the cave. She set up camp. She had a camp stove, a sleeping bag, and other supplies hidden in the cave.

Cat started to hike over to the big rock. Something didn't seem right. There weren't any animals around like there usually were. A putrid odor filled the usually fresh clean air of the hills. The fumes of ammonia, battery acid, and lye burned her eyes and nose. She knew it would be best to turn around and go home. She thought to herself, *I'll just get to the rock and see if I can find out the source that wretched odor.* After getting to the rock, she looked down the hill. She saw a black pickup truck with a small camping trailer hooked to it. The odor was coming from the trailer. Two guys were standing around a campfire. She backed up behind the rock. Her mind was racing. *What do I do? Go get help? Okay, calm down, get a better look.* She used the scope on her shotgun to get a better look. They were drinking. As she scanned the area, she saw another man beating a guy tied to a small tree. *Oh, this ain't good.* She got a better look at the guy tied to the tree. It was Officer Conrad. He had been badly beaten. Cat slid behind the rock again. Her heart was beating so hard she was afraid it would come out of her chest.

Talking to herself, she said, "Cat, calm down. Think this through. Do something stupid, and both of you will get killed. That'd really piss Mom off."

*****

"What's the matter, Warden? Want a drink?" one of the thugs said as he poured whiskey on the warden's head. He kicked him in the ribs. "Does that hurt? Teach you to mind your own business."

Officer Conrad could barely hold his head up, spitting out blood. "You can rot in hell."

"After you. I ain't the one tied up. I could be nice and put a bullet in your head, but I think I'll just let you die a slow death. We're about done with this batch."

One of the other dirt bags said, "Get over here and help unhook this trailer. We need to get some more ammonia and lye. We might as well cook another batch."

"All right, while you two are in town, get another bottle of whiskey. I'm gonna to stay here and play with the warden."

"That's all you need. Give me the warden's radio so we can tell if we've been reported."

As the other two left, he went back to the warden. The warden had passed out. "What's the matter, sleepy?" When he didn't get a response, he dumped some water on him.

The warden opened his eyes, "Go to hell."

"Maybe we will just force some meth down your throat before we leave you to die."

*****

After Cat calmed herself down, she looked through her scope again, thinking, *I know I can hit one, maybe two. No way can I get all three before they kill the warden. Maybe if I kill the one closest to the warden, it will give me time to hit the other two. No, probably not. At least one of the others would be a moving target.* Then she saw two of them get in the truck and leave. *If I shoot the one that's still here, the other two may hear the shot and come back.* Watching the thug beating the warden, she knew she had to do something pretty quick. As she was contemplating what to do, the thug headed back to the campfire. He took another drink and fell down. *Maybe he passed out. I'd better make my move.* Cat snuck down to the warden, walking up behind him. She put her hand over his mouth so that he wouldn't yell.

"It's me, Cat."

"Cat, what are you doing here?"

"Later, let's get out of here." She noticed they had handcuffed him to the tree; her knife was worthless.

"I have a key sewed on the inside of the collar of my shirt."

Cat found it and unlocked his cuffs. The thug started moving.

"Want me to kill him?"

The warden knew if he said yes, she would do it. It might have been safer for them if she would. Still, he didn't want that to be on her conscience.

"No, not unless you have to."

"Want me to cuff him?"

"No, he's still passed out. As much as he drank, he should be out long enough for us to get away."

The warden had been severely beaten, and one of his legs was broken. With Cat's help he was able to get to the cave. Cat opened her sleeping bag and helped him onto it. She loosened his shirt and belt, elevated his legs, and then folded the sleeping bag over his body. She placed a folded sheet under his head.

"I'll be right back. I'm going to cover our tracks."

"Be careful."

"Always."

She went outside and covered their tracks. Bushes hid the entrance to the cave, and with the clouds covering the moon, it would be hard for the thugs to find the warden. She went back in the cave. The warden was still conscious.

"That guy still passed out?"

"Yeah, I think he's down for the count. I'm going to get help. I will leave my 410 Rossi here with you. It's loaded. The hammer is back. Just flip off the safety, and it's good to go. Here are three more shells. Now, don't die on me."

"Don't plan on it. Be careful. The other two might spot you."

"Not to worry, I'm going out the back way."

"The back way?"

"See ya."

*****

Cat ran into the house.

"Mom, Dad, wake up!"

Dave jumped out of bed and ran out of the bedroom with Betty right behind him.

"Cat, what is it?"

"It's the warden! He's hurt bad!"

Dave, trying to get coherent, said, "Okay, Cat, slow down. Take a deep breath and tell me what's wrong.

Cat took a deep breath and let it out slowly. "It's the warden, he's hurt real bad. He ran into some drug dealers. They beat him up and broke his leg."

"Where is he now?"

"I hid him in the cave that I camped in. We have to get help!"

"All right. Betty, call Judge Bean. Tell him we're heading his way and the warden is hurt."

"You two be careful."

When Dave and Cat got to Judge Bean's house he was up, dressed, and drinking a cup of coffee to wake up. Cat explained everything.

Judge Bean said, "I'm going to call the state police, probably need to get SWAT."

Cat replied, "Make sure they don't use radios, because they have the warden's."

*****

The SWAT team met them at the courthouse. Judge Bean introduced Cat to the team commander.

"I'll let her tell you the situation."

Cat pulled a TOPO map out of her pocket as she told them what happened. "I usually get there by hiking through Dad's place, but there is a fire road to get you to the trail."

The commander listening to what she was saying asked, "There's a trail that goes down to that valley?"

"Yeah, it's overgrown, but I cleared out a path for a shortcut."

"May I use your map? You stay here, and we'll go get him."

"No, I'm going with you. I know that area like the back of my hand. The warden is scared, and I left my shotgun with him. He will recognize my voice."

The commander, knowing that this would go against proto-col, looked at Judge Bean. He smiled a little and nodded. The com-mander was quiet for a bit then said, "Sometimes you have to go with your gut."

Cat got into the SWAT van. As they left, Dave said to Judge Bean, "Good thing the wife ain't here."

"Yeah."

*****

Getting everyone and equipment to the cave by Cat's trail was not an easy task. The EMTs went into the cave with Cat. The SWAT team set up on the hill above the meth lab.

The SWAT commander said, "What dumbasses! As close as that fire is to the trailer, it could blow anytime!"

One of the officers asked, "What's the plan, boss?"

The commander looked through his binoculars, taking mental notes. The other two thugs had not come back yet. The third was still passed out by the fire.

"You two go down, cuff that bastard, and drag him back here. Make it quick. That trailer could blow anytime."

*****

Cat walked up to the warden. He was unconscious. He had one hand on the shotgun with his thumb on the safety. Cat carefully removed the shotgun from his hand, picked up the extra shells, then stepped back. The EMTs started working on him. They took his vitals then started an IV to get fluids back into his body.

One EMT said to the other, "We have to get him stabilized before we can move him."

Cat went over to the wall of the cave and sat down. She really did like the warden even if he had arrested her a few times. The adrenaline was wearing off, and she was getting tired. The only thing she could do now was stay out of the way of the professionals and to pray.

"Okay, Lord, I did my part with your help. Now the rest is up to you and the EMTs. Amen."

Within a few minutes she was fast asleep.

*****

After officers dragged the suspect back to the hill, the team watched the meth lab. They knew it wouldn't be long until the other two would show up.

One of the snipers said to the commander, "Boss, it'd be a lot easier just to shoot them when they get back, save the taxpayers a lot of money."

"Yeah, it would, but you know we can't do that. Plus, think of all the extra paperwork."

"I know. I'm tired of arresting these slime balls and then liberal judges letting them go on technicalities."

"It sucks."

"I think they're coming back."

The meth makers pulled up to the trailer and got out. When they got to the trailer, one of them put a cigarette in his mouth and pulled out his lighter. The SWAT commander was watching through his binoculars.

"No, you *dumbass*, guys, get down and cover your heads!"

When the lighter was lit, the trailer blew up. Pieces went flying everywhere. Fortunately, it had rained a couple of days ago, so the fire didn't spread far. The commander called the fire department, and then he said to the rest of the team, "That's one less case that'll be on the court docket."

The fire department showed and put out the fire. There was not much left of the pickup or trailer. Two of the SWAT members stayed at the crime scene while the investigators and medical examiner did their jobs. The rest of them went back to the cave to see how the others were doing. An ambulance was waiting outside the cave.

Inside the cave, one of the EMTs walked over to Cat, who was sound asleep. He shook her shoulder lightly saying, "Hey, girl, he's gonna make it."

Cat, waking up from a deep sleep, for a moment didn't realize where she was. "Huh?"

"The warden's gonna make it."

Cat rubbed her eyes, "Oh, good."

"Yes, we have him stabilized. His blood pressure and pulse are good. We're getting ready to load him in the ambulance. You can ride with us to the hospital if you want."

"Really?"

"Yeah, he came to for a minute and asked about you."

Cat stood up, picked up her shotgun, and responded, "That's great."

"I'll tell you what. How about you give your shotgun to one of the officers. I'm sure they'll give it to your dad when they go back to town."

"Yeah, I guess you're right." Cat opened the action and handed it to the officer. "Will you give this to Dad and tell him I went to the hospital with the warden?"

"Sure, I'll do that. You did a fine job."

"Thank you."

*****

Cat sat in the waiting room while the warden was in the emergency room. Dave and Betty walked in. Cat looked up.

"Hi, Mom, Dad."

Betty gave Cat a big hug. "Oh, I am so glad you're all right."

"Yeah, me too."

Dave said, "How's Conrad?"

"Haven't heard anything yet, the EMTs had him stabilized before he was put in the ambulance."

Betty hugged Cat again. "You sure you're okay? You just added more gray hair to me."

"Mom, I'm fine. I'm just worried about the warden."

Dave said, "Oh, by the way, they gave me your gun."

"Thanks."

The ER doctor came to the waiting room walked up to Cat. "I take it you're the one that's called Cat."

"Yeah, that's me. This is my mom and dad."

"The warden's left leg is broken. X-rays show two broken ribs and three cracked. We suspect some internal bleeding. He is in surgery now. After that we'll do an MRI to see if there are any head injuries. We need to get the bleeding stopped before we do anything else. Before we put him under, he told me to tell you thank you. I told him he can tell you himself when he wakes up. He said, 'I know, but just in case.'"

"I told him not to die on me."

The doctor cracked a little smile. "He'll be able to thank you himself. He'll probably be in surgery for at least two hours. By the time he gets out of recovery and to his room, it will be quite a while. Why don't you go home and get some rest and come back later in the morning. Leave your number with the desk, and we will call you if anything changes."

"I want to stay here till he gets to his room."

Mom said, "Now, Cat, you can't do anything while he's in surgery. Let's get you home. You can take a shower, get some clean clothes on, and grab a bite to eat. Your dad can bring you back after that."

"Well, okay." She looked at her dad. "You'll bring me back so I can wait here?"

"Yes, I'll bring you back."

The ER doctor said, "Well, I'll see you later. Be sure to leave your number at the desk."

5

It had been nearly a week since Officer Conrad had been taken to the hospital. Every day after school, Cat went to the hospital to visit him. It was more or less a one-way conversation. The warden was still quite heavily sedated. He would open his eyes every once in a while, crack a smile, and nod.

The doctor started weaning Officer Conrad off of the pain killers. Cat was hoping the nurse was right, that he would be more coherent this afternoon.

Cat walked into the Conrad's room. He was sitting up, eating, and watching TV.

"Glad to see you are back amongst the living."

"If you call it that." He lifted his arm. "Still hooked up to all these wires and tubes."

"Well, at least you are eating on your own."

"Yeah, Jell-O and chicken broth. I want some real food."

"It shouldn't be too long till your body can handle a steak and potato."

"So tell me, what were you doing out there that night?"

"Since you were there, you already know."

"Well, I had my suspicions."

"You know what I was doing. That's not the first time you saw me there."

"You're right, it wasn't."

"Why don't we leave this conversation for another time?"

"You're right. Anyways, I want to thank you. I heard you did a fine job getting me to the cave and covering me up. You saved my life. I don't know how I can repay you."

"Oh, I don't know. How about a 'Get Out of Jail Free' card?"

The warden smiled. He liked Cat. She had a heart of gold. "I'll see what I can do."

"I am glad you're awake. It was getting kind of boring me just doing the talking."

"I heard you've been up here every day."

"Yep, well, I had better get going. Have some chores to do at home. Let me know when your stomach can handle it, and I'll bring you a steak and potato."

"Venison?"

"Season's not in yet."

Conrad smiled. "See you tomorrow."

*****

Judge Bean went to the hospital to see how Officer Conrad was getting along. He walked into Conrad's room.

"You're looking a lot better than the night they hauled you in here."

"I would hope so. From what I hear, I was in pretty bad shape."

"That would be putting it lightly."

"Cat just left about an hour ago."

"You had her worried. She's been up to see you every day since you've been here."

"That's what the nurses told me."

"So what were the two of you doing out there at that time of the night?"

Conrad sat up in his bed. "You probably already know."

"I have an idea, but go ahead and fill me in."

"Well, you know how Cat likes to bend the law a little."

Judge Bean laughed. "A little?"

Conrad smiled. "I guess maybe more than a little. You know that Cat has been helping a lot of the poorer families in the area."

"Yeah, like Widow Johnson and her young'uns."

"I heard a couple of women talking to each other about how Cat was keeping their freezers full of meat. I stopped in to see old man Smith, who lives in that small cabin by the abandoned railroad depot."

"He tans animal skins and peddles them at rendezvous?"

"Yeah, him. He was tanning a fresh deer hide when I stopped by. He told me that he had a few left in the freezer from last season."

"You didn't think so?"

"No, I started putting two and two together and decided to start following her."

"And...?"

"I went down to the valley one night. Sure enough, there she was sitting by a rock with her shotgun. It was a pretty well-lit night. I stayed back and watched through my binnacles. A huge buck came into the area. I think it was the one all the hunters have been talking about, the one that disappears opening day. Cat raised her shotgun and looked through her scope. I sure didn't want to see him killed that way. Before I could do anything, she put her gun down."

"Then what happened?"

"The strangest thing I have ever seen. The buck nodded at her as though he knew she was there, then he walked away. Two minutes hadn't gone by when a yearling came in to view. She raised her gun and shot, the deer ran about twenty yards and fell over."

"You think that big buck lead that deer to her?"

"Had me wondering. I watched her clean that deer. It was the neatest job I had ever seen. She cut the meat off the bone, wrapped it in sheets, put in plastic bags, then packed it in her backpack."

"You didn't approach her?"

"No, I just watched. In the distance I saw some coyotes just sitting, waiting, and watching. Cat put her backpack on, went back, and picked up her gun. She walked across the valley then just disappeared."

"Went up that hidden trail?"

"I was told that Cat brought the SWAT team in that way. No wonder I never saw her leave. Anyway, after she left, the coyotes went and cleaned up what was left. It was like they knew. It was as though the wild had accepted her as one of their own. I observed this a couple of more times. The same thing happened."

"Why didn't you arrest her?"

"I don't know. I mean, she was helping people."

"So having a problem with what is legal and what is right?"

"It was starting to bother me. After all, she was breaking the law. I decided to bring her in. That's when I ran into that meth lab. That was my fault. Knowing that Cat wouldn't give me any trouble, I had let my guard down. Walked right into trouble, you know the rest."

"I'm glad to see you're getting better. Hey, I'll see you later. I need to stop by the office before I go home, see you tomorrow."

"All right, I ain't gonna be going anywhere."

Judge Bean opened a letter from the State that was left on his desk. It was the answer to his request for a DNR officer to fill in while Conrad was recuperating. He read the letter over. *Just as I figured, someone that hasn't been with the DNR very long. I'll call around tomorrow and see what kind of guy he is.*

*****

Mike installed new target holders and rebuilt the benches on his rifle range. It had been a long time since it looked this good.

Mike took his .308 Winchester rifle out of his safe and picked up a target and a box of cartridges. He hung a target at the hundred-yard mark. After squeezing off three shots, he walked down and checked his target. He took a dime and put it up to the holes. It didn't quite cover all three. "Not too shabby for an old man."

Mike put his rifle away and started to look over some old catalogs. There was a lot of catching up to do since he had been out of the game for a few years. He found some old papers he brought home from Camp Perry.

"I wonder if Jim is still shooting." Jim was twenty years younger than Mike. Mike had taught him a lot when they were shooting together. "I'll just give him a call, hope the number's the same." Mike looked up Jim's number and dialed.

"Hello."

"Hi. Jim?"

"Yes."

"This is Mike."

"Mike? The old guy that used to show up at Camp Perry, come hell or high water?"

"Yeah, that Mike."

"How the hell are ya?"

"Not bad, you still compete at Camp Perry?"

"Every year. Why, ya thinking about getting back in the game?"

"No. The reason I called was, I was wondering if you could send me some info on what's new in long-range shooting. There's a young girl that's interested, and I'm teaching her."

"Man! You gonna teach a young girl how to shoot? What happened to the 'I just want to be left alone'?"

"It's a long story. She found out that I was a sniper. She just kept coming over to my place and wouldn't let me alone, so I figured I might as well teach her."

"Like a stray dog?"

"Exactly."

"Sure, I can send you some info. I have plenty. I also have some CDs, you have a computer?"

"No, but I'm sure her brother does."

"Okay, I'll box up what I have here and send it your way. Good luck."

"Thanks. I'm thinking about taking her to Camp Perry next summer."

"That'd be great! I'll send you the dates next spring."

"Okay, talk to you later."

"Bye."

The next day Mike went out to his workshop to build Cat a practice rifle, one that would be as realistic as possible—weight, balance, length of pull, etc. He had an action and a stock. The local machine shop turned down a piece of steel with a threaded end he could use for a barrel. Cat could use this to practice her trigger squeeze and breathing. Everything he had was for a right-handed shooter. Her being a southpaw would take a bit of getting used to. The basics were the same. He would let her use his .308 Winchester to start off with. He would build her a rifle later. Left-handed equipment had gotten more available in the last few years.

The people in town were starting to notice the difference Cat was making in Mike's life. He was coming into town more often, not as grumpy. One said that they thought they heard him laugh. Another said they saw him smile.

*****

Cat was walking toward the diner when Judge Bean came up.

"If you have a minute, I'd like to talk to you. Can you stop by the office?"

"Sure, I'll come over right now. I can stop and see Mom after."

Cat followed Judge Bean over to the courthouse. After they were inside, Judge Bean pointed to a chair. "Have a seat."

Cat sat down. "Pretty nice day."

"Relax. As far as I know, you ain't in trouble."

"Good."

"I wanted to let you know that the state is sending a DNR officer to fill in while Conrad is laid up. Conrad will be getting out of the hospital soon, but it will be awhile before he'll be able to work full time."

"Them slime balls did put the hurt on him."

"Yes, they did. I got the letter from the state with the information on the new officer. He has been with the DNR for a little over a year. I called around. He is as I suspected—gung ho, goes by the book, and measures his success by how many arrests he makes. He does not take into account the human factor."

"I take it he won't be as nice to me as you guys have?"

"Or to the rest of the residents in the county. He's young, hasn't figured out that you can get more flies with honey than vinegar."

"I had better do a good job covering my tracks."

Judge Bean shook his head. "It'd be better you not make any tracks. Like I said, he measures his success by how many arrests and convictions he gets. It would put me in an awkward position. If I let you off with little punishment, he could send in a complaint to the state."

"Okay, I'll behave. What's his name?"

"Officer Shot."

"Is his first name *Big* or *Hot*?"

Judge Bean, doing his best not to laugh, said, "CAT!"

"Yes, Judge, I'll behave."

*****

Cat rode her bike into town to pick up some bait before heading over to Mike's to do some fishing. When Cat came out of the bait shop and started to get back on her bike, Officer Shot walked up to her.

"May I see your fishing license?"

"I ain't fishing."

"You have a pole and bait. I want to see your license, NOW!"

"How do you know I ain't going to a private pond?"

"I don't care. You have the equipment. I want to see your license."

"I'm going to a private pond, I don't need a license. It's on page 6, third paragraph down on the left side in the fishing regulation." *His first name must be Hot.*

"Look, *girly*, show me your license."

"I'm gonna report you for rape."

"Rape, I didn't rape you!"

"Well, you have the equipment, don't you?"

"Oh, we have a smart-ass kid, huh?"

"No, we have an arrogant half-bright game warden. Give you a badge and a gun and you think you're god. Creases so sharp in your uniform you could cut yourself. Boots so shiny, it's a wonder you don't blind yourself on a sunny day."

Shot glared at her.

Cat thinking to herself, *This oughta impress the judge. I'd better show him my license.*

With Shot still staring at Cat, she handed her license to him. "There, now if you see me on state ground, you won't have to ask me for it. As you can see, it has all the stamps."

Shot looked it over and then handed it back to her. As he turned around, Cat said, "Have a nice day. I will."

Officer Shot walked into the courthouse. Conrad was there visiting with Judge Bean.

Judge Bean said, "How's it going?"

"You sure have some smart-ass kids around here."

Conrad asked, "How so?"

"I just asked that girl out there for her fishing license. She started quoting fishing regs to *me*, page and paragraph."

Judge Bean responded, "That would be Cat. When she's around, we don't need to look anything up. We just ask her."

"She said she wasn't fishing. I told her she had the equipment."

"Then what?"

"She said she was going to report me for rape because I had the equipment!" Shot was still steaming as he left.

Conrad and Judge Bean held their laughter until Shot got outside.

Judge Bean said, "Report him for rape. I guess we don't have to worry about her. This might get interesting."

Conrad responded, "I'm gonna have to be careful not to tear any stitches from laughing so hard. Almost feel sorry for Shot, but on second thought, nah."

That story spread through the town faster than a forest fire on a windy day. Betty heard the story more than once while she was working at the diner that day.

*****

Cat was still mad as a wet hen when she got to Mike's. She told him about running into Officer Shot.

Mike listened to the whole story then burst out laughing. "You told him you were going to report him for rape 'cause he had the equipment?" He was laughing so hard he had tears in his eyes. He hadn't laughed like that for years.

Cat didn't think it was that funny. "I'm gonna see if the fish are biting."

Mike was still bent over from laughing. "Okay, go right ahead."

Cat went back to the pond. It wasn't long before she came back with a catfish, five nice bluegills, and a bass. She cleaned them, put them in a bowl of salt water, and set it in the refrigerator. Fishing or hunting always calmed her.

"There, that should make you a nice meal."

"You gonna fry 'em up for me?"

"Oh, I suppose."

"Well, come over here. I wanna check something out." Mike handed her his Winchester. "Hold this. I want to see how it fits you."

Cat was all smiles as she took a hold of it. It was a bit heaver and longer than her Rossi.

As Mike looked at her stance, he said, "Line up on something like the saltshaker on the stove." The stock could be a little shorter, but this would have to do for now." He took some measurements and wrote them down.

Cat handed the rifle back to Mike. "You gonna let me shoot this?"

"I know you're a southpaw, and this is for right-handed shooters, but we have to work with what I have. When do you want to start your lessons?"

"Yesterday."

"I guess we can start now." Mike cleared off the kitchen table then sat a couple of sandbags on it. He grabbed a target and taped it on the wall. Cat watched him in disbelief. Mike caught her out of the corner of his eye and started laughing.

"No, you're not gonna blow holes in my walls. You are going to start off with dry firing."

"Dry firing?"

"Yes, I want to see how your trigger squeeze and breathing are."

"Why do I have to do that? I know all about trigger squeeze and breathing control."

"If you already know, why you want me to teach you? Now, you gonna listen, or you wanna get a different coach?"

Cat looked toward the floor, knowing that she had better start listening if she wanted Mike to teach her. "Sorry, I'll be all ears."

Mike placed his rifle on the sandbags, having Cat sit in a chair behind the rifle. She put the stock up to her shoulder. He looked at her stance, moving her elbow closer to the rifle. "Looks pretty good. Now, where your cheek touches the stock is the spot weld. Every time you put the rifle to your shoulder, it has to be the same. This is important. The rifle needs to be an extension of your body."

"Like the rifle and I are one?"

"Yes. Later I will have you close your eyes and shoulder the rifle. It should be right where it needs be. No adjustments necessary."

"This is going to take a lot of work."

"Yes, it will. Now, let's check your trigger squeeze." Mike put a snap cap in the chamber and closed the bolt. "Now line up on the bull's-eye, take a breath, let some out till you feel comfortable, and squeeze."

Cat squeezed the trigger. The rifle moved just a little. After a few more times Mike set a dime on edge on the barrel. "Now try it and see if the dime stays there."

Cat squeezed the trigger ever so slowly. The dime fell off. "Ain't no way."

Mike had her get up. He put the dime back on the barrel, sat down, and squeezed the trigger. The dime was still sitting there.

Cat looked at Mike. "Will I be able to do that?"

"With enough practice."

"Well, I had better get home."

"Okay. Be back tomorrow to fry those fish?"

"And do some more practicing."

After Cat left, Mike looked over the material that Jim had sent him. A lot of advances have been made in long-range shooting, especially optics. Mike liked Cat being around; she was like a granddaughter he never had, plus her cooking was a lot better than TV dinners.

After Cat put her bike away, she walked into the house all excited. "Mom, Dad, guess what? Mike is going to teach me how to shoot!"

Betty replied, "Teach you how to shoot, don't you already know how?"

"No, I mean long-range shooting, a thousand yards."

Betty, not having a clue what Cat was talking about, replied, "That's nice of Mike."

Dave said, "He's a brave man."

"Well, supper's about ready. Cat, after you wash up, would you set the table."

"Sure, Mom."

After supper, Cat went to bed thinking how great it was moving down here.

*****

Officer Shot was always trying to nail Cat for something. This was starting to irritate her. One night she decided to keep him busy. Grabbing her backpack, binoculars, flashlight, and sketchpad, she headed toward the cave. She entered the valley so that Shot would see her. Cat sat up by the rock like she's done times before. It was a moonlit night; a light snow was coming down. She listened to the hoot owls as well as the coyotes howling in the distance. "This sure is pretty and peaceful." She scanned the valley. Before long, the monster showed up. He looked so magnificent standing there broadside, looking in her direction. His antlers reflected the moonlight. The light snow looked like glitter as it fell on him.

Officer Shot was watching her through his binoculars, talking to himself. "I knew it, you ain't getting away from me this time!"

Cat took out her sketchpad and sketched a picture of the buck. He stood there as though he knew what was going on. After she was done and had put her pad and pencils back in her backpack, the buck nodded and walked away, as if knowing she was done. As she picked up her backpack and started to leave, a yearling came into view.

"Not tonight, this is your lucky day. Sorry, coyotes. No free meal tonight."

She hiked over to the cave and went home the back way.

Officer Shot couldn't believe it. It was as though she had disappeared into thin air. He was talking to himself, as he walked back to his truck, "You got away this time, but I'll get you. There's a new sheriff in town. You ain't gonna get away from me, you little smart-ass."

Cat would lead Shot on more wild goose chases. It was getting personal with him. Every time he thought he had her, she would slip away. It became known as the game of "Cat and Warden." Officer Shot was getting no slack. When he walked down the street, somebody would yell, "Hey, Warden, I saw Cat with a fishing pole. Gonna ask her for her license?" The whole town was getting into the game. Young and old alike were on Cat's side. There was a board up on the barbershop wall that was keeping score. Every day it would be updated. You could bet on what the score would be at the end of the week. Put your guess and two dollars in an envelope, wait till the end of the week, and if you guessed it, you won the pot. If no one had the right answer, the money would be put in next week's pot. Most of the entries had the rookie at zero. Even the judge and Conrad played.

*****

Widow Johnson's oldest boy wanted Cat to take him deer hunting. It was too late for this season, but Cat would be able to get him ready for next year. On opening day, Cat killed a nice buck on her dad's property. She would have to tell the story to the boy every time she went over there. His mother would shake her head.

"The kids sure love it when you stop over. I appreciate all you have done. He can't wait till you can take him deer hunting. That's all he talks about."

"If it's all right, I can take him rabbit hunting."

"Sure, that'd be great. Bless your heart."

Cat smiled. "No problem."

"I have my husband's guns here, but they might be a little big for him."

"That's okay. I'll let him use mine."

"Bless your heart."

"I had better get home. I'm sure Mom has something for me to do."

"All right, come back anytime."

"Thanks, bye."

*****

After supper one night, Cat said to her mom, "I think I am going to take a bike ride."

"Gonna go to your second home, the woods?"

"Yeah, I haven't been out for a while. It's a clear night. There should be a lot of animals out tonight."

"You be careful."

"As always."

Cat was riding her bike to one of her favorite spots, a valley that had a lake and plenty of grass for the wildlife. It was a great place to relax, gaze at the stars, and watch the animals get a drink and graze on the grass. It was a good place to refresh her soul. She noticed Officer Shot's pickup alongside the road. Cat wasn't in the mood for games tonight, so she snuck by him.

Cat turned down a fire road toward the valley. When she got there, something just didn't seem right. She looked down toward the valley. There were two guys by a campfire. Off to the side was an old junky red pickup. Cat picked up her binoculars. What she saw made her more sick than mad. They had shot a small deer but had not killed it. They were poking it with a stick. She could hear it cry. The guys would just laugh and take another swig of whiskey. *They should be shot down like rabid dogs.*

Cat had a high respect for animals. The Good Lord put them on earth to use, not abuse and torture. She had no problem killing animals for food or their fur, or killing rodents and predators that were destroying crops and property. It was all natures predator-prey of the food chain. What these jerks were doing was not only illegal but just plain wrong. She sat there for a bit. So much for enjoying the moonlit night. *Now, what do I do? I guess it's a good thing I left my rifle at home.* She sat there a bit longer. *I've got it! Hot Shot wants to catch some slime balls. Here's his chance.*

Cat snuck back around Shot's truck. This time she rode past him, making sure he saw her. When he did, he started following her with his lights off.

Cat said to herself, "Trying to be sneaky keeping your lights off, huh?"

As she got to the turn off, she turned on her flashlight. She wanted to make sure he didn't get lost. Shot had taken the bait. Cat hid behind some trees to watch the show. When Officer Shot saw the guys at the campfire, he turned on his lights and sped toward the truck. The two jumped in their truck and took off. They drove about twenty feet, and both back wheels fell off.

Shot jumped out of his truck with his shotgun, pointed it at the two, and yelled, "Out of the truck, NOW!"

The two got out of the truck with their hands up and in full view. "Where's the girl?"

"What girl?"

"Don't give me any shit, scumbag, the girl that tried to warn you."

They started to put their hands down. "There ain't no girl here."

"Bullshit! Put your hands up. I followed her here."

"Look, pig, we don't know nutten about no girl."

"Get to the front of the truck." He held his shotgun with his right hand and grabbed his handcuffs in his left. One of the guys tried to hit him. Shot hit him in the face with the butt of his shotgun. While he fell to the ground spitting out blood and a couple of teeth, Officer Shot pointed the shotgun at the other. "You wanna try, dickhead?"

"Uh, no."

"Now grab one of those wheels that fell off your truck and set it by your buddy."

"What for?"

"Just do as I say. It would be a lot easier to just shoot ya."

He brought the wheel up and set it down by his friend.

Shot took his cuffs and threw them on the ground. "Pick 'em up. Put the cuff on your buddy's left hand, keyhole toward his body."

The guy did as he was told. "Now, what?"

"Put the other end through the wheel, and put the cuff on your left hand keyhole toward your body. That oughta keep you two from going too far."

Shot called the state police on the radio to pick up the suspects. While he waited, he walked up to the wounded deer and put it out of its misery.

Cat waited around till she heard the state police sirens.

The state police came, picked up the suspects, and took them to town. Judge Bean was waiting at the jail when the state police, and Officer Shot showed up with the suspects. As they took the suspects back to the cells, Shot kept yelling at them, "Where'd that girl go?"

"Like I said, asshole, there weren't no girl with us!"

Judge Bean said, "Calm down, Shot. While they're being put in the cell, come out here and tell me what happened."

Officer Shot sat down at the Judge Bean's desk and told him the whole story. He ended with, "I still say that Cat girl was with them."

Judge Bean rubbed his chin. "Now, let me get this straight. A girl that has been giving you the slip and staying one step ahead of you since you've been here just rode her bike past your truck like she never saw it."

"Yes, that's right."

"Then you started following her?"

"Yes."

"Okay, and then she turned her flashlight on, not knowing you were following her?"

"That's right. I told you, that girl's no good."

Judge Bean leaned back in his chair. "Now let me cut you in on something. Cat may bend the rules a bit, but there is no one in this county that respects wildlife the way she does. I know Cat pretty well. I would bet my last paycheck she didn't have her rifle, or there would've been a couple of dead bodies with the deer. You didn't follow her. She led you there."

"What, you think I'm that dumb?"

Judge Bean ignored the question. "Now go and write your report. You have a good case. Drugs and drug-making paraphernalia found in their truck. So you have a drug charge to go along with the animal cruelty charge. They are going to admit to everything so that they don't get charged with the kidnapping of an underage girl they've never heard of."

"All right."

"Clear your head, and be sure to read over your report after you're done. You don't want to look stupid." *Like he needs any help with that.*

"Anything else?"

"No, that's it. I'm gonna stay here tonight with the prisoners till the state transfers them in the morning."

Officer Shot left the jail and went to his truck. On the hood of his truck were two sets of lug nuts.

6

Cat went over to Mike's, hoping that he would let her shoot his Winchester. She knocked on his door.

"Come on in."

Cat walked in. "Hi, Mike."

"I figured it was about time for you to show up."

"How's that?"

"Well, it's been a few days since you've been over."

"Miss me?"

"Like the plague."

"When you gonna admit you like me hanging around?"

"Never. Come over here, I have something to show ya."

Cat walked over to Mike as he handed her the practice rifle he finished up the day before. Cat's eyes got big.

"For me?"

"Calm down. This is nonfiring. You can use it to practice your trigger squeeze."

"Wow, it sure looks real! You even put a scope on it."

"Want it to be as close to real as possible. You can take it home and practice."

"I will. When do I get to shoot your Winchester?"

"I figured that's why you showed up today. I don't see why we can't shoot today."

"Really?"

"Only if you want to." Mike picked up his rifle and cartridges. "Grab that target."

Cat smiled. "You had this planned."

"Not me. I have the bench set up at fifty yards. I will start you off there, then I'll move you back as you progress."

Mike hung the target and went back to the bench. He sat the sandbags on the bench then laid the rifle on the bags.

"Now sit down behind the rifle. The bench is a good place to start. Later, we'll get into prone, kneeling, and other shooting positions."

Cat was all smiles. She brought the rifle up to her shoulder and looked through the scope. "This is neat."

"All right, now make sure you hold the stock tight against your shoulder. This has a little more kick than your little Rossi. Think you're ready?"

"As I'll ever be."

Mike put a live cartridge in the chamber, and Cat closed the bolt. "Line up on the bull's-eye, and slowly squeeze the trigger."

Cat looked through the scope. When she had a good sight picture, she squeezed the trigger. The rifle barked. Cat found herself on the ground behind the bench.

Mike started laughing. "Didn't hold it tight, did ya?"

Cat got up and picked up her earmuffs. "Wow, guess not."

"Let's go see if you hit anything." Mike had loaded that cartridge on the hot side, not enough to be dangerous, just enough to get her attention. They walked down to the target.

"Look at that, right through the center!"

Cat was rubbing her left shoulder. "Not bad, huh?"

"That's pretty good. Shoot a couple more rounds, then we'll move back to the hundred-yard mark. That is if you don't want to quit."

"What, you think I'm some kind of sissy? Of course I wanna shoot some more!"

"That'a girl."

The rifle didn't seem to kick as much as it did with the first shot. Cat wondered if it was because she was holding the rifle tighter against her shoulder or if Mike had something to do with the first cartridge. Cat stayed around while Mike cleaned his rifle and put it away. Cat noticed some magazines and catalogs setting on the table.

"May I look at these?"

"Sure, a friend of mine that competes at Camp Perry sent me a whole box of stuff. He even sent me some CDs, but I don't have a computer."

"Ben has a laptop. Maybe he can bring it over next time."

"I'd sure like to know what's on them. Equipment has improved since I was in the game."

"You think I'll ever be able to compete at places like Camp Perry?"

Mike picked up a magazine and handed it to Cat. "Take this home with you, and read about how to control your breathing. That is very important. Then you can learn how to slow your heart rate down."

"I know about breathing, but heart rate...?"

"At a thousand yards, everything counts. You will need to be able to squeeze your shots off between heartbeats."

"I guess I have a lot of learning to do."

"Yes, you do. Take your practice rifle home and practice. I want you to be able to keep the dime still standing on the barrel after you squeeze the trigger."

Cat picked up her stuff and walked toward the door. "I'll see you later."

"All right, remember practice, practice, practice."

After Cat left, Mike poured himself a glass of lemonade and sat down at his kitchen table. It gave him a good feeling that he would be able to pass his knowledge down to the younger generation. Marksmanship demanded discipline from the shooter. This would help Cat with other challenges in life from schoolwork to life in general.

Mike picked up the phone and dialed Jim's number. The phone started to ring. It was answered, "Hello."

"Hello, Jim?"

"Yeah, this is Jim."

"Hey, this is Mike. How've ya been?"

"Pretty good. Had a chance to look over the material I sent you?"

"Yeah, I have some of it in front of me now. Cat shot my .308 Winchester. She didn't do too bad. I want to either build her a rifle or have one built. Wondering which caliber you recommend."

"There are a lot of good ones out there. Thinking one thousand yards or better?"

"Yeah, that's her goal, at least one thousand yards."

"Some guys are using the .50 BMG. The .418 Rigby ain't bad. Personally, I like the 6BR or the .338 Lapua."

"I was thinking about the .338 Lapua. From what I have read it's a good round."

"I like it. If you are looking for a gunsmith to build a rifle, there's a guy in North Manchester, Indiana, who builds rifles for competitions."

"Does he build them for southpaws?"

"That I don't know. I can send you his address and number. If not, Surgeon rifles build a hell of a rifle, might cost a little more for a left-handed action. Another thing you might be able to do is buy an action from Surgeon and have him build a rifle around it."

"That's an idea. I'll write him a letter and ask him. I'm thinking about taking Cat to Camp Perry next summer."

"That'd be great."

"Yeah, thought we'd stay through the centerfire competition."

"I can book you a room in the same hotel that I'll be staying at. My daughter will be there, Cat can stay with her."

"All right, I'll talk to ya later."

"Okay, bye."

*****

Cat rode her bike over to Mike's. Mike was sitting on his porch drinking a cup of coffee. As Cat walked up to the porch, Mike said, "A bit chilly for riding your, bike ain't it?"

"Was gonna say the same thing about sitting on the porch."

"Weatherman said it's gonna warm up later this afternoon. Maybe we can go back and see if you can put anything in the X-ring."

"That sounds good."

"What's the matter? You look like somebody shot your best coon dog."

"Is it that obvious?"

"You're not the easiest to read, but yes."

"I was over to Widow Johnson's yesterday. She is about out of meat. I've been teaching her oldest how to shoot, but I won't be able to take him deer hunting till next season."

"You've taking a liking to them, haven't you?"

"Yeah, her kids are great, and she is such a nice lady. I'd like to go out and get her a deer, but with Hot Shot still in town, I can't take the chance. He is bound and determined to catch me at something. It was a lot simpler when he wasn't here. Then I could just go to the meadow at night and get one."

"I figured that's how you were supplying Widow Johnson and a couple other families with venison."

"Yeah, that's what I was doing. I am sure you knew that. That's how I happened to be there when Conrad ran into trouble."

"Yeah, I did."

"I guess I could give her some out of our freezer."

"Hang on a minute, you still playing Cat and Warden?"

"Sure, anything to make him look stupid, not that he needs any help."

Mike had an idea. He didn't much care for Shot, especially with the way he was always after Cat.

"How do you usually take the venison to Widow Johnson?"

"I wrap it in old bedsheets that Mom has thrown out then put it in plastic bags. I put it in my backpack then take it to her house."

"Okay, tell you what. You go home, get your backpack, sheets, and plastic bags. Be back here in a couple hours."

"What you up to?"

"You'll see. Now get going."

"Okay, see ya in a couple hours." Cat jumped on her bike and headed home.

Mike went into the house, grabbed a couple of coolers, and put them in the back of his pickup. He drove over to a butcher shop in the next town. He walked in. A big guy came up to the counter.

"Hey, Tiny, how's it going?"

"Mike, is that you?" Tiny walked around the counter and shook Mike's hand. "Haven't seen you in a coon's age, thought maybe the buzzards got ya. How ya been?"

"Nah, not yet. Hey, I need some chunks of beef."

"What would you like? I'm just getting ready to cut up a front quarter."

"Just give me some chuck roasts. Cut it so it will fit in these coolers."

"Gonna have a barbecue?"

"More like a roast."

Tiny took the coolers to the back room. In a few minutes, he came back with the coolers filled with meat. He helped Mike carry them out to his truck. Mike went back inside and paid the bill.

"Thanks, Tiny. I'll see ya later."

"Thank you, hope that works out for ya."

"I'm sure it will."

*****

Widow Johnson and her kids were in the grocery store to pick up a few things.

The oldest boy asked his mother, "Is Cat ever gonna bring us anymore deer meat? I'm getting tired of cheap hotdogs."

"I don't know. She's been pretty busy."

The next aisle over, Officer Shot was listening. *I knew it. I'll get her before I leave town.* He left the store and staked out Widow Johnson's house.

*****

Cat was sitting on Mike's porch with her backpack when Mike pulled up. He got out of his truck and carried the coolers into the house.

Cat followed him in. "What are we going to do?"

"The way I see it, Shot wants to throw you in jail. I say let him."

"Say what?"

"Don't worry. He will have to let you out."

"I don't know if I like this plan."

"It'll be great. Now cut up this meat and put it in your backpack like you do the venison."

Cat was starting to get the idea. She cut it into pieces that would fit into the bags she brought then put in her backpack. "Now what?"

"Take it over to Widow Johnson's, and see if Shot takes the bait."

"This is a lot earlier than I usually go."

"Don't matter, I'd bet my last bullet he's already watching the widow's place."

Cat hiked over to Widow Johnson's place. Sure enough, Officer Shot was parked off the road behind a couple of trees. She walked along the side of the house to the back door, resisting the urge to sneak over and let the air out of his tires. She looked back. Shot was reading a book. *I don't think Hot Shot saw me. I had better walk around the house to make sure.*

Officer Shot looked up from his book just in time to see Cat walk down the side of the house. *I gotcha now, girly.*

Cat knocked on the back door. Widow Johnson came to the door. "Cat! My land girl, what'a doing?"

"I brought you some meat."

"You shouldn't have. You're gonna get yourself in trouble."

"I'll be all right."

Cat set the backpack down and started putting the meat on the table. Widow Johnson got a knife and freezer bags. "The boys are sure gonna be happy, but you're taking a big chance coming this early, especially with that game warden after you the way he is."

"Ah, don't worry, hard to outsmart me."

The back door opened. Officer Shot came busting into the kitchen. "Hold it right there! I finally caught you, girly!"

"Oh yeah, where's your search warrant?"

"Don't need one, probable cause."

"For what?"

"Illegal deer meat, I knew you were no good."

"I didn't do anything illegal."

"Yeah, right, get your hands behind your back." Shot put handcuffs on Cat.

Widow Johnson walked toward Cat. "Why you picking on this girl?"

"Shut up and get back, or I will charge you too."

Cat looked at Widow Johnson. "Don't worry, I'll be all right."

"Shut up, girly."

As Shot walked Cat out of the house, she turned to Widow Johnson and winked. Widow Johnson smiled to herself, wondering what Cat was up to. Shot put Cat in his truck, fastened her seat belt, and drove off.

*****

Judge Bean sat down to eat a steak and fried potatoes. "Finally, I get to relax and eat a decent home-cooked meal." After taking his first bite, he said, "Not bad if I say so myself."

The phone rang.

"Now what?" He answered the phone, "Hello."

"You let that girl go!" summoned the voice on the other end.

"What are you talking about?"

"Cat! That hotshot arrested Cat. Now you let her go!" continued the voice.

"I don't know what you are talking about. I just got home... trying to eat my supper."

"You get to town and release her."

"Calm down. I'm on my way."

Judge Bean put his supper in the oven. "Never fails." As he was getting his boots on, the phone rang again. "Hello."

"What you mean arresting Cat?" bellowed the caller.

"I didn't arrest her. I'm heading to town now."

Judge Bean hung up the phone, and it immediately started ringing again. "I'll let voice mail get it." He grabbed his coat and picked up his cell phone. It already had five text messages and six missed calls.

"Oh, this is going to be a long night!"

*****

A small crowd was forming around the jail when Shot and Cat showed up. He took her inside and locked her in the cell. The crowd booed Shot as he retrieved the backpack from his truck.

The crowd had grown by the time Judge Bean got to town. As he got out of his car, he heard, "Let Cat go."

He walked into the office. Officer Shot was sitting at Judge Bean's desk with the backpack.

"First thing, get out of my chair."

Officer Shot got up. "I told you that girl was no good."

"Okay, tell me what happened."

"I was at the store when I heard one of the widow's boys ask when Cat was going to bring them some more deer meat, so I staked out her house. Pretty soon Cat shows up with this backpack. I went inside the house, and they were cutting up the meat to put it in the freezer. That's when I arrested her."

"You just can't leave her alone, can ya?"

"She was breaking the law."

"All right, sit while I go back and talk to Cat."

"She'll lie to you."

Judge Bean went back to talk to Cat, wondering how she could've let Shot catch her. "What'd you do? I told you to be careful."

"All I did was take some beef that Mike had bought to Widow Johnson's place."

"You... Mike did what?"

"Widow Johnson told me she was out of meat, so I told Mike. He went out and bought some beef. I put it in my backpack and took it to her. Then Officer Shot shows up, busts through the door, and starts yelling that I had done something illegal."

"Did you tell him that it was beef?"

"No, he didn't give me a chance. He just kept yelling about how he finally caught me."

"If I had to guess, I'd say this was all Mike's idea."

Cat didn't say anything. Judge Bean walked back to the front.

Judge Bean opened the door and looked at the crowd. *This could get ugly. So this is how Matt Dillon felt.* He walked out of the jail.

"Everybody, calm down."

A voice from the crowd, "As soon as you let Cat go."

"Give me a minute."

The crowd had grown even larger than when he had entered the jail. Mike was standing by Cat's parents. Betty turned to Dave.

"What are we going to do? I knew she would get into more trouble, now she's in jail."

Mike turned around. "Don't worry. She'll be out in no time."

Judge Bean spotted Mike. "Mike, get your ass in here *now!*"

Mike turned to Dave. "Might as well come with me, y'all don't want to miss the show."

Mike, Dave, and Betty went inside. Judge Bean shut the door.

"Take a seat."

As Betty sat down, "What's this about?"

"That's what we're gonna find out. Officer Shot, why did you bring Cat in?"

"I caught her with illegal deer meat at the widow's place. The evidence is on your desk."

"I see."

"It's all right there. I told you she was up to no good."

"So how did you catch her?"

"I staked out the widow's place."

Betty stood up. "Don't you have anything better to do than picking on girls and widows?"

Judge Bean pointed to the chair. "Calm down, Betty, take a seat. We'll get this sorted out."

Officer Shot continued, "I saw Cat with a backpack go into the widow's house. I waited for a bit, then I went inside."

"So you just walked in with no search warrant."

"I had probable cause."

"You saw her kill a deer?"

"Well, no, but she was sneaking to the widow's place with her backpack."

"Sounds pretty lame to me."

"Don't matter, I caught her red-handed."

"You're sure it's deer meat?"

"What else would it be? I can have the meat tested."

"That probably won't be necessary. Mike, you have anything to say?"

Mike, trying not to laugh, said, "Yeah, I went over to Ribeye and Sons and bought some beef roasts for the widow. I told Cat to take it to the widow. Here is the receipt."

"Knowing full well that Officer Shot would be watching Cat?"

Mike said laughing, "Yep, he's such an easy mark."

Dave and Betty started laughing. Judge Bean was doing his best not to. Officer Shot was more than a little annoyed.

Officer Shot stood up. "We can charge them with interfering with law enforcement."

Judge Bean replied, "Have you seen that crowd out there? It would be best to drop this whole thing. You had better stop with this vendetta against Cat. You started gaining a little respect when you caught those slime balls, which, do I have to remind you, without Cat's help, you wouldn't have caught them?"

Judge Bean let Cat out of her cell. He turned to everyone, "Now, no more playing games. Officer Shot, go out and look for some real criminals."

"Yes, Judge."

"Mike, get this meat back to the widow's before it spoils. Now, since it's your fault my supper was interrupted, you owe me a steak dinner."

"Yes, Judge."

"Dave, Betty, take your daughter home."

"Yes, Judge."

"All of you, get out of my office, *now!*"

Mike grabbed the meat. The rest of them followed him out the door. When the crowd saw Cat coming out, they all cheered. As Officer Shot walked to his truck, an old woman walked up and hit him with her handbag. "Pick on somebody your own size, you big bully."

Cat asked her dad, "Is it all right if I go with Mike and help Widow Johnson with the meat?"

"You gonna stay out of jail?"

Cat smiled, "At least for a day or two."

Mike said, "I'll make sure she gets home."

Dave said, "I don't think the judge was too happy about his supper getting interrupted."

"No, probably not, but he'll get over it. I bet ole Hot Shot wishes he'd left Cat alone."

"It was entertaining."

"I'll say. Best money I've ever spent!"

7

Cat didn't really mind school even though it did cut into her shooting and hunting time. History, government, and gym classes were a breeze. Math, science, and English was a bit more of a challenge.

Cat had to take home economics this semester. She didn't want to take this class. What Mom hadn't taught her about cooking and sewing, she could learn on her own. The last thing she wanted was some health nut teaching her how to cook.

Cat thought it would be best to just keep her mouth shut and slide by. That worked for about two days. The teacher was showing the class how to make a healthy breakfast. She started out by showing them how to poach eggs. This was more than Cat could bear, ruin an egg by cooking it in water. Cat raised her hand. She wouldn't be able to keep her mouth shut on this one.

The teacher said, "Yes, Cat, you have a question?"

"Why would anybody want to cook an egg in water without the shell? That's crazy."

The class started to chuckle.

The teacher not amused. "And how would you cook eggs?"

Cat, more than happy to explain, said, "First I would get an iron skillet and fry up a pound of bacon. While the bacon was draining on paper towels and the grease was still hot, I would fry the eggs. That way the eggs would take up some of the flavor of the bacon."

"That is just way too much grease."

"You can always let the eggs drain a little before you put 'em on the plate."

"Still, bacon and eggs fried in grease are bad for your health, especially your heart."

"Maybe, but great for your taste buds."

The teacher finished teaching the class. Cat sat there thinking, *I will be lucky if I pass this class, let alone get a good grade.*

*****

There were a few new students that enrolled this semester. Cat noticed one in the cafeteria sitting at a table by himself. He was a skinny boy and looked geekier then her brother. He was made fun of quite a bit.

Cat walked up to his table, "Mind if I sit here?"

He looked up surprised, and suspicious, that anyone would want to sit with him, especially a girl. "No, go right ahead."

Cat set her tray on the table. "You one of the new kids?"

"Yeah, we just move here from Duluth, Minnesota."

"Is it true that the four seasons there are June, July, August, and winter?"

Breaking a smile, he said, "Yeah, that's about it. Aren't you afraid that you will be picked on being seen talking to me?"

"Nah, I've been here long enough for the troublemakers to know that I'll punch them in the nose."

The boy smiled. "You must be Cat."

"Yeah, how did you know?"

"We moved into the house next to Bob, the one that you gave a black eye and broken nose to."

Cat smiled back. "He never called me a girly-girl again."

"That's what he said. By the way, I'm Barry."

Cat thought to herself, *I wonder if it's razz or blue.*

"Why are you called Cat? Is it because you're cunning?"

"We'll go with short for Catherine."

Cat finished her lunch then told Barry she needed to get to her next class.

Barry, smiling again, said, "Okay, I'll see you later."

As Cat left for her class Barry thought to himself, *It looks like I'll have at least one friend at this school, I hope.* He had learned to be cautious of people that came out of nowhere to be friendly to him. More than once it had been a setup, especially with girls. But Cat seemed different; he would give her a chance.

*****

"All right, class," the home economics teacher said as she walked into the classroom, "the required project for this quarter will be a prepared dish. There will be three areas that will be graded on. One will be presentation, 2 tastes, and 3 is the recipe easy to follow? You may make up your own recipe. Get one from a cookbook, your friends, or family. If you tweak a recipe, both copies must be turned in with the changes marked. A journal will need to be kept while you are working on your project, how you came up with the idea, and what resources you used. This will keep you from having grandma fix it for you. This will be 20 percent of your grade this quarter. Any questions?"

Cat raised her hand.

Sighing, the teacher said, "Yes, Cat."

"Can I make anything I want?"

"That should be 'may I'? Yes, anything except desserts."

As Cat left the class, she thought to herself, *I can do this. I'll show Miss Bean Sprout-Tofu what good food is.*

Cat left school and stopped by the diner to see her mom.

As she walked through the door, Mom said, "Hi, honey. How was school?"

"Not bad, I met one of the new kids at lunch today. He is more of a geek than Ben."

Betty smiled, "Is that possible?"

"I know, hard to believe. I have a project I have to do for home ec."

"Your favorite class."

"Yeah, have to prepare a dish, anything except dessert."

"Have any ideas?"

"I was thinking about rabbit stew. There are plenty of rabbits around, and we froze plenty of vegetables from the garden."

"That sounds like something you can do. Want a cup of coffee?"

"Sure."

Betty poured Cat a cup of coffee. "I have to work later than I thought. You can go over to the library, and I will pick you up when I'm done."

"Okay, be all right if I fix supper till I get my dish perfected?"

"Gonna use your family for test subjects?"

"Sounds like a plan."

"Fine with me, it'll give me a break."

Cat finished up her coffee then gave her mom a hug. "I'm heading to the library."

"Bye." Betty wondered how three children from the same parents could be so different.

*****

Cat brought her lunch tray over to Barry's table and sat down. "Hi."

"Hi, doesn't it bother you to sit with me when no one else will?"

"Nope, we're the only ones that have our own table."

"I guess that's one way to look at it."

"So you say you're from Minnesota. How did you end up here?"

"My dad works for a mining company and got transferred down here."

"What does he do?"

"He is in environmental control. He makes sure the company is in compliance with the EPA regulations and anticipates new ones coming up. His job is basically to help with policies that keep the workers and the residents in the area safe from the operations of the mine. He summed it up one night by saying, 'I have to keep the EPA, the workers, the residents of the area, the company, and the stockholders happy.'"

"Sounds like a tough job."

"He said it's harder than being married."

They both laughed. Barry noticed a boy walking toward the table. "There's that boy that transferred from another school. He is a real bully, always picking on me. His name is Bill, doesn't like being called Billy. I found that out the hard way. He stuffed me in a garbage can."

"Did you tell anyone?"

"No, that would just make it worse."

Bill came up to the table then purposely knocked Barry's tray in his lap. "What's the matter geek? Can't eat without getting food all over you?" Bill laughed and continued to make fun of Barry.

Cat stood up. "Why don't you pick on somebody your own size and leave him alone?"

"And if I don't?"

Cat was getting ready to show him.

Barry interrupted, "Cat, it's all right. I wasn't hungry anyways."

"No, it's not all right."

"Cat, let it rest."

Billy said, "Cat, I've heard about you. I ain't 'fraid of no girl."

"Can't help it if you ain't too bright."

"Geek, I'll catch you later when you ain't got your girly body-guard with you. Maybe I'll stuff you in the fish tank next time and see if geeks can swim."

Cat started making a move.

Barry grabbed her arm. "Let it go."

Billy left. Cat helped Barry clean up the mess.

"Why did you stop me? I'm not that big, but I'm quick and hit hard. I know I could've given him a black eye and broke his nose before he knew what happened."

"After talking to Bob, I have no doubt. I don't want you to get into trouble for me. I have to figure out a way to fight my own fights."

"I guess I can understand that, but if you change your mind, let me know."

"Oh, I will! I didn't think I would be able to stop you after he called you girly."

"I restrained myself."

As Cat left the cafeteria, she thought to herself, *The only way Barry could win a fight with Billy would be to find him sleeping and hit him with a baseball bat. That is, if he could lift it.*

*****

As the family sat down for supper, Ben said, "I'll be glad when Cat gets her project done, can't be many rabbits left in the county."

Cat replied, "There's plenty."

"I was afraid of that."

"I only have three days left till I have to turn it in."

"Then Mom will start cooking again. Hopefully something without rabbit."

"Just shut up and tell me how this recipe tastes."

"About the same as the last ten."

"Yeah right. Which one's the best?"

"This one. Now we can have something different tomorrow?"

"Thanks a lot. Mom, Dad, what do you think?"

Mom, as she took another bite, said, "I think you may be trying too hard. You need to relax."

Dad put down his fork. "I think you have to think outside the cookbook."

Cat replied, "What do you mean?

"When my mom made beef stew, she would flour and brown the meat before she would add the vegetables. The browned flour would make it thick and add flavor."

"Thanks, Dad. I can do the same with the rabbit. I'll flour it and brown it in bacon grease. Why didn't I think of that?"

Ben whispered to Dad, "We have to all agree that the next try is the best. If I eat any more rabbit, I am going to start hopping. My ears are already getting longer."

*****

Cat sat in home ec class while one of the students, Lucy, brought her dish up to the teacher. It would be Cat's turn in two days. Lucy set the dish on the teacher's desk and turned to the class and explained how she made the dish.

"I am a vegetarian. I found this recipe on eathealthy.com. It is a vegetarian dish, low on fat."

After the teacher tasted it, she exclaimed, "Very good, Lucy. Are there any questions from the class?"

The teacher sighed when Cat raised her hand. "Yes, Cat."

"I just want to know if you are a vegetarian because you love animals, or is it 'cause you hate plants?"

The class started laughing.

The teacher said, "Cat, that was uncalled for."

"I was just wondering."

Lucy said, "I am a vegetarian because I think it is healthier."

"Fair enough."

Cat went home right after school and cooked supper using her dad's suggestion. If she were to be honest, she was also getting tired of rabbit.

The family sat down for yet another meal of rabbit stew. As Ben took a bite, "It ain't fair that Liz's not here to enjoy our pain."

Cat responded, "Oh, shut up."

After Dave took a bite, he smiled. "Cat, I think you've done it. This is the best."

Betty added, "Yes, this is the best."

Cat said, taking a bite, "Are you sure you ain't just saying this?"

Ben was already going for seconds. "Why didn't you make it this way first? It would've saved us a lot of suffering."

Cat knew that Ben was serious because there was no way he would be taking seconds if he didn't really like it. This was the first time that there weren't any leftovers.

Before anybody left the table, Cat said, "Thank you for helping me, and to reward you, Mom will cook tomorrow."

*****

As Cat was thumbing through one of Mike's magazines, she said, "Hey, Mike, what did you do in the Marines? I heard you were in the Special Forces."

Mike's face lost all expression. "I was a sniper in Force Recon. I did my best to keep my men and myself from getting killed while inflicting as much damage to the enemy as I could. Winning a war with rules is impossible. Our government would not let us fight to win, and then the media..." Mike stopped.

He hadn't given the war much thought since he met Cat. He realized that the Vietnam War was as far back to her as World War II was to him. He knew that Cat was probably just curious.

"You know, Cat, I really don't want to talk about that now, maybe some other time."

Cat wished she hadn't brought it up. "Oh, okay, didn't mean to upset you."

"You didn't upset me. It just brought up some memories that I try to forget. Now let's work on your breathing and trigger pull. I want to enter you in some competitions this spring. Maybe if the weather ain't too bad tomorrow we can go out back and shoot."

Cat smiled. "That'd be great."

*****

Cat invited Barry over to her house. Ben and Barry hit it off right away. They were talking so much geek that Cat couldn't keep up.

Barry looked at Ben's computer and asked, "What're you working on?"

"Cat wants to get into long-range shooting. I've been looking over some books and magazines that her friend Mike gave her. I want to see if I can develop a program to figure out bullet drop on different loads and bullet weight. Also, how the wind affects the flight of the bullet."

"How far does she want to shoot?"

"As far as she can, she wants to compete in thousand-yard matches or farther if possible."

"What's the fun in that? Why doesn't she just get closer?"

Cat came into the room. "Because it's a challenge and it's fun to see how far away you can hit a target."

"To each his own."

"What do you do for fun?"

Barry's eyes lit up. "I've been working on the next digit of pi."

"That's fun?"

"Oh, and I am writing a paper on how to breed apples so that they taste like grapes."

"What is the purpose in that? If you want the taste of grapes, do what I do, eat grapes."

"It's challenging to make one fruit taste like another."

"The next thing you know, you'll want a pear that tastes like a peach."

"Hey, never thought of that, the texture of a pear tastes like a peach."

"Just joking. I mean, what do you do for fun? Ever go fishing?"

"Fishing? That makes no sense. First you have to get a pole, bait, and find a place to fish. After that you have to wait on the fish to bite. If you catch any, you have to clean them and cook them."

"Well, yeah."

"Why do that? You can go to the store, buy fish that is in squares, put them in the oven, and when they're done, put them on bread. The squares fit perfectly on the slices of bread."

Cat shook her head as she left Ben and Barry to their geek talk, thinking to herself, *No wonder he gets picked on.*

Mom was in the kitchen fixing supper.

Cat walked in. "Mom, would it be okay if I asked Barry to stay for supper?"

"I don't see why not. I have plenty."

"Okay, I'll ask him."

As Cat walked into Ben's room, Ben said, "Hey, Cat, Barry says he can design a program for your shooting."

Cat looked at Barry. "You can?"

"Sure, all I need is all the variables that are involved. The more I have, the more accurate it'll be."

"I know some of them. I'll talk to Mike and get a list. I guess there are some advantages to having geeky friends."

"As soon as you get all that, give it to me, and I'll get started. I can use that for extra credit in computer class."

"No problem. Would you like to stay for supper? Mom says we have plenty."

"Sure, I'll have to call my mom and ask her if it'd be okay."

"There's a phone in the kitchen."

Barry called his mom then went back to Ben's room to play computer games until supper was ready.

After they were all seated, Betty said, "Cat, it's your turn to say grace."

Ben whispered to Barry, "The length of the prayer will depend on how hungry Cat is."

Cat folded her hands. "Lord, thank You for this food and also for me meeting Barry. I am sure that with Your help and his computer skills, I'll take some first places in rifle competitions next year. Amen."

Barry turned to Ben, "That sure is a strange table prayer."

"Oh, you ain't heard anything. If this was the day before deer season, she would've ask the Lord to lead a deer to her stand."

"This food sure looks and smells good."

"Thank you," Betty beamed.

Cat said, "It sure does. Mom knows how to cook a good venison roast."

Barry asked, "Venison?"

"Yeah, you know, deer meat."

As Barry took a bite, he said, "I've never had deer meat before. It has a good flavor, the texture is a little different from beef."

Betty said, "There's less fat than beef."

Cat said between putting bites of food in her mouth, "No wonder you're so skinny. You analyze your food instead of eating it."

Barry replied, "I don't know how you can taste anything as fast as you eat."

Cat grinned, as this wasn't the first time she's heard that. "I have fast taste buds."

After supper, Dave took Barry home.

Barry's mom said, "Thanks, we'll have Cat and Ben over for a cookout some time."

"They would like that. Bye."

"Good night."

*****

It was Cat's turn to present her project. She sat her Crock-Pot of rabbit stew on the teacher's desk.

"I made rabbit stew."

"It sure smells good."

"Thank you."

The teacher put some in a bowl. While it was cooling, she said, "Are there any questions you would like to ask Cat?"

Lucy raised her hand.

"Yes, Lucy."

"Why did you use rabbit? Do you hate rabbits?"

Cat grinned. "I guess I had that coming. No, actually I love rabbit, fried or otherwise."

The class started laughing.

The teacher said, "All right, class, now settle down." She took a bite of the stew. "This is very good."

"Thank you."

The teacher took another bite then got a strange look on her face. You could see the disappointment on Cat's face. As the teacher took something out of her mouth and laid it on her desk, she asked, "What's this?"

Cat looked at it. "Looks like a piece of number 6 lead shot."

"How did that get into your stew?"

"I must have missed it when I was preparing the rabbit."

"Why was it there to begin with?"

"I always aim for the head, but when using a shotgun, some pellets can get into the meat."

"You mean you shot the rabbit for the stew?"

"Well, yeah, you don't think I picked it up along the road, do you?"

The students started laughing.

The teacher said, "Okay, class, quiet down."

Cat laid her journal on the desk. "Here's my journal. I've outlined the project from start to finish." Cat went back to her seat disappointed.

On the way out of class, Lucy walked up to Cat and said, "That's too bad about your stew. I'm sure you worked hard on it."

Cat grinned. "Thanks, maybe I tried too hard."

"You know what I like about you?"

"I didn't know you did. I mean, I do eat a lot of meat. I could probably be a vegetarian if bacon grew on trees."

Lucy laughed. "It doesn't bother me if you eat meat. That's your choice. I am a vegetarian not a vegan. Actually, I am a semivegetarian. I eat some poultry, fish, eggs, and some dairy products."

"So what is it you like about me?"

"Never have to wonder what you're thinking. You speak your mind. You don't try to make people like you. If they like you fine, if not, that's fine too."

"Well, I've never been accused of sugarcoating anything."

Lucy laughed. "See you tomorrow."

"I'll be here."

At the end of the week, Cat got her grade. Fortunately, it was divided into two parts. She received a B for the journal but failed on the dish. The reason—a toxic substance in the food.

Cat knew it would do no good to argue. She figured she could do better on the next project, which was making an article of clothing. She just wanted to pass this class.

*****

Cat sat down at the lunch table with Barry.

"Hi, I have a list of the variables so that you can design that program."

"Great, now I can get started."

"I think that is about everything that can affect bullet flight."

Barry said, looking over the list, "It looks like you've included everything, wind speed, altitude, bullet weight, bullet speed, and even the rotation of the earth. How far do you plan on shooting?"

"The farther, the better. I hope to be able to work up to a mile or better. There are some thousand-yard matches I want to shoot in."

"What's this spin drift?"

"Oh, that's the distance that the bullet moves just from spinning."

"Okay, I will need the speed of the rotation."

"I'll ask Mike."

"I can still get started. I will set it up so all you have to do is punch in the numbers."

"That'll be great."

Lucy walked up to the table. "May I sit down?"

Cat replied, "Sure."

Ben walked up. "Have room for me?"

Cat said, "Yeah, I thought you ate in the other period."

"My classes got changed."

"Lucy, this is my brother, Ben, and this is Barry."

"Hi."

Ben asked, "Hi, you that vegetarian in Cat's class?"

Wanting to crawl under the table, Cat said, "Ben!"

Lucy said chuckling, "That's all right, I've been called worse."

Billy walked up to their table. "This must be the misfit-and-geek table."

Cat looked at Billy. "Why don't you go someplace where you're welcomed? Oh, that's right, there ain't no place."

"Looks like the only ones that welcome you are misfits and losers." He pushed Lucy's lunch off the table into her lap. "What's the matter, can't eat without getting it all over yourself?"

Ben and Barry each grabbed Cat as she started getting up. Ben said, "Easy, Cat, let it go."

Billy said, "Told you I ain't 'fraid of no girl. And you geek will take a swim in the fish tank this week." Pointing to Lucy, he said, "I might throw her in with ya." Billy left laughing.

Cat looked at Barry and Ben. "You know this needs to stop, and I can stop it."

Barry said, "I am working on a plan."

"I've already have a plan, called give him a knuckle sandwich."

"You have to let me fight my own fight."

Cat went over and helped Lucy clean up the mess. "Were you really gonna fight that guy?"

"Yep."

"He's pretty big."

"The bigger they are, the harder they fall."

"Still, aren't you scared?"

"He's a bully. Stand up to them, and 90 percent of the time, they'll back down."

"And the other 10 percent?"

"Then you have to *knock* 'em down."

*****

The weather was starting to warm up. Cat and Ben went over to Mike's to do some shooting. Ben knocked on the door.

"Come on in."

"Hi, Mike."

"What are you two up to?"

Cat replied, "I was hoping to do some shooting."

"You been practicing your trigger pull?"

"Sure have."

"Well, let's see how you're doing." Mike put some sandbags on the table. He sat his rifle on the bags and put a snap cap in the chamber. "Okay, let me see."

"What, no dime?"

Mike laughed as he got a dime and put it on the barrel.

Cat slowly squeezed the trigger. The dime stayed put. "See, I told you I've been practicing."

Mike decided she was ready for the next step. He had her try again. Just as she was ready to pull the trigger, he went up behind her and yelled. Cat knocked the rifle and everything else that was loose off the table. Mike and Ben started laughing.

Cat was not amused. "What the hell was that for?"

"Next step, you have to be able to block everything out and concentrate on shooting."

"Even from a raving lunatic?"

"Yeah, I had probably better sight in the rifle before we shoot."

"You mean we are going to shoot?"

"Yeah, it's a nice day, might as well."

They went out back to shoot. Mike fired three rounds to make sure that it was still sighted in, then Cat shot. Mike was impressed how fast Cat was catching on. They all went back into the house. After Mike cleaned his rifle, he said to Cat, "You're doing pretty good. You keep practicing your trigger pull and breathing. Ben, I want you to try and break her concentration."

"How?"

"Just do anything to mess her up, like I did. Just be annoying. I am sure you can do that."

Cat replied, "Yeah, he doesn't have to try to be annoying."

Mike grinned. "All right, you two go home and practice. I have entered you in a four-hundred-yard match."

"You have? When?"

"The third week of May."

"Great!"

Cat was starting to wonder about Mike's training program, but if it made her a great shooter, it would be worth it. Ben was getting excited about his part to help his sister. Let the fun begin.

8

Cat rode her bike over to see the old man Smith who lived in a small cabin behind an abandon railroad depot. Cat knocked on his door.

"Hey, old man, you home?"

"Yeah, young lady, come in. Now that we got our age differences out of the way, what ya want?"

"I need some tanned deer skin."

"Ya do?'

"Yeah, I am going to make a deer skin jacket for my project in home ec."

"I should teach you how to tan hides."

"Hey, I don't want to take away your fun."

Old man Smith picked up a jug, took a swig, then offered Cat the jug.

Cat shook her head, "Nah, better not."

"Best part of the corn."

"I had better stick to eating it instead of drinking it."

He sat the jug down. "Let's go out to the shed and see what I have."

Cat followed him out to the shed. He went over to a pile of skins, sorted out six nice ones, and handed them to her. "Here, these ought a do just fine."

"You think I need that many?"

"I'm sure you'll find use for what's left."

"Thank you, sure appreciate it."

"No problem, young'un. You have more than built up my supply."

"Well, with any luck, I'll be bringing you more."

"I'm sure you will. I could use a couple coyotes to sell at the rendezvous."

"I can do that. See you later, and thanks again."

"Okay, stay out of trouble."

*****

Whenever Cat had any free time and the weather was nice, she would be outside practicing her trigger pull. Ben was more than happy to help her. He would sneak up on her and yell. When that quit working, he tried firecrackers. A kid at school gave him some rattlesnake rattles. One day he snuck up behind Cat while she was in the prone position and started rattling them. Cat froze. She didn't move a muscle. It was all Ben could do to keep from laughing. He rattled them for a little bit then wait, then he would rattle them a little more. He kept that up for about a minute. He couldn't hold it in anymore. He burst out laughing.

Cat turned around. "*Not* funny!"

"I thought it was."

"You had better get out a here before I wrap this gun barrel around your neck."

*****

Cat went over to Mike's and knocked on the door.

"Come on in, figured you'd be here as nice as it is. Been practicing?"

"Yeah, I'm getting better. Ben is having too much fun bothering me." Cat told him about the rattlesnake rattles.

Mike burst out laughing. "That boy can come up with some good ones."

"It's not funny, I almost had to change my pants!"

"You be surprised how much that will help you. Wanna go back and shoot the Winchester? The match is coming up pretty soon."

Cat's face lit up. "Sure!"

"I have everything set up. Grab the rifle, and I'll get the ammo."

"Expecting me to come over?"

"You're getting pretty predicable."

Cat was hitting the 10-ring at two hundred yards. Mike moved her back to four hundred yards. "You know, Cat, you're getting pretty good. Next time we'll see how you do at six hundred."

After she was done shooting they went back to the house, cleaned the rifle, and put it away. Cat grabbed one of Mike's magazines and started looking through it.

"You think I'll be able to shoot like these guys?"

"With lots of practice and determination, I can't see why not."

Cat smiled. "I had better get home and do my homework."

"All right, see you later. Take that magazine with you."

*****

Cat, Ben, and Barry went over to Mike's. Cat introduced Barry to Mike. Barry showed Mike what he had completed on the program. Mike looked at it.

"All you have to do is punch in the numbers, and it will tell you the corrections needed?" asked Mike.

"When I am finished, it will tell you the trajectory and corrections needed to move the point of impact."

"That'll take away the guesswork."

"I'd like some information on the rifles, propellants, and projectiles that are going to be used. The more info, the more accurate I can make it. The weight and shape of the projectile is important. I will also need the speed and direction of the spin."

Mike went over to the box of stuff that Jim had sent him and handed it to Barry. "Rifles, powder, and bullets, this box of stuff should cover that."

"This will get me started. How was this done before computers?"

"Pencil, paper, and SWAG."

"SWAG?"

"Scientific, wild-ass guess."

Ben and Cat started laughing. Barry had a blank look on his face.

Cat picked up the box. "We'd better get going. I still have homework to finish."

Mike went to the kitchen, dished out some vanilla ice cream, poured some peach schnapps over it, saying to himself, "A girl that thinks Hoppe's No. 9 should be cologne, a couple of geeks, and an old man—what a team!"

Mike finished his ice cream and went to bed.

*****

Cat was sitting in the cafeteria waiting on Barry. Barry came in soaking wet. Cat looked at him.

"What happened?"

"Billy threw me in the fish tank. Go ahead and eat. I am going to change clothes. I have a dry set in my locker."

"You had better come up with a plan pretty soon or let me use mine."

"I have one. Can you stop by my place after school?"

"Sure."

After school, Cat went over to Barry's, wondering what kind of plan he had. She knocked on the door. Barry's mom opened the door.

"Hi, Cat. Come on in."

"Barry home?"

"Yeah, he's on his computer in his room."

Cat went to his room and knocked on his door.

"It's open. Come on in."

"Hi, what's this plan you have?"

"Over here on my computer."

Cat walked over and looked at the computer screen. It looked like a computer game of two people fighting.

"This is your plan, challenging Billy to a computer game?"

"No, don't be silly. I've been using my phone to record when Billy attacks me or fights someone else. I loaded it on my computer."

"How's this gonna help?

"I have about all his moves on the computer. Now, all I have to do is come up with countermoves."

"Whoa, slow down. You plan on fighting Billy?"

"Yep, that's my plan. Would you teach me how to fight?"

"Now, let's be realistic here. You would have a hard time fighting your way out of a wet paper bag."

"The way I figure it, I'll use the element of surprise and leverage to make up for my strength. All I have to do is find somebody to teach me the moves. You seem to know a lot. Will you teach me?"

"I don't think I can. I've read self-defense books, but when I fight, I just do it. I'm not a very good teacher."

"Do you know anybody that would teach me?"

"I can see if Mike will."

"Thanks."

*****

Cat walked up to the front of the classroom. Finally, the day was here for her to show off her jacket. She handed it to the teacher.

"This is a deer-skin jacket I made."

The teacher looked it over. "It looks well made. Put it on, and show the class."

Cat put it on and turned around so the teacher could see how it fit. As the teacher looked at it, she said, "A deer skin jacket, I suppose you shot the deer."

"Well, yeah."

"Why is it tied together with fringe instead of being sewn? Were you trying to be fancy or too lazy to sew?"

Cat said, staying calm, "It would've been a lot easier to have sewn it, but you don't want to sew deer skin because that will let the water through. The fringe keeps the water from running up your sleeve. The same with the fringe on the bottom, it keeps the water away from your body."

"And you know this how?"

"I watch the History Channel and read books about mountain men and the American Indians."

"The jacket is well made, but the requirements were not met."

"I figured as much. I bought some denim and used my mom's sewing machine to make this shirt to go with the jacket."

The teacher looked over the shirt. "This is well made. You did this all yourself?"

"Mom helped me lay out the pattern and set up the sewing machine. Everything else I did."

"I'll accept the shirt, the jacket will be considered extra credit."

*****

Barry was in the math lab writing equations on the chalkboard. Billy walked in.

"What's this, geek? Looks like a bunch of scribbles." He took an eraser and erased half of it. About that time, Cat was walking by. She walked into the lab. "What's going on?"

Billy said, "None of your business, *girly*."

Barry said, "I was getting some extra credit designing your program."

"Looked like a bunch of scribbles to me, *geek*."

Cat asked, "My shooting program?"

Barry answered, "Yes."

This was more than Cat could take. She picked up an eraser and hit Billy square in the nose. She hit him hard enough to make his nose bleed. The mixture of chalk dust and blood made Billy look like something out of a horror movie. For good measure, she punched him in the gut, knocking the air out of him.

Barry yelled, "Cat, I told you to let me fight my own fights."

Cat yelled back, "That is *my* program you are working on, so that made it my fight."

The principal walked in the room, looked at Billy, then Cat. "What is going on?"

Cat started explaining, but the principal ignored her. "Bill, go down to the school nurse." He looked at Cat. "You go to my office. I am going to call your parents. This school doesn't need troublemakers like you. I will not tolerate this type of behavior." He looked at Barry, "And where are you supposed to be?"

"Right here, working on extra credit."

Cat was sitting in the office, and the principal came in. "I have called your parents to come get you. You will be suspended for three days."

"What about Billy? He started it."

"He likes to be called Bill. You hit him. There is no excuse for that. Now sit in the chair outside my office till your parents get here."

Dave came to the school. While they were waiting for the principal Cat told her dad what had happened. The principal walked out of his office, looked at Dave and Cat, and said, "You can come in now."

Dave and Cat followed him into his office. He shut the door. "Have a seat."

Dave and Cat sat down.

The principal looked at Dave. "Your daughter attacked one of our students. This school will not tolerate that."

"Just out the blue, Cat attacked someone?"

Cat joined in, "Billy started it. He erased Barry's work. He has been picking on Barry since he started school, and you haven't done anything about it."

The principal replied, "I have no knowledge of that."

"You must be blind! All the teachers and students know about it. I think you're scared of him."

"That's enough! You still don't have the right to hit him. Violence is not the answer!"

Dave said, "Depends on the question. If you had been paying attention and did your job, we wouldn't be here now."

"Doesn't matter, I'm in charge. Cat will be suspended for three days. You'll not be able to make up any tests or work from those days."

"What about Billy?"

"I see no reason to do anything to him. He's suffered enough already."

Dave thought it best to leave before he ended up in jail. He looked at Cat. "Let's go."

114

"All right, Dad."

On the way home, Cat looked at her dad. "Sorry, Dad, I don't get it. Billy gets away with everything. He is just a big bully."

"Yeah, it doesn't help when the principal doesn't do anything about it. Have any plans while you're off?"

"Thought I'd go camping and collect my thoughts. This couldn't have happened at a worse time. I am supposed to take a test in math and history tomorrow."

"Your mom can use some help. She wants to paint the kitchen."

"Anything to help you out, you know how much I like painting."

"Atta girl, you'll still have time to camp."

"You know, I'll be glad when Mr. Wilson gets back. His replacement has no clue. He would not put up with Billy. When do you think he'll be back?"

"I don't know, depends on how fast he recuperates. Heart attacks are no joke. He's lucky to be alive."

"I've been to his office a few times, but at least he was fair."

As Dave pulled into the driveway Cat asked, "What do you think Mom will say?"

"The usual."

*****

The first day of Cat's suspension, she helped her mom paint the kitchen. That evening the phone rang. Betty answered it.

"Cat, Barry's on the phone."

Cat took the phone, "Hi, Barry."

"Hi, how are you doing?"

"Pretty good now, since the kitchen's painted, what's up?"

"Not much, just wanted to let you know that the math and history tests have been postponed till Tuesday."

"That's great! Did they say why?"

"They said that the printer was broken. I think it was the teacher's version of 'my dog ate my homework.'"

Cat laughed. "That's pretty good from a geek."

"Thanks. Either they like you or else they don't want you in their class next year."

"Probably a little of both."

"Yeah, probably. Mom says supper's ready. Talk to you later."

"Okay, bye."

*****

Cat and Barry went over to Mike's. Cat was getting excited about trying out Barry's program. They walked up to the door and knocked.

"Come on in."

Cat walked in first. "Hi, Mike."

"What are you two up to?"

"Not much, Barry brought over his program to show you."

"Have it done already?"

"Not completely, I have some fine tuning to do yet. I want to see how it works with some real numbers."

"I have some books here. Let's punch in some numbers and see how close the answers are. Then we can go out back and see how it works on the range."

Barry looked over the books and put the numbers in his computer. The answers were very close. "Looking pretty good, let's go back and try it out for real."

Mike picked up a box of cartridges and targets. "Cat, get the rifle."

As Mike went down to hang up the targets, Cat sat up the sandbags. Barry took the information off the ammo and entered it in his computer. Mike came back to the bench.

"We ready?"

Barry replied, "I think so, we're at six hundred yards."

"Yep, the scope is zeroed at a hundred."

Mike fired three rounds using Barry's calculations. They were in a tight group, but a little high. Barry wrote down some notes and made some changes in his computer. Mike tried again. This time he hit dead center.

Mike said, "Not bad. We'll have to try this on a windy day."

Barry replied, "Oh, there's still a lot of work to do on it yet. I needed to see what it was like on the range. It'd help if you can shoot at different ranges."

"That won't be hard to do."

"When I get done making some changes, I'll come back, and we can give it a try."

"Sounds good."

They went back to the house, cleaned the rifle, and put the equipment away.

Mike asked, "You want anything to drink?"

Cat said, "Sure, what do you have?"

"Water, iced tea, and lemonade."

"I'll take lemonade."

Barry said, "I'll have tea, thanks."

Mike went out to the kitchen and came back with the drinks and handed theirs to them.

Cat said, "Thank you. We have another favor to ask you."

"And that would be?"

Cat told Mike the problems they were having with Billy, especially Barry.

"You don't plan on shooting him, do ya?"

Cat laughed, "No, Barry wants to learn how to defend himself, although shooting him would be easier."

Mike looked at Barry. "So how big is this Billy?"

"Pretty good size, I do have a plan."

Mike said, "Well, let's hear it."

Barry asked Mike to look at his computer. "I have been recording Billy whenever he picks on me or fights someone else. I figure if you can teach me counter moves, I will program them into my computer then practice them."

"Make up for your size with knowledge and surprise, I like it. Knowing what he does is a big help. While he's off balance, that's the time to make your move. One thing I will tell you, once you start, don't stop and don't second-guess yourself. You will have one chance. You sure you want to go through with this?"

"Yes, this has to stop one way or the other."

"All right I'll teach you. Stop by two or three nights a week for lessons. The other nights, practice at home."

"Great, thank you."

*****

Cat and Ben went over to Mike's. Cat knocked on the door."
Come on in, ready to do some shooting?"
"Yep."
Mike looked at Ben. "Bring your laptop?"
"Yes."
"Cat, how you doing on your trigger pull?"
"Good, I've been able to block out Ben's yelling and the fire-crackers. I always wonder what he'll come up with next."
"Sounds like you're ready for the next step."
"What's that?
"You'll find out. Go out and do some more practicing. I want to look over some of the CDs that Jim sent me."
Cat went outside. Mike started looking at the computer.
"It'd be easier for me if this was on paper."
"I can go to the library and print out some of this. Just write down the page numbers you want."
"That sounds good. Did you bring a change of clothes for Cat?"
"Yeah, what did you want them for?"
"The next step."
"Next step?"
Mike went over to the refrigerator and took out a bucket of water. "Sneak up on your sister, and dump this water on her"
Ben smiled. "I'm glad that she can't chamber live ammo in that rifle."
"Yeah, that's probably a good thing."
Ben took the bucket of water and waited till Cat was in her bubble. Just when she was ready to squeeze, the trigger he dumped the whole bucket on her. The cold water took her breath away. She froze. Ben stood there for a moment. When Cat started to move, Ben

decided he had better run. After Cat got her breath back, she got up and started chasing Ben.

"When I catch you, I'm gonna stuff you in that bucket!"

Cat was gaining on Ben as he made it through the door, then Mike stepped in front of Cat, laughing, "Easy, girl."

"What the hell was that for?"

Mike still laughing, said, "The next step, keep the dime on the barrel?"

Cat still mad. "Yeah, right now I have to go home and change clothes. How do you expect me to shoot soaking wet?"

"Might as well get used to it, competitions don't stop unless there's lightning."

"Great."

"Calm down. Ben brought you a change of clothes. Go in the bathroom, dry off, and put on some dry clothes."

While Cat was changing clothes, Ben began looking over the CDs. "Mike, it looks like a lot of math is involved in shooting. I love math."

"There is. I figure you and Barry can help me make Cat a top-notch shooter."

"You think Cat will let us after today?"

"I'm the coach, she doesn't have a choice."

Cat came out of the bathroom. "I'm ready to do some shooting."

"All right, grab the rifle. You know, Cat, you really have to work on your temper."

"It'd be a lot easier if I wasn't tested all the time by a bunch if raving lunatics."

Mike laughed, "All to make you a better shooter."

They went back to the range and did some shooting. After they were done and had the rifle cleaned and put away Ben and Cat went home. Mike sat down at the table. He was going to inspect the empty brass. He figured he had better do some reloading tomorrow. Cat was producing plenty of empties. The phone rang.

Mike answered, "Hello."

"Hi, Mike?"

"Yeah, this Jim?"

"Yeah. How's your girl doing?"

"Pretty good, her brother and a friend are computer geeks and math wizards. They've been helping."

"What are you doing, building a dream team?"

"Yeah, as long as they don't kill each other. She's been doing real well on the trigger squeeze, been putting more in the 10-ring than not."

"What range?"

"I have her shooting at six hundred yards, that's about all I can get at my range at home. I'll have to find someplace else to shoot any farther."

"There's a new range that's gonna open up not too far from you. It should be advertised in *Long Range Shooter*'s next issue."

"I'll make sure I get a copy."

"The reason I called is, I wanted to let you know that there's a six-hundred-yard shoot about fifty miles from you, coming up in the near future, if you think she's ready."

"Thanks. I have entered her in a four-hundred-yard match. I'll see how she does there. Thanks for calling."

"Yeah, no problem. I'll talk to you later. Bye."

9

Mike was keeping busy with Cat shooting and teaching Barry how to fight. It seemed as though he had reloaded more brass in the last few weeks than he had in a lifetime. He didn't mind. He enjoyed working with Cat. He was impressed on how well she was progressing. The next challenge would be teaching her the rules and regulations put in place for the safety of the competitors and spectators.

Cat was at Mike's doing some shooting. Mike walked up to her while she was checking her target. "Well, you think you're ready to compete?"

"About as ready as I'll ever be."

"Good. I've entered you in a local shoot this weekend."

Cat smiled. "How you think I'll do?"

"We'll see." Mike handed her a booklet. "Here's a list of the regulations for the shoot."

Cat looked over the safety rules. "What, they think we're a bunch of idiots?"

Mike was expecting that reaction. "These rules are there for the safety of everyone. You follow them, or you get disqualified or worse yet, get banned from competing in matches all together."

"Okay, I'll read them. Like I have a choice."

"That's my girl."

"How's it going with Barry? You think he has a chance?"

"He does have determination, I'll give him credit for that. The way he calculates every move, I do believe he has a chance. One big thing he has going for him is the element of surprise. No way will Billy expect a skinny geeky kid to fight him."

"That's for sure, I don't think anyone will."

"Time will tell."

"I hope he don't get killed before he finishes my program."

Mike laughed, "Only you."

Cat smiled. "Well, I'd better get going. See you later."

"All right, be sure to read those rules."

*****

Mike went to town to pick up a few things. As he walked down the sidewalk, Judge Bean stopped him.

"How's Cat doing with her shooting?"

"Oh, her shooting's ready, just have to work on her etiquette."

Judge Bean laughed. "I'm heading to the diner for a cup, I'll buy you one."

"I'll take ya up on that."

They walked into the diner and sat down at the counter.

Betty walked up. "Coffee?"

Mike and Judge Bean answered, "Yes, thanks."

Judge Bean turned to Mike, "So she's doing good on her shootin'?"

"Oh yeah, puts 'em in the 10-ring most of the time. I entered her in a shoot this weekend."

"Well, you must think she's ready?"

"Like I said her shootin's good. She just needs to work on her etiquette. It's like training a junkyard dog to win a blue ribbon at a dog show."

"And keep 'em from biting the judge?"

"That's putting it mildly."

"Well, Mike, if anyone can do it, you can. Good luck."

"I'll need it and plenty of prayers."

"You know, you're having the time of your life."

"Yeah, I guess. Hey, I haven't seen ole Hot Shot lately, he gone?"

"I can see you've been paying attention. He left a while ago. The doctor released Conrad a few weeks ago."

"Good, where'd he go?"

"Eastern part of the state, a DNR officer got shot in a meth raid. They needed somebody to fill in, so I recommended him."

"What the hell did they ever do to you?"

Laughing, he said, "I just wanted to get rid of him."

"I had better get going. Thanks for the coffee."

"You buy next time."

*****

On her way to the cafeteria, Cat turned the corner of the hallway and saw students starting to gather. She worked her way through the crowd. Barry was standing with his back to his locker. Billy was standing in front of him.

"What's it gonna be geek, the trash can or fish tank?"

Barry stood there.

Billy continued, "Geek I'm talking to you. You deaf?"

Cat stood there watching. *Is this the day? I hope Barry's ready.*

Billy said, "Well, geek, make up your mind, trash can or fish tank? What's it gonna be?"

Barry stared at Billy. "Neither, not today."

"Getting brave or stupid?"

As Billy took a step back, Barry put his head down and charged him like a mad bull. He caught Billy off balance and knocked him to the floor. He remembered what Mike had said about not stopping after you start. Barry was right on top of him. He used Billy's head like a punching bag. Billy's nose started bleeding. His lip was cut. Then Barry moved down and started punching him in the ribs. There was no stopping him. He had turned into a mad man.

Cat and everyone else stood there in awe. Then Cat thought she better pull Barry off before he killed Billy. She grabbed Barry but couldn't hold on to him. She tried again, this time locking his arms behind him. She pulled him away. It was all she could do to keep him off of Billy.

Cat yelled, "BARRY, settle down!"

Barry stood there looking at Cat as though he had come out of a trance.

Cat slapped his face. "What did you do, eat a bowl of spinach instead of cornflakes this morning?"

"Uh, no, Wheaties."

The principal and a couple of teachers worked their way through the crowed.

"All right, break it up." He looked at Billy lying on the floor then at Barry. He looked at Cat. "Should have known you'd be involved, you and Barry, to the office, now!" He turned to one of the teachers, "Help Bill down to the nurse."

As Barry and Cat walked to the office, Cat said, "You sure put a whuppin' on Billy."

"I can't believe it, once I started, I couldn't stop."

"I'll say. I hope you never get mad at me. You didn't even get a scratch on ya."

Barry looked at his knuckles. "Can't really say that, it'll take a while for the skin to grow back, but it was well worth it."

The principal walked into the office; he was not pleased. "I've called your parents and Bill's dad. When they get here, this is going to get sorted out. If I have my way, you two will be expelled."

Cat asked, "What about Billy?"

"You never give up, do you? Why do you insist on picking on him? Don't you think he's been through enough?"

"No."

"That's enough. You two go to the conference room until your parents get here."

Cat and Barry's parents came into the conference room. While they waited for Billy's dad and the principal, Cat explained what happened. All of them looked at Barry in disbelief.

Barry's mom broke the silence, "You know, I'm not a fan of fighting, but sometimes there's no choice especially when school officials won't do anything about it."

Barry's dad asked, "Why didn't you tell us this was happening?"

"There comes a time when I have to fight my own fights."

The door opened, and in walked Billy's dad followed by the principal. Billy's dad was a big man. He nearly filled the doorway as he walked in. The principal closed the door.

"John, sorry I had to bother you, but there has been an incident today."

"Where's Billy?

"Bill is with the school nurse. He is fine. He'll be here after he gets cleaned up."

Cat was thinking to herself. *John? Dad listens to a song called Big John. Wonder if they're related? I thought he didn't like being called Billy.*

"Like I said, there has been an incident. Bill was attacked."

It was all Cat could do to keep her mouth shut. Dave grabbed her arm helped.

John, still standing looking around the room, said, "So what exactly happened?"

The principal started to explain, "Bill was standing in the hall when..."

John interrupted, "Were you there? Did you see it?"

"Well, no, but I got there right after."

"Was anyone there to see what happened from the start?"

Cat took the opportunity. "I was."

"And you are?"

"I'm Cat, a student."

"Cat? You're that girl from New York."

"Yes."

"No longer than I've been in the area I've heard of you. Seems like everybody in this area either knows you, knows someone that knows you, or knows about you."

"I didn't know that I was that popular."

"The way I understand it you have a heart of gold but won't take shit from anybody don't matter who they are."

The principal interrupted, "We don't need that kind of language here."

John ignored the principal and asked Cat, "Is it true you broke a boy's nose for calling you a girly-girl?"

"Uh, yeah, Bob."

"You hit my boy?"

"No, not me, but I saw the whole thing."

"Well, young lady, tell us what happened."

The principal interrupted, "You're not gonna believe this trou-blemaker, are you?"

"Why not? She said she was there from the beginning. She has no reason to lie."

"Still…"

"Now let's just see what she has to say."

Cat asked, "You want to know what happened today or from the beginning?"

"I have plenty of time. I'd like to hear it all. What about the rest of ya?"

Barry's parents replied, "We don't have anyplace to be."

The principal started to protest.

John looked at Cat. "Okay, tell us the rest of the story."

Betty whispered to Barry's mom, "This is going better than I expected."

"I'll say."

Cat told the whole story from when Billy knocked Barry's tray in his lap until she pulled Barry off Billy.

After Cat finished, John stood there for a moment, rubbing his chin. He looked at the principal. "Why wasn't I informed of what my boy had been doing? I should have known something was wrong when he came home with blood and chalk dust on his shirt."

"I didn't want to bother you. I called him to the office and explained to him that he shouldn't pick on other students. I think he is just misunderstood."

Cat couldn't let this go. "Misunderstood? I understand him per-fectly. He's a big bully who likes to intimidate the weak. The only language he understands is the language that Barry used."

Cat and Barry's parents chuckled a little.

John said, "I've never heard it put that way before, but you have a point."

The principal said, "Violence is not the answer."

John looking directly at the principal, he said, "Let me cut you in on something. I can't do anything about my boy if I ain't informed. I need to know what's going on. His mom ran off with a used-car salesman when he was little. The court decided he'd be better off with his mother. When he got older and she couldn't handle him, guess who got the chore to finish raising him? If I had been informed, we wouldn't be here today."

The nurse brought Billy to the conference room.

John looked at him then looked at Barry. "You did this?"

Barry, a little scared, said, "Yes."

John turned to Billy. "Underestimated your opponent, didn't ya, boy?"

Billy didn't say a word.

John looked at Barry again. "Now I know why I quit betting on fights."

The principal said, "Cat and Barry are going to get suspended for causing a disturbance in the school."

Cat asked, "What about Billy?"

Before the principal could answer, John said, "Five-day suspension." Then he looked at the principal and said, "Any problem with that?"

"Well, uh, I think that's a little excessive. It might hurt his self-esteem."

"No wonder we're having trouble with kids today, worried about hurting they're feelings. You need to grow a pair and discipline when needed."

"Uh, okay, five days."

John turned to Billy. "Son, the Marine recruiter is stopping over Wednesday. I highly suggest you sign up on the delayed enlistment, study hard, and graduate. Be an asset to society, not a burden."

"Yes, Pa."

John turned to the principal. "If he causes any more trouble, call me."

"Okay."

"Well, I guess we're done here."

When they got outside the school, John went up to Cat and Barry's parents. "Sorry, my boy caused your kids problems. I didn't know. Hopefully, the Marines will straighten him out."

Dave said, "Well, if they can't, maybe Cat can."

John chuckled then looked at Barry. "I'll say one thing, yours must be made of brass."

Barry stood there with a goofy look on his face. "What's made of brass?"

Laughing, Cat said, "Your dad can explain that to ya."

*****

Cat knocked on the Mike's door.

"Come on in."

Cat and Barry walked into the house.

"Why ain't you two in school?"

Cat answered, "We got suspended for three days."

"How did ya do that?"

Barry showed Mike his knuckles. "The training paid off."

"I heard you put a whuppin' on that Billy kid."

Cat said, "You heard about that already?"

"It's the talk of the town."

"You should have seen it Mike. One second Billy was threatening Barry, the next Barry was on him like white on rice. I had to pull him off before he killed Billy."

Mike looked at Barry. "Like it's been said, 'adrenaline makes the body strong.'"

Barry said, "I couldn't believe how well I did. I did just what you told me. Once I started, I didn't stop. I shouldn't have any more trouble with Billy."

"Not if he has any sense. Well, since you're here, we might as well go out back and practice."

After Cat did some shooting, they all went back to the house.

Mike asked Cat, "Think you're ready for Saturday?"

"About as ready as I'm gonna be."

As Cat and Barry left, Mike said, "I'll be over to pick you up around five Saturday morning."

"I'll be ready, bye."

*****

Saturday Mike went over to pick up Cat to go to the competition. Cat was ready to go. She got in the truck.

"Morning, Mike."

"Good morning, read over the rules?"

"Yep, I even made a checklist to follow."

"That's a good idea."

"Thanks."

Cat didn't fair too well. She didn't even place in the top ten. On the way home, they stopped to get something to eat.

After they sat down, Mike asked, "What happened? You were putting them all in the 10-ring and some in the X-ring at home."

"I really don't know. I got so nervous with so many shooters and all those people watching. I couldn't get my breathing right, kept worrying that I'd mess up."

"You did pretty good at the rimfire competitions."

"There were a lot fewer people shooting and watching, most of them I knew."

"Stage fright?"

"There were people from all over the state shooting. Not only that, their rifles were out of this world."

"The person that placed sixth was using a .308 Winchester like you were using."

"I don't know what happened."

"I'd say you didn't stay in your bubble. You need to just have one thing on your mind when you shoot. Ben said you were doing good when he was working with you."

"Well, yeah, he's my brother. It's easy for me to ignore him."

Mike laughed. "Well, now you know what you have to work on."

"I guess."

"There'll be time. School will be out pretty soon, and there'll be lots of competitions within a day's drive. You'll have to do three things—practice, practice, and practice."

Cat smiled. "I hope you have a lot of ammo."

"If not, I'm sure I can get more."

*****

Cat was sitting in the cafeteria eating her lunch. Barry came up and sat down. "Hi, Cat."

"Hi, how ya doing?"

"I'm doing great, aced my calculus test. I love math."

"So does Ben. I don't see what's there to love about math. I think it's boring."

"*Boring?* Not to me! How did you do shooting Saturday?"

"I don't want to talk about it."

"Not good, huh?"

"Mike said it was stage fright."

"How could you get stage fright?"

"I said I don't wanna talk about it."

"All right, I've tweaked your program. You think we can try it out soon?"

"Sure, I guess it's a good thing you find math exciting."

Billy avoided their table as he walked by. Cat looked at him, then turned to Barry and said, "I doubt he'll be bothering you anymore."

"No, I don't think he will. You know, it seems like everybody is treating me different now. No more standing in front of my locker so I can't get to it. They don't even lock the door to make me late for class like they used to. The girls are even talking to me. I don't get it, it's like they're scared of me."

"You don't get it? You need to take human behavior 101."

"Huh?"

"You put one hell of a whuppin' on the biggest bully at school, of course you're gonna get treated different."

"Still, I don't want people to be scared of me. I just wanna be left alone."

"Well, if it helps any, I ain't scared of ya."

Barry smiled, "Thanks."

"I don't think there'll be a problem with anybody messing with you anymore. Just don't let it go to your head."

"I won't, I don't like fighting. My knuckles still hurt."

"I'm sure not as bad as Billy's head."

Lucy walked up to the table. "Hi, Barry, mind if I sit down?"

"No, go right ahead."

Lucy smiled and sat down.

Cat said, "I have to get going, see you later."

As Cat left the cafeteria, she was thinking to herself, *Great, Lucy's interested in Barry. I hope he gets the program perfected before he starts spending a lot of time with her. Boys!*

*****

Cat was spending all her spare time over at Mike's practicing. Mike was spending all his spare time reloading brass. Mike entered her in as many matches as possible. Her performance was improving. She came in third at a four-hundred-yard match.

Cat was helping Mike clean some brass when she asked, "Mike, what's a Black Ops?"

"I told you, when I'm ready I'll tell you about Nam."

"I know you did, but Ben found this on the web," she said as she handed Mike some papers.

His face lost all expression; his eyes went stone-cold as he started reading the papers. "Where did he get these?"

"He said he found them on the History Channel website."

Mike knew that was a lie. This mission would have never been declassified. He looked at Cat.

"Don't lie to me, Cat."

"Okay, he was checking out some government sites."

"You mean hacking?"

"Yeah, I guess so."

"Tell him to stop. He doesn't know how serious this can be. People have been killed for knowing less."

Cat started getting scared. "Okay, I'll tell him."

"Tell him to destroy what he has and stay away from the government websites."

"Okay, I'll tell him."

"Better yet, tell him to come over with his laptop and all the printed pages he has."

"You want him to bring it over tonight?"

"That would be best, but it's getting late. Tomorrow will be fine. Now go home and tell him."

"Okay, I will. Bye."

Cat picked up her stuff and went home, wishing she hadn't brought it up.

Ben was in his room on his computer when Cat walked in. Ben asked her, "Did you ask Mike?"

"Yeah, you really screwed up. You could be in big trouble. He said to stay off the computer and bring everything you have, including your computer, to his place no later than tomorrow."

Ben kind of laughed. "You serious?"

"Ben, I've never seen Mike like that. He really scared me."

"Oh okay, I'll go over as soon as I get out of school if you think it's that bad."

"Yeah, you better listen to Mike."

*****

Mike was looking over the papers that Cat had left. He was hoping that Ben would listen to his sister. The more he read, the madder he got. He had always suspected that this particular mission had been compromised, and it looked as though it had. He still had nightmares about it. Two men were killed; the lieutenant was captured. After Mike got his men and the bodies of the fallen back to the EZ (extraction zone), he went back to find the lieutenant. He found him being held at gun point by a VC (Viet Cong). Mike looked through his scope. It would be a tough shot; he could see the lieutenant's head in the scope. He had to take the shot, better the lieutenant be killed than be tortured. If roles were reversed, that's what he would've wanted. After the shot, two more VC came into view. Mike shot them. He had to get back to the EZ before the chopper took off. To this day, he still didn't know if his bullet hit the lieutenant or the enemy. Cat had caused some memories to come back that he had tried to bury.

"Why now?"

*****

As soon as Ben got home from school, he ate a sandwich. He gathered up the papers and laptop and went over to Mike's.

Ben knocked on Mike's door.

Mike answered, "Come on in."

Ben walked in. "Cat said you wanted to see me."

"Yeah, sit down."

Ben laid the papers and his laptop on the table and sat down.

Mike said, "How did you find this stuff? It didn't come from the History Channel."

"I was checking out some government sites about the Vietnam War, and I came across them."

"You didn't just come across them."

"Well, no, the stuff I was reading, I could have gotten from old news stories. This file was secured."

"How did you get in?"

"I tried using passwords that are common in the government, but after my third try, I was locked out."

"So how did you get in?"

"I found a backdoor."

"Backdoor?"

"Yeah, sometimes people will create a backdoor so if they lose their job or get locked out, they can get back in. Kind of like an insurance policy, especially if they're afraid of becoming a scapegoat."

"So there is probably somebody else out there with unauthorized access?"

"That would be my guess."

"This is some dangerous information. There have been people killed for knowing less. We need to destroy everything you've downloaded."

"Okay, if you say so."

"Don't say a word to anyone, understand?"

Ben was starting to get a little scared. "Okay."

"Now we can burn the papers, but what about your computer? Can you delete it or what?"

"I can delete it, but it'll still be on the hard drive. I can do a wipe, but that would take some time, plus somebody could tell there had been something on it."

"What's the best way to get rid of it?"

"Destroy the hard drive. I can buy a new one."

"All right, we'll go with that. I'll take it to my workshop and cut it up with my torch."

"That'll work, give me a minute to take it out of my computer."

After Ben removed the hard drive, they walked to Mike's shop. Mike lit his torch and turned the hard drive into a molten mess.

Mike asked, "Is that destroyed enough?"

"Yeah, I don't think even Abby could get anything out of it."

"Abby?"

"Yeah, that gal on that TV crime show."

On the way out of the shop, Ben asked, "What's covered up on the bench?"

"Oh, that's what I'm building for Cat." He took the cover off. "I bought the action from a gunsmith from North Manchester, Indiana. Cost me a pretty penny. The stock is custom built for Cat."

"She has no idea?"

"Nope, and I wanna keep it that way. I am having the barrel cryogenically treated. It should be back soon."

"What's that?"

"In layman's terms, freezing the barrel in liquid nitrogen."

"What does that do?"

"It relieves stress, makes the barrel more uniform and produces a microsmooth surface."

"Wow, you are going all out!"

"Well, I want your sister to be the best she can be. The right equipment will help."

"If she can't do good with this, it'll be shooter error."

"I also ordered a rifle from Surgeon. Have to have a backup."

"Wow, two rifles! Cat will be ecstatic!"

"I've got something else. Let me get it out of the safe." Mike walked over to the safe and pulled out an AR-15 Flattop and handed it to Ben.

"This is nice. I'd like to shoot this, but it doesn't have a scope. Cat won't like that."

"No, it doesn't. I want Cat to shoot at an 'Across the Course' competition."

"What's that?"

"Oh, they're fun. You fire at three different ranges, different positions, slow and rapid fire."

"Sounds interesting."

"Well, what ya say we go in and have a bowl of ice cream?"

"Sounds good."

They went into the house. Mike got the ice cream and bowls out.

As they were eating, Ben asked, "You want me to help you burn these papers?"

"No, I'll burn 'em later."

After Ben finished his ice cream, he said, "I'd better get going. Thanks, and sorry I got nosy."

"Well, at least we got rid of it before you got in any trouble. See ya."

*****

Mike looked at the pile of papers that Ben had left. He could not resist the temptation to read through them. It looked as though his unit he was in had been used for hire to the highest bidder by some in the US government. He knew he should stop, but he couldn't something caught his attention. *Could it be possible the lieutenant had made it out alive and still be living?* He sat there for a moment.

Mike got up, went to his closet, and pulled out a box of stuff he had kept from the war. He had not looked at it for years. He opened it. There were his medals, a small bottle of bourbon, and a coin. Even though he knew that there was to be some distance between officers and enlisted men, he and the lieutenant became close. War will do that to you. One day, they each had a coin made. Each coin had their initials and their draft lottery number on it. Before every mission, they would give each other their coin with the understanding that after the mission, it would be returned to its rightful owner. The idea was, they wouldn't go back to the States with the other's coin. Also after the mission, if everyone made it back alive, they would share the bourbon. If someone didn't make it back alive, the bourbon would be poured on the ground.

Mike picked up the bourbon. Would it be possible after all these years the lieutenant was still alive? He picked up the coin. Did the lieutenant still have his?

Mike sat there wondering what to do. If he wanted to find him, he would need Ben's help. How would he be able to ask him after he just got done telling him to forget about what he had found? Should he let it lie or ask Ben to help him, knowing it could put Ben and his family at risk? It was close to three o'clock in the morning by the time he got to bed.

10

With school being out for the summer, Cat was spending more time at Mike's than she did at home. When she wasn't competing, she was practicing. She finally started to relax and enjoy herself. She was placing in the top ten in many matches. She hadn't placed first yet.

On Saturday, Mike went to pick up Cat for another match. It was about seventy miles away.

As Cat got in the car, Mike asked, "Gonna take first place today?"

"That's my plan."

"Atta girl."

"I told you it'd be easier as time went along."

"You were right."

They got to the match a couple of hours before it started. It was a great day, hardly any wind and the temperature was in the midseventies.

Talking to herself, she said, "I'm gonna get first place today. I can feel it."

It was going great. She was on her last ten shots. She had a really good chance to take first. There were nine holes in her target, five in the 10-ring and four in the X-ring. She was thinking to herself, *Just one more and I've got it. This will make Mike happy.*

She lined up on her target; the wind was perfect. She took a breath, let half of it out, held it, and then slowly squeezed the trigger. The bullet hit the X-ring.

"I did it!"

She checked the target with her spotting scope. There were only nine holes in her target.

"What happened?"

She looked at the target in the lane next to her; it had six holes in the 10-ring and five in the X-ring. She had cross-fired. This mistake put her toward the bottom of the scoring.

After the scores were announced, an old man came up to her and said, "Thank you, you're welcome to shoot next to me anytime." He kind of chuckled and walked away.

Cat didn't say what she was thinking. She had no one to blame except herself. Mike walked up to her as she was picking up her rifle and spotting scope.

He looked at her and said, "Ready to go?"

"Yeah, I guess."

"Let's get this stuff loaded."

Cat didn't say anything as they loaded the car.

A few miles down the road, Mike asked, "Wanna stop and get something to eat?"

"Nah, I ain't hungry."

"Cat ain't hungry? That's a first. I had better write this down."

"I just don't feel like eating."

"It could be worse."

"How? I did something stupid and lost first place? How could I have shot at the wrong target?"

"Oh, the dreaded cross fire. You know, Cat, there are two groups of rifle shooters. Those that have cross-fired and those that will. Today you just changed groups."

"Still, I don't see how I could've done that. Have you ever cross-fired?"

"More than once, but that ain't the stupidest thing I've ever done."

"Oh yeah, care to tell me and cheer me up?"

Mike smiled. "I might as well. It was back in high school."

"That was a while ago."

"You really didn't have to remind me."

Cat smiled. "Yeah, I know."

"I was on the football team. We were undefeated the whole season. It was the championship game, last quarter, thirty seconds to go. The score was tied. We had possession of the ball. I caught the ball and ran toward the goal, then I got hit hard. They spun me around. I managed to stay on my feet. I held the ball tight, kept running, and made the winning touchdown."

"So what was wrong with that?"

"When I had stopped spinning, I was heading in the wrong direction but didn't realize it. I scored for the other team."

Cat smiled. "Yeah, I guess that was pretty stupid."

"I would bet that the newspaper article is still hanging on the wall in the coaches' office."

"I guess you were remembered."

"To add insult to injury, my cousin was on the other team. He sent me a thank-you card."

"That's just mean."

"He sends me one every year. I still get one, probably will till one of us dies."

"With friends like that, you sure don't need any enemies."

"No, I don't. Feeling better?"

"Yeah, I'm getting a little hungry now."

"A little hungry? I'd better stop at a buffet."

*****

Barry's mom invited Cat and Ben over for a cookout. Barry answered the door.

"Come on in."

They followed Barry into the kitchen.

"You remember my mom."

Cat and Ben said, "Hi."

Barry's mom replied, "Hi, glad you could make it."

Barry said, "I'll introduce you to my dad. He's in the study working on some papers for work."

They walked into the study.

"Hi, Dad, Cat and Ben are here."

"Hi, I have some work I want to get finished."

Barry said, "Mom said you're cooking on the grill."

"Yeah, she wants me to cook some hamburgers on the grill. I don't understand why. She has a perfectly good stove in the kitchen. She is cooking the rest of the meal there anyway. Now I have to go and light the charcoal because it makes the food taste better. Not only that, she bought bulk hamburger, and now I have to make patties. She could have bought frozen patties which are all the same size and fit on the bun perfectly."

Cat said, "I'll cook the burgers. I love cooking on the grill."

"Be my guest, if you don't mind. I need to get these papers done by Monday."

Barry said, "She doesn't mind. She's kinda weird."

Cat laughed. "Show me where the grill and charcoal are, and I'll get started."

"Okay, it's in the backyard."

As Cat and Barry walked toward the grill, Cat said, "I can see the nut didn't fall far from the tree."

Barry gave Cat a goofy look. "Huh?"

Barry's mom laughed.

Cat turned around and saw Barry's mom. "Uh, sorry."

"Can't be mad about something I agree with."

Barry said, "I don't get it."

"You're just like your dad."

"Oh."

Cat said, "I said I would cook the burgers."

Barry's mom was shaking her head. "He got out of grilling again."

"I don't mind."

"Okay, when you get the charcoal lit, come in the kitchen and I'll help you make the burgers."

"Sure."

Barry said, "I'll find Ben and show him my new computer games."

Cat went to the kitchen, made the burgers, and then put them on the grill. After they were finished eating, Cat helped Barry's mom clean up. Ben and Barry went to his room and played some more games.

As Cat and Ben got ready to leave, Cat said, "Thanks, we had a good time."

Barry's mom replied, "Good, we'll have to do this again."

"Sounds good, bye."

"You kids be careful on your way home."

*****

The next day, Cat and Ben went over to Mike's. Mike was in his yard when they pulled up. As they got out of the car, Mike said, "Come over to shoot?"

Cat replied, "That was my plan."

"Follow me out to the shop. I have something to show you."

Cat and Ben followed Mike. Mike went to his safe and pulled out his AR-15 and handed it to Cat.

"Here, I have a new one for you to try."

Cat looked at it. "Where's the scope?"

"You're gonna shoot this one without."

"You know I don't like to shoot without a scope."

"Yeah, I know, but I want you to shoot in an 'Across the Course' match."

"Okay, if I must."

"Let's go out back and give it a try."

They went back to the range. Mike showed Cat how to shoot it. After she shot a few rounds, she looked at Mike. "You're right, I like this."

"I thought you would. Go ahead and shoot for a while. Ben, come back up to the house. I need your help on something."

"Sure."

Mike and Ben went back to the house.

After they got in the house, Ben asked, "What do ya need?"

"I would like you to check something out for me. If you don't want to get involved, I understand."

"What is it?"

"Before I burned the papers, against my better judgment, I read them. I think there is a possibility that the lieutenant that I served under is still alive and living in the States. He was listed MIA. I would like you to see if you can find him. I don't want to say any more than that. The less you know, the better."

"I'll have to hack into some government computers."

"Like DOD, IRS, and DOJ?"

"Yeah, and probably a few more."

"You want some time to think on it?"

"No, I'll do it, it'll take a little time. What am I looking for?"

"I think the government changed his identity."

"Okay, where should I start?"

"See if you can find out if someone just appeared out of nowhere. They would do their best to make it look like they hadn't, but something is always overlooked. Narrow it down to a family with a husband, wife, and one daughter. I've written down his name, date of birth, the approximate ages of his wife and daughter, and the time period this probably happened. If you find nothing, widen the search by two years."

"I'll start with military records, then go to tax records. After that, I'll check birth and death records."

"You sure you want to do this?"

"Yeah, it'll be fun. You might want to destroy my hard drive when I'm done."

"I can do that."

"Those hard drives ain't cheap."

Mike pulled out his wallet and handed Ben some cash. "Will this cover it?"

Ben looked at it. "Oh yeah!"

"Thanks, now let's see if your sister shot up all the ammo."

"Okay."

They started back to the range. Cat was already walking toward the house.

Mike asked, "All the ammo gone?"

Cat smiled. "Yes, it is. You were right. I like this rifle."

*****

Ben was running out of ideas to disturb Cat while she was dry firing. She was able to block out everything from getting water poured on her to firecrackers going off. Even the rattlesnake rattles wouldn't bother her. He had to come up with something new.

Ben was in the sporting goods store looking around the hunting and trapping section. On the scent shelf, he saw a bottle of pure skunk scent. He thought to himself, *This will work.* Ben took it up to the counter to pay for it.

As the cashier rang it up, he said, "Be careful with this stuff. A little bit will go a long way."

Ben paid for it then replied, "Oh, I will."

As luck would have it, when Ben got home, Cat was lying on the ground in the prone position dry firing. Ben thought, *This is as good of a time as any to try this stuff out.*

Cat was just getting ready to squeeze the trigger when Ben snuck up beside her and poured half the bottle of the skunk scent right beside her. She didn't flinch. The dime stayed on the barrel. When she went to cock the rifle, her eyes started watering.

"What's that smell?"

Ben replied, "One-hundred-percent pure skunk scent, just wanted to see if that would mess ya up."

"Well, you don't have to try that again."

Ben, wiping the tears from his eyes, he said, "Don't have to worry about that."

Ben should have checked the direction of the wind before he tried that stunt. The wind blew the scent toward the house. Betty had the windows open and clothes on the line.

As Cat and Ben walked toward the house, Betty yelled, "What is that smell?"

Cat replied, "Ben dumped skunk scent right beside me while I was practicing."

Dave arrived in the middle of Betty yelling at the kids.

He asked, "What's going on?"

Betty yelled, "You know what *your* kids did?"

"No, but I am sure you are going to tell me what *my* kids did."

"They can tell you. I'm going to town till you and your children get rid of this smell."

Betty went in the house, got a few changes of clothes, and got in the car and left.

"Okay, what did you do?"

Ben answered, "I dumped some skunk scent beside Cat while she was practicing. I should have checked the wind direction first."

"Some? How much is some?"

"Half the bottle. How are we going to get rid of the smell?"

"I don't know, but we'd better figure out something pretty quick."

Cat said, "Maybe Mike can help us out."

"You two go over and ask Mike if he has any ideas. I'll get these clothes off the line."

Cat and Ben went over to Mike's. After listening to them explain what happened, Mike started laughing then said, "I ain't never heard of skunk scent being used to train a shooter. Did it break her concentration?"

Ben answered, "No, she didn't even notice it till after she pulled the trigger."

Mike was still laughing.

Cat said, "It ain't funny. Mom's madder than a mule munching on bumblebees. You have any ideas on how we can get rid of the smell?"

"Yeah, I bet your mom is not a happy camper. You two go back home. I'll go to town and see if I can find something to get rid of the smell. I'll be over as soon as I find something."

"Thanks, Mike, we'll be waiting on you."

"Bye, be over in a bit."

Mike shook his head and thought to himself, *"Dream team."*

Mike showed up with some bottles and spray cans. "This stuff is supposed to be able to neutralize any odor. I guess we'll find out."

Cat said, "I hope it works."

"Well, let's get started. Ben, you take this bottle and pour it over the area you put the scent and work it into the dirt with a shovel. Put some fresh dirt on top when you're done. Cat, take this bottle and put some in the washing machine with the clothes. Dave and I will use the spray cans and spray the house. I hope this is enough. I bought all they had."

The stuff worked pretty well. The smell was almost all gone by the time Betty came back. She didn't say a word about what happened, and no one else brought it up.

*****

Mike had finished building Cat's rifle. When she came over to Mike's, he said to her, "Follow me out to the shop. I have something to show you."

Cat went with Mike to his workshop. They walked up to the work bench. Mike pulled the cover off the rifle. "What'd ya think?"

Cat stared at it then said, "Wow! That is nice!"

"I put it together myself, the action was custom-built. The barrel is the best one money can buy. The scope is the best money can buy. It's chambered in .338 Lapua. You should be able to keep it in the X-ring with this."

Cat didn't hear a word he was saying.

Finally, Mike said, "Earth calling Cat."

"Huh?"

Mike shook his head then repeated everything. After that, he asked, "So you wanna try it out? I started breaking the barrel in. We can shoot five rounds before I clean it."

"Sure, I want to try it."

They went back to the range. After Cat shot five rounds, she looked at Mike and said, "Now this is a rifle! I am in love!"

Mike smiled. "I thought you'd like it."

"No, love it!"

*****

Mike opened his door after he heard a knock. "Hi, Ben, come on in. You by yourself?"

"Yeah, I think I may have located your friend."

Mike, with mixed emotion, asked, "Is he still living?"

"I believe so."

"Well, tell me about it."

"I started with the dates you gave me. I looked for families that seemed to appear out of nowhere. There were quite a few. Most of them were eliminated through immigration records. That left four families that had a daughter. I included another family that also had a daughter and a son. The reason I included them was that was the only thing that would eliminate them. The son would have joined the family after he had gotten back to the States."

"It's possible they could've had another child. Go on."

"I checked to see if any of the men drew an early pension. Three of them did, two of them are drawing disability pension. That left the family that also had a son. His name is Mark Weatherspoon. He started drawing a pension in his midthirties."

"That's pretty good to draw a pension that early in your life. Where did he draw it from?"

"That's another strange thing. I couldn't find anything on the Internet about the company he supposedly worked for. The deposits to his bank account come from nowhere. It's like they just appear every month."

"It is probably a company invented so that the government can pay him under the radar."

"I also found out that Mark's wife died five years ago. He is in a nursing home. His daughter visits him every day."

"You hacked into the nursing home's computer too?"

"Yeah, it was easy compared to the others. Visitors sign in on a computer screen, and the record is kept on their computer."

"You're pretty sure this is him?"

"Yes, I'm almost positive. I checked old obituaries and found out that when Mark Weatherspoon was seven years old, he and his parents died in a bad car accident. Their bodies were cremated because they were so badly burned. I checked records at the county courthouse, and there was nothing about the Weatherspoons. I figure the government destroyed the county records but didn't think about the newspapers."

"Wow, is there anything else?"

"Yes, I checked the military records, and he is still listed as MIA. His wife and daughter died in a house fire caused by a gas leak. Their bodies were so badly burned that they couldn't be identified, at least that's what the newspaper said. Here is a printout of the newspaper article."

"Sounds like you found him. Thank you."

Ben reached into his pocket and pulled out a hard drive. "We'd better go give this the torch test."

"Yeah, we'd better. Let's go to the shop and do that now."

They went to the shop. Mike destroyed the hard drive.

"That should do it."

"Yeah, I'd say. Mike, what are you going to do with this info? Are you gonna try and find him?"

"I don't really know. I'll have to think on this long and hard."

"You do what you think is best. Your secret is safe with me. If you need any more help, let me know."

"I will. I want to thank you again."

"You're welcome, I will see you later."

Mike went back to the house. He went to the closet and got out the box of things he had from the war. He sat down at the table and went over the information Ben had found. He opened his box. There was a newspaper article of the house fire of the lieutenant's family. Mike had forgotten that he had put that in there. Other items had been added, such as a sympathy cards when his wife and son died. Instead of a signature, "Semper Fi" was written on them. Mike was torn. Should he pursue this or let it lie? He put everything back in the box.

11

Mike was sitting at his kitchen table drinking a cup of coffee and reading a magazine. He found an interesting article on a thousand-yard rifle range being built about eighty miles from them. Mike needed to find a place where Cat would be able to shoot at one thousand yards or better. There wasn't enough room at Mike's to shoot that far. The best he could do was to use reduced-size targets. This place might be the answer. Mike's thoughts were interrupted by a knock at the door.

Mike yelled, "Who is it?"

Cat answered, "Your favorite people."

"Think so, huh? Come on in."

"Hi. Wondering if I could shoot the .338 today."

"I don't see why not. I have it broken in."

"Great, Barry has some time and wants to work with his program."

"Give me a minute, and I'll get the rifle and ammo. I loaded up some rounds I'd like you to try."

They all went back to the house after the ammo was gone.

Mike said, "Sit down. I'll get some lemonade. I just got done reading an article about a thousand-yard rifle range opening up soon. Thought maybe we could go and check it out in the next couple of days."

Cat's eyes got big. "Really, that'd be great!"

Barry asked, "Is it all right if I go too?"

Mike answered, "Sure, all of ya can come along. I'll let ya know when I'm going."

Ben said, "We better get going. I told Dad that I would help him stack firewood."

*****

Ben walked by Cat while she was dry firing in the prone position. Once again, he was running out of ideas on how to break her concentration. He walked into the shed and saw his BB gun hanging on the wall. *Yeah, this will do it.* He grabbed the BB gun, snuck behind Cat, aimed at her left butt cheek, and pulled the trigger. The BB hit the mark.

Cat jumped up. "Ben, you idiot, that hurt! When I catch you, I'm gonna wrap that BB gun around your neck!"

Ben didn't stick around to hear the rest. Cat chased Ben up to the house, trying to rub her butt at the same time. Ben made it to the house, ran inside, and locked the door.

Cat started pounding on the door and yelling. Betty came out of the kitchen to find out what the commotion was about. She let Cat in. Cat started right for Ben. Betty grabbed Cat's arm and stopped her.

"Now what's going on?"

Ben said, "I was just trying to break Cat's concentration while she was shooting."

Cat replied, "Yeah, by shooting me in the butt with a BB gun! It still hurts."

Betty yelled, "Dave, get in here and do something about your children."

Dave walked in. "My children?"

"Yes, your children."

Cat and Ben started talking at the same time.

Dave said, "All right, one at a time."

After Dave heard the story, it was all he could do to keep from laughing. He looked at Cat and asked, "Are you able to put yourself in a bubble as you call it?"

"I'm doing fine. I'm able to block everything out, then this idiot comes up with something else. What's he gonna do next, run over me with a truck?"

"I hope not, because I ain't got the money or the time for a funeral."

"Dad!"

Dave looked at Ben. "I don't think Cat needs any more *help*."

"But, Dad, it's so much fun."

"I don't want you two to kill each other."

"Yeah, I know. You don't have time for a funeral."

Betty came back into the room and asked, "Everything settled?"

Dave answered, "Yep, we're all one big happy family, right, kids?"

"Right, Dad."

Betty replied, "Yeah, one big happy and crazy family. No wonder I am getting gray hair."

Dave said, "At least you ain't losing yours."

"Not yet."

*****

Mike drove over and picked up Cat, Ben, and Barry. They were going to visit that new rifle range that Mike had read about. As Mike pulled into the driveway, they were all waiting and ready to go. As they got into Mike's car, Cat asked, "Did you bring the rifles?"

"No, I just want to drive up there and see what it's like, see if it's open or if you have to buy a membership."

"I can't wait to actually shoot at a thousand yards."

Barry said, "Yeah, then we can really put my program to the test."

Mike pulled into the parking lot of Thousand Yard or Better Rifle Range. "This must be it."

They all got out of the car and went inside. A man walked up to them and said, "Hi, I'm Don. May I help you?"

Mike replied, "I'm interested in shooting at your range."

"Sure, let me gather up some information for you. It'll take a minute."

As Don was getting the information together, Mike and the kids started looking at the pictures on the wall.

Cat commented, "This looks great."

Mike said, "Yeah, it does."

Don came back. "Here is a book on the rules and membership prices. Are you a member of the NRA?'

"Yes," replied Mike.

"Great, are these your grandkids?"

"No, but might as well be."

"Okay, with minors, either a parent or guardian must be with them or have permission slips from their parents."

"I'm sure I can get that."

"Here are the permission forms." Don handed the forms to Mike. Don continued, "I should be able to put you on the family membership. I'll check with the owner and let you know when you come back."

"Thanks. Any way we could see the range today?"

"Sure, jump in my Blazer and I'll show you around."

They all got in the Blazer. As Don drove them around the range, he explained, "We hope to open part of it in two weeks. You can call and check before you drive out here. It's gonna start out self-serve for a while. On the west side we are going to put in some pits so we can have regulation matches. The east side will be for practice only. The outside benches are completed. We should have the building completed by fall. That way you'll be able to shoot in the winter without freezing your ass off. There'll be a deck on top for shooters who want to shoot prone."

"This looks like there was a lot of planning in this."

"Yeah, there was. The permits were a nightmare. We are trying to buy some more land so we can put a 2,500-yard lane in. That will probably be awhile. Getting ready for regulation matches is our next priority."

"What calibers are allowed?"

"Anything under the .50 BMG. After the 2,500-yard lane gets put in, we'll allow that also. So who's the shooter?"

Cat said, "I am."

"What do you shoot?"

"I started out with Mike's .308 Winchester. He just built me a .338 Lapua."

"That's a popular round."

Don drove back to the office. As they all got out of the Blazer, Don said, "Look over the information, and if you're interested, I'll see you when you come back."

Mike said, "Oh, I'm sure we're interested. I'll give you a call next week."

"Okay, see you later."

"Thanks, bye."

They all got back in the car. On the way home, Cat wouldn't shut up about the range.

She asked Mike, "What do ya think? Can we get a membership?"

Mike responded, "Well, I don't know, you think I should?"

"Well, yeah."

*****

Ben stopped over at Mike's. He wasn't in the house. Ben walked out to the shop, opened the door a little, and called, "Mike, you in here?"

"Yeah, come on in. What are you up to?'

"Oh, I thought I'd stop by and see how you're doing."

"Not too bad, I'm loading the brass that your sister shot. It's good therapy for me."

"Yeah, she's probably keeping you busy. Need any help?"

"No, I can get it, but I wouldn't mind the company."

"Okay, I ain't got anyplace I have to be. Thought any more about whether or not you're gonna try to find the lieutenant?"

"I haven't made up my mind yet. I would like to see how he's doing, but then again maybe it's best to let a sleeping dog lie."

"I can see how that'd be a double-edged sword."

"Yes, it is."

"Only you can decide."

"Yep. Will you hand me that bucket of brass?"

"Sure."

"I filled out the membership application and mailed it in for the range."

"That'll make Cat happy."

"I'm sure it will. Would you take the permission forms home and have your parents sign them and give one to Barry for his folks to sign?"

"Sure. No problem. When are we going up there?"

"I called, it should be open next week. I thought we'd try for Thursday. I'll check before we go."

"I'll tell Cat. That should make her day."

"Well, I think this is enough for tonight."

"All right, I'll see you later."

*****

Mike picked up Cat, Ben, and Barry. They were going to the range.

As they got in the car, Mike asked, "Have the permission forms?"

Cat handed them to Mike. "Yep, all filled out and signed. Do we have to stop at the office first?"

"No. Don said we can sign in at the range then drop the forms off on our way home. Did you read over the rules?"

"Yep, I have them memorized."

"That's good."

"They're pretty simple. Safety is the main concern."

"That's very important in the shooting sports, as is being considerate of other shooters."

Mike parked the car. They all got out and carried the rifles and equipment to the bench. Cat was setting up the Lapua when she noticed two other shooters setting up.

She walked over and said, "Hi."

They looked at her and returned the greeting.

Cat noticed they had a bunch of glass bottles with them. She asked, "What are you gonna do with them?"

One of them said, "None of your business, but if you must know, we are going to set them up to shoot."

"Didn't you read the rules? No glass bottles, only paper or other approved targets."

"We don't care. What are you gonna do about it, *girly?*"

Cat was getting tired of being called girly. She looked at them and answered, "Nothing, I guess."

Mike overheard the conversation. *She took that pretty good.*

The other shooters were setting up their bottles at the fifty-yard line. Mike noticed Cat was looking through the rifle scope. The firearms were to be in a safe position when other shooters were in front of the firing line. He didn't worry too much about it since the bolt was opened. Out of the corner of his eye, he saw Cat chambering a live round. *Oh shit!* He walked over and covered the scope with his hand then said, "What the hell are you doing? You gonna shoot somebody because they pissed you off? You have to control your temper, young lady."

"I was just going to speak to these boys in a language they'll understand. I'm not gonna hurt him. I was just gonna shoot the bottle out of his hand."

"Now just be cool. We can talk to Don when we get done. Let him take care of it."

"Okay."

The boys walked back toward the firing line laughing and making fun of Cat. Cat picked up the AR-15, loaded a twenty-round magazine, shot half the bottles, dropped the empty, loaded another, and shot the rest.

Mike looked at Cat and yelled, "What are you trying to do, get a war started?"

"The rules say no shooting glass bottles. I ain't gonna let anybody break the rules."

Mike was trying to find the logic in that statement when the two guys came up and started yelling at Cat.

Mike said, "Calm down, boys. You know that you ain't supposed to use glass as targets."

"We're gonna report *her!* She shot the bottles, not us."

They picked up their guns and left.

Doing his best not to laugh, Mike looked at Cat and said, "You trying to get us kicked out on the first day?"

"I guess that's not the smartest thing I've ever done."

"No, it isn't. We might as well shoot since we're here."

Cat shot a few rounds but couldn't keep her mind on her shooting. She looked at Mike and said, "We might as well go. Probably won't be allowed back anyway."

"All right, let's go clean up that glass. There's an outside chance they didn't report us."

"I guess I should clean it up. I did make the mess."

Mike got some garbage bags out of the car, and they all went and cleaned up the glass.

Mike said, "Go ahead and put the bags in the car. I'll throw them away at home. That way, if nothing was said, there won't be any broken glass around here."

Mike pulled up to the office. As they got out of the car, Mike looked at the kids and said, "If anything is brought up, let me do the talking."

Ben said, "You think they're dumb enough to say anything when they're the ones that brought the bottles?"

"You never know."

They walked into the office.

Don said, "Well, what did you think?"

Mike replied, "It's very nice. I take it you got the check I mailed. Here are the permission slips for the kids."

"I'm glad you liked it, but we had a report that a girl was shooting glass bottles. If you had read the rules, you know that's not allowed."

"So they did report it." Mike went on to explain what happened. When he was done, he said, "I understand if you want to give me my check back and tell us to leave."

"Don't get too hasty. One of my employees was doing some wiring while you were there. He has a pair of tactical headsets that amplifies sound and reduces harmful impulse noise like gun fire. He heard the whole thing."

"I didn't know there was anybody else there."

"He would've been easy to miss. He was wiring ventilation fans in the roof. He saw and heard the whole thing. I appreciate you cleaning up the mess."

"Well, Cat did make it."

"My employee said he was enjoying the show. He was waiting for her to shoot the bottle out of his hand. It's probably a good thing you stopped her."

"I don't need a lawsuit."

"Shooting glass is still against the rules, so if you want to keep your membership, I'm gonna have to fine you and suspend you from the range for a few days. When did you plan on coming back?"

"I was hoping next weekend."

"All right, your fine is five dollars, and you are suspended from using the range for three days. Sign here."

Mike handed him five dollars and signed the ticket. "I can handle that."

"I thought you could, oh, and here's some information you might be interested in. There's a weekend match that I think she'll enjoy, but it ain't till next spring. The entry fee is reasonable."

"Thank you."

"Here's another competition. It won't be for at least another year. They're putting up a state-of-the art range, it's not even finished yet. It is going to be limited to five hundred shooters. Entry fee is $2,000 plus application fees. The prize money is good."

"I would hope so at that price."

"The visitation center is supposed to open next month so people can see what it is going to look like. There will be an article about it in next month's *Long Range Rifle Shooting.*"

"Thanks, I'll look this stuff over."

As they headed to the car, Don walked up to Mike and asked, "Could she have shot that bottle out of his hand?"

Mike chuckled a little. "I wouldn't bet against it. She once shot a knife off her brother's belt after he pissed her off while they were squirrel-huntin'."

Don laughed. "I'll see you guys later."

On the way home, Mike said to Cat, "Well, you skated through that."

"Yeah, I guess so. You gonna take me up here again?"

"If you promise me you won't cause any more trouble."

"I promise."

*****

Mike pulled into Cat's driveway.

Cat came out and said, "Hi, Mike."

"Hi, is your dad around?"

"Yeah, he's in on the back porch."

Mike walked around the house. "Hi, Dave."

"Hi, Mike, you want a cup of coffee?"

"Sure."

"Sit down. I'll get you a cup, black, right?"

"Yep."

Dave came back and handed Mike his coffee, "So what you up to?"

"Well, I was wondering if it'd be okay to take Cat to Camp Perry this August."

"I'll talk to her mom, but I'm sure it'll be all right. She'll love that."

"A friend of mine, Jim, and his daughter go every year. I'll have him book another hotel room. Cat can stay with her. I can stay with Jim and catch up on old times."

"Like I said, I'll talk it over with Betty. I'll go down and get a paper notarized that she has permission to be with you and get her medical attention if needed."

"That's a good idea. I don't want to get locked up for taking an underage girl across statelines."

"That's all you'd need."

"Thanks, Dave. I won't say anything to Cat till you've talked it over with Betty."

Mike finished his coffee then said, "I'll see you later."

Cat came into the house and asked her dad, "What'd Mike want?"

"It's a surprise."

12

As Cat and Ben were driving over to Mike's, Cat asked, "I wonder what Mike wants?"

"I'm sure we'll find out when we get there." Ben had an idea.

Cat knocked on the door.

Mike answered, "Come on in."

As they walked in, Cat asked, "What's up?"

"I'm gonna be gone for a few days. I was wondering if you two would look after my place."

"Yeah, we can do that. Is everything all right?"

"Oh yeah, I want to visit a friend of mine I haven't seen for years."

"Be okay if I practice while you're gone?"

"Yeah, just be careful. No shooting apples off your brother's head."

"Like he'd let me."

"I have all the brass loaded up. If it's okay with your folks, you're welcome to stay here while I'm gone."

"That'd be great."

"Here's a key. I'm leaving Tuesday."

Cat walked toward the car.

Ben walked up to Mike. "You're gonna go see if you can find him, ain't ya?"

"Yes, I need some answers."

"Just use cash for your trip, be less of a trail that way."

"You don't have to convince me. I saw what you can find on the computer. That put a whole new meaning on Big Brother."

158

"I'm sure Mom and Dad will let us stay here."

"Thanks, there's plenty of food in the house."

"Even for Cat?"

Mike laughed. "Yeah, I think there's even enough for her. If not, she can kill or catch something."

"I'll see you later, have a good trip."

After Cat and Ben got home, they walked into the house.

Dave asked, "What'd Mike want?"

Cat answered, "Mike is going out of town for a few days. He wants us to keep an eye on his place."

"He is? Is something wrong?"

"No, he said he wants to visit a friend that he hasn't seen in years."

Ben said, "Mike said that if it was all right with you and Mom, we can stay there while he's gone."

"I'm sure that will be okay. I'll have to ask your mom."

Betty walked in. "Ask Mom what?"

"Mike is leaving town for a few days. He wants the kids to keep an eye on his place. He said they were welcome to stay there while he was gone."

"Is everything okay? It's not like him to take off by himself like that."

"I guess he has a friend that he wants to visit. He hasn't seen him in years."

"That's still kinda strange, all of a sudden like that."

Ben felt bad not being able to tell them the whole story. He was hoping Mike was making the right decision.

Cat asked, "Well, Mom, is it okay if Ben and I stay at Mike's?"

"It's okay with me if your dad thinks it's all right. You two won't be that far away. Still, it is strange Mike taking off like that. Did he say how long he is gonna be gone?"

"No, all he said is that it'd be a few days. I'm gonna go and pack my bag."

Ben said, "He ain't leaving till Tuesday."

"I know. I just want to get that out of the way."

*****

Monday night Mike packed his clothes. He took his credit cards out of his wallet and put them in his desk drawer. He went over to the closet took his box out, opened it, and looked through it, wondering if he should go through with this. Would he find out something he didn't want to know? He took out the coin and put it in his wallet.

Tuesday morning, Mike got up and put everything in his pickup. He had not been on a trip this far since he quit going to Camp Perry. Mike stopped and rented a motel room when he got fifty miles from the nursing home. Before he went to bed, he took his coin out of his wallet. Would he finally be able to return it after all these years? Thoughts of going back home entered his mind, but he had already come this far. If he turned back now, he was sure he'd regret it.

Mike woke up the next morning, still holding onto the coin. He walked to a diner and ate breakfast. He came back to the motel and looked over the maps that Ben had printed out for him.

What kind of deranged person would name a nursing home 'Over the Hill Nursing Home'?

Mike left the motel; it wasn't long until he saw an exit sign that read, "Over the Hill Nursing Home," next right. He took the exit. The road went up a big hill, and on the other side was the nursing home. He pulled into the parking place. *So that's how it got its name, not because old people live here.*

Mike parked his car and went inside. He walked up to the information desk and asked about a Mark Weatherspoon.

The receptionist replied, "You a friend or relative?"

"Old friend, I have something to return to him."

"Okay, sign the guest register. He doesn't have many visitors. This will be a surprise. He is in room 231. The elevator is down the hall on the left."

Mike signed the electronic pad, making sure he didn't look up. He didn't want the cameras to get a picture of his face. He signed the pad Jacob Spralling, hoping they wouldn't ask for ID.

As Mike walked toward the hall, the receptionist called out, "Mr. Spralling?"

Mike turned around. *She's good.* "Yes."

"I'm sorry. That elevator is out of order. You will need to use the one at the other end of the hall."

"Okay, thank you." Mike walked to the other elevator. *That was close.*

Mike got off the elevator and walked toward room 231. He was starting to get a little anxious. The door was closed. Mike knocked on it lightly.

A voice from inside said, "Come in."

Mike walked into the room. It was nice, looking more like an apartment than a nursing home room. Sitting at a table was an older man reading a paper. He looked up a bit startled. He was expecting his daughter.

"May I help you?"

Mike could tell he was nervous. He reached into his pocket and pulled out the coin. As he handed it to him, he said, "LT, I have something to return to you."

The old man took the coin, looked at it, and quietly asked, "Sarge?" A tear ran down his face.

Mike had a feeling of relief. This was him. Mike stood there in silence, wondering what to say next. The silence was broken when a woman came through the door, yelling, "Who are you, and what do you want? Get out of here!"

She looked over to Mark, exclaiming, "Dad, you have to be careful. You can't just let anybody walk in here."

Mike was getting ready to leave when Mark said, "Mary, calm down." He showed her the coin.

She looked at the coin turned to Mike, "You Mike?"

"Yes."

"Sorry, I yelled at you. How did you find us?"

Mark said, "Mary, bring me that box on the dresser."

Mary handed it to Mark. He opened it, pulled out a coin, and handed it to Mike.

Mike looked at it and smiled, "Semper Fi."

Mark took his coin and put it in the box. Mike put his in his pocket.

Mark said, "After all these years, finally the coins are home."

"Finally," Mike replied.

Mary said to Mike, "Go ahead and visit with Dad for a couple hours, then meet me down at the coffee shop on the corner of Fifth and Main. When you leave the parking lot, turn left instead of right. You can't miss it. I'll see you then."

"Okay."

Mary walked over to her dad and gave him a kiss on the cheek. "See you later, Dad. Enjoy your visit, love you."

"See ya, Mary, love you too."

Mark said to Mike after Mary left, "She's a bit overprotective. So how have you been?"

"I'm still living in Kentucky. My wife passed away a few years ago. Six years ago, my son was killed in a car accident. Other than that, I am doing okay."

"My wife passed five years ago. Mary is the only one left. She has been taking care of me. I moved here a couple years ago. I didn't want to, but glad I did. There is plenty to do here. There's a wood-shop I can use. I go fishing in the lake. I really enjoy that."

"You always liked fishing."

"Yeah, what's great is one of the maintenance men clean them for me. Mary will fry them for me."

"That sounds pretty good, just catch 'em and eat 'em."

"You live alone?"

"Yeah, I have a house on a few acres with a woods and lake plenty of fish and game."

"Sounds like what you always wanted."

They talked some more about their civilian life, hobbies, family, and friends. The war was never brought up. Mike did want to know how Mark got back to the States; hopefully Mary would tell him. The time flew by. Mike knew this would be the last time he would see Mark.

Mike stood up, extending his hand to Mark. "LT, it's been good to see you. I'd better get going. Don't want to keep your daughter waiting."

Mark shook Mike's hand. "Sarge, don't know how you found me, but I'm glad ya did. I've wanted to see you for years. Mary will fill you in on how I got back to the States."

"I enjoyed our visit. I wish it had been sooner."
"I did too, bye."

*****

Mike walked into the coffee shop, looked around, and saw Mary sitting at a table with her laptop. Mike walked over to her table.

"Does everybody carry a computer around with them?"

"Just about. Have a seat."

"It was sure good to see your dad, sorry I scared you."

"You probably have a lot of questions."

"A few. I'd really like to know how your dad got back to the States and was able to live off the grid all this time."

"It hasn't been easy. Had some help from the government but more from my mom's side of the family. Did you know anything about my mom?"

"I remember your dad telling me he had married an Italian gal whose dad was a little more organized than the government liked."

"That's one way to put it."

"I know he really loved your mom, kept a picture with him all the time. It nearly killed him that he wasn't home to see you born."

"He called me the 'home on leave' baby."

"Yeah, I remember him telling me that."

"Grandpa really liked my dad."

"I may sound paranoid, but I have a feeling I've been followed since I left the nursing home."

"You were."

"Oh."

"That's why I wanted to meet you here. I'm a Realtor, and this is where I meet a lot of my clients."

"An actual Realtor, one that sells property?"

"Yes, you watch too many movies."

"After Mom died, Dad told me what had happened in the war. He said if it hadn't been for you, he would've been killed."

"I came to the conclusion that your dad was dead even though something in the back of my mind said that somehow he'd survived. I passed that off as wishful thinking."

"We figured it would be safer for us if it was thought we were all dead."

"What did happen, and how did your dad get back to the States?"

"Like I said, after Mom died, he told me the story. Dad became suspicious of some of the missions that were carried out. He found out that some higher-ups had been selling the use of his unit to the highest bidder."

"Great."

"Dad had gathered up a lot of information on what was happening. He didn't tell anyone. He buried it at the base you were operating from. He had orders to go back to the States. His plan was to take the information with him. Two days before he was to leave, he got orders to go on one last mission. Dad started putting two and two together."

"It was meant to be the last mission for us."

"Yes, the whole unit was to be destroyed to cover up the whole mess."

"We would've just been a casualty of war."

Mary turned her lap around to Mike and said, "How about this place?"

He looked at it. "I'd like some more woods and a lake."

"I might have something, let me check."

"How did some of us survive?"

"Dad looked at the operation plan and changed the time and approach to the village."

"We got ambushed before we got to the village."

"Yes, you ran into the ones that were to finish you off on the way out."

"Your dad was captured. I wanted to follow them, but there were two dead and three wounded. We had to get to the EZ. After we got them there, I went back to get your dad while the rest of the men waited on another chopper."

164

"You went back?"

"Yes, the first choppers evacuated the wounded and the dead. Three men waited on me and another chopper."

"You took a chance going back."

"I wasn't gonna leave your dad."

"Then what happened?"

"I found your dad. The VC was trying to use him to lure his men back. I looked through my scope." Mike's mind started going back to that time. "The gook had a gun next to your dad's head, trying to get him to call out. This was going to be a tough shot. I could see your dad's head in my scope. I had to take the shot. I knew how our men were tortured. You would end up dead anyhow. After I shot, two more gooks came into view. I took them out. I still didn't know if my first shot hit the mark or killed your dad. I heard the chopper, so I had to get to the EZ."

"Dad said that he knew it was you because you were the only one he knew that had the skill and the balls to take a shot like that. After you shot the other two, the others started following you to the chopper. This allowed time for dad to escape."

"It was close. The door gunner provided cover fire while I climbed into the chopper. My tour was over so I went back to the States. I never got ordered back, nor did I volunteer."

"Dad was ever grateful for what you did. Many times he wanted to contact you, but he didn't want to put you in any danger."

"So how did your dad get back to the States?"

"The story he told me was that he snuck back to the base and retrieved the info he had gathered. After that, he waited and stowed away on a cargo plane. He said that it was a long, cold flight."

"I could use another coffee, you?"

Mary turned her computer around again. "How about this place? And yes, I'd like another coffee."

Mike got the waitress's attention asked for two more coffees, then looked at the computer. "That's more like it, but a little out of my price range."

After their coffee was brought to the table, Mary continued, "After Dad got back to the States, he made copies of what he had.

He sent one to the DOJ, DOD, the speaker of the House, and to the White House. He put one copy in a locker at the bus station. He kept it from the media, hoping the government would take care of it. He then went to the FBI headquarters in DC. He walked past the guards, busted into the director's office, and put the papers on the desk. Two agents tried to stop him. Dad promptly disarmed them and cuffed them to each other, using their own cuffs."

"Diplomacy was not one of your dad's virtues."

"He told the director to look at the papers, then he would let the agents go and surrender. The director started reading them looked up and asked, 'Does the media know anything about this?' Dad replied, 'No.' He told him where the other copies were sent and that he had one copy hid. Dad released the agents. He was then put into what he hoped was protective custody."

"He did have them by the short hairs with the copy he put in the locker."

"That's what he said. It went pretty high up. The investigation took a while. Six men were indicted, including a cabinet member and two senators. Dad was placed in protective custody. Mom and I were taken to a safe house. The trial of the first two ended up in an acquittal. That scared Dad, and he figured the jury had been tampered with. He knew he would not be safe, even with a new identity."

"What happened after that?"

"The two that were acquitted were shot in front of their office buildings. Their lawyers died in car crashes. The other defendant's lawyers quit. They pled guilty to all charges the next week. They were sentenced to life."

"I didn't see any of that in the news. Somebody did a good job of keeping it out of the media."

"Yes, they did. The government staged our deaths in a house fire and kept dad listed as MIA and got us all new identities. Dad opened a small bait-and-tackle shop near a lake. He always wanted his own shop. With that and his pension, we did pretty well. Only Grandpa and a select few knew we were still alive. We're still being protected even though Grandpa died two years ago. I feel a little better now that the last of the defendants died in prison last month."

"So that's why I was followed."

"Oh yeah, you were being watched as soon as you asked about Dad."

"I'm glad they didn't decide to take me out."

"They had an idea of who you were."

"Oh?"

"Dad made me promise to give you your coin after he passed. So we had to keep track of you. It was pretty easy since you never moved."

"The flowers and sympathy cards for my wife and son…?"

"Yes, they were from Dad."

"I wondered."

"So how were you able to find us?"

"A high school kid back home was snooping on some government websites about the war and asked me about it. One thing led to another."

"You mean hacking, not snooping. Our whereabouts were in the records? I thought they were destroyed."

"The birth and death records were destroyed, but an obituary in a newspaper had Mark Weatherspoon being killed in a car crash when he was seven." Mike told Mary how Ben used the process of elimination to narrow down where her dad could be.

"Pretty smart kid."

"I want to thank you for everything. I've found answers to a lot of questions I've had over the years. I won't visit your dad anymore. I hope I haven't caused any problems."

"No, I'm glad you were able to see Dad. He talked about you a lot. He didn't want you to get dragged into this mess. Now, when the time comes, he'll be able to go in peace."

"I know now I made the right decision to look up your dad. One more thing. When your dad goes, I'd like you to let me know. I won't go to the funeral, but still I'd like to know."

"I'll do that."

"I had better head home. Again, thank you."

"You're welcome. Now, when you leave, you will be followed. On the way out of town, stop at the gas station on the corner of Main and Burdock, and fill up with gas."

Mike stood up and shook Mary's hand. "Tell your dad I enjoyed the visit, goodbye."

"Goodbye, and have a safe trip home."

Mike went to the restroom. When he came out, Mary was gone. He got into his truck and headed for home. Mike looked in his mirror. He was being followed as Mary had said. Mike pulled into the gas station as Mary had instructed. He pulled up to the pump, went inside to pay for the, gas and bought a cup of coffee. As he was pumping his gas, he noticed his tail was parked across the street. Mike finished pumping the gas, got back into his truck, and left. He looked in his mirror; his tail had turned around.

Mike drove for another three hours before stopping at a motel for the night. It had been a tiring day for an old man. Before he went to sleep, he looked at his coin. He would put it in his box when he got home. Finally, after all these years, the coins were in the hands of their rightful owners.

*****

As Mike pulled into his driveway he heard rifle fire. *Cat must be shooting*. He drove back to the range and got out of his truck. Cat and Ben walked up. "Hi, Mike, have a good trip?"

"Yes, I did. I take it I have a lot of reloading to do."

"Only three buckets of brass, I kept them separated."

"Which rifles did you shoot?"

Cat smiled. "All of them."

Mike smiled back. "I'll get started on it tomorrow."

Cat went back to the bench to gather up her equipment.

Ben walked up to Mike. "Was it him?"

"Yes, I'm glad I went. Later, I will tell you what I can."

"I'm glad it worked out for you. I can stop by tomorrow and help you clean the brass."

"Okay, go help your sister, and then I'll take the two of you home."

13

Cat was sitting at the kitchen talking to her mom and dad, anxiously waiting for Mike to pick her up. She was finally going to the thousand-yard matches at Camp Perry. As Mike pulled into the driveway, Cat grabbed her suitcase and headed out the door. Dave and Betty followed her.

Mike got out of the car, looked at Cat, and said, "Ready to go?"

Dave replied, "She's been sitting at the kitchen table since she got up this morning waiting for you."

"Yeah, I'm running late. Jim called me and gave me the name of the hotel he's staying at."

Cat said, "Here's my suitcase."

As Mike opened the trunk, "Only one suitcase?"

"Yeah, we're only gonna be gone a week."

"Most women I know need at least four."

Dave said, "I think she stuffed three suitcases of stuff in that one suitcase!"

Betty gave Cat a hug, "You be careful and have fun."

"I will, love you."

Dave walked over to Mike and said, "Here's some money to help with food."

Mike replied, "Nah, that's okay. I've got it covered."

"You sure? That girl can eat when she gets excited."

"Yeah, I'm sure."

"I hope you know what you're getting into."

"We'll do fine."

As they left, Cat said, "This is great. I always wanted to go to Camp Perry. Carlos Hathcock won the Wimbledon Cup in 1965."

"So how did you know that?"

"I read *Marine Sniper: 93 Confirmed Kills*. After I read it, I did some research on him. He's still a legend in the Marine Corps."

"You really like reading about long-range shooters, don't you?"

"Yep, all the way back to Thomas Plunkett."

"Thomas Plunkett?"

"He was an Irish soldier in the British Ninety-Fifth Rifles. In 1809, he shot a French general at six hundred meters, and to prove it wasn't a fluke, he reloaded and shot the general's aide. That was some shooting for the rifles of that era."

"I'll take that back. You're not interested, you're obsessed."

Cat smiled, "Yeah, I guess so. Another is Billy Dixon."

"Now that one I know, 1874 Adobe Walls. He shot an Indian off of his horse almost a mile away with a borrowed 50/90 Sharps. He didn't think his 45/90 would reach that far."

"Yep, after that, the Indians left the settlement alone."

"I think we'll stop at the next rest area. I need to stretch my legs."

"Sounds good."

Mike pulled into the rest area. They went inside and used the restrooms. Mike stopped to look at the map inside the building, and Cat went outside to look around. Besides a few semitrucks, they were the only ones there. Cat walked over to a table to do some stretches. As Cat was stretching, a car pulled up and three guys got out. They started walking toward Cat. She reached into her pocket and pulled out a pencil she kept for defense when there wasn't a firearm handy. It was a number 6 drafting pencil sharpened to a fine point. She had put an eraser on one end and kept a cap on the sharpened end so that it wouldn't put a hole in her pocket. She took the cap off put it in her left hand with the eraser in her palm and the pencil between her third and fourth finger. She held it down and behind her leg.

As the thugs got closer, the one in the center pulled out a revolver, pointed it at Cat, and said. "Hey, little girl, give us your money."

Cat looked at the revolver and could tell that it was loaded. She replied, "Ain't got none."

The other two pulled out knives and said, "Maybe we'll just take something else."

"Ain't gettin' none of that either."

The one holding the gun said, "Hey, guys, we have a feisty one here. This will be fun."

Cat wasn't ready to meet her Maker. She had a lot of things she wanted to do while she was on earth. One thing was for sure, if she was going, at least one of them was going with her. The thug holding the gun started walking toward her. This was good. At least this would give her a little time.

Cat was going over everything in her mind of what she had read about using a pencil as an improvised weapon. Since there were three of them, she would have to put the one holding the gun out of commission. Her plan was that when he got close enough, she would ram the pencil through the bottom of his jaw with enough force to drive it to his brain. She would take a step to the right as she made this move. That would keep her from being in front of the muzzle if the gun fired, hoping after he fell on the ground with a pencil stuck in his neck, the other two would clear out. She planted her feet firmly on the ground and began timing his steps as he came closer. Only having one chance for this to work, she started counting to herself to when she would make her move.

Five, four, three…

Her concentration was interrupted when she heard Mike, "What'd ya up to, boys?"

The thug with the gun said, "Stay out of it, old man."

"Can't do that."

"What you gonna do? There's three of us."

"I've got a little help." Mike pointed a lug wrench at them.

They started laughing at him; even Cat was wondering if Mike had lost his mind.

"You think that lug wrench is gonna help you?"

"I didn't get this at Auto Parts R Us." Mike pointed it at their car and shot a hole through the left quarter panel. "The next round is going through your head. Now drop your weapons and get the hell out of here!"

The thugs just stood there. Mike aimed at the leader's head. "Cat, back away. I don't want to get blood and goo all over you when his head explodes."

This got their attention. They dropped their weapons, ran to their car, and took off. As they left, Mike shot out the left taillight. Cat looked at Mike and asked, "A shooting lug wrench?"

"Yeah, I designed it myself. I took a four-way lug wrench and a .380 automatic and put it together. I spray painted it black then put a couple of scratches on it. It works pretty good, just have to make sure it's unloaded when you're changing a tire."

"Yeah, I guess so. I thought you had lost your mind!"

They walked back to the car. Mike opened up the trunk, placed the wrench on top of the spare tire, and tightened up the tie down bolt. He looked at Cat and said, "See, can't tell it's any different from a normal wrench."

Cat was impressed. She turned to Mike and asked, "We gonna call the state police?"

"Nah, we won't have to. I'm sure them idiots will call 'em."

"You think?"

"Oh yeah, go put this blanket over the weapons, and we'll just wait."

Mike pulled the car to a parking space close to where the thugs dropped their weapons. He looked at Cat and said, "We'll just wait here till the state police show up."

"We won't get in trouble, will we?"

"Don't know for sure. It will look better for us if we wait instead of them looking for us."

"I guess so. I'm gonna get a drink from the cooler."

"Grab me one too."

*****

A police car pulled up behind Mike's car. An officer got out of the car, walked up to Mike's car, and tapped on the window.

Mike rolled down his window, "Yes."

"Would you two get out of the car please?"

Mike and Cat got out of the car. As they did, another police car pulled in.

The officer said to Mike, "We had a report that and old man with a girl shot at someone here. Do you know anything about it?"

"No, the only thing that happened here was three guys tried to rob us."

"Tried?"

"Yeah, I pointed my lug wrench at them, and they dropped their weapons and took off."

"A lug wrench?"

"Yeah, must have spooked them. Their weapons are under that blanket over there."

The officer walked over and moved the blanket looked at the gun and knives lying on the ground turned back toward Mike and asked, "You didn't shoot at them?"

"No, they just got in their car and took off."

"Can you describe the car?"

"Sure, it was a blue midsized Ford sedan. The left taillight was broken, and there was a hole in the left rear quarter panel."

"May I see that lug wrench?"

"Sure." Mike opened the trunk, pointed to his spare tire, and said, "There it is on top of the tire."

The officer shone his flashlight into the trunk focusing the beam on the wrench. He could smell the faint odor of gunpowder.

The officer turned to Mike and said, "Okay, you may close your trunk. Why didn't you report the attempted robbery?"

"I was just getting ready to do that."

"If I had to guess, I'd say that you didn't want a record of your phone number on the 911 log."

Mike didn't say a word.

The officer continued, "You two are lucky, there have been reports of a group robbing and beating motorist at rest areas. Where you headed?"

"Camp Perry."

"You competing?"

"No, just watching."

"Well, you two be careful. You're free to go."

"Thank you. I bet if you put an unmarked car here and wait, them idiots will come back for their weapons."

"That's what I was thinking. They ain't very smart if an old man holding a lug wrench scared them."

Mike smiled. "I hope you catch them."

The officer smiled back. "Me too, you two have fun."

"Thank you."

Mike and Cat got in the car and left.

As they were driving away, Cat said, "Do you think he believed you?"

"He believed what he wanted to. He knows we're not the problem. If he couldn't smell the gunpowder in the trunk, he has no sense of smell."

"Is that the reason you didn't call the police, so that there wouldn't be any record?"

"Yep, did you notice he didn't ask my name? He didn't call in my plates either."

"I guess he figured it'd be better use of time to catch them thugs instead of wasting time with us."

"Yeah, that's how I figure it. Say, what were you going to do with that pencil?"

"I had read in one of my self-defense books that a pencil was a good weapon. Before you showed up, I was going to ram it up through his lower jaw. I was hoping the book was right about being able to hit his brain. I was sure relived when I heard your voice."

"You sure know a lot for no older than you are."

"I read a lot."

"I will say one thing, your parents don't have to worry about you being able to take care of yourself."

"Nah, guess not."

"That was exciting. What you wanna do next month?"

"Oh, I don't know, go to Afghanistan and hunt terrorists?"

"Nah, we better not. The United Nations would accuse the United States of having an unfair advantage."

Cat liked Mike's sense of humor. It was as goofy as hers.

"Mom and Dad probably wouldn't let me go anyways."

"Probably not. You wanted to know if that pencil trick works, it does."

Cat thought it best to change the subject. "I'm getting kind of hungry."

"Yeah, me too, we can stop and get some breakfast."

"That sounds good to me."

Mike stopped at a truck stop, filled with gas, and parked the car. He and Cat went into the restaurant and sat down. The waitress walked up to their table.

"Good morning. Coffee?"

Mike and Cat replied, "Yes."

The waitress brought their coffee and asked, "Ready to order?"

Mike ordered bacon, eggs, and hash browns. Cat ordered steak, four eggs, ham, bacon, sausage, and hash browns. Mike looked at her and asked, "You sure that's enough?"

Cat thought for a second and then replied, "I'll also take a short stack of pancakes with maple syrup and butter."

"I had to ask."

Mike shook his head when the waitress brought out the food.

Cat looked at Mike. "I get really hungry when I'm excited."

"That's what your dad told me. I hope you calm down pretty soon. I don't want to have to take out a loan to feed you."

"Don't worry, it should just last a couple of days."

Mike was thinking, *Maybe I should've taken that money Dave offered me.*

As Cat was finishing up her breakfast, she said, "We have much farther to go?"

"No, I figure we should get to the hotel between four thirty and five o'clock this morning. I'll call Jim when we get closer and wake him up."

Cat finished her cup of coffee. "Ah, now I feel better."

"I hope so, that much food would've lasted me a week."

*****

Mike pulled into the hotel's parking lot. He called Jim to let him know they were there. Jim told Mike he would meet them in the lobby. Cat and Mike got their suitcases from the trunk and walked into the hotel. Jim walked up to Mike and shook his hand.

"Hey, Mike, good to see ya. This must be that gal you were telling me about."

"Yeah, this is Cat. Cat, this is my old friend Jim."

Cat shook Jim's hand. "Glad to meet you."

"Well, let's get up to the rooms. Cat, you can share a room with my daughter, Sherry."

Mike said, "That way, Jim and me can catch up on old times."

They went up to the rooms. Jim knocked on Sherry's door.

Sherry opened the door. "Hi."

Jim said, "Well, they made it. This is Cat. Cat, this is my daughter, Sherry."

Sherry replied, "Hi, come on in. So you're the one that likes to shoot."

"I take it Mike has told you quite a bit."

"Mostly to Dad, I know one thing, he does like you. He told Dad that you were like a granddaughter to him."

"He would never admit that to me."

"No, he wouldn't go that far. Did you want to take a nap or stay up and talk? I can put on a pot of coffee. We have around three hours before we have to leave."

"I'm too wide awake to sleep. I'll take a cup of coffee."

"Okay, it'll take a few minutes. What have you been shooting?"

"I started with Mike's .308 Winchester. He just finished building me a .338 Lapua."

"That's a nice round, very accurate. You shot it yet?"

"Yes, but I haven't competed with it yet. Are you competing here?"

"No, not this year. I had surgery on my shoulder last month, so I'm gonna sit this year out."

"You think I'll ever be good enough to shoot here?"

"Practice enough, have the will, and you'll make it here someday."

*****

Jim opened the door and followed Mike into his room. Jim set Mike's suitcase down.

"Mike, it's good to see ya. Have a new bottle of bourbon, care for a shot?"

"Little early, ain't it?"

"The sun ain't up yet."

"You ain't changed a bit. I'll take one."

Jim got out the bottle and a couple of glasses. As he poured the drinks, "I'm glad you decided to come out this year."

"It's good to be here."

"Tell me, what you've been up to?"

"Well, as you know, I've been teaching Cat to shoot. She's been keeping me busy. I think I've done more reloading this last year than I've done in my life."

"You always say you can't practice too much."

"Yeah, but did my own reloading."

"You'll have to teach her how."

"I don't really mind. It's good therapy for me."

"Get that rifle built?"

"Yep, a .338 Lapua, you were right, that is a nice round."

"Yeah, I thought you would like it."

Mike and Jim sat for the next two hours talking.

Jim looked at his watch and said, "Sherry should be knocking on the door pretty soon."

"You shooting today?"

"No, not today."

There was a knock on the door.

Jim said, "Come in."

"Dad, it's about time to go. You and Mike have a good visit?"

"Yeah, how about you and Cat?"

"That is some girl. I wish I had half her energy."

"Give us a couple of minutes, and we'll meet you down at the car."

"Okay, I'll get Cat and meet you there."

*****

Jim parked the car. Cat got out and looked in awe at everything.

Jim looked at Cat and said, "Well, what do ya think?"

"I've died and went to heaven."

Jim laughed. "There's lot to see around here. Today is the last day for the high-power rifle matches. Tomorrow starts the long-range matches."

Sherry asked Cat, "You want to go with me to Commercial Row? I'm sure you'll like it. It's like a strip mall for gun and shooting enthusiasts. I'm helping one of the food vendors, *American Gypsy Dog*. I'm sure I can talk them out of a dog and cup of coffee for you."

Mike said, "You got her attention, food and guns."

Cat said, "Sure. Like Mike said, food and guns!"

Jim said, "Okay, we're gonna go watch the shooting."

Sherry asked, "Where you think you'll be?"

"Probably around lane 65."

"Okay."

Cat and Sherry walked over to Commercial Row. Cat started looking at the vendors that were set up. She had never seen so many gun dealers and manufacturers in one place at one time. Sherry was right. It was a strip mall for shooters, everything from reloading supplies to actions, barrels, and optics.

Sherry said to Cat, "You go look around while I give them a hand here at the hotdog stand. Meet me back here in a couple of hours, then we'll find Dad and Mike."

"Okay."

Cat started looking around, picking up brochures, flyers, and literature from about every table. She was having the time of her life. There were people from everywhere.

*****

178

Jim said, "You think you'll be here someday watching Cat shoot?"

Mike replied, "If I live long enough."

"If she can shoot as well as you say, it won't be long."

"No, it won't. I'm gonna enter her in as many matches as I can next summer."

"Tomorrow I have to work in the pit, you want to join me?"

"Yeah, it's been a while since I've had bullets flying over my head."

"Great, I'll put you on the list."

Jim and Mike watched the shooting continuing the conversation they had started in the hotel room about what they had been doing since they had last seen each other. Sherry and Cat found Jim and Mike. Sherry handed Mike and Jim some food.

Sherry said, "I thought you two might be hungry."

Jim said, "Thank you. You have to go back?"

"No, they said they have it covered for the rest of the day."

Mike took a bite of his hotdog the best he could and said, "I think I need a knife and fork to eat this. What's this called?"

Sherry handed him a package that had a plastic fork, knife, and napkin in it. "That's called a 'Hippy Headband.'"

"Where do they come up with these names?"

"They're friends I met in college. He lost his job and decided to try food vending, invested in a food cart and started *American Gypsy Dog*. I always accused them of being leftover hippies."

Mike looked at Cat and said, "You ain't eating?"

"I already had three."

Sherry said, "I don't know where she puts all that food."

"That's why I stop at buffets when she's with me."

Cat just smiled. "This place is great! I've collected a lot of stuff to read."

They spent the rest of the afternoon walking around Commercial Row then went back to the hotel. Jim poured Mike a drink. Sherry got Cat and herself some lemonade.

Jim asked Cat, "Did you enjoy yourself?"

"Oh yeah, can't wait to go back tomorrow."

"Mike and I will be helping in the pit tomorrow, so you'll be hanging around with Sherry."

*****

Cat was having the time of her life. When Cat wasn't with Mike, she was out making new friends. Mike's old buddies couldn't stop laughing when they found out how Mike and Cat met.

When they all came back together, they sat down to watch the match.

Cat looked at Jim and asked, "What're those yellow things on the rifles?"

"Chamber flags. When you are done shooting or a cease-fire is called, you have to open the bolt and put a flag in the chamber so the range officials know the rifle is safe."

"A safety rule?"

"The last thing we need is for someone to get hurt."

A voice over the loudspeaker said. "Cease-fire, cease-fire, there's an idiot on a jet ski in the restricted area."

Cat asked, "What's going on now?"

Mike answered, "Someone crossed over the buoys into the restricted area. We have to wait till the Coast Guard clears the area."

"If they're that stupid, they deserve to get hit."

Jim laughed, "That wouldn't be good for public relations."

"Yeah, the antigun crowd would eat that up."

After the shooting was done for the day, they all went back to the hotel.

Mike said to Jim, "I'm gonna take Cat to that steakhouse I promised her."

"Okay, Sherry and I want to see some friends before they leave. I'll see you back here."

Mike turned to Cat and asked, "You want to go get that steak?"

"Well, yeah, sure."

"You still excited?"

"I haven't been this excited since I shot my first deer."

"That's what I was afraid of." Mike checked his wallet. "I had better stop at the ATM."

Mike parked the car in front of the steakhouse. "They should have plenty of food here."

"I hope so. I'm hungry. I haven't eaten anything since breakfast!"

"What you ate for breakfast would have lasted a normal person for a week."

"That's the difference. I ain't normal!"

"Truer words were never spoken."

The waitress seated them and asked them what they wanted to drink. While waiting on their drinks, they looked over the menu. The waitress came back to the table and asked, "Ready to order?"

Mike ordered the rib eye steak, baked potato, and a salad. He handed back the menu and waited to see the expression on the waitress's face when Cat ordered.

Cat looked at the waitress and said, "I'll take the 32-ounce porterhouse for two, medium rare."

"But he already ordered."

"I know, this is for me."

"It comes with two baked potatoes and two salads."

"I know that too. I'll take ranch on one and French on the other. Oh, butter and sour cream for the potatoes."

The waitress looked at Mike in disbelief.

Mike smiled and said, "You should see what she eats when she's hungry."

As they were waiting on their food, the news came on the TV.

The officer being interviewed said, "We've apprehended three suspects that we think are responsible for the attacks and robberies at the rest areas in the state."

The interviewer said, "One of the suspects said that an old man with a young girl shot at them with something that looked like a lug wrench."

"The only thing I know is that an officer was parked in the rest area when a car pulled up. One of the suspects got out and started picking something up off the grass. The officer walked over and seen them picking up a gun and two knives. The other two took off. He radioed in, and they were stopped about two miles from the rest area."

"You're pretty confident these are the guys committing the crimes at rest areas?"

"Yes, we found some weapons and stolen purses in their car."

"Okay, thank you."

Cat looked at Mike. "Well, I guess we won't have to worry about them on the way back."

"No, I guess not."

The waitress brought out their salads. Cat was starting on her second one before Mike was finished with his. He looked at Cat and said, "Slow down, girl, that food ain't gonna run away from ya."

"That's what Dad tells me."

"It's a good thing you hunt and fish, or your parents couldn't afford to feed you."

"Dad tells me *that* too."

The waitress brought out their steaks. Mike looked at Cat's steak, wondering where she put all that food. Cat looked up and said, "Boy, this steak looks good."

"Yes, it does."

Cat had eaten part of her steak and was putting butter and sour cream on her second potato when a twenty-something woman walked up to the table. Cat looked up as the woman said, "That is way too much red meat and butter for you. That will plug up your arteries, causing you a heart attack, or worse yet, a stroke. It's not healthy for you."

Mike was getting up to go to the restroom but sat back down. He didn't want to miss the show.

Cat looked at her and said, "Not nearly as unhealthy as inter-rupting my meal with your unwanted advice."

Mike chuckled.

The woman looked at Mike. "And you why are you letting her eat that much unhealthy food? You are contributing to her unhealthy lifestyle. This is child abuse."

"If you're brave enough, you take her food away."

Cat turned to Mike in a quiet voice, "I'll take care of this."

Mike mumbled to himself, "That's what I was afraid of."

Cat took another bite of her steak, looked at the woman, and asked, "So do you exercise?"

"Well, yes, I go to the gym twice a week, but I also watch what I eat."

"What does your diet consist of, baked skinless chicken breast and dry salad?"

"Fried, fatty foods are not good for you."

"Even though it's none of your business, I am going to tell you what I do to keep in shape. I run three miles at least three times a week. It's not on a treadmill, I run through the hills of Kentucky. I ride my bike almost everywhere I go."

"Well, still, you need to eat a proper diet."

Cat took another bite of her steak and continued, "I'll tell you what. If you want to challenge me to a bike race or a marathon, let me know. I'd also be glad to compare my health records with yours. My cholesterol is good, my blood pressure is good. The doctor says my pulse and heart rate are excellent. There is no reason to fix something that ain't broke. Besides that, it ain't none of your business what I eat."

"You still shouldn't be eating like that. It will catch up to you."

"Why don't you go back to eating your tasteless dinner, and I can finish mine before it gets any colder. Oh, and one more thing, in case you care, I'll be ordering dessert."

The woman left in a huff.

Cat looked at Mike. "Why can't people mind their own business?"

"I don't know."

The waitress came back and asked if they wanted any dessert. Mike said, "No, I'm full."

Cat replied, "Yes, I'll take a piece of apple pie à la mode."

Mike looked up and seen that Miss Nosy was still looking at them.

Mike smiled and said to the waitress, "On second thought, I'll take the same."

*****

The next morning, Cat and Sherry got up and went over to Jim's room to have some coffee before they went to Camp Perry.

As they walked into the room, Jim and Mike said, "Good morning."

Sherry and Cat replied, "Good morning."

While Cat and Sherry were getting a cup of coffee, Jim and Mike were watching the news. There was a repeat of the apprehension of the, rest area attack suspects.

After it was over, Jim looked at Mike and asked, "You still have that custom-made lug wrench?"

Mike smiled.

They finished their coffee and decided to stop for breakfast on their way to Camp Perry.

The waitress came to the table and asked, "Coffee?"

"Yes," they all replied.

The waitress came back with the coffee and asked, "Ready to order?"

Cat said, "I'll take the three-egg special with bacon, hash browns, and pancakes."

Mike looked at her. "Off your feed?"

"Oh, I've calmed down."

"Thank the Lord for small favors."

While they ate breakfast, Cat told them that she was glad that she and her family moved to Kentucky. They were amazed at how she had saved the game warden and they couldn't stop laughing about the run-ins with Officer Shot. Jim and Sherry got a kick of how Cat won Mike over.

Cat said, "I'm glad that I was able to talk Mike into teaching me how to shoot. At first I didn't know if I was going to be able to get through that brick wall he built around himself. He is pretty stubborn."

Mike said, "That's the pot calling the kettle black."

"Just because the pot calls the kettle black doesn't mean it's not true."

Jim said, "She has a point there."

"I can't win," muttered Mike.

Everyone laughed. They finished up their breakfast and went to Camp Perry. They watched the competition for a while then looked around Commercial Row. After another full day, they all went back to the hotel.

Cat knocked on Mike's door.

"Come in."

Cat walked in and said, "I'm gonna go and run. I have to wear off some of this food I've been eating. I don't think my sit-ups are gonna be enough."

"Okay, be careful."

"You know me."

"Yes, I do. Be careful."

Cat smiled and went outside. She had mapped out a route before she left. Cat had run about a half mile when she noticed two people running behind her. She didn't want to get paranoid, but the incident at the rest area, plus being in a strange town is making her nervous. *Maybe I should have seen if somebody would've come with me.* She didn't know whether to try to lose them or slow down and see who they were. She decided to slow down and conserve her energy. She was pretty confident if she had to she could outrun them back to the hotel. When the runners caught up with her, she was relieved. It was a couple she had met at Camp Perry, friends of Jim and Sherry.

The guy said, "Hi. Aren't you that girl staying with Sherry?"

"Yeah, Cat."

The girl asked, "Mind if we run with you?"

Cat, glad to have someone running with her, answered, "No, that'd be fine."

"How far are you planning on running?"

"If the map is right, three miles."

"That sounds like a good jog."

"Did Mike ask you to run with me?"

The guy said, "Can't put one over on you."

The girl said, "Actually, it was Sherry, she knew we were going out."

At first Cat was a little upset, then after thinking about it, she realized how fortunate she was to have friends that cared.

After they got back to the hotel, Cat asked, "You guys gonna run tomorrow night?"

"Plan on it. We'll stop by your room if you want to run with us."

"Sure, see you tomorrow."

*****

As Cat and Mike were putting, their suitcases in the car Cat said to Mike, "I can't believe it's time to go home already."

"Yeah, those ten days went by pretty fast."

Jim said to Mike, "Glad you could make it. Next year come earlier so you can watch some of the other matches."

"We'll see. I might have to take out a loan to feed her."

They all laughed then Sherry said to Cat, "You have my e-mail address, keep in touch."

"I will, hope to be back next year."

Jim said, "You two be careful. Cat, good luck on your shooting."

"Thank you."

"Keep Mike in line."

They all shook hands, then Mike and Cat got in the car and headed for home.

Mike asked, "Did you have a good time."

"I sure did!"

"You know there's a lot of rifle competitions out there. If you continue to practice and improve, you'll be the one to beat."

"Think so?"

"Yeah, just keep practicing."

"Now that school is getting ready to start in a couple of weeks, I won't be able to practice as much."

"What grade will ya be in this year?"

"I'll be a senior. Of course, Ben graduated last year."

"Is he going to college?"

"He said something about taking some online classes this year. He thinks sitting in a classroom is boring."

Mike stopped to get some gas. While Mike was filling the car, Cat went inside and looked around the gift shop to see if she could find something for her mom. As she was looking through the books, *How to Cook All Wild Game* caught her eye.

She was looking at it when Mike walked up and asked, "Find something interesting?"

"Yeah, Mom would love this cookbook, but it's a little more than I have."

"Let me see it."

Cat handed it to him, and he looked through it. "I'll get it for you."

"I can't ask you to buy this so I can give it to Mom. You've already done too much for me."

"You didn't ask, I offered. Besides that, I'll consider it an investment. I expect to be invited over for a meal. I'm sure your mom's a good cook."

Cat grinned, "Thanks, Mike."

Once back on the road, Cat began looking through some of the flyers she had picked up at Camp Perry. She asked Mike, "What's a PALMA Shoot?"

"Looks like you got bit by the shooting bug."

"That happened a while ago."

"A PALMA shoot is where you shoot prone at 800, 900, and 1,000 yards. Fifteen rounds each, limited to .308 and 155 grain bullet. The weight of the rifle cannot exceed 14 1/2 pounds."

"What scope can you use?"

"No scope."

"No scope at those ranges. I can scratch that off my list."

Mike laughed and said, "You don't do too bad with the AR-15. Sherry shoots PALMA."

"I know, but I'd rather use a scope. What's F-class?"

"That's kinda a cross between PALMA and bench rest shooting. It is limited to .223 and .308. You are allowed a scope."

"I suppose I had just better stick with the long-range matches for now."

"Yeah, that'd be best."

*****

Mike pulled into Cat's driveway. Dave walked up as Cat was getting out of the car.

She looked at Dave and said, "Hi, Dad."

"See you made it back. Have a good time?"

"Yeah, it was great."

Cat went into the house to see her mom. Dave helped Mike get Cat's stuff out of the trunk. Mike looked at Dave.

"You know, Cat is a very good shooter. I think she has the ability to be one of the top shooters in the country."

"That's always been her dream."

"The shooting sports have become more popular in the last few years. I would like to continue to take her to matches."

"She would love that. Aren't the shooting sports pretty expensive? I mean, with the rifles and equipment?"

"Don't worry about that. You have a top-notch shooter there, and I would hate to see that talent wasted."

"I hate to see you spend all your money on her."

"I have quite a bit of money in my 401(k) that I didn't know what I was going to do with. I get enough from my pensions to live on. I enjoy taking her shooting."

"I'm sure that will be a dream come true for her. You know, the kids think of you as a grandpa."

"I sometimes catch myself thinking of them as grandchildren."

Betty came outside and said to Mike, "Will you stay for supper? I've made plenty."

"Sure. I'll tell you what. That girl can eat."

Dave laughed, "I told you."

They all went into the living room to visit while the ham finished baking. Liz is there. She just returned from a mission trip overseas. Cat was glad to see her even if it did mean sharing the bedroom again. Cat handed the cookbook to her mom and said, "Here, I got ya something."

Betty took it and asked, "What's this?"

"It's a wild game cookbook."

Betty sat down and started looking through it. "This looks like a nice book, thank you."

Cat smiled and said, "You're welcome."

Betty started going through the book and to Cat's surprise and shock started tearing out pages. Cat looked at Mike and shrugged her shoulders. Betty went through the whole book. After she was done, she took the pages that she had torn out and threw them away.

Cat waited till Mom came back to the room and asked her, "Mom, why did you tear out those pages?"

"I don't mind cooking venison, rabbit, squirrel, and catfish. In fact, I like venison but there ain't no way I am going to cook raccoon, muskrat, opossum, or woodchuck."

"You didn't have to tear the pages out."

"I don't want to be looking for a recipe for a roast and come across a picture of a roasted muskrat."

"Well, okay, I guess. It is your book."

"Yes, it is. You gave it to me, and I'll use it."

When Betty went back to the kitchen to check on supper, Dave asked Cat, "That big rabbit you shot last fall, it was a rabbit?"

Cat just nodded. Dave knew better. They all sat down for supper. After they were done, Mike said, "Thanks for supper. I'm gonna head home."

Cat replied "Okay, I'll see you later. Thanks for everything."

"You're welcome."

14

Cat knocked on Mike's door.

Mike answered in his usual way, "Come in."

"Hi, Mike."

"How's school going?"

"It's going."

"That good, huh?"

"Oh, I don't mind school."

"Be honest, it cuts into your shooting time."

Cat smiles, "And hunting time."

"I've been going over your scores from the summer. You've come a long way."

"I'll take that as a compliment."

"It is. Now it's time to focus on what to do before a match."

"Like what?"

"You exercise regularly, which is good. You need to watch what you eat before a match."

"Watch what I eat? You think I'm getting fat?"

"Just like a *woman*! No, you're not getting fat. What you eat and drink before a match will affect how you shoot. You need to watch your sugar and caffeine intake the morning before."

"I have to give up my coffee *and* pancakes?"

"No, you don't have to give them up. The morning before a match, have just one cup of coffee instead of the standard three or five, skip the pancakes and syrup. You'll be able to figure it out."

"You're right. That day I ate all those pancakes and four cups of coffee for breakfast, plus I drank two colas right before the match, I didn't do too well."

"Everyone is different. You'll figure it out."

"I guess I'll just add it to my do and don't list."

"You'll do fine. So what else you up to?"

"I wanted to know if it'd be okay to bring Widow Johnson's boy over here to practice. I'm gonna take him deer hunting this season."

"Sure, anytime."

*****

Cat hiked into the woods and picked out a tree to set up a tree stand for her and Widow Johnson's son. It would give them a good view of a well-used deer trail. She walked over to a big rock and sat down. *This is a good day to relax and enjoy nature. It has been a busy summer.*

Cat liked the fall of the year with the leaves changing color and falling to the ground. Soon the trees would be naked; the only color would be the evergreens. It wasn't long before the area became busy with the squirrels running around chattering and gathering food for the winter. A hawk swooped in and grabbed a squirrel for his meal. A flock of geese flew over. The days were getting shorter; the air getting colder signaling winter is right around the corner. How she wished she had lived in a time when she could have found a piece of land, built a house, and made it hers. Sure, it would be hard work, but it would be hers. Moving down here was as close as she would be able to get to that in the modern world.

Cat awoke out of her daydream when a big buck deer came into view. It was the monster. This surprised her; she had never seen him in the daylight. His antlers sat on his head like a pair of giant oak trees. *How is it possible to grow something that big every year?* He looked her way. His antlers reflected the sunlight, and he stood proud with his head up. This was his territory, and he was king. He looked at Cat, knowing she would do him no harm. She had seen him many times while she was poaching. Was it possible that he had led the younger deer to her?

Soon another buck came into view, a proud, younger buck, not quite as large. He had the same build as the monster, possibly one of his offspring. The younger one put his head down and ran toward the monster. The fight was on. Would this be the year the monster lost his territory? Clashing antlers broke the silence of the cool, quiet air. First, the younger one would push the monster one way, and then the monster pushed him back. Their antlers would lock, then after they broke free, they would back up like two prize fighters going to their corners. Then, as if a bell rang, they started fighting again. Cat sat there as if she were watching a boxing match. Both of them were working up a sweat, foam coming from their mouths and snot from their noses, and neither one was giving up. Both of them started tiring. The monster couldn't take any more. He was exhausted. He had been defeated. He turned toward Cat as though he knew she had been watching the whole fight. He put his head up, looking at Cat for a moment. Cat could see the disappointment in his eyes. He put his head down and walked away as though he had no reason to live. The title had been passed on.

Cat wondered what would happen to him now. This once-proud buck walked away defeated. Would he fight another day or lie in the brush and starve? How long ago was it that he fought his predecessor? How long would it be before the young buck would be defeated? Cat couldn't help feeling sad, but this was nature's way of making sure the species stayed strong.

*****

Cat went over to Widow Johnson's place. The sun wouldn't be up for another two hours, but opening day was here. Cat hoped that all the practicing that the widow's boy had been doing would pay off. She knocked on the door.

Widow Johnson answered, "Come on in, Cat."

"Hi, is he ready?"

"Oh yeah, he's been up and ready for two hours."

"I can understand that, nothing like your first deer hunt."

"He had been out with his dad before but only watched. He was getting excited about the next season, his dad was going to let him hunt." Widow Johnson looked down trying to hide the tear in her eye. "His dad died before the next season came."

"I'm sorry."

Widow Johnson wiped her face and said, "You needn't be. I'm glad he can go this year."

Widow Johnson's boy ran into the kitchen, looked at Cat, and said, "I'm ready!"

"Okay, you have your vest?"

"Yep."

"Okay, let's go! Mike helped me put up the stand. It's big enough for both of us."

It was a challenge for Cat to get them there without making too much noise. She knew it would be hard, being his first time. When they got there, Cat put some deer scent around the area. They climbed up into the stand and got situated. Cat made sure he could aim his shotgun in whatever direction that the deer may be coming from.

After they got comfortable, Cat said, "Okay, now all we have to do is wait. We still have about forty-five minutes till we can shoot."

"You think we'll see some today?"

"If we're quiet, we will."

It seemed like a week went by until it started getting light. The sun began peeking over the horizon. It wasn't long until a couple of does walked under the stand. The boy looked at Cat. Cat shook her head no. He seemed disappointed, but Cat knew a bigger one would come by. Another hour went by. Cat saw some movement out in the distance. She looked through her binoculars, and what she saw nearly took her breath away. The monster was walking right toward them.

She thought to herself, *What is he doing? He has to know that all the hunters are after him. Why would a buck that had made it all these years avoiding hunters, poachers, vehicles, not to mention the wildcats and coyotes, walk out in the open like that? How could he be so stupid?* Cat had built a relationship with the buck. She resisted the temptation to stand up and yell to scare him away.

Cat turned to look at the boy just as he saw the buck. The boy's heart started beating so hard and fast that Cat could almost hear it. His hands were shaking so bad that Cat didn't know if he would be able to shoot straight.

Cat put her hand on his shoulder and whispered, "Calm down. Slow your breathing."

The buck continued slowly toward them. He stopped thirty-five yards from the stand. He looked up at Cat, turned broadside, and held his head high. Cat couldn't help but wonder if this was the way he wanted his journey to end.

She turned to the boy, who was staring wide-eyed at the buck, and said, "He's not gonna stand there all day. Remember what I taught you."

The boy shouldered his shotgun using the rail of the stand to hold himself steady. He looked through the scope and slowly squeezed the trigger. The slug left the muzzle then tore through the heart and lungs of the buck. Cat saw the hair move when the slug hit. She knew it was a well-placed shot. The buck didn't run as she had expected. He just walked a few steps and fell down. This was one of the few times she had feelings of happiness and sadness at the same time.

Cat looked over at the boy. His grin stretched ear to ear. He said, "Let's go see how big he is!"

"No, we want to wait a bit to make sure he's dead." Cat knew he was already dead, but she wanted to get him in the habit for future hunts. It was a lot easier to wait a few minutes than to trail a wounded deer.

After waiting for a few minutes, they climbed down from the stand and walked toward the deer. As they got closer to the deer, Cat explained, "You want to walk up behind him that way you have less of a chance of getting hurt if he's still alive."

"He sure is big!"

"Yeah, he's a nice one. Take your gun barrel and touch his eye with it. If he blinks, shoot him again. The taxidermists hate that advice, but better safe than hurt."

The boy walked up and touched the buck's eyes with his gun barrel. The buck's eyes were wide open. He didn't move. The boy then looked at Cat, "I'd say he's dead."

"Good. Fill out your tag, then I'll show you how to gut him."

After the boy filled out his tag, Cat field dressed the buck explaining what she was doing and why. After they were done, he attached the tag to the deer. Cat looked at the buck and said, "I think we're gonna need a little help."

"Mike's probably at the diner. He's always there during deer season drinking coffee and listening to stories from the hunters."

"That's a long hike."

"I need to walk off some of this excitement. I can take the logging road up to the county road…probably be able to catch a ride to town."

"All right, I'll wait here."

"Maybe another deer will come by and you can get yours."

"Maybe." Cat knew the excitement the boy felt was not only because he got his first deer but also that he was able to help his mom with the food.

*****

As expected, Mike was in the diner drinking coffee and swapping hunting tales with some of the other guys. In through the door ran Widow Johnson's boy.

He ran up to Mike, yelling at the top of his voice, "Mike!'

"Yeah, what is it, everything all right?"

"Yeah, great!" He was talking so fast that nobody could understand him.

Finally, Mike said, "Okay, boy, calm down, speak a little slower so I can understand you."

Widow Johnson's boy told Mike about the big deer he had shot and how he needed help getting it out of the woods.

Mike looked around and asked, "Who's going with me to give this young man a hand?"

A couple of guys volunteered. They jumped in Mike's truck and headed to the woods. Mike drove down an old logging road and got as close as he could. They would still have to drag the buck about a quarter mile.

When they got to the deer, Cat said, "Hi, Mike, he's a big one. Might not be a record, but it's a wall hanger."

Mike and the other guys looked at it, and one of them said, "Son, that's a nice deer. I've hunted over thirty years and never got a chance for one this size. Good job."

Mike said, "It is a nice buck. Let's get it to the truck."

Halfway to the truck Mike looked at the boy and said, "Ya know, you could've shot him a little closer to the road."

Cat said, "Don't pay attention to him, at least it wasn't down in a valley."

After the buck was loaded, Mike drove to the check station. Widow Johnson's boy was enjoying all the attention that he was getting. After the metal tag was placed on the buck's leg, Mike drove to Widow Johnson's place.

The boy ran up to the house, yelling, "Mom, Mom, come look at the buck I got!"

Widow Johnson walked out to the truck and said, "Boy, that's a big one."

Smiling, "Yeah, he walked right up to the stand."

"We'll have plenty to eat this winter."

Mike and Cat hung the deer in the shed. On their way out, Widow Johnson walked up to Cat, "I want to thank you, you made his day."

"He made mine too. I'll be back tomorrow to show him how to skin it."

"Thank you."

As Mike got into his truck, Cat said, "Mike, I have a favor to ask you."

"This is gonna cost?"

"Well, a little."

"What would you like me to do?"

"Well, you know, Widow Johnson doesn't have much money. It would make her boy real happy to have that deer head mounted."

"You want *me* to pay for it? Why would I do that?"

"Because deep down inside, probably real deep, you have a heart."

"Think so, huh?"

"I know so, and you know that it would be a shame not to have it mounted."

"You think you know me pretty good, don't you?

"Yeah, I do."

"Can't fool you any. After you skin it out, take the head and hide down to Billy Bob's Beer, Liquor, and Taxidermy. Tell him Mike will pay for it."

Cat gave Mike a funny look. "Beer, Liquor, and *Taxidermy?*"

"Don't let the name fool ya. He's one of the best in the county. He closed his taxidermy shop, bought the liquor store. He kinda missed taxidermy, so he does a few every year in the backroom. He'll do it for me."

"I'll need somebody to haul it over there."

"Is there anything else you want me to do?"

"No, that should be about it. If there is, I'll let you know."

"I'm sure you will. Give me a call when you have the head and hide off."

"Okay, thanks, Mike."

"Now, don't tell anybody. I don't want anybody to think I'm getting soft in my old age."

"Your secret is safe with me."

*****

It was suppertime when Cat got home. She washed up and sat down at the table. As she wolfed down her supper, she told her family about the day she had."

Betty said, "Slow down, girl. That food ain't gonna run away from you."

"I know, but I haven't eaten since morning."

"Sounds like you had an exciting day."

"I did, you should've seen Widow Johnson's son's face when he walked up to that buck. There was no way you could get that smile off his face. I'm gonna go skin it tomorrow. Mike said he'd have the head mounted for the little guy."

"That's nice of him."

"Yeah, don't tell anybody, he doesn't want people to think he's getting soft."

"Okay, I won't."

"Is it okay if Widow Johnson stores some of the meat in our freezer? I doubt her freezer is big enough."

Dave said, "Boy, it must be a big deer."

"You should see it. It's a monster."

Cat helped her mom with the dishes then said, "With the moon so bright, I think I'll get my sketch pad and see what's happening in the woods. I bet there'll be a lot of activity tonight."

"All right, you be careful."

"I will, love you."

*****

Cat went back to where Widow Johnson's boy killed the buck. She sat down by a big rock. Coyotes were working on the gut pile. One of them with blood on its nose looked up at Cat then continued to enjoy the free meal. It seemed so peaceful with the snow putting a white coat on the ground. It made the fur of the coyotes sparkle in the moonlight. What a pretty picture this would make in an outdoors magazine. The coyotes knew Cat would do them no harm tonight. Later, at another place and time, they might fall prey from a bullet or a trap set by her. Their fur would be used to trim the hoods of parkas or made into coats. A big one might be taken to a taxidermist then placed in a wildlife display. Tonight none of this would happen. For tonight, there was a truce.

As she was sketching this scene, her thoughts went back to the fight between the bucks, about how the big one had lived. He had lived a full life, outsmarting hunters, predators, winters, and vehicles.

Now the meat from him would feed a family. Even the coyotes got a free meal. His head will be mounted, and all the people in the area will know that this buck once roamed the hills. He would never be forgotten, especially by Cat and Widow Johnson's family.

How long would the younger buck make it? Would he be smart enough, strong enough, or lucky enough to last as long as the older one had? As she watched the coyotes finish up their dinner, her thoughts went back to the younger buck. Would this be the way his life ended, or would he fall to a poacher's bullet, die of old age and be eaten by scavengers, or get hit by a truck? Nature is simple, but so brutal.

Even though it was late when Cat got home, her mom was still up. As she walked in the door, her mom asked, "Pretty night?"

"Yes, Mom, it is so peaceful out there in the moon light." She handed her the sketch pad. "What do you think of these?"

Betty looked at the drawings. "You know, with this talent, you could make a career out of art."

"I know, but if it became my job, I might not enjoy it as much."

"I guess you have a point there. You would rather want to instead of have to."

"I'm gonna go get some sleep, I'm going over to Widow Johnson's and skin that buck in the morning."

"Okay, good night, love ya."

"Love you too, good night."

The next day, Cat went over to Widow Johnson's to skin the buck. When she got there, the boy was in the shed admiring the deer.

Cat walked up to him, "He's a dandy."

"Yeah, I think it'll fill the freezer. Have you ever gotten one this big?"

"No, I haven't. I'll show you how to do this, then the next one you get, you can skin it."

When Cat finished skinning the buck, she called Mike to pick up the head and hide so he could take it to the taxidermist. The weather was cool enough to let the meat hang a few days. She would come back later to cut it up and put it in the freezer.

*****

Saturday morning Cat rolled out of bed, drank a cup of coffee, ate some breakfast, and went over to Widow Johnson's to cut up the deer. Cat knocked on the door.

Widow Johnson answered, "Come on in. We've been waiting on ya."

Cat walked in. Widow Johnson had a cutting board and freezer bags already on the table.

Widow Johnson said, "I dug out my old meat grinder. The boys want some burger."

"Okay, I guess we'd better get started."

Cat went out to the shed and cut off a front quarter and brought it in the house. As they were cutting it up, Widow Johnson said, "I sure appreciate everything you've done for us."

"Glad to do it."

"How did you ever get Mike to come out of his shell? Everyone thought he'd die a grumpy old man. I thought he'd be found dead sitting in his chair."

"I don't know. I guess I'm a little more bullheaded than he is."

"I didn't think it'd be possible to be more stubborn than that old man."

"Talk to my parents."

They all started laughing. With everyone helping, they got the meat cut up and put in freezer. There was quite a bit left after they filled the freezer.

The oldest boy said, "Wow, this is a lot of meat!"

Widow Johnson said, "Yes, it is. You boys should have plenty to eat for a while."

Cat said, "I'll call Dad to come over and get the rest of it. Mom said there'll be plenty of room in our freezer."

"Tell your mom thanks."

"I will. Is it okay if I take a couple of steaks over to Mike's?"

"Of course it is, and tell your mom to use some of it. It's the least I can do."

"Thanks."

Dave came over and picked up the meat. After they got it loaded in the car, Cat said to her dad, "I'm gonna take some steaks over to Mike's. I'll see you at home."

"Okay."

*****

Cat was driving over to Mike's to return his .308 Winchester as well as some empty brass. It was a nice spring day. Flowers were starting to bloom. She had the car window down, enjoying the fresh spring air. She passed a parked car along the road, thinking to herself, *That looks like the home ec teacher's car.*

Her thoughts were interrupted by a scream. She turned the car around and pulled up behind the car. As she got out of her car, she heard another scream. She looked out into the field. The home ec teacher was standing with a little girl beside her. In front of them was an animal about the size of a dog. Cat opened the trunk of her car and took out her rifle and sandbag. She sat the sandbag on the hood of her car, laid her rifle on the bag and looked through the scope. Standing in front of the teacher and little girl was a fox. The fox was snarling and foaming at the mouth.

Cat was talking to herself, "He must be rabid. I wish they'd stop screaming."

Cat opened the bolt and placed a live round in the chamber, closed the bolt, looked through the scope, flipped off the safety, lined the crosshairs up on the heart/lung area of the fox, and squeezed the trigger. The bullet found its mark; the fox jumped then fell dead. Cat chambered another round and walked toward the teacher. The little girl had her arms around the teacher's legs, still screaming and crying. Cat walked to the fox and tapped the body with the gun barrel. The fox didn't move. His eyes were wide open and with foam around his mouth.

Cat walked over to the teacher and girl and said, "You're okay now. He won't hurt you."

The teacher replied, "What is that? We were just looking at the wildflowers when it walked up to us and started snarling."

"That's a fox. I think he's rabid. They usually run away when they see humans. Did he bite either one of you?"

"No."

A state policeman driving down the road heard a shot. He pulled up behind the cars. He exited his car with his shotgun and walked toward Cat. Cat turned around and saw the officer. She held her rifle with the action facing the officer and the barrel pointed toward the sky and said, "Chamber's open."

The officer walked up to Cat and asked, "What happened?"

"I heard a scream as I drove by, so I stopped. I looked toward the creek and saw a fox getting ready to attack these two. He looks like he may be rabid."

The officer looked at the fox and agreed. "Let's go back to the car. I'll get a pair of gloves and a bag to put it in. I'll take it to the State Board of Health and have it tested.

"Okay."

The teacher said, "Cat, I don't know how I'll be able to thank you."

The officer asked, "You're Cat?"

"Don't tell me that even the state police know who I am?"

The officer laughed and replied, "I'm a friend with Judge Bean and Officer Conrad. I was in town visiting with them. They were telling me a little about you."

"I hope they didn't tell you everything."

"Probably not, I was only there a couple hours."

"Still, I'm sure it was enough."

"Enough to know you're unique."

"I guess I can't argue that."

"That's a nice rifle, Winchester?"

"Yeah, .308, Mike lets me use it."

"Grumpy Mike?"

"I'm sure the judge told you about me and Mike."

"A little, heard he built you a .338 Lapua."

"Yes, he did. That rifle is sweet."

The officer got the bag and gloves out of his trunk, looked at Cat, and asked, "You shot that fox from here?"

"Yes, not much over a hundred yards."

"Still, that's a ways, considering how close he was to the teacher."

"There was at least five feet between them."

"That's still pretty close."

"I didn't have many options."

"You have a point. You all stay here while I go get that fox."

While they waited, the teacher said to Cat, "I want to thank you again."

"You don't have to thank me. I just did what had to be done."

"Are you all right? Why do you look so sad?"

"Oh, it just doesn't seem right that the fox had to be shot that way."

"What do you mean?"

"He's a predator, he should've been shot killing somebody's chickens, been tricked into stepping in a trap, or been shot by a hunter when his fur was prime."

"I don't understand, he'd be dead either way."

"That's not the point. It's the way he'll be remembered. If his fur was prime, it could have been made into a stole. If he'd been shot killing chickens, he would have been talked about for years, especially if he'd been mounted and sat on somebody's fireplace mantle. Not this guy, he'll be tested for rabies, which I'm sure will be positive. Then his body will be incinerated like garbage."

"I still don't quite understand."

"Have you seen the deer head hanging in the Corner Store in town, the one that Widow Johnson's boy shot?"

"Yeah, I saw it but didn't pay much attention to it. I think it's terrible to kill such a beautiful animal like that then hang its head on the wall."

"How is that terrible? I watched that deer when he was in his prime. I would go out at night to observe him. It was a beautiful sight, the snow falling on his antlers in the moonlight. He stood there strong and proud. One morning as I was watching him, a younger, stronger buck, probably one of his offspring, challenged him for a doe. The older one fought his best, but he was getting old and tired, he lost the fight. He walked away with his head down, defeated."

"I still don't get your point. Why should his head be on the wall? I think the boy just wants to brag about killing a defenseless animal. I can't see how anybody can enjoy that."

"You have to look at the whole picture. After losing the fight to a younger buck, several things could have happened. He could have wandered off, eaten very little, gotten sick, and died. What the coyotes and buzzards didn't eat would have rotted. A lot of people wouldn't have known that he even roamed the hills. That's not what happened. He walked up to the tree where the boy was sitting and stood broadside."

"You think he did that on purpose?"

"You could argue that he felt his life was worthless. Maybe he was depressed and just started wandering around. Either way, the boy placed a perfect shot. That deer fed Widow Johnson's family. The head was mounted so everybody knew that at one time he roamed the hills outsmarting hunters and predators alike. Even the coyotes weren't left out. They got to clean up the gut pile."

"That is a different perspective to look at it from."

"Nature is not a utopia where everything is cute and fuzzy. It would cease to exist. A lot of times it's cruel, but that is the only way wildlife will survive."

The officer came back with the fox. He had heard part of the conversation. He said to Cat, "That was good. Ever consider writing for an outdoors magazine?"

"Thought about it."

After putting the fox in trunk, the officer said to the teacher and Cat, "After I get the results back, I'll send a copy to Conrad."

*****

Cat made it to Mike's. After she told him what had happened, Mike looked at her and said, "Excitement seems to follow you everywhere."

"Either that or I cause it."

"Plan on doing some shooting today?"

"Planned on it, want to get ready for that weekend competition."

"Which rifle you gonna use?"

"I think I'll use your Winchester."

"I thought you'd use the Lapua."

"Nah, it's just a five-hundred yard match, I thought I'd use the Winchester. I don't want it to feel left out. I'll save the Lapua for the long ranges."

"I wouldn't worry about that too much, rifles ain't like women. They don't get jealous."

Cat laughed. "I guess not."

"There's an old-time shoot coming up. I thought you, Ben, and Barry would like to go. It is pretty close to that new state-of-the-art shooting range they're building."

"The B&C?"

"Yeah, I thought we could stop and check it out before we came home."

"Sounds good to me. I'll ask Ben and Barry."

15

Monday morning Jimmy-John pulled up to the guard shack and noticed a railcar on the tracks by the old maintenance tunnel. This was unusual since the track had been put out of service after 9-11. An upgrade to the dam made the tunnel obsolete. Every three months the tunnel was inspected for damage and leaks. The plant hadn't been able to get the permits to permanently fill in and close the tunnel.

As Jimmy-John handed the guard his ID, he asked, "What's with the railcar?"

"It was put there over the weekend."

"By who?"

"A contractor that finished a job at the mine."

"Okay, see you later."

Jimmy-John parked his truck and slowly walked toward the plant resisting the urge to check out the car before his shift started. It didn't make any sense. He made a mental note to call a friend of his that worked at the mine. When he got to the time clock, his boss said, "Jimmy-John, take these new manuals and safety updates down to the control room."

"Okay. Say, do you know anything about that railcar parked by the old maintenance tunnel?"

"I got a memo that a contractor from the mine wanted to park it there for a couple of weeks. Maybe they're finally going to fill in that tunnel and close it for good."

"Did you check with Corporate?"

"No, I'm sure they know about it. They don't like to be bothered."

"Still, that track has been closed since 9-11."

"You worry too much. You think there's a terrorist under every rock."

As Jimmy-John went to the control room, he couldn't get the railcar out of his mind. Why would they allow a car to sit there? His gut was telling him something was up, and it wasn't good.

Jimmy-John handed the updates to the control supervisor. The supervisor took the papers. "You know anything about that railcar by the old maintenance tunnel?"

"Nope, maybe they're gonna finally close that tunnel."

"Yeah, maybe." Jimmy-John still not convinced.

At lunchtime Jimmy-John grabbed his lunch and went outside to the picnic table near the tracks. While eating his sandwich, he wandered around the railcar. Someone had been walking between the railcar and the tunnel entrance. He walked over to the tunnel door. It had been opened recently, and a new lock had been installed. New conduit ran from the tunnel on top of the concrete to a phone company's junction box outside the fence.

Jimmy-John walked back over to the door of the railcar to get a look inside. The smell of bad breath made him turn around.

A big, burly guard with night stick in hand gruffly asked, "What are you doing here?"

"Just looking at this railcar. What's it here for?"

"None of your business."

"They plan on closing the tunnel?"

"You have no need to know."

"All right, I'm leaving. You need some breath mints."

"Leave, now."

Jimmy-John hurried back to the plant. As he clocked in, his boss walked up behind him. "You're a little late from lunch."

"Sorry, boss, I was just looking at that railcar. Somebody is up to no good."

"You just worry about your job."

"Okay."

*****

Jimmy-John walked into his house, threw some leftovers on a plate, and put it in the microwave. He couldn't get the railcar out of his mind. He picked up a notepad and pencil and drove back to the plant, leaving his supper in the microwave. Jimmy-John parked his truck outside the fence by the junction box he had noticed earlier in the day. He was taking a chance; you were considered trespassing being on company property outside working hours. He looked over the phone company's junction box; it had been put in recently. Nearby, he found a spot where animals had dug under the fence. With a little more digging, he is able to get under.

Jimmy-John snuck over toward the railcar; he noticed some movement. He hid under the railcar to see what they were doing. Three guys, plus the guard, were carrying containers to the tunnel. Jimmy-John had seen enough to know the dam was a terrorist target. It was time to leave. When he slid out to see if the coast was clear, he placed his hand out a little too far, and one of the men stepped on it. Jimmy-John quickly bit his lip to keep quiet. After what seemed like hours, the man finally moved. When the four men went to the far end of the railcar, Jimmy-John crawled out, got on his feet, and ran toward the fence. Stones and dirt were spraying up around him; he was being shot at. He slid under the fence, got into his truck, and sped off. He heard something hit the left quarter panel of his truck. After he pulled into his driveway, he looked at his truck. The left taillight had been shot out, and there were two more bullet holes in the fender above the tire.

He was shaking so bad that he could hardly get the key in his door. He got inside, sat at the table, and offered a prayer of thanks. Going over in his head of what just happened, he realized that he hadn't heard gunfire when being shot at. This meant they had suppressers on their rifles. He couldn't go to the sheriff yet because he would have to explain why he was at the plant. To cover up the bullet holes, Jimmy-John backed his truck into a tree by his driveway. He hit the left taillight then continued along the left side until the fender was dented in. He pounded the fender back out a little so that it wouldn't rub the tire.

CAT

Jimmy-John drank a couple of beers, hoping it would calm him down enough to get to sleep. After a few hours of restless sleep, Jimmy-John rolled out of bed, started a pot of coffee, and turned on the TV to listen to the morning news. A terrorist cell had been broken up in Montana. This caught Jimmy-John's undivided attention. He filled his coffee cup and sat down to listen. When searching the cell's house, the authorities found plans to blow up three railroad bridges simultaneously. C-4 explosives along with recipes for liquid explosives similar to what was used in rock quarries were also found. Jimmy-John remembered reading about some C-4 and surface to air missiles being stolen a few months back. Could this be the same cell? Could that have been C-4 that they were carrying into the tunnel?

Jimmy-John turned off his TV, refilled his coffee cup, and made himself some breakfast. While he was eating breakfast, he went over in his head what he had seen the night before. Were those containers filled with explosives? He looked at the clock; he still had a little time before he'd have to leave for work. He picked up the phone and called a friend of his that worked at the phone company. After the third ring, it was answered, "Hello."

"Shorty?"

"Yeah, who's this?"

"Jimmy-John."

"Haven't heard from you in a while, how you been?"

"Not too bad. Have a couple of questions. Did you guys put some new lines in at the plant recently?"

"Don't think so, why? I can check when I get to the office."

"I noticed a new conduit running from the old maintenance tunnel to a junction box outside the fence."

"I'm sure that wasn't us. All of our lines come from the other side and are underground. I'll go ahead and check anyways and make sure."

"Thanks."

"No problem, I'll let you know if I find out anything."

*****

Jimmy-John arrived at the plant a little early. He scanned through the sign-in log to see if any outside contractors had been there in the past few weeks. An electrical company employee had signed in a couple of weeks ago. He knew most of the companies that did work at the plant, but not this one. He scanned his ID card and walked into the control room.

His boss said, "Jimmy-John, keep an eye on generator 4."

"Problems?"

"Not sure, been getting some strange readings."

"Do you know what work was done here a couple of weeks ago? I've never seen that company here before."

"Some government safety updates that had to be done right then, couldn't wait till scheduled maintenance time."

"Why the new company?"

"That's the company the government sent. Now get that conspiracy shit out of your head and keep an eye on that generator."

"But, boss, do you think it's a coincident that we're having trouble on the generator that they worked on?"

"Just do your job. I ain't got time for this shit."

Jimmy-John finished up his workday getting more questions than answers.

*****

On the way home, he stopped at the local bar and grill to get himself a couple beers and burger. He walked in and sat down.

Jenny, the waitress, brought him a beer and asked, "The usual?"

"Yeah."

"It'll be ready in a minute. I put the order in when I saw you walk in the door."

"I'm that predictable?"

"Oh yeah. How you been?"

"Not too bad."

"What you been up to?"

"Not much, just working and going to school."

While the waitress went back to get Jimmy-John's food, a friend of his came to the table and sat down.

"Hi, still working at the power plant?"

"Yep, still there, probably be there till they fire me."

"Have you been by Falling Rock Ridge lately?"

"No, it's been a while. Why?"

"Looks like they're doing some work on top of the ridge. There was a drilling rig up there for about a week. The ones they use to take core samples. Maybe they plan on widening the road or something."

"That doesn't make sense, just last year new utility poles were put in. Those would have to be moved."

"That's the government for ya. Talk to you later."

Jenny brought Jimmy-John's burgers and another beer and set them on the table. "Figured you'd want another beer."

"Yeah, thanks."

Jimmy-John took a bite of his burger and stared at his beer. *Unscheduled maintenance, the railcar, the generator acting up, and a drilling rig along the highway…this is not a coincident.*

Jenny stopped by his table. "You all right?"

"Oh yeah, just thinking about something." He gave Jenny a twenty. "Keep the change."

"Thank you. I'm off Thursday. If you ain't doing anything and would like a good meal, stop over. I'll rent a movie, and we can watch it on my new TV."

"I'll let you know."

"You have my number. Give me a call."

Jimmy-John drove home, walked into his house, and sat down at his computer. He got on the county's government website and researched work projects. He couldn't find anything about work being done along the highway. He did the same on the state's website, same results. The feeling in his gut was getting stronger. He couldn't go to law enforcement with just a gut feeling. He would be laughed out of the office like the last time. No, this time he would have hard evidence before he went to the authorities. He started a journal on his computer, made a paper copy, put it in an envelope, and taped it under the kitchen counter. He drank a couple of beers before going to bed. This was the only way he could get any sleep at all.

*****

Jimmy-John clocked in and asked his boss, "Will I be able to leave at noon on Friday?"

"Let me check. I'll get back with you."

A half hour before quitting time, the boss came up to Jimmy-John and said, "I found someone to cover for ya Friday afternoon."

"Thanks, boss."

Friday afternoon, Jimmy-John loaded his ATV and camping supplies into his truck. He sat up camp on the state forest then drove back to the highway. He pulled his truck off the highway by a bridge that went over a dry creek. He unloaded his ATV. Even though this creek was prone to flash floods, he took the risk because this was the only way to get to the top unnoticed. When he made it to the top, he started looking around. A road had been made along the top of the ridge. He drove his ATV on the road and finds areas where drilling had been done. He looked around one of the sites and found a wire coming out of the bore hole. He drove to other sites and found the same.

Jimmy-John spent the night up on the ridge to see if there would be any activity during the night. He hid his ATV in a brush pile and picked out another place to put his sleeping bag. He placed some pine branches over his sleeping bag, climbed in, and went to sleep. In the middle of the night he was awakened by voices of a foreign language. He snuck out of his sleeping bag and crawled toward the voices. He hid behind a tree and watched as two men strung wires from one bored hole to another. After the men left, he crawled back to his sleeping bag. Before he went to sleep, he looked across the highway toward the mountains. Something shiny was on top of the mountains. He couldn't tell if it were lights or the reflection of the moon. He doubted anybody would be up there; the only way to the top was straight up the side.

The bright morning sun woke Jimmy-John. He climbed out of his sleeping bag and rolled it up. He walked over to where he had seen the men and brushed some of the dirt away from the bored hole. Sure enough, under the dirt were wires connected to the ones coming out of the bore hole. The wires went in both directions. He wondered how many holes had been drilled on the ridge; there wasn't time to follow the wires. He went back to the brush pile and pulled his ATV out, strapped on his sleeping bag, and headed back down the dry creek.

Jimmy-John heard thunder in the distance; he knew he had better hurry because that dry creek would soon be full of rushing water. He sped down the creek. As he pulled up on the bank, the water rushed by and, a tree limb hit the rear of his ATV, rolling it over. Luckily, it didn't catch it and drag it into the creek. He got up, turned it right side up, and pushed it further up on the bank. After he loaded it in his truck, he turned around and watched the water carrying limbs and other debris down the creek. He opened the truck door and noticed something on his windshield; it was a ticket for illegal parking. He put the ticket in his pocket and drove back to his campsite. He cooked some breakfast, and while eating he wrote in his notebook what he had discovered. The light he saw on the mountaintop bothered him; he wanted to get a closer look. He drove his truck to a rest area in the median strip of the highway.

Jimmy-John sat his spotting scope on one of the picnic tables and looked at the top of the mountain. A camp had been set up. It reminded him of a forward tactical military camp. Generators-supplied power and under the camouflage netting were computers, radios, and a board with maps. He made some notes, picked up his scope, got in his truck, and drove back to his campsite. He looked over his notes while he was eating lunch. Somehow everything from the railcar to the camp on top of the mountain was connected.

It was late when Jimmy-John got home; he backed into his driveway and parked. He made himself a sandwich, grabs a beer out of the refrigerator, and sat down in front of the computer. Checking out the news before opening his journal file, he read about a burglary at a stone quarry in Indiana that occurred four weeks ago. Blasting caps, electric fuses, and dynamite were stolen. After entering the new information in his journal, he printed a copy and put it in the envelope under the counter. Adding the news of the burglary to the information he had gathered, he thought, *This has to be a terror plot.*

*****

Monday morning Jimmy-John was having a hard time keeping his mind on his job. The railcar was gone earlier than expected. He was staring at the control panel, thinking about what he had found.

His boss came up behind him and asked, "Is everything all right?"

"Uh, yeah, everything looks good."

"Don't lie to me. You are a million miles from here. Keep your mind on the control panel, or you'll be looking for another job. Understood?"

"Yes, boss."

"Another thing, I received a work order. The tunnel is going to be filled in next month, the contractor wanted to unload their supplies here instead of taking it back to the shop. The railcar is gone."

"Why rail? Trucks would make more sense."

"Enough of this conspiracy shit. Get your head out of your ass."

"All right, still…"

"You want to start looking for another job?"

"No."

"I can arrange it."

"Yes, boss."

*****

Jimmy-John stopped at the bar and grill on the way home to get a bite to eat. As he sat down, Jenny brought him a beer and said, "Your order's on the grill."

"You know me better than I do."

"I do. Say, since you were *too busy* to make it last Thursday, how about this Friday? I have it off. I can order a pizza, and we can watch a movie."

Jimmy-John thought for a moment. Jenny was one of the few people that he could trust and would not think he was crazy. "You know, that does sound good, what time?"

"Really?"

"Sure, if you're serious."

"Well, yeah, it's just I've asked you many times, and you always turn me down."

"I need to get my mind off work and start having a little fun."

"Great! Eight o'clock work for you?"

"Sounds great."

He finished his meal and handed Jenny a twenty. "Keep the change."

"Thank you. See you Friday." She walked away thinking, *Finally he said yes!*

She remembered the first day she met him… He had come in just before her shift ended. She went over to tell him that she was off work and that another waitress would help him if he needed anything else. He looked at her and said, "I think this will do it." He handed her a twenty and said, "This should cover it."

"That will more than cover it."

"Well, if you ain't in no hurry to go, you're welcome to sit down and visit while I finish."

Breaking one of her self-imposed rules, she paid the check and sat down. "I have a few minutes."

"Want a drink?"

"Sure, a beer sounds good."

Jimmy-John ordered two beers. As they sat there, Jenny said, "I haven't seen you here before."

"Good reason, first time I've been here. I just started working at the power plant. Didn't feel like fixing supper when I got home."

"That's a good reason."

They talked for about an hour, and then he walked her to her car.

"Good night."

"You be stopping back again?"

"Sure. Food's good, beer's cold, and a good-lookin' waitress."

Jimmy-John stopped a couple times a week. When Jenny's shift was over, they would visit for a while, then he would walk her to her car. He never did ask her out no matter how many times she hinted. A couple of times she asked him to go to a movie or come over to her place. He would always take a rain check. She always looked forward to talking to him.

*****

Jimmy-John's living room started to look like a FBI investigating room. Photos, drawings, and newspaper clippings were taped to one of the walls. On a table were maps marked where he had found the bore holes and camp. To get another perspective, he started to think as a terrorist. He drifted back and forth between the table and wall trying to come up with a plan for a terror strike. An hour went by, still nothing made sense. Needing a break, he poured himself another cup of coffee and turned on the TV. *The Late Show* is interrupted with breaking news. An apartment had been raided by the FBI, and the only thing found was bomb-making residue. Other residents told the FBI that three men left with suitcases an hour before they got there. With that and an increase in radio chatter, the threat level was raised.

Jimmy-John turned off his TV, refilled his coffee cup, and went back to the maps. He backed away from the table to see the big picture. Staring at the maps for ten minutes, he yelled, "That's it!" Dropping his coffee cup, he continued, "Block the highway at the low end, and close off any escape back up the highway. Threaten to blow the dam if demands aren't made."

Jimmy-John wrote the plan on the map and highlighted the area. He took a picture of the map and entered it in his computer. He moved all the files to a flash drive and put printed copies in the envelope under the counter. He went to bed for another sleepless night. Was he becoming too paranoid?

*****

At the power plant Jimmy-John spent his lunch and breaks checking sign-in logs and work orders to see if he could find anything out of the ordinary. Everything seemed to be routine except for the new girl—a pretty brunette, supposedly an observer from Corporate. Her job was to make sure the employees followed government safety regulations. She spent most of her time in the control and security rooms, ignoring the rest of the plant. This raised suspicion; Corporate would want to know what was going on throughout the plant. Her accent led him to believe that she hadn't been in the country very long.

Jimmy-John was in the break room eating his lunch and writing in his notebook. The observer lady sat down at his table and said, "Hi."

Jimmy-John put his notebook in his inside jacket pocket and replied, "Hi."

"I heard that you were asking about me."

"Yeah, just wondering who you are and what your job is."

"Could have just asked me."

"Yeah, could have, so who are you?"

"I'm Vicky. I'm from the Energy Regulatory Commission. I'm doing an audit."

"So how long's that gonna take?"

"A couple more weeks. What's your job?"

"You should know. I relieve the operators for their breaks and fill in when someone calls off."

"That's why I see you in different places throughout the day. I noticed you write a lot in your notebook."

"Yeah, it's easier for me to remember if I keep notes."

"Are they work-related?"

"Some are, others are notes to myself."

"May I see it?"

Jimmy-John was getting suspicious looks at her and replied, "A little nosy, ain't ya?"

"I work for the government, it's my job. Can't be too careful."

Jimmy-John reached into his jacket pocket, took out his notebook, and handed it to her. "Just as well let you look at it. If I don't, I'm sure I'll get called into the office."

Vicky took the notebook. As she was looking through it, she asked, "A grocery list and to-do list?"

"Turn over three more pages, you'll see the list of break times I cover for the day."

Vicky handed his notebook back and said, "Thank you, I'll be seeing you around."

Jimmy-John put the notebook back into his pocket, glad that he had both notebooks in the same pocket. Something set off his radar; he didn't trust her.

*****

The next evening after work Jimmy-John drove to the mountain where he had spotted the camp. After parking his truck along a utility road he, hiked to the base of the mountain. A pile of brush between two trees caught his eye. He moved some of the brush, and neatly stacked were four crates of handheld ground-to-air missiles along with military-grade radios. *These are probably the ones stolen from the Army depot.* He quickly wrote the numbers in his notebook, put the brush back over the crates, and ran back to his truck.

Jimmy-John had a hard time keeping his mind on his driving and was given a ticket for running a red light. After he got in his house, he removed the envelope from under the counter and updated his flash drive.

*****

Jimmy-John walked up to the operator on generator 4.

The operator turned around and said, "Glad to see you!"

"Rough night?"

"Yeah, number 4 generator acts a little different than the rest. I haven't been on this one in a while. Something doesn't seem right. Oh, and I found some kind of switch towards the top of the side panel. It doesn't have a label, like we're not supposed to see it. Have any idea what it's for?"

Jimmy-John looked at it. "I have no idea. Did you tell anyone?"

"No."

"Let's keep this quiet, I think something is going on."

"I got an eerie feeling when I found it."

"Yeah, let me see if I can figure out what that switch is for."

Vicky walked up and said, "Good morning."

Jimmy-John replied, "Good morning."

"Everything okay?"

The operator started to say something about how the generator was acting.

Jimmy-John interrupted, "You have the log filled out and signed?"

"Yeah, right here."

Jimmy-John looked at it and signed it, "You better get home and get some sleep. I'll see you tonight."

"Yeah, these twelve-hour shifts are a killer."

After the operator left, Vicky asked Jimmy-John, "Were there problems last night?"

"Not really. This generator is acting a little different since the upgrades."

"That's all?"

"Yeah, I'm sure when they upgrade the rest, they'll all act the same."

"Okay, let me know if there are any issues."

"Sure thing."

After Vicky left, Jimmy-John looked at the switch that had been installed. No way was this switch official. He knew that Vicky did work for the government, but the question was, which government?

Jimmy-John left work as soon as his relief took over. He hurried home, took the envelope from under the counter, and spread the contents on the table. He knew that he only had a few more pieces of the puzzle to put together; then he would take it to the FBI. After entering everything into his computer and putting the files on two flash drives, one for his money belt and the other for his wallet. He removed the hard drive and then installed a new one in. He put the hard drive and envelope in a box and taped it shut. As he sat the box on the counter, he looked at the clock. *Oh shit!* He went immediately to the phone to call Jenny.

Jenny answered the phone, "Hello."

"Hi, Jenny? This is Jimmy-John. I'm running a little late. Soon as I get a shower, I'll head over."

"I figured you'd be late, after all you are male."

"See you in a bit."

"Give me a call when you leave, and I'll order the pizza. I picked up some movies this afternoon. Don't worry, they're not chick flicks. I don't want you to fall asleep. I'm not a clueless blond."

"I know. You're a redhead."

"Never mind, get your shower."

*****

Jimmy-John pulled into the driveway of Jenny's house, walked up to the door, and rang the doorbell. He left the box of papers in his truck. He knew he could trust Jenny, but he didn't know about getting her involved. He liked Jenny. They could sit and talk for hours. Maybe after he found out what was going on at the plant, he'd ask her out on a real date.

Jenny answered the door, "Hi. Come in."

He looked at her. "Wow!"

"I clean up pretty good, huh?"

"I'll say."

"Well, stop staring and get in here. The pizza will be here in ten minutes."

Jimmy-John followed Jenny inside to the living room. She handed him three movies. "I think you'll find one here that'll interest you."

Jimmy-John looked at the movies. *Yeah, I've got get out more. There's more to life than working.*

Jenny asked, "Find one?"

"Yeah, *First Twelve Hours in Afghanistan.*"

"Thought that'd be the one you'd pick." The doorbell rang. "Pizza's here."

220

She went to the door, got the pizza, and came back to the room. "I think you'll like this one, it has every kind of meat they have on it."

"You know me pretty good, don't ya?"

"I just pay attention." She set the pizza down, went to the fridge, grabbed a couple of beers, handed one to Jimmy-John, and sat down.

"Can't get any better than this—pizza, beer, and watching a movie with the prettiest girl in town."

Jenny smiled, "Flattery will get you everywhere."

After they ate the pizza and watched two movies, Jenny said, "It's getting pretty late. Why don't you stay the night? I'll cook you breakfast in the morning."

"Bacon, eggs, and hash browns?"

"I'll even fry the eggs in the bacon grease."

"Can't turn that down." He would wait till morning to talk to her about the box. He was starting to feel bad about involving her, but she was the only one he could trust.

*****

The aroma of bacon woke Jimmy-John out of a deep sleep. He opened his eyes and looked around. *This ain't my house.* He pinched himself. *Nope, I ain't dreaming.*

He walked out to the kitchen. Jenny was frying eggs.

She turned around, saying, "Good morning." She poured him a cup of coffee. "Eggs will be done in a minute."

Jimmy-John sat down, took a sip of coffee, and said, "I could get used to this."

Jenny put the food on the table and sat down, "See what you've been missing."

"Yeah, I guess I should've caught on sooner."

"Oh, you caught on, you're just scared to get into a relationship."

"How can you tell?"

"I'm female."

"That you are."

Once they finished breakfast, and as Jenny was cleaning up the kitchen, Jimmy-John said, "I have a favor to ask you."

"Is that why you came over last night, to ask me a favor?"

He could see this going south in a hurry. "No, well, kinda. I had a great time last night. It's just you're the only one I can trust."

"Oh great, you're in trouble!"

"No, wait here." He went out to his truck, got the box, and brought it back inside.

"What's this?"

"I don't want to tell you too much. I have an errand I have to run tonight, and if I'm not back by Monday, take this box to the police department and drop it off."

"What have you gotten yourself into?"

"There are some things around the plant that just don't seem right. I've written it all down. Don't open it. Just drop it off."

"Great, I finally get you to come over, and now I find out that you could be in danger—not only that, you're dragging me into it."

"I'm sorry, I just don't know who else I can trust."

"Just my luck."

"Next Friday night, I'll take you out to dinner any restaurant, your choice."

"Promise?"

"Yes."

Jenny had a bad feeling about this. She had finally found the man of her dreams, but now he was telling her he could get killed. Why else would he ask her to do this? In a weird sort of way, it gave her a good feeling that she was the only one he trusted.

She looked at him and said, "Okay, I'm gonna hold you to it."

"Thank you, you're the best."

"Don't you forget it."

*****

Jimmy-John drove home, walked inside, picked up his flashlight with the red lens, and put it in his pocket. He grabbed his .380 and two loaded magazines. He put one magazine in his pocket and the other in the handgun, chambered a round, and clipped it onto his belt. On his way to the base of the mountain, he stopped at the plant. As he walked in, the supervisor asked, "What you doing here?"

"I left my jacket in my locker."

"All right, get it and get going. I don't want to explain why you're here when you ain't scheduled."

"Sure thing."

Jimmy-John went to his locker, grabbed his jacket, took the flash drive out of his wallet, and taped it inside his locker, hoping if he didn't show up to work, somebody would find it.

As Jimmy-John continued his drive to the base of the mountain to gather more evidence, thoughts kept going through his mind. Should he have gone to the FBI instead of getting Jenny involved? His gut was telling him yes, but he ignored it. He had to have enough information so they would take him seriously. He couldn't get it out of his mind what had happened when he was laughed out of the sheriff's office years ago. Then, after the crime was committed, they wouldn't leave him alone. He was even a suspect in that bank robbery. The thoughts of Jenny came back. Why didn't he ever ask her out when she was hinting all the time? Scared it wouldn't work out? How would he ever know?

Jimmy-John parked his truck along the utility road and hiked toward the base of the mountain. The night was clear with some moonlight. When he got to the place where the crates were stored, one was missing. He looked toward the side of the mountain. Barely visible, one of the crates was being pulled up the side of the mountain.

Jimmy-John turned around. *I had better get out of here.* He hurried back to his truck. As he approached his truck, he sensed a presence behind him. He pulled his .380 from his belt, but a hand covered his mouth, and simultaneously he felt the cold steel of a knife penetrate the left side of his body. The knife went under his ribs toward his heart. He pointed his .380 behind him and fired two rounds, hoping to hit his assailant before the knife severed his aorta. Jimmy-John floated away as his life blood was drained from his body. He watched as his assailant put his lifeless body in the truck and drove off to a nearby lake. The assailant put Jimmy-John's body in the driver's seat, fastened the seat belt, and let it roll into the lake. As the truck was sinking into the depths of the lake, Jimmy-John heard a voice calling his name.

"Jimmy-John."

"Yeah, who is it?"

"It's me, your brother Jim."

"Can't be, you're dead."

"Everything will be all right."

"Does this mean I'm dead?"

"I've been watching you. You did all you could do."

"What about all those people? They'll all be killed. What about Jenny?"

"There's nothing you can do now, let's go."

"I have to do something."

"No, it is forbidden. It is up to those that are left."

"But..."

"Let's go, they'll figure it out."

"This ain't a dream, is it?"

"Afraid not."

*****

Sunday afternoon came, and Jenny still hadn't heard from Jimmy-John. She turned on the TV news. The anchor reports that a man was found dead along the highway with two gunshot wounds to the abdomen. He had no identification; he was in his midthirties and of Arab descent.

Jenny stared at the box that Jimmy-John had left with her. She was hoping for the best but feared the worse. She knew Jimmy-John carried a gun sometimes. Maybe he got away.

Monday morning at the plant, the boss asked an employee, "Have you seen Jimmy-John?"

"No, I haven't. He's usually here early."

The boss opened the door to the office and asked the secretary, "Did Jimmy-John call in?"

"No, I tried his home phone, and all I got was his answering machine, and his cell went straight to voice mail."

"Just ain't like him."

"Want me to call the police?"

"I don't know."

"It couldn't hurt to see if an officer would drive out to his place and check."

"Yeah, go ahead, it just ain't like him to be a no call, no show."

*****

Jenny was listening to the radio as she got ready for work. A news report came on about a break-in where the house had been ransacked. The only thing they could tell that was taken was the computer. The resident had not shown up for work and had not been seen since Saturday when he showed up at the plant to pick up his jacket.

Jenny sat down in a chair, knowing that she would never see Jimmy-John again. She went over to the box, picked it up, threw it against the wall, and cried. "Why, why did you have to be so stupid? I could kill you." After she calmed down a little, she picked up the box, put it in her trunk, and went to work. She drove past the police station but just couldn't stop. In her mind, if she dropped the box off, there would be no hope.

Jenny had been at work for about a half an hour when she realize that she just couldn't stay. She went home sick. The next day she drove to the police station. She carried the box up to the desk sergeant.

He looked at her. "May I help you?"

"Yes, a friend of mine told me if he didn't return, I should drop this off at the police station."

"And your friend's name…?"

"Jimmy-John, uh, John McCray."

"Fill out this form with his name, your name, and why you are dropping it off."

"All I know is that he asked me to do this. He's been gone since Saturday, and his house has been broken into." After saying that, she left.

The desk sergeant put the box in the bottom drawer of the file cabinet.

The search for Jimmy-John went on for the next three days, but every clue led to a dead end. It was as though he vanished. Jenny was interviewed by the authorities, as were Jimmy-John's coworkers. The box of evidence that Jenny had taken to the police station never made it to the detectives, and Jenny didn't bring it up during the interviews. Before long, Jenny couldn't take it anymore. She quit her job, sold her house, and moved to another state. The hope was to eventually forget about Jimmy-John, but down deep inside, she knew for certain that would never happen.

16

Mike was sitting at the kitchen table sipping a cup of coffee when the phone rang. It was Crazy Jane's gun shop letting him know that his .338 Lapua Surgeon rifle was in. He finished the rest of his coffee in one gulp and drove to town. He walked into the gun store.

Crazy Jane looked at him and said, "That didn't take ya long."

"I don't live that far away."

"I think it's more like a teenager on Christmas morning."

"Yeah, maybe, is the scope in?"

"Yeah, it came in last week. Didn't see no sense calling ya till the rifle came in. That scope costs more than most rifles I sell."

"If Cat wants to win, she needs the best."

"I thought you built her a rifle."

"I did, but always need a backup."

"I think you're more excited than her sometimes."

Mike smiled, "Probably so."

Crazy Jane handed Mike the 4473 form to fill out. Mike filled out the form, signed it, and gave it back to her. Crazy Jane took the form. "Now's the hard part."

Mike handed her a wad of cash. "Yeah, count out what you need."

Crazy Jane counted the money, handed Mike the receipt and change, and said, "I can close for the rest of the week with this sale."

Mike picked up the rifle and scope and said, "Glad I could help. See ya later."

"Bye. Need anything else, let me know."

Mike went back home. He laid the boxes containing the rifle and scope on the table. He opened the box, took out the rifle, and put it on his gun rest. He looked it over, talking to himself, "Maybe I am like a kid on Christmas." He pulled the scope out of the box and looked through it. "She'll be able to count the whiskers on a prairie dog at a mile and a half with this."

Mike mounted and bore sighted the scope. He put a snap cap in the chamber, looked through the scope, and squeezed the trigger. *Sweet.* He looked up at the clock. *I've got some time, might as well start breaking in the barrel. Cat ain't got the patience to clean the barrel after every shot for the first thirty rounds.* He picked up the rifle and a box of ammo. *Her idea of breaking in a barrel is shooting till the ammo is gone.*

Mike stepped outside and took a few steps toward his workshop when a big black SUV with tinted windows drove up his driveway. It stopped ten feet from where he was standing. Two men get out—one riding shotgun and one from the back driver's side. *Now what, two guys wearing $1,500 suits getting out of a black SUV?* The men walked up to Mike, stopping in front of him.

One asked, "You Mike?"

"Yes."

"Come with us."

"Sure. Let me put my rifle back in the house."

The one doing the talking pointed to the other. "He'll hold it."

Mike handed his rifle and box of ammo to the second man and followed them to the SUV. When they got to the back door behind the driver, the first man opened it and motioned Mike to get inside.

Mike looked inside.

"Hi, Mike. Get in."

Mike got in. The man shut the door and stood outside the SUV.

"Hi, Mary."

"Hope we didn't startle you."

"Well, it ain't everyday a shiny, black SUV pulls in my driveway and two 'businessmen' get out."

Mary chuckled. "Probably not. You asked me to let you know when Dad passed. He passed last week. We buried him next to Mom."

"Sorry to hear that. You didn't have to drive all the way out here. A letter would've been fine."

"He was so glad that you took the trouble to look him up. He brought that up many times." Mary reached out on the floor and picked up a briefcase and handed it to Mike. "Dad wanted me to give this to you."

"I'm glad I got to see him." Mike looked at the briefcase, then at Mary, then back at the briefcase, wondering if he was to open it now or later.

Mary looked at Mike and started chuckling. "I think you've been watching too many movies." She took the briefcase back and opened it. "See? No boom."

Mike laughed. "Maybe I have."

Mary took a book out of the briefcase. "This is a journal that Dad kept after he got back to the States. It's up to you whether you read it or not. Either way, it'd be best for you to burn it."

"Is there more there than what you've told me?"

"That I don't know. I've never read it. There are papers and photos from the other side of the pond in here also. I never knew what was in here till the week before Dad died." She put the stuff back in the briefcase and handed it back to Mike.

"Sorry to act so suspicious."

"I understand. One more thing…" Mary handed him a business card. "Keep this with you. If you get into any trouble, call the number on the card."

"Okay."

"Dial the area code first, then dial the last three numbers next. When you dial it as written, you will get the bank. Dial it the way I told you, it will be answered by a stern, not-so-friendly voice. Tell him that you were a friend of Mary's dad, where you're at, and what kind of trouble you're in. It'll be taken care of."

"Thanks. I hope I never need to call."

"It's there if you ever need it, and it's good for life. Don't be afraid to use it."

"Thanks again."

"There's no strings attached. Like I said before, my granddad thought the world of Dad and anyone that helped him the way you did."

"I probably won't see you again. You take care."

"You too, just tap on the window twice, and he'll open the door for you."

Mike tapped on the window; the door opened. He shook Mary's hand and exited the SUV. The man holding his rifle handed him the box of ammo, which Mike put in his pocket, and then he took the rifle. The first man looked at Mike and said, "That's a fine-looking rifle, you looking for employment?"

Mike felt the hairs on his neck rise and very politely said, "No, thank you."

"Very well."

The two men got into the SUV. Mike stood there as he watched it turn around and leave his driveway. He walked back to his house and went inside. He laid the briefcase and box of ammo on the table and leaned the rifle in the corner of his kitchen. He sat down at the table and opened the briefcase.

"And I thought CIA spooks were scary."

Mike took the journal out of the briefcase and laid it on the table, debating whether or not to read it. He continued laying out the items on the table—a bottle of bourbon, a copy of Mark's obituary, newspaper clippings, and old photos. As he looked through the photos, he stopped when he saw one of a young Vietnamese woman holding a baby. This brought back memories that he had tried to forget, but seeing the photo caused his mind to wander back to an earlier time.

He had finally gotten the paperwork from the state department to get her and the child back to the States. When they went to the village to tell her the good news, they were twelve hours too late. The VC had come and destroyed the village. She had been raped and beaten to death. It was done to serve as a warning to other villagers who were being friendly to the US troops. The destroyed village, and the corpse of the young woman was more than Mike could take. Once he returned to camp, he loaded up with a few supplies and as much ammo as he could carry and went hunting, returning only when he ran low on ammo. He was facing court martial, but Mark talked to a major he knew and convinced him that Mike was too valuable to lose. The punishment was reduced to an Article 15.

A year after Mike returned to the States, he married. He didn't tell his wife about the woman in Vietnam until nightmares kept him up at night. Finally, she got him to talk about it. He was afraid she would leave, but she stayed and helped him through it. No one else besides his wife knew about what had happened. He folded up the photo and put it in his wallet. Old wounds were being opened. Maybe it would have been better if he'd just burned the briefcase and forgot about it.

*****

Mike drove over to Cat's place. He was picking up Cat, Ben, and Barry. They were going to a competition near the B&C shooting range—or so they thought. Mike was taking them to an old-time rendezvous. As Mike pulled up to the house all of them were waiting and ready to go.

Mike got out of the car and asked, "You all ready?"

Cat replied, "Yep, all we have to do is load up."

Mike looked at the pile of stuff on the driveway and said, "We're only going to be gone for a few days."

Cat replied, "Don't look at me, I have everything I need in one bag. Ben and Barry seem to think they have to bring all their electronic junk."

Mike shook his head and said, "I'm glad we ain't gonna be gone for two weeks. I guess I had better invest in a trailer and take the truck next time."

Mike didn't know how he did it, but he got everything loaded into the car and still had room for them to sit. Cat and Ben said bye to their mom and dad, and they were off.

Mike hadn't driven very far when Cat asked, "Are we going to stop and get something eat?"

"Get something to eat, you hungry already?"

"I think I was born hungry."

Mike laughed and said, "Yeah, we can stop pretty soon. I'm a little hungry myself."

Mike stopped at a small café. They ate and then were on back on the road. Mike drove through some country that the kids had never seen. Mike turned onto a highway that ran past a dam.

Cat asked, "Does this dam produce electricity?"

Mike replied, "Yes, it does." Then he explained how the river was on one side of the mountain and the highway on the other.

"The river used to fork at the mountain. It would flow on either side and eventually come back together. The river was widened on one side of the mountain and an earthen barrier was put in place to divert the river. A dam was built to produce electricity. Flood gates were installed, so if needed, the water could divert to a concrete ditch alongside the highway down to a park that was built to hold flood waters. This way the water can be controlled to reduce the damage to the towns below. If the dam is ever breached, the force of the water would destroy the earthen barrier and cause a lot of destruction."

Cat asked, "Would that hold all the water?"

Mike replied, "The highway has been reinforced to handle the water if goes above the ditch."

"That looks like a waste of a lot of concrete."

"There has been some talk of modifying it so it can be used as a carpool lane during heavy traffic times. There's a skateboard race down it every year in the summer. The shoulder is packed with spectators. There has been talk of even having a race in the dark."

"That would be interesting."

"Yeah, it would as long as the do-gooders don't get it outlawed."

"Why would it be outlawed?"

"Nanny-state politics."

"Sounds like a bunch of killjoys."

"That's a polite way of putting it."

*****

Mike pulled into the rest area which had been built in the median; that way one rest area could be used for traffic going either way. He parked the car, and they all got out. They went into the building and used the restrooms. The kids started reading a plaque with the history of the building of the dam and highway inscribed on it. Mike bought them all a drink, and they headed back to the car. Cat walked by a table where three young men of Arab descent were sitting. One of them was looking through a pair of binoculars while another was writing in a binder. The third one was reading what looked like a textbook, although Cat couldn't see the title.

As Cat walked closer, she said, "Nice day to be studying."

The men put down the binoculars, closed the binder, and turned over the textbook. They all looked at her and didn't say anything.

Cat said, "Well, have a nice day."

The men started talking in a foreign language and then began laughing.

Cat went back to the car. As she was getting inside, she said, "Them guys were sure rude. All I said was, 'Have a nice day,' and they started laughing at me."

Mike replied, "Not everyone is as friendly as you are."

"Guess not."

"Probably here on student visas."

Barry said, "Mike, drive by their table slow, and I'll take a picture of them with my phone."

Cat asked, "What for, so I can make targets out of them?"

"Well, I guess you could do that, but no. They're acting weird. I wanna run them through the terrorist database."

"How you gonna do that?"

"I could take it to the FBI, to have them do it, but they'd probably ask too many questions. It'd be easier to hack into their computers."

"Should have known."

Mike pretended not to have heard that conversation. He drove past the men, and Barry took the pictures. After Mike got back on the highway, Barry asked, "Do any rocks fall off the sides of the mountains?"

"Once in a while, that's how it got its nickname, 'Falling Rock Highway.'"

Toward the end of the highway, the road was blocked by a police car. Mike stopped his car. When the officer walked up to his car, Mike asked, "The road gonna be closed for long?"

"Nah, shouldn't be too long, just long enough for the wrecker to pull a pickup to the road from the lake. They have it on the shore."

"Somebody run into the lake?"

"Workers were cleaning out an overflow pipe. When the water went down, they noticed the truck."

"Anybody in it?"

"Yeah, they've already taken the body. The ME said it looks like foul play. We'll know more later. I'm sure it'll be in the paper. Where you headed?"

"Don't Blink."

"The rendezvous?"

"Yeah, but the kids don't know it."

Cat was watching them pull the truck out, and the boys were buried in their electronics, too busy to hear the conversation.

After the pickup was pulled to the shoulder so it could be loaded onto a flatbed, the wrecker moved out of the way. The officer waved Mike on, "Have fun."

"Thank you."

Barry asked Mike, "What's the name of that town we're going to?"

"Don't Blink."

All three kids asked, "What?"

"Don't Blink."

Ben asked, "How'd it that name?"

"Well, if you're going forty miles per hour and blink, you'll miss it."

Cat asked, "Is it much farther?"

Mike pointed to a sign in the shape of an arrow that read, "Don't Blink" and said, "No, we're about there."

"Good."

Mike drove a couple of miles and passed a sign, "Welcome to Don't Blink Population." There was a bar and grill, a gas station, and a grocery store.

Ben asked, "That's it? I guess you could miss it."

Mike replied, "There used to be a post office, but it was closed."

Cat asked, "Where's the competition being held?"

"Just down the road."

It wasn't long until they saw a field filled with motor homes, trucks, campers, and cars.

Cat said, "I thought you said that this was a small competition."

Mike replied, "It is."

Ben asked, "You think you'll be able to find a place to park?"

"No problem."

Barry said, "Don't look like there's any parking places left."

"Only need one."

"Good luck."

Mike drove a little farther until he recognized a motor home. Beside it was an open parking space with the hand-painted sign "SAVED FOR MIKE."

"See, I told you I'd find one."

Mike parked the car. Cat got out and looked around in amazement. It was as though she had stepped back in time. There were all kinds of old-style tents, as well as people walking around in deer skin clothing and coon skin hats. The men were carrying muzzle loaders. There were even people in Indian style clothing.

Cat looked at Mike and said, "I thought you said this was a rifle shoot."

"It is. I just didn't tell you what kind of rifle."

"Looks like an old-time rendezvous."

"It is."

A man dressed in deer skin and a coon skin hat carrying an old flintlock rifle walked up to Mike. He spit some tobacco juice on the ground, put his hand out, and said, "Well, Mike, glad you could make it. Ain't seen you in a coon's age."

Mike shook his hand, "It's been a while, Sam. Glad I could make it."

Sam looked at Cat. "This must be that filly you were telling me about."

Mike gave Cat a 'Don't say what you're thinking look.' "Yes, this is Cat. Cat, this is my old friend, Sam."

"Hi, glad to meet ya."

Sam asked Mike, "Were you able to find everything she'll need?"

"Yeah, it's all in the trunk."

"Well, go get it. I'll go tell my wife you're all here."

Mike and Cat walked over to the car. Mike opened up the trunk, and took out two muzzle loaders. One, a Hawkins .50 caliber and the other a Kentucky long rifle, both of them flintlocks and left handed. When Sam got out of earshot, Cat asked, "Who is that old man, and why did he call me a horse? With that scraggly hair and beard, he looks like an old goat, and he kinda smells like one too."

Mike laughs, "Easy, girl, you've always said that you wanted to go back in time. This is as close as you can get without a time machine. There isn't anybody alive that knows more history about the mountain men and Indians than Sam. He is going to teach you how to shoot a flintlock."

"Still, calling me a horse..."

"Could be worse. He could've called you girly. Take it as a compliment."

"I guess you're right."

Mike continued unloading the trunk—deer skin clothing, moccasins, powder horn, a knife, and a few other things.

Cat looked at the stuff on the ground. "I have to wear this stuff?"

"If you want a true taste of history, you do. This is the biggest rendezvous in the country. I'm sure you'll enjoy it."

Cat started picking up the clothes and smiled. "You bet I will."

The people wearing clothing of the era had more freedom to move around camp. Ben and Barry walked up to the car and started looking at the stuff on the ground.

Mike said, "I brought some clothes for you two if you're interested."

They looked at Mike, then Ben said, "Nah, I think I'll just stay in the twenty-first century."

Barry joined in, "Me too."

"Well, if you change your mind, let me know."

Sam came back with his wife and said, "Everybody, this is my wife, Rose."

They all introduced themselves.

Rose said, "Cat, you can use the motor home to change."

"Thanks." Cat went to the motor home.

Rose looked at Mike and said, "You two gonna stay out of jail this time?"

"Yeah, plan to."

"Famous last words."

Cat came back to the car in her outfit. She looked at Mike all smiled, "How do I look?"

"Looks like you just walked out of the history books."

Cat smiled, "Feel like it too."

Sam said, "When you're ready, come over to the fire. Supper will be ready soon."

"Okay," replied Mike.

Cat said to Mike, "This is great!"

"You'll learn a lot from Sam. He lives this lifestyle. He took an early retirement, sold his house and what he couldn't take with him, and bought the motor home and a trailer. All him and Rose do now is travel around to rendezvous and sell skins he tans himself."

Mike and the kids went over to Sam's campsite for supper. Sam had a big piece of meat cooking over an open fire, and Rose was boiling potatoes in a cast-iron pot.

As they sat down on a log, Sam said, "I hope you're all hungry."

Cat replied, "I am."

Ben said, "Everybody else better get theirs first."

Rose answered, "I'm sure there's enough for everybody."

"You haven't seen Cat eat."

As they were eating supper, Sam asked Cat, "Think you can shoot a flintlock?"

"If it spits lead, I can shoot it."

"Well, tomorrow morning, you'll get a chance."

After supper, Sam said, "Mike, you and the boys can sleep in the motor home."

Rose said, "Cat, you're welcome to sleep in our tent. There's plenty of room."

"It looks like it's gonna be a clear night. If it's all right, I'll just sleep under the stars."

"Sure, that's fine. I'll get you some blankets."

Mike and the boys went to the motor home to sleep. Cat laid the blankets on the ground and lay down. She stared at the stars, thinking about how it must have been back in this time period.

*****

Cat awoke to the aroma of frying bacon. She got up and walked over to Rose, who was cooking breakfast. Rose asked, "How did you sleep?"

"Fine, it sure was a nice night."

"I hope you like bacon."

"It's my favorite food group."

"That's good. It'll be a bit yet. I still have the potatoes and eggs to fry. There's a basin of water over there if you want to wash your face."

Cat washed her face and went back to Rose, "That woke me up."

"Yeah, cold water does that to ya. I hear you're quite a hunter and trapper."

"Yeah, I like anything to do with the outdoors. The first year we moved to Kentucky, I knew that was the place for me. An old trapper loaned me some of his traps and showed me how to set a trap line. He was planning on giving up some of his area anyway, so he let me have it. I gave him some of my animals for the use of his traps."

"How did you do?"

"I was told I did good for a rookie. Mom wasn't too keen on me being gone for two or three days at a time. I would always leave a TOPO map marked of where I'd be. One time I stayed a day longer than I said I would. Mom sent the game warden after me. I was where I said I would be. After that, I made sure I was home when I said I'd be."

"What about school?"

"I would check my traps before I went to school and when I got out. On the weekends, I'd just stay out in the woods."

"I bet you give your parents gray hair."

"Just Mom. Dad's already lost most of his."

Rose chuckled.

Sam walked up to the fire and asked Rose, "Is breakfast ready?"

"Won't be long, you can wake up the guys."

Sam went over to the motor home and woke up Mike and the boys.

As they were eating breakfast Sam said, "After we eat, you all can check out the traders. Cat, be back here around ten o'clock, and we'll see if you can shoot a rifle as good as Mike says you can."

Mike and the kids wandered around the venders. There were all kinds of furs, skins, and handmade crafts for sale. Cat was really interested in the blacksmith. He could bend metal into any shape wanted.

Cat said to Mike, "I have to meet Sam back at his tent."

"Okay, we'll see you later. Have fun."

*****

Sam was waiting for Cat when she got back.

Sam asked, "You ready?"

"Yep."

"Which rifle you gonna use?"

"I'm gonna use the Hawkins."

"Okay, let's go."

Cat picked up the Hawkins, powder horn, and possible bag, and followed Sam to the shooting area. Sam showed her how to load the rifle.

"Make sure you have the ball tight against the powder, or you could blow it up."

"That would ruin my whole day."

Sam laughed, "That it would."

Sam set up a paper target and shot his rifle. The ball went dead center of the notch.

"That's some good shooting."

"This is easy. Wait till we drive nails, cut a playing card in half, or break a chain link."

"Drive nails?"

"Yeah, we pound a nail into a board and then shoot it in the rest of the way without bending it."

"I'd better start with paper targets."

Cat practiced the rest of the day. She caught on pretty quick. She was able to put one ball on top of another when shooting paper targets, but the nails and playing cards were a different story. She watched in awe as Sam pounded nails in with one shot, never missing a chain link or playing card. Cat's shoulder was staring to get sore, but she wasn't going to let Sam know that.

Finally, Sam said, "Well, I'd say it's about time to head back to the tent. You think you'll be ready for tomorrow?"

"About as ready as I'll ever be."

"We'll eat supper, get a good night's sleep, and practice a little more in the morning."

When they got back to the tent, Mike asked Sam, "How'd she do?"

"You were right. She catches on quick."

Cat smiled and said to Mike, "This is fun, but you said this would help me when shooting center fire rifles, how?"

"Flintlock lock times are a lot slower. They're measured in thousands of seconds. Center fire lock times are measured in milliseconds. If you can hold steady till the ball leaves the barrel of a flintlock, you'll have no problem holding steady till the bullet leaves the barrel on a center fire. Movement after the trigger pull is the most common shooter error."

One of Sam's friends walked over to the tent and said to Sam, "There's a bull session over by the tepees if you wanna come over."

Sam looked at Cat and asked, "You wanna sit by the fire and listen to a bunch of tall tales and Indian folklore?"

"Sure."

"What about you, Mike?"

"Nah, you two go on."

"Boys?"

Ben answered, "I think I'll just stay over here in the twenty-first century."

Again, Barry agreed, "Yeah, me too."

Sam and Cat walked over to the tepees and sit down by the fire. Cat was all ears listening to all the wild stories, knowing most of them were just tall tales and shaggy dog stories. The stories that impressed her were the ones told by the Indians, which she knew had been passed down from generation to generation and never written down. Cat's thoughts were interrupted by a big man with a shaved head and a necklace made of bear claws.

He looked at her and the knife she had on her belt and asked, "Can you skin, Griz?"

Cat pulls out her knife, held it in front of him, and replied, "I can skin 'em as fast as you bring 'em, 'Jeremiah Johnson.'"

"Too bad there weren't any around. I'd bring ya one."

Sam said, "She'd probably skin it."

*****

The aroma of breakfast cooking on an open fire woke Cat. She got up, washed her face, and walked over to Rose.

Rose asked, "Have a good time last night?"

"It was great. I'd never get tired of listening to those stories even if 99 percent of them were made up."

"That's something missing in our society today. With radio, TV, movies, and computers, a person doesn't have to use their imagination anymore. I think that's sad."

"It does seem to make one lazy."

Sam walked up. "Smells good, ready soon?"

Rose replied, "Yeah, will you wake up the guys?"

"Sure."

As they were eating breakfast, Sam said, "There's a dance tonight, you all wanna go?"

Mike replied, "I guess we can stay for another night then leave in the morning."

"Great, after breakfast I'll take Cat for a little more practice before the shoot."

Cat asked, "What time's the shoot?"

"Noon."

A crowd had gathered around where the shoot was to be held. It didn't matter what century you were from to watch. Sam explained the rules to Cat.

"You get ten shots. There are three nails, two playing cards, one chain, and a paper target. A perfect score would be to drive in all the nails, cut the cards in half, break the chain, hit the center of the notch on the paper, and have three shots left. The paper target is the tiebreaker."

Cat replied, "Oh, that's all?"

"Yep, that's all."

Cat enjoyed the shoot even though she came in second to last. The only reason she wasn't last was because she hit the center of the paper target. Sam took second with two shots left. The winner had three left. Cat had nothing but respect for the skill these shooters had with old-type rifles.

They all went back to Sam's campsite to eat supper before the dance.

Sam asked Ben and Barry, "You boys sure you don't want to change clothes and join us?"

Ben replied, "Nah, I don't think so."

Barry joined in, "I think I'll just play my video game."

Sam looked at Mike. "What about you? I have an extra coon skin hat."

"As long as you don't talk me into shooting lanterns off of the poles in front of the other tents, like last time. I don't need to spend any time in jail."

"No worries. Rose dumped out my jug when she heard you were coming. Have to admit though, it was fun."

"Yeah, but the rest of them didn't see any humor in it."

Two teenage Indian girls dressed in deer skins walked by and smiled at Ben and Barry. They smiled back.

Ben said to Barry, "You know, Mike did go to a lot of trouble to find them clothes for us. It's rude of us not to wear them."

"Yeah, I guess you're right, hate to hurt his feelings."

Ben said to Mike, "We decided to change clothes and join ya."

"What changed your mind?"

"Well, you did go to the trouble of bringing them along."

Mike smiled then handed Ben the car keys. "They're still in the trunk. Those young Indian girls didn't have anything to do with you changing your mind, did they?"

Ben smiled, "Uh, no."

Ben and Barry went to change.

Sam said to Mike, "Nothing like a pretty young filly to change a young man's mind."

"Yep, when you're that young, you don't know what kind of trouble women can cause ya."

After everyone was dressed and ready, they walked over to the dance. It was a nice moonlit night. A big fire and lanterns added additional lighting. Ben and Barry spotted the Indian girls.

Ben said to Mike, "We're gonna ask those girls to dance."

"Okay, have fun."

Sam, said, "Be careful you two. See that big Indian beating on the drums over there?"

Ben said, "Yes."

"That's their father. You may want to ask him if you may ask his daughters to dance."

You could see the color drain out of their faces.

Barry said, "What's the worst that could happen? He says no?"

Ben said, "He could scalp us."

Sam said, "Treat them girls with respect, and you won't have any problems. Asking him for permission is the first sign of respect."

Mike said to Sam, "Think they'll have the balls?"

Sam pointed, "Looks like it. I hope they didn't piss their pants when he showed them his tomahawk."

"I guess that'd test your nerve."

Ben and Barry walked over to the girls after talking to the girls' father.

Sam said, "They must've past interrogation."

Mike replied, "Must have."

Rose walked up. "Looks like the boys are having a good time."

Mike said, "Yeah, have you seen Cat?"

"Yeah, she's over talking to some of the guys. I thought you two could talk a line of bull. She can give you two a run for your money."

Mike wandered over to where Cat was standing. "I hear you can put out a pretty good line of bull."

"I learned from the best."

Sam came up to Mike. "Rose and me are headin' back."

"I think I'll get the kids and be there pretty soon."

"Good luck getting the boys to leave."

"That shouldn't be a problem. I saw the girls' father talking to them, so they'll be leaving soon."

"Keeps you from being the bad guy."

"Now all I have to do is drag Cat away."

*****

Once more Cat woke up to the smell of breakfast cooking. She was kinda sad knowing that they would be leaving today. She got up, washed her face, and walked over to Rose who was just finishing up breakfast.

Rose asked Cat, "Have a good time last night?"

"I've had the time of my life, wish I didn't have to leave."

"Maybe Mike will bring you back next year."

"That'd be great!"

"Sam went to wake up the guys. They should be here pretty soon."

After breakfast, Sam helped Mike load the car.

Sam asked, "You heading home?"

"No, we're gonna run over and check out that new shootin' range that's supposed to open next year. According to the map, it's not far from here."

"Oh, you mean, the B&C Shooting Range?"

"Yeah that's it. I've read that it's supposed to be state-of-the-art, a shooter's dream."

"I read some about it, two guys that met in a bar came up with the idea. Construction is coming along. A visitor's center is complete. You can take a look at their plans."

"Two guys in a bar came up with that idea?"

"Yeah, you wouldn't believe their names, Boon and Crocket."

"Descendants of Daniel and Davy?"

"If I had to guess, I'd say yes."

Mike said to Sam, "Good to see ya again. Maybe we can come back next year."

"Let me know, and I'll save you a parking spot."

"All right, I'll do that."

As Mike drove off, he asked, "Did everyone have a good time?"

Cat said, "That was the best time I've ever had."

Ben replied, "I had fun too. I have the e-mail address of that girl."

Mike asked, "You don't know her name?"

"Yeah, it's Spotted Fawn."

Barry said, "I have an address also. Her name is Dancing Doe."

Mike laughed, "I'm glad you all had fun."

Cat asked, "What about you, Mike?"

"Yeah, I had a good time too. It was good seeing Sam and Rose again."

*****

Mike drove until he saw a sign with an arrow that read "B&C Shooting Range—2 Miles." Mike turned and drove up to a building. He parked the car. They all got out and walked to the building. The door was open, so they walked inside.

A man standing inside said, "Hello."

Mike replied, "Hi, we were in the area, so we thought we'd stop in and check this place out."

"Come on in. I'm Bart, the manager."

"I'm Mike. This is Cat, Ben, and Barry."

"You all shooters?"

"I don't shoot much anymore. Cat's the shooter. Ben and Barry are more into computers. Barry developed a program for bullet flight."

"You almost need something like that the way this sport is advancing."

"We'd like to look around if that's all right."

"Sure, I ain't too busy today. I can show you around. In the next room is a scale model of what is planned here. Be sure to tell your friends. The more who know about this place, the better."

They all walked into the next room. If the range was going to be anything like the model, it would be the state-of-the-art.

Bart pointed at the model. "We're finishing up the long-range section now. We started there because it's the most popular. Next will be the shorter ranges for rimfires and pistols. There is even going to be an old western town built for Cowboy Action Shooting."

"Wow!" Cat exclaimed.

Mike asked, "Will it be ready for the big shoot next year."

"It should be… Contractors get a bonus for every day they beat the deadline."

"What about the western town?"

"They want that done because they are going to put in hotels and saloons."

"Sounds great. How'd this get started?"

"Well, Boon and Crocket met in a bar one night and started talking. They found out each of them made it big when the Dot Com stocks were hot. They were talking about what to do with all the money they had accumulated when a story came on the TV about how long-range shooting was becoming popular. Boon wrote some notes on a napkin and talked Crocket into a partnership."

"It all started in a bar written on a napkin?"

"You could say that. They traveled around to competitions taking notes, asking shooters what their ideal shooting facility would be. When they got done, they had almost three hundred pages of notes."

"Sounds pretty good."

"There are some flyers and pamphlets you're welcome to take along. Take plenty and pass them around. You interested in competing in the big shoot?"

Cat replied, "Yes!"

Mike said, "Can't tell she's excited, can ya?"

"Put your name and address in this book, and we'll send you the information, application, and rules when they are finalized. The first one is going to be a little expensive, but the prizes are good. They hope to bring the prices down in following years."

"How they plan on doing that?"

"They're thinking about selling advertising of arms and ammo companies on the different shooting lanes."

"Have any idea what the entry fee is going to be for the first one?"

"Yeah, $2,000. The first place prize is $750,000. There are money prizes for the first ten places. It will only be open to 500 shooters, 490 must win qualifying matches, and 10 will be winners in an essay contest sponsored by Savage and Winchester. Other arms and ammo companies are putting up some of the prize money."

"Thanks for the information. I'll be waiting to hear from you."

"Sure thing. Don't be afraid to give us a call if you have any questions."

They all got in the car and headed for home.

Mike asked Cat, "Well, what d'ya think?"

"I want to give it a try."

"It'll be a lot'a work and dedication."

*****

When they got back, Mike stopped at Barry's house first, then to Cat's. Ben and Cat walked into the house.

Cat said, "We're home."

Betty said, "Hi. You have a good time?"

"Yeah, Mike took us to a rendezvous."

"Mike told us where he was going to take you. We thought you'd like it."

"And you didn't tell me?"

"He wanted to surprise you."

Dave walked into the room. "I thought I heard familiar voices. Have a good time?"

Cat gave her dad a hug. "Yeah, it was great!"

"Oh, Conrad came by. He got the report back from the board of health on that fox. It was rabid."

"I was sure it would be."

Dave handed Cat the "Letter to the Editors" page of the newspaper and said, "You might want to read this."

Cat took the paper and read it aloud.

I want to thank Cat publicly for saving myself and niece from a rabid fox last week. I had always thought of her as an unruly and wild child. I thought that any child that hunted and trapped wild animals as someone who didn't care about wildlife. Anybody that would kill animals would grow up to be a killer. After talking to her that day, after she shot that rabid fox, I knew I was wrong. There is no one that respects wild animals, nature, and the outdoors the way she does. Hunting and trapping is not for me. I will not look down on others that participate in the sport, especially if they have the respect for wildlife as she does. Again, I want to thank her for not only being there that day, but also for opening my eyes to the other side of the issue.

Signed: The Home-EC Teacher

"Looks like you changed somebody's mind."

"Yeah, now, if she'd let Mom teach her how to cook."

Betty said, "Speaking of that, supper's ready."

Ben said, "Good, I'm starved."

17

With the end of summer coming, Cat knew she'd have to get ready for the upcoming school year. The only good thing she could see about summer ending was that the hunting seasons would be opening soon. Squirrel season was already opened. The weekend shoot that she had been practicing for would be here soon.

Cat, Ben, and Barry went to a football game that was held every year before school started. It was against their school's longtime rival. The tradition was said to have been started when the quarterbacks got into a fistfight in the middle of Main Street. The sheriff of the time broke it up and told them to save it for the field. As soon as the sheriff turned around, they started fighting again. The sheriff locked them up in the jail. He called their coaches and told them the best way to settle this feud would be a game. If they would agree, he would drop all charges. The coaches decided to have a game; neither one of them wanted their quarterbacks suspended for the season. A tradition was started.

Cat's high school won the game by a last-minute field goal. Ben and Barry went to play video games after the game. Cat didn't have anything to do and was bored. As she left the game, a girl that she knew but didn't hang around with came up to her.

"You doing anything tonight?"

"No, not really, why you ask? It's Suzie, isn't it?"

"Yeah, and you go by Cat?"

"Yeah."

"Some of us are meeting at the woods on the knoll off Two Forks Road. We're gonna cook some hamburgers and hotdogs."

Cat was kind of suspicious, being that they had never associated with her before. She was always snubbed when she tried to talk to them in school. Her gut was telling her to just go home, but temptation overrode her common sense.

"Sure, I'll go home change clothes and meet you there. Do I need to bring anything?"

"Nope, just you, it's starting around nine."

"See ya there."

*****

Cat went home changed her clothes and let her parents know that she was going to an after-game party that she was invited to. She rode her bike to the knoll. There was already a large group of teenagers there. A couple of guys were cooking burgers and hot dogs on a grill.

Suzie walked up to Cat and said, "Hi, Cat, glad you could make it. You want a burger or hot dog?"

"I'll take a burger."

Suzie handed her a burger then said, "Chips and drinks are over there."

"Thanks."

Cat took the burger, grabbed some chips and a drink, and then sat on a log by the fire that had been built. She started wondering if this was such a good idea and was getting ready to leave when Suzie and a couple of others sat down beside her.

Suzie said, "Nice night, you want another burger?"

"Sure."

When Suzie got up to get Cat another burger, a boy scooted over toward her and said, "Hi."

Cat gave him a stare and returned the greeting.

"Having a good time?"

"So-so."

Suzie came back, handed Cat her burger, and then sat down beside her.

The boy handed Cat a pint-size mason jar with clear liquid in it and said, "Here, this will help."

Cat took the jar; she had an idea what is in it. The smell proved it. She took a drink and handed it back to him.

Suzie asked, "Doesn't that burn?"

Cat shrugged her shoulders and said, "A little."

Cat had tasted bourbon before. Her dad had thought he would cure her of drinking by letting her taste it. That plan backfired; she liked the burn. It was the same with coffee. Mom got over Cat drinking coffee, but not the whiskey. Every once in a while, when Mom wasn't around, Dave would let her have a shot.

"That's pure corn whiskey."

"I can tell it ain't water."

The boy handed her the jar again. Cat took another swig. This time she didn't hand it back. The boy sat there waiting.

She looked at him, "I'm sure you have more."

"Ah yeah, I do." He went and got a quart jar and started passing it around. When the jar got to Cat, she poured some into her jar.

It wasn't long until the boy put his hand on Cat's leg. She grabbed his hand, put her thumb in the pressure point between his thumb and index finger, and pressed.

She looked him directly in the eye and said, "I ain't that drunk, keep your hand on your own leg."

"I'm just trying to be friendly."

"Well, I ain't interested in that kind of friendship."

Suzie put her arm around Cat and said, "Calm down, you might like it."

Cat grabbed Suzie's finger, bent it back, and asked, "Is this why you invited me, to get me drunk and make a fool out of me?"

Suzie stared at Cat. That had been the plan—to get Cat to the party, get her drunk, and make her the joke of the party. They thought it would be easy if she drank enough moonshine. They thought wrong.

Suzie and the boy grabbed her. "Easy, we just want to make you the life of the party."

The rest of the group made a circle around them, cheering and yelling. Cat felt all alone, like an elk calf surrounded by a pack of wolves. She wondered how she was going to be able to get herself out of this situation. The alcohol was starting to take effect, slowing her down. Then all of a sudden, everyone took off, leaving her there by herself. She sat back down, took another drink, and wondered what scared them off.

Conrad walked up to Cat. "Cat, what a' you doing here."

"Oh, hi, Warden."

Conrad took the jar from Cat, smelled it, then asked, "You been drinking?"

"Uh-huh."

"Why did you come up here?"

"I was invited. I thought they wanted me to be their friend."

"Some friends, they left you hanging."

"Yeah, I guess I was wrong."

"Well, come on, get in my truck."

Cat stood up and tried to walk. As she stumbled and started to fall, Conrad said, "Here let, me help you."

He walked her to his truck, helped her in, and buckled her seat belt.

"How did you get here, your bike?"

"Yeah, I'll go get it."

"No, you stay here. I'll get it."

"It's by the tree."

Conrad went and got the bike and put it in his truck along with the mason jars of moonshine he found, including the half-full one that Cat had been drinking from. The fire had burned down. He dumped the charcoal from the grills on the firepit and threw some dirt over the coals. He tossed the grills into the truck. They might come in handy. He would come back in the daylight and pick up the rest of the stuff, if it was still there.

As Conrad left the knoll, he said to Cat, "I can't believe you didn't hear me coming. I came through there like an elephant through a glass factory."

"Guess I wasn't paying attention."

"More like you're drunk. This ain't like you. What's got into you?"

"I don't know, bored I guess."

Conrad turned to say something else and saw that Cat was passed out. He dialed Judge Bean's number.

In a sleepy voice, Bean answered, "Hello."

"Hello, Judge. You won't believe who I'm taking to the jail, *drunk*!"

"Cat."

"How did you know?"

"If it were anyone else, you would've waited till a decent hour instead of calling me at 1:00 AM."

"Yeah, I guess you're right. Sorry, I'll put her in a cell and let her sleep it off."

"Since I'm awake, I'll call Mike and meet you there."

"See ya then."

*****

Conrad pulled up to the jail and woke Cat up enough to get her into a cell and on a bunk. He took her shoes off and covered her up with a blanket. He went back to the truck and got two of the mason jars and set them on the judge's desk.

Mike and the judge showed up.

Mike asked Conrad, "Cat passed out?"

"Yeah, I got her back to the cell. She won't be awake for a while."

They all went into the judge's office where Conrad told them that he had gotten a call about a party up on the knoll. When he got to the campfire, everyone except Cat took off. He pointed to the jars on the desk and said, "I found these."

Mike asked, "Know where these came from?"

"No."

The judge said, "Only one way to find out."

The judge and Mike each took one of the jars, opened it, and took a sip.

They said at the same time, "This is Pete's moonshine."

Conrad asked, "Pete's?"

The judge replied, "Yeah, taste it. He's the only one I know that can make corn liquor that smooth. I think he uses a little rye in his recipe."

Conrad took a sip and said, "Yep, that's Pete's. I'll have to go out and see him and let him know his boys got into his stash."

The judge took a ten-dollar bill out of his wallet, handed it to Conrad, and said, "While you're out there, pick me up a jar."

"No need, I have a case and a half in the truck."

"That ought a last me a while."

"You think we should call her parents?"

"No, not yet, I'll make a pot of coffee. No sense waking them up yet."

Mike said, "I'll go over to the diner after it opens and get some food."

"Hope Betty ain't working this morning."

Mike, Conrad, and the judge talked about what they should do about Cat. They knew something had to be done. A few ideas were brought up, but probably none of which would faze Cat. They talked until 7:30 AM, and then Mike went over to the diner and picked up some breakfast. When he got back, Conrad and the judge ate while Mike took some coffee and food back to the cell for Cat. She was still sleeping.

He woke her up and asked, "How do you feel?"

"Like I've been run over by a truck."

"Here is some food and coffee. Whatever possessed you to go drinking with that bunch? You have nothing in common with them."

"I don't know. I was bored after the game, and I was invited to a party."

"Weren't you suspicious?"

"Yeah, but I couldn't see what it'd hurt. I thought maybe Suzie wanted to be my friend, but I was wrong. I'm in big trouble, ain't I? Call my parents yet?"

"No, not yet, getting ready to. Do you want us to tell them, or do you want to see if something can be worked out?"

"No, tell them. That way I won't have to worry about Mom finding out, and she will."

"Okay, well, eat your breakfast. If you want more coffee, just yell."

Mike went back to the office to eat his breakfast. Conrad dialed Cat's parents.

Betty answered the phone, "Hello."

"Hello, Betty?"

"Yes."

"This is Conrad."

"Is Cat all right?"

"Yes, she's fine, we have her in jail. She was picked up for drinking."

"Okay, we'll be there."

Conrad could hear Betty yelling at Dave before she hung up.

Mike asked, "Get ahold of them?"

"Yeah, Betty answered the phone and said that she and Dave would be right down."

The judge said to Conrad, "Bring Cat up here. I want to talk to her before her parents get here."

Conrad brought Cat to the Judge.

Cat sheepishly said, "Hi, Judge."

The judge replied, "How you feeling?"

"Been better."

"Trying to out drink the locals?"

"Yeah, that wasn't such a good idea."

"Who was there?"

"I don't really know."

"You don't know or ain't gonna tell?"

"I don't know, and besides, it wouldn't help if I did know."

"All right, go back to your cell. I'll come get you when your parents get here."

The judge knew that Cat wasn't going to rat. He was hoping it wasn't because she was going to take care of it her way.

Betty came running through the door, yelling, "Where is she? I'm gonna wring her neck!"

Dave was right behind her, saying, "Honey, calm down. Let's find out what happened."

"Don't honey me. It's all your fault."

"My fault?"

"Yes, you never punish her, and you let her have a shot of whiskey when I'm not around."

"Now, dear."

Betty turned around and glared at Dave.

The judge said, "All right, both of you, sit. This is *my* jungle."

Dave and Betty sat down. "Yes, Judge."

"Conrad, tell them where you found Cat."

Conrad told them where and when he found her and that he brought her back to the jail.

Betty asked, "May I see her?"

The judge said, "As long as you don't kill her. I don't need a murder in this town."

"All right."

"Conrad, go get Cat."

Conrad went back to the cell and brought Cat up to the office. Cat stood in front of her mom and dad feeling lower than a snake in a wagon wheel rut. She looked up at her parents and said, "Hi."

Betty said, "You go get drunk, and that's all you can say!"

"Sorry."

"What were you thinking? You could've been killed!"

"I guess I wasn't thinking."

"Part of the blame is your dad's. 'Oh, I'll just let her have a taste. It'll burn, and she'll never touch it again,' like that worked!"

The judge said, "Okay, we ain't getting anywhere yelling."

Dave asked, "What do we do now?"

"Well, we haven't charged her yet."

Betty said, "Lock her up and throw away the key."

Dave said, "Betty!"

"What, you have a better idea?"

The judge said, "Let's just all calm down."

Betty looked at Cat and said, "What's next, a tattoo on your ass?"

Cat had the look of a kid getting caught with her hand in the cookie jar.

Betty looked at her and said, "You *don't*..."

"Don't what?"

"Have a tattoo on your backside."

"Why, no, why would you think that?"

"That look you gave me, like you got caught with your hand in the cookie jar. Don't lie to me!

Dave, Mike, and the Judge looked at Cat, then at Betty.

Mike said in a whisper, "This is getting more interesting by the minute.

Betty looked at Dave and asked, "Did you know about this?"

"No. I had no idea. Anyways, we still don't know." Dave was hoping Cat didn't have one.

"If you did, you wouldn't tell me."

Cat said, "All right, I have a buck deer on one side and a timber wolf on the other side."

Betty said, "You have two tattoos? What on earth for?"

"You know how I like wildlife."

"Animals or partying?"

"Animals. I wanted a predator-prey theme."

"And who was supposed to see this art?"

"Just me when I looked in the mirror."

"I give up! What's next, green spiked hair?"

"Oh, Mom, don't be silly."

Betty looked at Dave. "You take care of this. Of course, you won't do anything about it! I still say, keep her locked up till she's twenty-one. I'm going home!"

Dave said, "Wait a minute, we rode together."

"I know. I have the keys. I'm sure you can get one of your buddies to give you a ride home." Betty stormed out of the door.

Cat said, "I think Mom's kinda mad."

Dave replied, "What was your first clue?"

Mike said, "I sure wish she hadn't sugarcoated it and told us how she really felt."

Dave looked at Mike and said, "Would you mind giving me a ride home?"

"Sure, as long as I can drop you off at the end of the driveway!"

"Mind if we stop and get something to eat?"

"No, that'll be fine."

Cat said, "If it's all right, I'll just spend another night in jail."

The judge replied, "That will be okay. Go on back there now. I want to talk to your dad, Mike, and Conrad."

Cat went back to the cell. The judge said to Dave and Mike, "We'll all meet back here and see if we can come up with some sort of punishment that will satisfy Betty."

Dave said, "Short of hanging or life in prison, I don't think we can."

Mike said, "Come on, Dave, let's get something to eat, then I'll take you home."

*****

When Dave got home, Betty was in the kitchen baking away; she already had ten dozen cookies baked and was working on some pies. Baking was a better way to work off steam than putting holes in the wall, but Dave was wondering what he was going to do with all the baked goods. He had never seen her that mad. He walked into the kitchen. Betty didn't turn around.

"Where's Cat."

"She's still in jail. I'm going back tomorrow."

"Is that it, one night in jail?"

"No, we're gonna figure out some form of punishment for her."

"Probably won't be enough. I need you to go get me some more flour and sugar."

Dave went back to town to get some more flour and sugar for Betty. He stopped at the bakery and diner and told them he'd bring some baked goods in for them tomorrow.

The owners looked at Dave and asked, "Betty mad again?"

"Oh yeah, you'll have plenty!"

"I'll put a sign in the window."

Dave drove back home and took the flour and sugar into the kitchen. He walked into the living room, and just as he had suspected, there were blankets and a pillow on the couch. Oh well, at least it was inside.

*****

Dave showed up at the jail around nine the next morning. Mike was already there.

Conrad came out and said, "The judge said to come on in."

They all walked into the judge's office and sat down.

Mike asked Dave, "Couch comfortable?"

"About the same as last time."

"The bakery is gonna have home baked goods tomorrow?"

"Yeah, the bakery and diner!"

"I think everybody in town gains ten pounds when Betty gets mad."

"Probably twenty this time."

The judge said, "All right, we have to figure something out that will punish Cat. The problem with her type is she always takes everything in stride. It never seems to bother her."

Mike said, "Yeah, I know. When I caught my boy drinking, I bought a bottle of the most rot-gut whiskey I could find, opened it, threw the cap away, and we drank it till it was gone. He never touched the stuff again for over ten years."

Dave said, "I don't think that'll work with Cat."

"Yeah, it might be embarrassing if she outdrank me."

The judge said, "We have to find something that will really bother her."

They sat there for a while thinking. Then the judge opened up his bottom desk drawer and pulled out the two mason jars that he had placed in there the night before. He set them on the table with four glasses.

"Maybe this will help us think of something."

Dave asked, "Have any cigars?"

Mike said, "Ain't supposed to smoke in here."

The judge opened the top desk drawer, pulled out four cigars, and passed them around, "Like I said, this is *my* jungle."

The judge opened up a window; they all lit their cigars and filled their glasses. Every time one of them would come up with something, the other three would shake their heads and say, "Nah, that wouldn't work."

When they were about three-quarters done with their cigars, Mike took a long drag on his then said, "I've got it! Sentence her to a weekend in jail."

The judge replied, "That's it, one weekend?"

"Not just any weekend, but the weekend of the fifteenth and the sixteenth.

Dave said, "The weekend of that shoot she's been practicing for?"

"Yep, if that don't get her attention, nothing will. She's been looking forward to it all summer."

The judge said, "That sounds like a winner. Conrad, go get Cat. I'll put the glasses and jars away."

Conrad brought Cat into the office.

Cat said, "I didn't think you were supposed to smoke in here."

The judge looked at her.

Cat said, "It is your office."

The judge said, "Cat, sit down. I have come up with a sentence for you."

"And that is?"

"You will spend a weekend in jail."

Cat looked relieved. "That's it?"

"Not just any weekend. You will show up here on the evening of the fourteenth and leave the evening of the sixteenth."

"You mean the weekend that I have been practicing for? There's gonna be shooters there from all over. Not that weekend. I'll do any other weekend, or even two, just not that one."

They knew they hit a nerve.

The judge replied, "You will serve what I said and stop whining, or you will serve every weekend next summer."

Mike added, "I'm not going to spend all this money and have you screw it up by going out and getting drunk. How well do you think you've done if you pulled that stunt the night before a competition?"

"Not very well."

The judge said, "Well, I guess that's settled. Cat, since you started whining, you can spend tonight in jail. Your dad can come get you in the morning."

Cat knew that it would be useless arguing. "Okay," she said and started back toward her cell.

The judge said, "Oh, Cat…"

"Yes."

"If I were you, I think I'd wait till you move out before you finish that wildlife mural on your backside."

"Yeah, I think you're right. Nobody was supposed to find out about it."

*****

Dave drove back home. As he walked into the house, Betty asked, "Decide what to do with Cat? Where is Cat?"

"We can pick her up in the morning."

"That's all? How is she ever gonna learn?"

"No, that's not all, she has to spend another weekend in jail."

"One weekend, like that will do anything."

"On 14, 15, and 16."

"The weekend of the competition? She's been looking forward to that all summer. How could you guys be so mean?"

"You just told me yesterday that I wasn't stern enough, that she gets away with murder."

"Yeah, but that's gonna kill her."

"I'm sure she'll survive."

Ben walked in and asked, "Where's Cat?"

Dave answered, "She's spending the night in jail."

"I knew she'd get off easy."

Betty added, "Oh, that's not all. Ask your father what else."

Dave said, "Why don't you tell him."

Betty said, "Your sister has to spend the weekend she has been looking forward to all summer in jail."

Ben asked, "You mean the weekend of that competition?"

"Yes."

"I can't believe you guys are that mean."

"I can't either. I'll go pick her up in the morning. She probably doesn't want to see you."

Dave replied, "I can't win… Don't punish her enough, you bitch. Punish her more, you bitch. I wish you'd make up your mind. What do you want me to do?"

Dave walked to the cupboard, opened it, and pulled out a bottle of bourbon and a glass. He looked at the bottle then put the glass back. He grabbed a couple of cigars and went out to the porch and sat in his chair. He took a long sip of bourbon, lit a cigar, and thought, *Is there any way to please this family? Probably not.* Dave finished the bottle and cigars then went inside. The blankets and pillow were still on the couch.

The next morning, Betty drove to the jail.

As she walked in, Conrad said, "Hi, Betty, here to get Cat?"

"Yes, is she ready?"

"Yeah, sign these release forms, and I'll go get her."

Conrad walked back to the cell and brought Cat to her mom.

Betty asked, "Hi, honey, ready to go home?"

Cat was more than confused. Yesterday she wanted her locked up for life. Today Betty was asking her if she was ready to go home.

"Yeah, I'm ready."

"Good, I thought we'd stop and get something to eat on the way home."

"Okay."

*****

While they were eating, Betty said, "I can't believe you have tattoos on your butt."

"You weren't supposed to find out. The tattoo artist said I had the firmest butt she had ever worked on."

"I can believe that with all the exercising you do."

"At least I didn't break any needles."

"What's your husband gonna say when you get married?"

"He'd better like wildlife as much as I do."

They both laughed. "I bet in less than a year, he'll wonder what he got himself into."

"Don't all husbands?"

"Yeah, I guess you're right."

"I love you, Mom."

"I love you too, let's go home."

18

Mom knocked on Cat's bedroom door even though it was open. Cat was at her desk reading. She turned around.

"Hi, Mom, come in."

"Hi, honey, you busy?"

"Not really. I'm just reading about how the American Indians thought they had a spiritual connection with the animals. I can understand how they thought that."

"How's that?"

"Sometimes, when I'm in the woods, it seems like the animals and I are able to communicate. Like that buck Widow Johnson's boy shot. I saw him lose a fight with a younger, stronger buck. When he walked away, he looked at me as though he had let me down. Opening day, he walked right up to our tree stand and looked right at me, as though he knew that I would not let him be forgotten."

"He would be right about that. I still hear the customers at the diner talking about that big deer."

"And like the coyotes the night I watched them clean up that gut pile. They just looked up at me, and it was like they knew that I wasn't gonna hurt them and then continued eating."

"You're not questioning your faith, are you?"

"Oh no, Mom, my faith is as strong as ever. You don't have to worry about me dancing around a fire, half naked, asking the Great Spirit to bring buffalo."

Betty laughed, "That's good."

"It could be that I'm just more attuned to nature then most people."

"You'll get no argument from me."

"So was there something you wanted to talk to me about?"

"Yes, there is, your tattoos."

"Yeah, I know, I should've said something to you first, sorry. I won't get any more till I move out and am on my own."

"Easier to get forgiveness than permission?"

"Usually, but when you found out, I was wondering."

Betty laughed. "It's just that I worry about you. Where did you get them? Was the place clean and sanitary? I don't want you to get an infection."

"Mom, it was very clean and neat. She has all the modern sterilization equipment."

"Where did you find someone that would sell you a tattoo being underage?"

"One day I was at the taxidermist checking on that deer head. I noticed someone walking out of the back room. I got curious and went into the room."

"Curiosity killed the cat."

"Yeah, but satisfaction brought him back."

"You did have to find the second line of that saying, didn't you?"

"Anyway, as I was saying, Billy Bob's daughter does tattoos in the backroom. All she does is wildlife, I was admiring the art work she had on the wall when she came in. She was a little upset at first then we started talking. She likes wildlife and nature as much as I do. I noticed a predator-prey theme on the wall and asked her about it. She said that she wouldn't do it unless I had parental consent forms signed."

"How did you talk her into it, or did you forge my signature?"

"No, Mom, we started talking, and I found out she was looking for a nice fox that she could have her dad mount to add to her collection."

"And you just happened to have one."

"No, not then, but I made a deal with her if I could get a fox she liked, she'd do the tattoos for free. I couldn't beat that deal."

"Well, there ain't much I can do about it now. I'm having a hard time with you growing up. You *are* my baby."

"I guess I am a challenge."
"To put it mildly."

*****

Mike picked up Barry then went over to pick up Cat and Ben. They were going to the range to practice. Mike stopped at the office to pick up a pass. As they walked in, Don greeted them.

"Hi, gonna do some shooting?"

Mike replied, "Yeah, It's a nice day for this time of year."

Don looked at Cat, "Not gonna shoot any bottles out of anybody's hand, are ya?"

Cat looked down, "No. Am I ever gonna live that down?"

Mike laughed, "I doubt it."

Don said, "Oh, by the way, we were just notified that we're one of the ranges that will be having some of the qualifying matches for the Big Shoot."

Mike replied, "I haven't received any information yet. Have the rules been set?"

"They're not finalized yet. They're trying to get enough ranges to handle all the shooters. It looks like it's gonna be bigger than they expected. There have been inquiries from other countries, especially from the UK, Australia, and Canada."

"It looks like this is just what the shooting sports need to boost the popularity."

"If this doesn't, nothing will."

Mike drove to the range. The kids took the rifles and equipment to the benches. Cat set up the rifle, Ben the spotting scope, and Barry set up his computer. Mike handed Barry a list of the loads Cat would be shooting.

Barry asked, "What range is she gonna be shooting today?"

"She's been doing pretty well at five hundred yards. We'll stretch it out to eight hundred today."

When the range was clear, Mike and Cat set up the targets at the eight-hundred-yard line. When they returned, Barry handed Cat the windage and elevation corrections she would need. Cat fired three rounds.

Ben looked through the spotting scope and said, "Windage is good, but she hit two inches low."

Barry rechecked the range with the range finder. It was correct. He punched some more numbers into his computer, handed Cat the corrections, and said, "Try this."

Cat said, "This takes too much time. Why can't I just raise the elevation where I think it should be?"

"I'm learning too. When I get the information entered and saved for all the distances and different loads, all we have to worry about then is the wind."

"I guess it'll save time later."

Cat fired three more rounds. Two hit the 10-ring, and one just nicked the X-ring.

Mike looked at Cat. "Not bad, I have a rifle I bought from Surgeon I want you to try. I already broke it in."

"Another rifle, why?"

"Always have to have a backup."

Cat did well with that rifle also. She was grinning from ear to ear.

Barry looked at her. "I don't see the big deal. I tell you how to set your scope. All you do is pull the trigger."

"All right, Einstein, you think it's so easy, show me."

"Sure."

Mike, shaking his head, thought, *Never a dull moment with these kids.*

Cat said, "What distance you wanna try?"

"It's set up for eight hundred."

Ben went down range and set up a new target. Mike showed Barry how to sit and hold the rifle then said, "Put the crosshairs on the center of the target and squeeze the trigger. Be sure to hold it tight against your shoulder."

Cat said to Mike, "You didn't have to tell him that."

"Now, Cat."

Barry fired a round. Cat looked through the spotting scope. "We can use that target again, there ain't no holes."

Barry said, surprised, "What? I missed that big target?"

"Try again."

Barry fired five more rounds. One hit the target way outside of the rings. He looked at Cat. "I guess it ain't as easy as it looks. I don't get it."

"I do. You think you put all the information in the computer, and that's all you need. You forgot one important thing, the human factor. So why don't you stick to what you know—the computer, programs, and the rest of the geeky stuff. I'll stick to what I know, putting the bullet in the X-ring."

"You don't have to be such a smart-ass. Do you really want to piss me off? After all, I do give you the information, and I could accidently punch in a wrong number at a critical time."

Cat thought for a moment. "Point taken, I guess we'd better work together. If you want to learn how to shoot, you can use my .22. That's what I started with."

Mike said, "Well, I think that's enough for the day. We had better be going. They loaded up the car and headed back home.

On the way home, Mike said, "I read over some of the info Don gave me. It looks like you have to shoot a minimum of five and up to seven quantifying matches. They average the top five. The top 490 will be allowed to enter."

Cat asked, "Think I can do it?"

"What do you think?"

"I can."

"That's a girl. I guess I had better invest in a trailer to haul all this stuff around."

"Can I go with you?"

"So you can pick it out?"

"Yeah."

"Might as well, it'd be a boring drive by myself."

*****

268

Mike went over to pick up Cat early Saturday morning. They were going to a dealership about two hundred miles away. Ben had done a web search for Mike that showed this particular dealership had the best selection and prices.

Mike pulled into the driveway and stopped.

Cat got into the truck and said, "Morning, Mike. I'm usually not awake this early unless I'm going deer hunting."

"Or coming back from one of your night hunts."

"I haven't done much of that lately."

"So you haven't quit?"

"Nah, I wait till somebody asks me to get them some meat. It's just too much fun to give it up completely."

"You're gonna get yourself into some real trouble if you keep it up."

"Might, but I still have my 'Get Out of Jail Free' card."

With that, they pulled out of the driveway and headed out of town.

*****

"I received some information from the B&C Shooting Range. It looks like it is going to be a theme park for shooters like Bart said. They plan on having the old western town finished before the Big Shoot. They've applied for alcohol and gambling permits."

"Maybe we can go to one of their Cowboy Action Shoots."

"Yeah, I'd like that. There's also gonna be shooting leagues like bowling."

"Too bad we didn't live closer."

"That does sound like fun. They sent a fee schedule and application along. It is $2,000 to enter the Big Shoot. You have to qualify first, that's $100 a match. You need at least five. I have a list of the places that have signed up so far. You get an hour to shoot three targets. You can't shoot all your qualifications at the same shooting range. There must be at least three different ones and no more than one at the B&C. If you don't make it in the top 490, you get your application fee back, but not the qualification fee."

"I hope you can keep this all straight."

"I should be able to. All you have to do is be one of the top 490."

"I thought it was 500."

"It is, but ten places have been reserved for the essay contest sponsored by Savage and Winchester."

"I'd probably have better luck shooting than writing."

"Yeah, probably. I'm hungry, how about you?"

Cat looked at him. "You really need to ask?"

Mike laughed as he took the exit. He stopped at a restaurant that was not far from the dealership. They ate a bite then drove to the dealership. Mike parked the truck. Cat got out and started looking around.

A salesman came out. "May I help you?"

Mike replied, "Yeah, I'm looking for a trailer."

"You've come to the right place. If you can't find one here, you ain't gonna find one anywhere."

"I'm looking for an eight-footer, enclosed."

"We have a great selection over there in the third aisle."

"Okay, thank you."

"Just pull it up to the office when you find what you want. I'll hook up the lights and get you the title."

After they looked around a while, Mike called Cat over. "I think this one's just the ticket. It has a side door along with the one in the rear. It's sturdy enough. I can build cabinets in it to keep everything from moving around. The tag says it even comes with an inside lighting kit."

"It sure looks nice."

"Yeah, and it should be easy to tow. I think it's small enough that your dad's van will be able to pull it. Watch me back up to it, and we'll hook it up."

Mike pulled the trailer up to the office, and the salesman came out and said, "I see you found one."

"Yeah, this is what I'm looking for."

After they agreed on a price, the salesman said, "I'll get you the inside lighting kit and paperwork, hook up the lights, and check the brakes."

The salesman hooked up everything and made sure the lights and brakes worked. "Give me a check, sign here, and it's all yours."

"Cash work?"

"Cash is good."

Mike handed him the money, signed the paperwork, and put the receipt in his pocket.

The salesman said, "Thank you. Tell your friends about this place."

Mike said, "Will do, bye."

Cat said, "This is great! We can leave some of the stuff in the trailer and not have to load it every time we go to shoot."

"Yeah, I think it'll be handy. Speaking of shooting, you've got a lot of practicing to do if you want to get qualified to enter."

"I know, I'm not gonna let you down."

"I won't let you."

"Hey, I saw a sign that read there's an ice cream shop at the next exit."

"Trying to tell me something?"

"Yeah, I want some ice cream."

Mike laughed. "Ice cream does sound good."

Mike pulled into the parking lot. He parked toward the back to make it easier to get out. As they walked into the shop, Mike asked, "You want to eat it here or take it with us?"

"Both. I'll get a banana split to eat here and a large chocolate cone to take with us."

"Should have guessed."

They walked up to the counter.

Mike told Cat, "Tell the gal what you want."

"I'll take a banana split to eat here and a large chocolate cone to take with me."

"Okay, I'll wait till you're ready to leave to fix your cone." She looked at Mike and asked, "And you?"

"I'll take a chocolate malt made with vanilla ice cream."

They went to the restroom while they were waiting on their ice cream. When Mike came back, he went to the counter, picked up their ice cream, took it to the table, and sat down. Once back, Cat finished her split while Mike still had half of his malt left.

He looked at her. "I don't know where you put all that. Go tell the gal that you're ready for your cone. I'll take the rest of this with me."

Cat went up and got her cone, then they headed for the truck. When they were within twenty feet of the truck, a car sped toward them, stopping between them and the truck. Three men jumped out.

One of them pointed a gun at Mike and said, "Is this your truck, old man?"

"Yes."

"*Was*, give me the keys."

Mike quickly thought the situation over and decided it would be best to just give him the keys. Mike reached in his pocket to get them. The man hit Mike on the side of his head with the pistol and knocked him to the ground. Cat kneed the one in front of her in the groin. When he bent over, she grabbed his head and brought her knee up and broke his nose. The third thug hit Cat on the side of her head, knocking her down; she fell on her right arm, breaking it. He then started kicking Cat in the head and ribs. The thug that hit Mike went to get the key out of his pocket. When he got close enough, Mike reached up and grabbed the thug's Adam's apple and squeezed with all his strength and held. He concentrated only on crushing the thug's windpipe; he didn't let up his viselike grip. If Mike was going to die, he was going to make sure he took the thug with him.

Cat would black out then come to, only to be hit again. Unbeknownst to anyone, a truck pulled into the parking lot. A big man got out and walked up to the thug beating Cat. Cat came to just in time to hear what sounded like someone cracking their knuckles. Her attacker fell to the ground. She was able to turn her head enough to see the one that she kneed going toward Mike to help his friend. The stranger walked up behind him. Cat heard the sound again, and the thug fell to the ground like a rag doll. The stranger walked back to Cat and checked to see if she had a pulse. She looked up and recognized the stranger. She managed a very feeble, "Thank you."

"Help's on the way." He then went back to check if Mike had a pulse. Mike looked up with his hand still wrapped around the thug's windpipe. "Help's on the way, Semper Fi."

The stranger got back into his truck and left. Cat passed out again. Mike could hear the sirens coming toward them.

A patrol car showed up with two officers—Officer Franklin, who had been on the force for fifteen years, and Officer Darby, who was a rookie. Franklin walked over to Cat and checked to see if she had a pulse. Darby walked over to Mike and checked him for a pulse.

Franklin yelled to Darby, "This one's alive, check to see if the ambulance is on the way."

"Have a live one here to,; the ambulance is on the way. I called for a second one."

Franklin walked up to the thugs and checked for a pulse; they were dead. He yelled to Darby, "Better make a call for the medical examiner. Tell them to bring two body bags along."

"Better make that three."

"Did we lose that one?"

"No, check this out."

Franklin walked over to Darby. When he saw Mike's hand still around the thug's windpipe, he said, "He wasn't going by himself."

"I can't loosen his hand."

"Let the EMTs do it. I'm going back to the girl, you stay with him. I think these guys picked on the wrong people."

A rescue van showed up; three EMTs got out. Two began helping Cat; the other went over to Mike. Soon after, the ambulance showed up. Cat was in bad shape. Her blood pressure was critically low, pulse rate 43, breathing shallow, and her eyes were unresponsive to light. As bad as she was beaten, the EMT suspected internal bleeding. This wouldn't be able to be confirmed until they got her to the hospital. They quickly and carefully put her on the gurney, started an IV, and gave her oxygen. After she was loaded into the ambulance, the EMT radioed the hospital and told them to get an operating room and surgical team ready.

*****

Franklin walked up to the ME and said, "Broken neck?"

"Yeah, just like the one over there. Whoever did this has done it before."

Darby came up to Franklin and said, "I ran the plates on the car. It's the one carjacked at the state line where the woman was left for dead. A gun was found, could be the same one used before."

"Anything else?"

"Yeah, the lady in that car parked over there said she pulled into the parking lot just when the fight started. She called 911. She also said that a delivery truck pulled up and a big man got out and walked over to the fight. In no time the two thugs were lying on the ground. He then knelt down as though to see if the ones that had been attacked were all right. After that, he got in his truck and drove away. That may be the one that broke those guy's necks. She gave me a description and license number of the truck."

"I'm gonna go in the ice cream shop and look at the surveillance videos."

"Do you want me to put a BOLO out on that truck?"

"Why, you think he'll tell us anything different than what we will find on the camera?"

"Well, no, but we can't let people take the law into their own hands."

"Answer this question honestly, then you decide what to do."

"Okay."

"Let's say this would have been your father and daughter here tonight. What would you want the investigating officers to do?"

Darby thought for a minute, handed the paper with the information to Franklin, and said, "I'll tell her thank you, and if we need any more information, we'll contact her."

"Remember, you need to be able to look yourself in the mirror every morning, knowing that you not only upheld the law but also did the right thing the day before. If we would find this guy and bring him in, no jury would convict him. It would be a waste of resources that could be better used to prosecute violent criminals. You can stay out here while the area is being cleaned up. I'm gonna see what I can find out in the ice cream shop."

"Okay."

*****

Franklin walked into the ice cream shop, looked at the girl's name tag, and said, "Beth, I'm Officer Franklin."

"Hi."

"I'd like to ask you a few questions about what happened in the parking lot tonight."

"Sure. Would you like anything to drink?"

"Water would be fine."

Beth got two glasses of water, "We can sit down at this table."

They sat down, then Franklin said, "Tell me what you saw."

"Sure. After the man and girl left, I walked over to the table to clean it. I looked out the window when I saw a car driving toward them. When it stopped, three guys got out. It looked as though they were going to rob them. I went to the phone and called 911. By the time I got back to the window, I saw a truck leaving the area. It wasn't long after that I heard the sirens."

"Do you have security cameras in the parking lot?"

"Yes, but the boss has the key. I called him, he's on his way."

"You here by yourself?"

"No, my coworker Brian is here. He's in the back cleaning up."

"I'd like to talk to him."

"Sure." Beth turned her head and yelled, "Brian, will you come out here?"

Brian walked to the table. "Yeah?"

Franklin said, "Would you sit down? I have a few questions I'd like to ask."

Brian sat down, "Okay."

"Did you see anything tonight?"

"No, I was taking the trash out to the dumpster. When I got back inside, Beth told me what was going on. I thought it best to just stay inside."

The boss walked in, looked at Beth, and Brian and asked, "You two all right?"

They answered, "Yes, we're fine."

Beth said, "This is Officer Franklin. He'd like to look at the tapes."

"Sure, Brian, if it's all right with the officer, you can go home."

Franklin said, "Yeah, that's okay. If I need to talk to him, I'll call."

Brian said, "Okay, see you tomorrow."

The owner said, "Let's go into the office and look at the tapes."

"Okay, you know that I'm gonna take them with me?"

"Yeah, I figured."

The owner took the tape out of the recorder, and as he put it in a player, he said, "This is from the camera at the light pole in the back part of the parking lot."

He rewound it until Mike and Cat came into view. They watched it from the time that the thugs got out of the car until the stranger was checking on Cat, then it quit.

The boss said, "Tape ran out, it has a changer. I'll get the other one."

He put the tape in the player, and they continued watching. After the stranger was done checking on Mike, he looked straight into the camera, then left.

Franklin asked, "Do you recognize him?"

Not wanting to admit it, he said, "Yes, he stops in here when he delivers out this way, which is about once a week."

"Do you know his name?"

"No, but he always buys a half gallon of 'Rocky Road.' Sometimes he eats it here, once in a while he takes it with him. He always calls us a half hour before he stops to have us set it out of the freezer so that it'll be soft by the time he gets here."

Franklin looked out of the office door and saw a half gallon of ice cream sitting on the counter. The boss noticed it also.

The boss yelled to Beth, "Did the 'Rocky Road' guy call tonight?"

"Yes, he called right before the man and girl left, but he never showed up."

Franklin said, "He probably saw all the commotion and decided not to stop."

"Probably." Beth went back to cleaning.

The boss said to Franklin, "You know, he's not a bad guy. One night he was in here eating his ice cream when this punk was giving Beth a hard time. Something about that he didn't want nuts on his ice cream. He was getting real nasty. On my way to the front, I heard the 'Rocky Road' guy in a very polite but firm voice say, 'Young man, no need to be rude.'

"The punk replied, 'Mind your own business, old man.'

"With that, 'Rocky Road' stood up. You don't know how big he is till he stands up. He walked over to the punk and said, 'I bet if you just ask this nice lady, she'll make you another sundae without nuts.'

"The punk just looked at him and left, never saw him in here again."

"I know who this guy is. I pulled him over for speeding once. I noticed a Marine sticker on his cab. I asked him if he was a Marine. He said, 'Nam vet, my boy is training to go to Afghanistan.' We talked awhile. My boy is in Iraq. I just gave him a warning. Two weeks later, he comes speeding past me again. I pulled him over and said, 'Didn't you see me there?' He said, 'Yes, but I was wondering how your boy's doing.' I said, 'You mean you sped by here so I'd pull you over so you could ask me how my boy's doing?' He replied, 'Yeah.' We talked awhile about our boys. I gave him my cell number and told him to give me a call when he was in the area, and we'd talk."

"He sounds like a pretty good guy. I hate to see him get into trouble for helping someone."

"What happens if you forget to put the second tape in the recorder?"

"It just stops, I've done it before."

"So you forgot to put the tape in this morning."

"You know, there was something I was supposed to do this morning."

"I'll put that in the report. If I have to change it, I'll let you know."

"Thank you."

Franklin put the one tape in an evidence bag and sealed it, the other he put in his pocket. He went back out to the scene of the crime.

When Franklin left, Beth said to her boss, "It was the 'Rocky Road' guy that helped that man and girl, wasn't it?"

"Couldn't really tell, I forgot to put the backup tape in. It quit recording before we could see who it was."

"What should I do if he calls again?"

"Set out his half gallon and give it to him when he shows up. You might as well take that ice cream home with you. We can't sell it."

"Okay, thank you."

*****

Franklin asked Derby, "How's everything going?"

"They got the girl stabilized enough to move. She's hurt pretty bad. It'll be touch and go."

"What about the man?"

"He seems to have fared a little better. It took a little while for the EMTs to get his hand relaxed enough for him to let go of the thug's wind pipe. They ended up giving him a shot. He was coherent enough for me to get some information. He gave me his keys and asked if I would drive his truck to the hospital. I told him that would be fine. The wrecker left with the car."

"Did he give you a number where we can reach the girl's parents?"

"Yes, he did, but he also gave me a number of a judge. He said this judge knows the family well, and he would make sure they got to the hospital safe. He doesn't want them to get in a wreck."

"That sounds reasonable. Go to the ice cream shop and see if they'll let you use their phone. I want to talk to the ME before he takes off. When you get back, I'll follow you to the hospital."

*****

The judge, awakened out of a deep sleep from the phone ringing, answered, "Hello."

"Judge Bean?"

"Yes."

"This is Officer Darby. Do you know a man named Mike and a girl that goes by Cat?"

The judge's heart fell down to his stomach. "Yes, I do."

"They were victims of an attempted carjacking. They're both still alive. They've been taken to the hospital. The girl is in critical condition. Mike asked me to call you to see if you would tell her parents and make sure they got to the hospital safely."

"Sure, thanks for calling."

The judge hung up the phone after Darby gave him the address of the hospital.

The judge put on a pot of coffee and took a shower. After his shower, he got dressed, packed a suitcase, drank his coffee, and went over to Dave and Betty's.

Dave, being awakened by the pounding on the door, went to answer it. He opened the door.

"Judge, what's wrong?"

Before the judge could answer, Betty came to the door. When she saw the judge, she started screaming, "Oh my dear Lord, what's happened to Cat?"

The judge said, "May I come in?"

Dave said, "Sure. Did something happen to Cat and Mike?"

Betty asked, "Is she alive?"

"Calm down. Let him tell us."

The judge said, "Some guys tried to carjack them, they're both in the hospital." The next words were difficult for him to say. "Cat's in critical condition."

Betty cried, "Oh no, my baby!"

The judge said, "I'll drive you up there. It's gonna take around three hours. Betty, why don't you get some personal items together for Cat while I run over to Mike's and get some stuff for him."

"I want to leave now."

"It's gonna be a while before you can see her. So go ahead, wake up Ben and get ready. I'll be back soon."

Dave said, "Okay, we'll be ready. We can take the van, it's full of gas."

"All right, I'll be back soon."

After the judge left, Betty prayed, "Oh, Lord, save my baby."

*****

Cat was rushed into surgery as soon as she arrived at the hospital. As they were examining Mike, he asked, "How's that girl doing that came in with me?"

The nurse replied, "I'll go check."

"Thank you."

In a few minutes, she came back and said, "She's in surgery, but they can't do a whole lot till they get the parents' permission."

"Where're my pants?"

"Right here."

"Hand me my billfold."

The nurse gave Mike his billfold. He opened it up, pulled out a piece of paper, and handed it to the nurse.

"Here is a notarized paper that gives me the authority to sign permission forms for medical treatment."

"This is great!" said the nurse. "I'll get a copy of this and bring you the forms to sign."

"I'll be here."

The nurse left to get forms. She brought them back for Mike to sign.

Franklin and Darby came into the ER. Franklin asked, "How you doing?"

"A lot better than I was. My arm and wrist is a little sore."

"I bet it is. The EMT told me that they almost had to pry your hand apart finger by finger."

"Yeah, if there was ever a good time for my hand to cramp close, that was it."

"You two were very fortunate. We've been looking for those guys for two days. They carjacked a car yesterday and left a pregnant woman for dead."

"How is she?"

"She'll make it. The baby had to be taken early and put in an incubator. She is slowly improving."

"That's good."

"My partner parked your truck in the hospital parking lot."

"Thanks."

"Did you get a look at the guy that helped you?"

"No. All I remember was him telling me that help was on the way."

"Okay, I'll let you get some rest."

"They want to do an MRI on my head and keep me for a couple of days."

"I'll be back tomorrow. I want to talk to the girl."

"See you tomorrow. Say, I wouldn't spend too much time looking for that guy."

"Don't really plan on it."

*****

Cat was taken to recovery after three hours of surgery. She had a ruptured spleen, which had to be removed. She also had a broken rib; three others were cracked. Her liver was bruised, but it would heal. Fortunately, the rest of her organs were fine. Her arm was left in the air splint; a cast would be put on later. The professionalism of the first responders, surgical team, and hospital staff and the fact that Cat was in great physical health would ensure her a full recovery.

19

As the judge pulled up to the hospital entrance, he said to Dave, "You and Betty go on in. I'll park the van, wake up Ben, and catch up with you."

"Okay, thanks."

Before the van had come to a complete stop, Betty jumped out of the van and ran toward the hospital entrance. Dave caught up with her at the desk.

She was at information, asking excitedly, "Where's my daughter? Is she okay?

"Uh, ma'am, I need a name."

Dave said, "Calm down, go over and sit down, and I'll find out where's she's at."

"I don't want to sit down. I want to see my baby!"

"Okay, just hold on, let me find out."

Dave talked to the receptionist and got the information. He turned to Betty. "She has just been taken to her room."

"Let's go."

Dave and Betty took the elevator to the floor where Cat was. Dave found the floor nurse.

"We're looking for Cat. We're her parents."

"The one that was beat up by the carjackers?

"Yes."

"I'll take you to her room. She's still groggy from the anesthetics and painkillers."

Dave and Betty walked into the room and proceeded to Cat's bed.

Betty kissed Cat. "I love you, honey."

At that, Cat woke up and said, "Mom…Dad."

"Yes, we're both right here."

Dave asked, "How are you feeling?"

"About as well as I look." She drifted back to sleep.

The nurse said, "She'll be a little more coherent after she sleeps a while more. There's a visitors' lounge down the hall with some chairs and a couch. I'll keep you updated on her condition."

Betty asked, "May I stay with her?"

"Sure, there's a chair on the other side of the bed. I'll get you a blanket."

"Thank you."

Dave said, "I'll go to the lounge and wait on the judge and Ben."

*****

The judge parked the van, then yelled to Ben, "Wake up, we're at the hospital."

Ben opened his eyes, "Where's Mom and Dad?"

"I dropped them off at the door. Come on, let's go."

After finding out where Dave was, the judge and Ben went to the visitors' lounge.

Ben asked Dave, "How's Cat?"

"She's sleeping. Your mom is staying in the room with her."

They all went to Cat's room and looked in. Both Cat and Betty were asleep.

Dave said, "I think we should just let them sleep."

The judge said, "I found out where they put Mike. He's on the same floor but in a different wing. Want to go check on him?"

Dave said, "Might as well."

Mike was sitting up in bed watching TV. He looked up when they walked in.

The judge asked, "You still awake?"

"Yeah, but my arm's killing me, and if I lie down, my head hurts. The painkillers make me sick. I told them to just get me a bottle of bourbon."

"Besides that, how are you doing?"

"I can tell you one thing, I'm getting way too old for this shit."

They all laughed, then Mike asked, "How's Cat doing? They told me she was in pretty bad shape."

Dave said, "She's sleeping now. Her nurse said the surgery went fine and that they're going to put her arm in a cast tomorrow. The surgeon was gone when we got here, he's going to talk to me tomorrow."

"Maybe I can talk one of the nurses into wheeling me down to her room when she feels up to talking."

"I'm sure she'd like that."

Dave, Ben, and the judge visited with Mike for a while then went back to the lounge and sat down. It wasn't long before they were asleep.

Betty was awakened by Cat. She stood up, looked over her, and said, "Honey?"

"Mom, when did you get here? Is Dad and Ben here?"

"Yes, we got here last night. You were pretty out of it when we arrived."

"I must have been. Is Mike all right?"

"Yes, he's doing fine. He'll probably talk a nurse into wheeling him down here to see you."

As Cat and Betty were talking, the doctor came in and said, "Good morning. How are you feeling?"

"A little sore."

"I bet. You took quite a beating, but everything is looking good."

"When can I leave?"

The doctor laughed and said, "It'll be a while. The nurse will be coming to get you to take you to orthopedics to have a cast put on your arm."

The doctor turned to Betty and brought her up to date on Cat's condition.

"That girl's lucky to be alive. Her being in shape helped a lot. I will be back later."

Betty replied with a sincere, "Thank you."

*****

284

After interviewing Cat, Franklin walked out of Cat's room. The judge walked up to Franklin.

"You the officer that was at the scene?"

"Yes."

"I'm Judge Paul Bean, a friend of Cat's."

Franklin extended his hand. They shook hands, then Franklin said, "She's quite a fighter."

"Yes, she is. If you have some time, I'd like to talk to you about what happened."

"Sure, I'll be back at the office in an hour. I have something I think you'll be interested in seeing."

"I'll get me a bite to eat and be over."

"Sounds good, see you then."

After the judge got something to eat, he drove over to the police department. He walked in, and the officer at the front desk asked, "May I help you?"

"Yes, I'm Judge Paul Bean, here to see Officer Franklin."

"Have a seat, and I'll let him know you're here." He called Franklin to let him know that the judge was there to see him.

Franklin walked out and said, "Hi, come on back to my office."

The judge followed Franklin back to his office and sat down.

Franklin asked, "You still on the bench?"

"I'm kinda semiretired. I take care of traffic tickets, game violations, and other misdemeanors. Felonies and jury cases are tried at the county seat. It helps keep the backlog down."

"I have the security tape from the ice cream shop. I'd like to show it you."

After the judge and Franklin viewed the tape, the judge said, "Wow! Mike and Cat sure gave them a good fight. They wouldn't have needed any help if there had been only two thugs. Any idea who the Good Samaritan is?"

Franklin pulled a tape out of his desk drawer and said, "Yes, I do, but this tape doesn't exist."

After watching the second tape, Franklin asked, "You know him? He lives in your county."

"Yeah, that's Big John."

"Ever caused any problems?"

"No, he's only been there a little over three years. The only problem we've had is his son at the high school. When John found out about it, problem solved. I think his son joined the Marines."

"Yes, he did, about the same time my son joined up."

Franklin told the judge about how he and Big John had met and kept in touch."

"I never talked to him much. He would always come in to town every Friday to get groceries. The owner of the bar and grill said he would stop in there and get a ham sandwich and onion rings. He would drink two beers and a shot of whiskey. He never drank any more than that. Once, he was offered a drink on the house, to which he replied, 'No, thank you. If I drink any more than that, somebody gets hurt, and I get into trouble.'"

"I did a background check on him. He served in the Marines during the latter days of Nam. He spent some time in Angola and other wars that the US was not involved in. I did some more checking and found out he would've received quite of a few more medals, except he was on missions that didn't happen."

"I really don't think he's a danger to society."

"Probably more of an asset. I'll destroy the tape."

"Sounds good to me. Thanks for taking your time. I'll see you later."

Franklin shook the judge's hand. "Thanks for stopping by. See you later."

*****

Cat heard a knock on her door.

The nurse wheeled Mike into the room and said, "Cat, I brought someone to see you."

Mike said, "Gonna lie in bed forever?"

"Not if I can help it. You couldn't walk down here?"

"I could've, but I'm not gonna turn down a ride by a pretty nurse."

"Nurse, would you help me sit up?"

"Sure." She helped Cat sit up. "You two visit for a while. Call if you need me."

"Thank you."

"Feeling better?"

"A lot better than I did a few days ago. You?"

"Had a pretty bad concussion from that hit on the head. My arm and wrist is still sore from trying to crush that thug's windpipe. According to the ME, I succeeded."

"Where was your .380 you always keep in your pocket."

"I left it at home since we were going across state lines. Where was your pencil?"

"I left it at home 'cause I figured you had your .380. Where was your lug wrench?"

"Behind the seat. We'd have made it to the truck in time if we didn't have to wait on your cone."

"We'd have made it too if you hadn't parked so far away."

They started laughing when they realized they were arguing like a couple of first-graders.

Finally, Mike said, "I am so glad you're all right."

"I'm glad you're okay too. I'd hate to think that I'd have to load my own ammo."

"I bet you would."

"I hope I'll be well enough to shoot the qualifiers."

"I'll enter you as late as possible. It'll just mean they'll be close together and not much time to practice between them."

"Just so I get a chance."

"I'm gonna go back to my room now and let you rest."

"Okay, bye."

After Mike left, Betty and Ben came in.

Betty asked, "Feeling better?"

"Not too bad. Mike was here a little bit ago. I am glad he's doing okay."

"He was worried about you. He had stopped down a couple of times, but you were sleeping."

"He could've waken me."

"He wanted you to get your rest. Your dad is bringing Liz and Barry up tomorrow."

"That's good. How did Liz take the news?"

"She was worried, wishing she could've gotten here sooner."

"I'll be glad to see her."

After they visited a little while, Ben said, "I'm gonna go to the hotel and take a shower. I'll be back later."

Cat asked, "Hotel?"

Betty said, "Yeah, the judge and Mike rented a hotel room for us while you're here. The judge said he got a good deal."

"That was nice of them. I'll see you later, Ben."

After Ben left, Betty walked up to Cat's bed and started tearing up a little.

Cat asked, "What's the matter, Mom?"

"Oh, Cat, I'm so glad you're all right. I don't know what I would've done had you been killed."

"I do."

Betty gave Cat a puzzled look, "You do?"

"Sure, provided my body was found. You would've spent way too much on a casket and headstone. You would have had the funeral home tear out all that fancy cloth in the casket and had it replaced with deer skin. If I didn't have enough, you would ask old man Smith for some more. He's the guy that lives by the abandoned railroad depot. You would take the fox skin I have on my bed and have it placed under my head. My feet would be covered with mink and muskrat skins. My hands would be under a raccoon skin. You would ask Widow Johnson's boy to display that deer head at my viewing."

Betty looked at Cat in disbelief, "How are you so sure?"

Cat, in a matter-of-fact tone, replied, "Because you would go to my room to pick out some clothes for me. You would go to my desk and look through my binder that I keep my sketches and journal in. In the front pocket of the binder, you would find a sealed envelope. Curiosity would cause you to open it. Everything I've told you is written down."

"How come you have never talked to me about this before?"

"'Cause every time I'd bring it up, you'd say 'It's too morbid.'"

"How can you take something so complicated and make it sound so simple?"

"No, you take something that is simple and make it complicated."

"I guess. Oh, you didn't say what clothes I'd pick out for you."

"I left that up to you. Mom, life is as simple or as complicated as you want it. You can make it exciting or boring, it's your choice."

"But you're so young. It would've been terrible for you to die at such a young age."

"Mom, look at what I've done already in my life. I've probably had more fun and exciting experiences than people twice my age."

"I love you."

"I love you too. Life goes on no matter what happens. I'm getting a little tired."

"All right, I'll let you rest. Do you mind if I sleep at the hotel? That chair is a bit uncomfortable."

"No, Mom, you need your rest too. See you tomorrow."

"See you later, honey."

*****

The nurse walked into Cat's room and said, "Good morning."

"Good morning."

"There are two FBI agents that would like to talk to you. Your mom went to the cafeteria. Would you like to wait till she comes back?"

"Nah, I'll talk to them."

The FBI agents walked in and introduced themselves and showed their badges and IDs. They started to put them away when Cat asked, "May I see them?"

The agents looked at each other, nodded, and then handed their IDs to her.

She looked them over, gave them back, and said, "Real live FBI agents! How do I rate a visit from the Feds?"

"We'd like to ask you a few questions about the carjacking."

"Can't you just read the police reports?"

"We read them. We just wanted to hear it from you."

"One of the thugs pointed a gun at Mike. They were planning to take his truck. Mike reached into his pocket to get the keys, and that's when he hit Mike on the head."

"Probably thought he was reaching for a gun."

"I knew then that we were going to get killed no matter what we did. So I kneed the one in front of me in the nuts, I mean…"

The agents started laughing. "Yeah, that's what the report said. Did you get a look at the guy that helped you out?"

"Nah, couldn't get a good look at him. It was dark, and I was trying to keep from passing out."

"You wouldn't tell us if you did see him."

"No, I wouldn't."

"Don't blame ya, I wouldn't either."

"I owe him my life."

"The conventional wisdom has been to not fight back, but I've always questioned that logic. If you two had cooperated, your chance of survival would've been zero."

"Odds didn't look a whole lot better the other way either. A slim chance is better than none."

"Those guys that attacked you were a bad bunch. They were on the top ten wanted list. They had carjacked three cars, killing two people. The last car they took, a pregnant woman was left for dead."

"The Lord had angels watching over us."

"I believe that. There's a reward for information leading to the capture and conviction of them. Looks like the capture and conviction has been taken care of."

"Mike should get the reward."

"It will be split between the two of you. Since you're underage, one of your parents will receive it on your behalf."

"That's great! It'll help with the doctor and hospital bills."

"I'm gonna put in a suggestion that yours and Mike's bills be paid. Don't say anything till it's a fact. When we get back, we'll send in our report and request. You should hear something in two to three weeks."

"That's great."

"All right, thank you for talking with us. You have a speedy recovery,"

"Thank you."

The FBI agents left the room and walked toward the coffee machine.

One agent said to the other, "As far as I'm concerned, this case is closed. The old man's story was about the same as the girl's."

"Suits me fine. I don't want to waste my time arresting someone that saved us a lot of time and paperwork." He put some change in the vending machine then asked, "Coffee?"

"You buying?"

The agent handed him the cup then said, "You get the next one."

Betty walked into Cat's room and asked, "Who were those guys?"

"The FBI, they wanted to talk to me about the carjacking."

"Did they seem satisfied with your story?"

"Yeah, I'll have to ask Mike if they talked to him too."

"I'm sure they did. Everything I've heard has been secondhand. I'd like to hear it from you."

"Sure, Mom, I don't mind."

Betty listened intently as Cat told the story from the time they stopped at the ice cream shop until the EMTs showed up.

After Cat was finished, Betty said, "Wow! I don't know if you were brave or crazy."

"More like scared."

"I can understand that." Betty gave Cat a big hug and said, "I love you. I am so glad I didn't have to pick out a casket."

"Yeah, me too. Love you."

*****

Dave had little time to spare. He would work during the day and get the house ready for Cat's return in the evening. He still found time to drive to the hospital to see Cat. The judge helped him with the house. Mike, after being released from the hospital, helped Dave as much as he could. Mike would stay at Dave's place for a day or two and then catch a ride back to the hospital to visit with Cat.

The town went together and bought a treadmill, small weights, and other items so that she would be able to build back her strength. Mike wanted Cat to start practicing as soon as possible. Knowing that it would be a while for her body to be able to take the strain of shooting live ammo, he wanted a place for Cat to dry fire. There was just enough room to fit his portable shooting bench by a window. He hung a target on the shed, which was about one hundred yards from the house. This would enable her to practice her breathing, trigger squeeze, and also build muscle memory.

*****

Liz arrived at the hospital two days after Cat had gotten hurt. She made arrangements to take her classes online while Cat was recuperating. Liz talked Betty into going home for a couple of days. Betty had to talk to the school about Cat's schoolwork and let her boss know when she could go back to work. Her boss told her to take all the time she needed. The school gave her Cat's schoolbooks and a list of assignments. Everyone in town was understanding and supportive. Betty still wanted, and financially needed, to work when Cat returned, but this would be hard for Betty. Her natural, motherly instinct was to hover over Cat. Betty knew this would benefit neither one of them; there was only so much she could or should do for Cat.

*****

Betty walked into Cat's room and said, "Good morning, honey. How are you feeling this morning?"

"Not too bad, waiting on breakfast, if you can call it that. Yesterday I ordered bacon and eggs. I got two measly pieces of bacon, two eggs that were cooked in water, one pat of fake butter, and skim milk. I swear the home ec teacher is the head cook here. I'm gonna starve to death if I don't get some real food soon!"

Betty laughed, "Not everybody eats the way you do."

"I guess. The coffee wasn't bad."

"It shouldn't be too long, and you'll be home."

"I can't wait."

There was a knock on the door. "Food service." A lady walked and said, "Ready for breakfast?"

"Sure am."

The lady set the tray on her table and took the top off. She could tell that Cat was disappointed after she looked at it, "Ain't much there, is there?"

"No, but I guess that will have to do till I get out of here. That is, if I don't starve to death first."

The lady took a tray from the second shelf of her cart and set it on Cat's bedside table, "Maybe this will help. I heard that a young lady was complaining about not getting enough to eat, so I volunteered to take this wing this morning."

Cat took the top off, and sitting on the plate was a sandwich. It had two slices of tomato, two pieces of lettuce, and more pieces of bacon than she could count. Cat looked up. "Wow! That's the way I like it. Is that real mayonnaise?"

"Yes, it is."

"How did you know?"

"That old guy that used to be in my wing told me."

"That must have been Mike."

"Yeah, he stopped by last night and asked me to bring you something you'd like. This was easier than getting you a two-pound steak."

"This is great! Thank you."

"No problem, enjoy."

Cat finished her sandwich and was drinking her coffee when she heard a knock on her opened door. She looked up, and a man standing in the doorway said, "Hi. I'm the hospital chaplain. May I come in?"

"Sure, I ain't going anywhere."

"I'd like to visit with you for a few minutes."

"Might as well sit down, 'cause I like to talk."

The chaplain sat down. "That's fine. I'm not very busy today. I heard that you and a friend of yours were attacked by carjackers."

Cat told the story one more time.

The chaplain asked, "So Mike, is he a relative?"

"No, he's just a good friend. I guess I could call him my coach."

"You're into sports?"

"Yes, long-range shooting. I've been accumulating a lot of gear. That's the reason Mike was buying a trailer. It'll make it a lot easier to haul my gear to the matches."

"How far do you shoot?"

"I really like thousand-yard competitions, but there ain't many ranges set up for that distance. Although more are being built as the sport becomes more popular. I have competed in quite a few three-hundred to six-hundred-yard matches. There's a big competition coming up limited to five hundred shooters. My goal is to compete in that match."

"What else do you like to do?"

"Whenever I get the time and the chance. I like to hunt, fish, trap, and camp."

"I take it you like the outdoors."

"Yep. If I could, I'd live in a cabin and live off the land. That's hard to do in the modern world, but that is my dream someday."

"It doesn't bother you to kill God's creatures just for their skins?"

"Uh, no, why should it? When God gave Adam and Eve the boot from the garden, the Good Book says he clothed them with animal skins, not leaves and twigs."

"Well, yeah, but we live in different time. Things change."

"The world has changed, but God hasn't. He gave man dominion over the animals."

"That still doesn't give man the right to destroy the earth for profit."

"Man is not perfect, but hopefully, we learn from our mistakes."

"The buffalo nearly became extinct because of profit."

"Yes, the start of the industrial age fueled the buffalo kill. The hides were used for belts in the factories. The mind-set of that time didn't think the buffalo would run out. Besides that, how would the west get settled with thirty-five million buffalo roaming around."

"So you think that was right?"

"No, but we learned from that."

"It doesn't seem like it. There are still a lot of animals that face extinction, and industry is destroying the earth."

"With the technology that has been developed in this country, we are able to get what we need with minimal damage to the environment. This would not have been possible without people being rewarded for their work."

"Still it's not fair that some people have a lot more than others."

"Why? Why shouldn't we be able to keep what we make?"

"Jesus said we should take care of the poor."

"Yes, we—not have the government take from the rich and give to the poor."

"You sure have faith in your fellow man."

"I trust my neighbor before I do the government. The government is like Judas. They don't care about the poor. They just want to control the money box. Like Judas, they are thieves."

"I still don't think hunting has a place in today's society."

"If it wouldn't be for the hunters, there would be no wildlife."

"How so?"

"With the self-imposed tax on hunting equipment, firearms, and ammo. Also hunting, fishing licenses, and stamps. This is all used for wildlife habitat."

"What about cutting down all the trees?"

"They don't cut down all the trees. When forests are managed correctly, it benefits wildlife. Some wildlife needs young forests to survive, such as grouse and other ground birds. Take the spotted owl. When the trees are cut down, grass grows and seeds are produced. Seeds feed the mice, mice feed the owl. It is so simple."

"I don't think it's as simple as you think."

"Yes, it is. If you want to save an endangered species, put it on the menu. Don't see any shortages of cattle or chickens, do you/ Want to save something? Put a profit into saving it. No shortage of Christmas trees. Profit is the most efficient method of moving goods and services to where it is most needed."

"Okay, how about we get back to what happened. Were you scared?"

"Well, yeah, I was scared. I was praying that we'd get help."

"So you think praying helps?"

"Well, yeah, if I didn't think it'd help, I wouldn't waste my time praying. The Lord did send someone to help us."

"You believe the Lord sent someone to kill your attackers?"

"The Lord answered my prayer by sending someone to help us, period."

"I have other patients to visit. I've enjoyed talking to you. Good luck in your adventures."

"Thanks, I'll see you later."

As the chaplain left, Betty was coming into the room. The chaplain said to Betty, "Hi, I was just talking to your daughter. She is a very interesting girl, quite opinionated."

"That she is. You should raise her."

"No thanks. I firmly believe the Lord will not give me more than I can handle."

"He must think I'm pretty strong."

"You have a good day."

"Thanks, you too."

Betty asked Cat, "Why is it every new person that meets you tells me that I have an interesting daughter?"

"'Cause you do."

*****

The nurse walked into Cat's room and asked, "How you feeling this morning?"

"Pretty good, but I'll feel a lot better when I get out of here."

"I have some good news."

"I'll get dressed."

"Not so fast. What I was going to tell you is, it looks like two more days."

"Oh."

Dave, Betty, Liz, and Ben walked into the room. Excitedly, Cat said, "Two more days and I'm outta here!"

Betty replied, "That's great."

The nurse said, "Yes, the doctor has ordered an X-ray of her arm and an MRI of her neck and head."

"Another MRI on her head?"

"Yes, he just wants to make sure her head is okay before he releases her. She did get hit pretty hard."

Liz said, "You don't need an MRI. We already know something is wrong with her head."

They all laughed, then Cat said, "Very funny."

Betty replied, "Aw, honey, you know we all love you."

"Yeah, I guess."

Ben said, "I'm gonna get something to eat. Wanna come along, Liz?"

"Sure."

After the nurse left, Betty said to Cat, "Well, that's good news."

"Yes, it is! I'll be glad to get out of here so I can start practicing again. I'm gonna win that competition."

"Whoa! Slow down, girl. Don't overdo it."

"I won't, but I have to get started. Mike already has me entered in the qualification shoots. The first one is just two weeks after I am supposed to get my cast off."

"Can't he change it?"

"No, Mike said that the schedule is filling up fast."

"Just don't hurt yourself."

"I won't. Mike said that he would reduce the loads so I won't hurt my shoulder."

Betty, having no clue what she meant, said, "I just wish you'd give your body time to heal."

"I will."

"That competition is pretty important to you, ain't it?"

"Well, yeah, you just wouldn't believe the money. There has never been this much prize money in a shooting competition, ever."

Betty chuckled, "What you gonna do with all that money?"

"Depending on where I place, I'm gonna pay Liz's school bill, buy Ben a new computer, and pay off you and Dad's bills."

"What about you?"

"Oh, I'm sure Winchester, Remington, Ruger, Savage, or Kimber has something I'd be interested in."

Betty laughed. "I'm sure they do."

"I want to finish my schoolwork so Dad can take it back with him."

"Okay, I'm gonna get me something to eat."

"See you later."

*****

Cat was sitting in her chair doing schoolwork when she heard a knock on the door. As she looked up from her books, she saw black boots so shiny she could see herself in them. Her eyes continued upward. The creases in the pants were sharp enough to cut. The sleeves of his shirt had the same sharp creases with a collar that looked as though it was molded just for him. The front of the shirt was so stiff it looked as though the buttons were glued on instead of holding the shirt closed. The patches and American flag were positioned perfectly. Everything was perfect, not a wrinkle in sight. *It can't be*, she thought to herself. Her eyes wandered over to the name tag; it was him. She looked at his face.

"Officer Shot?"

"Hi, Cat."

"Usually, when I see you, it ain't good news. You don't have any outstanding warrants for me, do you?"

Shot started laughing. "No, I don't."

"You know, I've never really liked you."

"Oh, you've made that clear more than once."

"So then what do I owe this visit to?"

"I heard about an old man and young girl that fought back against some carjackers. I was wondering if it was you. I did some checking, and well, I thought I'd see how you two were doing."

"Broke my right arm, broken rib, a couple cracked ones, and they had to remove my spleen. Besides that, I'm doing okay. Mike has been released. He fared better than me."

"I'm glad you're doing well. What else you been up to?"

"As soon as I get out of here, I'm going to start practicing. I want to enter in a big shooting match."

"The one that the B&C is putting on."

"Yep."

"I admire your determination."

"So what you been up to?"

"I have an office in a small town not far from here. I have my own district, been there for three months."

"You haven't been run out or shot yet?"

Shot chuckled. "No, I haven't. It's been rough since my reputation preceded me. They even had flyers up that said I'd arrest my own mother."

"If she is half as mean as you, you'd need backup."

Shot laughed. "Never have to wonder what you're thinking."

"Nope."

"I learned a lot filling in for Conrad. When that old lady hit me in the head with her handbag, it woke me up."

"Gotta admit it, you fell for that one hook, line, and sinker!"

"At least Widow Johnson got some beef out of the deal."

"Yeah."

"It hasn't been easy, but I am starting to get the trust of the people. It finally hit me the night I caught a guy poaching a deer. He didn't have much, and all he wanted was to feed his family. His pride wouldn't let him ask for help. As I was taking him to jail, it hit me. I ended up taking him home instead, dumped the deer in his driveway, and told him to take care of his family. Ever since then, the people started to be more cooperative. It definitely makes it a lot easier when I need information on serious crimes. Now I'll overlook a game violation any day, if it'll help me keep meth labs out of the county."

"It is always easier to get flies with honey than vinegar. Most of the times treat people right, and they will return the favor."

"Yeah, it took a teenage brat to teach me that."

"I'll take that as a compliment."

"It was meant as one. I have to get going. You take care, and good luck with your shooting."

"Okay, thanks. See you later."

Betty walked into the room and asked, "Was that Officer Shot?"

"Yes."

"What'd he want?"

"He heard about the carjacking and came to see how Mike and I were doing."

"Really, that's strange. All he ever wanted to do was throw you in jail."

"Yeah, he has his own district now. He said he learned a lot filling in for Conrad. He sounds like he really cares about people. Hard to believe he can change."

"People can change. Sometimes they just need a push in the right direction."

"I guess you're right. I hope I get out of here tomorrow. I need to start eating real food and exercising. I'm getting weak just lying here."

"We'll see what the doctor says. The test results should be back soon."

*****

Cat was dressed and ready to go. All they were waiting for was the doctor to talk to them. He finally walked in and asked Cat, "Ready to go?"

"I've been ready for a week."

"Well, everything looks good. Your arm is healing well. Don't take that cast off yourself. Your MRI looks good. Have you had any more headaches?"

"No."

Betty asked, "You telling the truth?"

"Yes, Mom, why would I lie?"

"To get out of here."

The doctor said, "The MRI didn't show any signs that she'd be having any headaches, so all we can do is believe her. Make sure she sees your family doctor. I'll have all the records sent to him. Any questions?"

"No," Cat replied.

"Then you're free to go. A wheelchair will be here in a few minutes."

Dave said, "I'll go get the van."

Cat was wheeled down to the hospital entrance where Dave had parked the van. After they put Cat in the van, Betty said to Ben, "You ride up front with your dad. I wanna sit back here with Cat."

"Sure, I love riding shotgun."

They were finally heading home. Now would come the hard part: getting ready for the competition.

Cat asked, "Mom, have you been keeping up on the news?"

"No, I really haven't had the time, why?"

"Oh, Homeland Security said on the news that there was some chatter picked up over the airwaves but not to worry about it. If we're not to worry about it, why bring it up?"

"It doesn't make sense, but I'm sure they'll find any terrorist cell before they cause any trouble."

"I hope so. I'm getting a little sleepy."

"Go ahead and sleep. I'll wake you up when we get home."

*****

Betty woke Cat as Dave pulled into the driveway. The judge, Conrad, Mike, and Barry were there to greet them. When Dave stopped the van, Ben got out and opened the side door to let Cat out.

Mike said to Cat, "Welcome home."

"Thanks, glad to be home."

Judge Bean said, "Let me help you to the house."

As Cat walked into the house, she saw the treadmill and other excising equipment and asked, "Where did this all come from?"

"You have a lot of friends in this town."

"I guess I do."

Mike said, "Come over here. I have something to show you."

Cat walked over to the shooting bench Mike had set up. She looked at the bench and the target on the shed. "I don't think Mom is going to like me shooting inside the house. Not only that, I'm sure Dad isn't going to like me putting holes in his shed."

Mike laughed. "You're not going to use live ammo. You're going to use a snap cap so that you can work on your breathing, trigger squeeze, and build muscle memory. It's going to be a while before the doctor will let you fire live ammo, even with reduced powder charges."

"This is great! I want to thank everyone. Mom, are you going to fix supper tonight?"

"Sure, honey, what would you like?"

"Fried chicken, mashed potatoes, and gravy made with the chicken drippings."

"Haven't lost your appetite, I see."

"Nope, it'll be good to eat some food that has some taste to it. I think that stuff they tried to pass off as chicken broth at the hospital didn't even have a beak or feet pass through it."

They all laughed. It was sure great to have Cat back home again.

20

The aroma of bacon frying found its way to Cat's room. As she rolled over and realized that she wasn't dreaming, she got out of bed. She got dressed, washed her face, and she walked into the kitchen.

"Good morning, Mom."

"Good morning, honey. Frying bacon works better than an alarm clock for you."

Cat smiled. "Yeah, it does, coffee ready?"

"Yeah, get ya a cup. Breakfast will be ready in a few minutes."

"Thanks, I'll be sitting on the porch till it's ready. Where's Dad and Ben?"

"They went to town, and Liz is visiting some friends. I have to go to work pretty soon. You be okay by yourself?"

"Sure, Mom. I'll be fine."

Cat went out and sat on the porch until Betty told her breakfast was ready. She walked back into the kitchen and sat down.

"Besides the bacon, what's for breakfast?"

"I fried you some eggs and potatoes."

"In the bacon grease?"

"Yep, just the way you like it. Made you some pancakes too."

"Ain't worried about clogging my arteries? I was there when the dietician was talking to you."

"Well, I talked to your doctor, and he said that your blood work was great. I told him, 'If you would see what she eats, you would swear the tests were wrong.' He replied, 'No sense trying to fix something that ain't broke.'"

"I guess I'm one of the lucky ones that can eat what I want."

"Yeah, I guess you are. The doctor said one reason you're so healthy is that you are so active."

"So I just have to burn off all the fuel I eat."

"That's one way to put it. Anyways, I figure if them carjackers couldn't kill you, a little bacon and eggs won't either."

"I didn't realize how much I missed this place. It's great to be home."

"I'm glad you're home. Now enjoy your breakfast."

While Cat ate her breakfast, Betty got ready for work. As Betty was leaving, she asked Cat, "What are you going to do today?"

"Oh, I thought I'd ride my bike to town."

"You think you can ride your bike with your cast?"

"I've been riding it up and down the road the last few days."

"I don't know what I'm gonna do with you, child. You've only been home a week and a half. I was hoping you'd use the treadmill.

"Ain't much you can do. I've been using the treadmill. I just wanted some fresh air."

"Well, I can't keep you tied up. Just be careful."

"Yes, Mom, I'll make sure I have my cell phone with me."

Betty gave Cat a hug. "I'll see you later."

"Bye, Mom."

After Betty left, Cat did her morning exercising routine, took a shower, got dressed, and went outside. She went to the shed and got her bike out. It was so good to be able to get outside in the air. It would take some time before she would be back to the way she was before the attack. Working on the treadmill was helping her physical state. The bike rides did more for her attitude. It was a nice day. The sun was brightly shining, a light breeze blowing. Being outside in always brightened her day. Today was no different.

She rode her bike toward town. She stopped by an old oak tree to rest. The squirrels were chattering. She looked at them. "You're pretty brave now knowing that season ain't in."

The squirrels just kept chattering and eating nuts. One walked toward her with a nut in its mouth, stopping about two feet from her.

Cat said, "Oh, you're really brave."

The squirrel chewed on the nut and then ran up the tree and barked at her before disappearing into its nest. Friend-enemies would probably the best way to describe Cat's relations with the wildlife.

Cat got back on her bike and rode to the town park. She got off her bike and walked over to the first bench she had painted and sat down. *The paint is holding up pretty well.*

She started thinking about when her family first moved here. Her thoughts were interrupted when she felt a newspaper tap her on the head and heard, "What ya doing sitting on my bench, brat?"

Cat turned around, "Hi, Mike. Is your name on it?"

"You should know. You put it there."

"Yeah, I guess I did. Good to see you."

"I'm glad to see you up and around, even if I do have to get my own donut."

"This ain't Saturday."

"I know. I had to stop at the post office and pick up a couple of packages. So how you feeling?"

"Not bad, considering. I've put a few miles on the treadmill. It's helping, but it just ain't the same as being outside. I can't believe how tiring riding my bike can be."

"It's gonna take a bit to get your body back to where it was. I imagine you got a little weak lying in the hospital."

"I know, but I sure tire easy. I haven't said anything to Mom 'cause she is so worried about me."

"That's what mothers do, especially with their baby."

Cat and Mike sat on the bench and talked about everything from the time they met until they got attacked.

Mike said, "You do look a little tired. Let me put your bike in the truck. We can go over to the diner, and I'll buy you a cup of coffee."

"I'll take you up on that. I can let Mom know that you're giving me a ride home."

Mike and Cat walked into the diner and sat down at the counter.

Betty said to Cat, "I see you made it. How you feeling?"

"I'm a little tired. Mike said that he'd buy me a cup of coffee and then take me home."

"You sure you're all right?"

"I'll be okay. I just need some time."

"Well, all right, you have a doctor's appointment next week. We'll see what he has to say."

"Oh, Mom, you worry too much."

"That's what moms do. Mike, thanks for taking her home. Make sure she gets in the house all right."

"Oh, Mom, I'm okay."

"Just the same, we'll talk to the doctor. I want to make sure."

Mike said, "I'll make sure she gets home safe and sound."

*****

Betty took Cat to the doctor for a checkup. After they took an X-ray of her arm, Cat and Betty went back to the room to wait for the doctor. The nurse came in and took Cat's vitals.

"Everything looks good. The doctor will be in shortly."

The doctor came into the room carrying a saw. The nurse followed. Cat started getting excited. Maybe she would get her cast off early. The doctor could tell what she was thinking.

He looked at her. "Now, don't get too excited. I'm gonna put new cast on. By the wear on your cast, I'd say you've been pretty active, which is good."

"Do you have to put another one on? My arm feels fine."

"It still needs a little more time. You break it again now, the healing process will have to start all over. With any luck, the next time I see you, it'll come off for good."

Cat, not being able to hide her disappointment, said, "Okay, I guess. I've waited this long. I can wait a little while longer. Can I start shooting full loads yet?"

"You better wait till you get the cast off. Stick with the rimfire and reduced powder charges for now."

Betty said, "Now, just don't get in too big a hurry. You have plenty of time before the first match."

"But, Mom, I have to start practicing soon."

"Just listen to the doctor."

As they left, the doctor said, "Keep up the good work. I'll see you later."

Cat replied, "I will. Bye."

After they got home, Cat said, "Mom, I'm gonna ride over to Mike's."

"Okay, be careful."

"I will."

Cat rode her bike to Mike's place. She knocked on the door.

Mike, in his usual manner, said, "Come on in."

"Hi, Mike."

"Well, what did the doctor say?"

"I still have to wear this cast. He still doesn't want me to shoot full loads yet."

"That's all right. You've been practicing dry firing."

"It's not the same. I have had my .22 out, but I want to fire the Surgeon."

As Mike opened up a gun case, "In due time... Here, I bought something I think you'll like." He pulled a rifle and handed it to her.

"A .17 rimfire Magnum?"

"Yep, I was down at Crazy Jane's gun shop."

"I bet she likes to see you show up."

"Yeah, I always leave with less money than I show up with."

"When can I shoot it?"

"How about now?"

Cat grinned from ear to ear. "Great!"

"I thought this would be just the ticket for you to practice at a hundred yards till you're able to shoot the Lapua. It'll give you a chance to shoot without the recoil."

"That, or you wanted an excuse to buy another rifle."

"I really don't need an excuse."

"I always wanted one of these for squirrels."

"I suppose I could let you use it for squirrel hunting, as long as you give me some."

"You have a deal."

They went out back and shot. Cat was still keeping them in the 10-ring.

After they were done, Mike asked, "Want me to give you a ride home?"

"No, I'm feeling pretty good. I'll ride my bike."

Cat got on her bike and headed home. As she left, Mike thought to himself, *Maybe this is all she needed... Could be that depression is making her tired.*

*****

It was the end of May. A major milestone in Cat's life had finally come. She was sitting in the school auditorium waiting for her name to be called so that she could receive her diploma. The gown was anything but comfortable. She started to think about the hard road she had taken to get here, especially her senior year. The school had been more than accommodating, letting her do her schoolwork at home while she was recuperating from the attack at the ice cream shop. She had been able to go to school in its last few weeks in session. Not that she wanted to, but she thought she should since she was able to get around. It would be a little hard to explain why she was able to go out hiking and shoot her .22 and not able to get to class. Her thoughts drifted off to the qualification shoots starting soon. As she was dreaming about receiving the first-place trophy, the student sitting next to her nudged her.

"Cat, they called your name."

Cat replied, "Huh?"

"They called your name."

"Oh."

Cat jumped up and walked toward the stage. Upon receiving her diploma and shaking the principal's hand, she walked back to her seat, hoping the rest of the ceremony wouldn't take much longer.

*****

Cat was slowly regaining her strength. Every day she would spend a little more time on the treadmill, ride her bike a little farther. She started hiking some of the trails, which made Betty a little nervous. She even got out her trusty .22 and did some plinking. She was deadly on empty pop cans. Dave would tease her that they didn't weigh as much when he went to sell them at recycling center.

When Mike thought Cat was ready, he had her start shooting the Lapua again. He started her out on reduced powder charges to see how her shoulder would hold up. Everyone could see Cat's spirits lift after she started shooting again. It wasn't long until she was shooting full powder charges. Mike had her practice with both rifles, the one he built for her and the Surgeon. She liked both rifles but knew she had to pick which one would be her spare. She decided to use the Surgeon as primary rifle.

Mike was looking over the dates that he had signed Cat up for. The first qualification was coming up fast. He had sent in the application and check for the Big Shoot. He also sent in the applications and checks for five of the qualification matches.

Mike thought it was time to get Cat to the range to see how she'd do at a thousand yards. He had built some shelves and cabinets in the trailer. This would be a good time to try it out. He drove his truck pulling the trailer over to Cat's house. As he pulled up, Cat, Ben, and Barry came out to meet him.

Mike got out of the truck and said, "Hi, kids, thought we'd get the trailer loaded tonight. That way we can get an early start in the morning. It probably won't be as busy in the mornings."

Ben asked, "How soon we leaving?"

"I want to get started by five. The early bird gets the worm."

Barry replied, "Yeah, but the second mouse gets the cheese."

"Can't argue that."

Ben said, "I'll put the grills and charcoal in now."

Mike asked, "We going to shoot or cook out?"

"Both," replied Cat.

Betty came outside and said to Mike, "You might as well stay for supper, there's plenty. Barry's staying the night, so you won't have to worry about waiting on him."

"Now that sounds good."

"Keep an eye on Cat. I hope she ain't starting too soon. The doctor says she's ready, but I'm not so sure."

"She'll be fine. I'll watch her."

*****

Mike pulled into the parking lot at the range. The range had made some changes since the last time they were there. The office was moved closer to the shooting area. The parking lot was expanded. A picnic area with tables and grills had been built.

Don came out, shook hands with Mike, and said, "Glad to see ya. I thought maybe the girl gave up shooting."

"There's no way she'll give up shooting."

Mike went on to tell Don about the incident with the carjackers.

"Wow! I had heard something on the news. I hadn't realized it was you two."

"That was us. I see you've made a few improvements since we were here last."

"Yes, this place is becoming popular, especially with the qualification shoots starting soon. We want to make this place as family friendly as possible. The picnic area will keep people from eating in the parking lot. It also gives people a place to gather and talk away from the firing line."

"The sport is growing."

"The girl gonna try to qualify?"

"Yeah, that's why we're here… Wanted to get some practice in."

"Send in your paperwork yet?"

"Sent in the $2,000 and have five qualification matches nailed down."

"Have any here?"

"Yeah, her first one is here. I might have jumped the gun. I don't know if she'll be ready."

"She can shoot up to seven."

"I know. Spots are filling up fast."

"Stop by the office. I might be able to get her in for another one. You're allowed two at the same range. Did you get a spot at the B&C?"

"Yeah, I lucked out, five weeks before the match."

"I guess you did. They are going to close the range four weeks before the competition to get ready."

"Are they getting more applications then they expected?"

"I think so. They hired an accounting firm to handle the money and applications. I've heard that more than two thousand shooters have applied and more coming in every day. They're coming from all over the world. I may have to start taking reservations for practice and limit it to two hours."

"It looks like Cat will have her work cut out for her."

"Looks like it. Stop at the office after you're done, and I'll see if I can get her in for another qualification match."

"Okay, thanks."

By the time Mike was done talking, Cat and the boys had everything set up.

Mike walked up to the bench and asked Cat, "Ready?"

"As well as I'll ever be."

"Don said it's gonna be getting busy. Over two thousand have entered so far."

"I guess I had better get started."

Barry said, "I'm ready."

Mike watched as Cat shot. The first group wasn't as tight as she had hoped. Barry entered the results into his computer. It was going to take some time to figure out which loads would work best. By lunchtime they had it narrowed down to three.

Mike walked over to Ben, who was cooking lunch, "Lunch about ready?"

"Yeah, I was just ready to come get ya."

Cat and Barry walked up to the grill.

"Should have known that Cat's nose would smell the food. Hamburgers and hot dogs are done. Chips and drinks are on the table."

After lunch, Cat shot some more. Mike could tell she was getting worn out. He decided to call it a day.

Mike said to Ben, "Get the stuff loaded. I'm gonna talk to Don."

As Mike walked into the office, Don said, "I have some good news. There's an opening for the girl. It's toward the end of the qualification time."

"I'll take it."

"You still want to sign her up for the seventh one?"

"Sure, but that makes two for here."

"Yeah, I know, but there's another range that just got certified."

"Might as well."

"It doesn't make any difference when you shoot. None of the scores are going to be public till the qualification period is over."

"That will make it interesting."

"Yeah, it was a rule that just posted. They figure it'll be fairer that way."

"Makes you do your best, not knowing who you have to beat."

"I'll tell you what… Never seen anything like it."

"Well, thanks. We'll be seeing you. I'll make sure I call to reserve some practice time."

"All right, tell that girl good luck."

After they got home, Cat took a shower and went straight to bed. It was going to be a long road to the championship.

*****

Cat was doing her best to keep up with her practicing. Getting time at the range was becoming harder to do. The participation was more than anyone had expected. Temporary thousand-yard ranges were being set up anyplace that was safe. Between practicing at Mike's and going to the range, there wasn't much time to relax. She knew she had to perform well at her first match and improve from there.

One morning she was sitting on a bench in the town park. This was one of those rare days that she didn't have anywhere she had to be and could relax. She tried to keep it from her mom that she was tired all the time, but she knew she couldn't hide it from her.

She was off in her own world when she heard a voice, "Hey, brat, you sleeping or what?"

"Oh, hi, Mike, no, just thinking."

"You gonna be ready for that first match?"

"I hope so."

"I found out there's gonna be some practice time before the match. Not much, just thirty minutes. I reserved you a spot."

"Thank you."

"You feeling all right?"

"Yeah, I'm fine, just tired and nervous."

"Why you nervous?"

"Found out not only Mom and Dad are going to the first match, but Barry's folks are also driving up to watch."

"Stage fright?"

"I guess."

"Well, you have two days yet. I think it'd be best for you to relax and get some rest."

*****

Mike pulled into Cat's driveway.

Cat walked up to his truck and said, "Good morning Mike."

"Good morning. How are you feeling this morning?"

"Not too bad, I still feel tired."

Betty said, "You shouldn't be tired all the time, especially as young as you are."

"I'm okay, Mom."

"Well, I still think I should take you to the doctor."

"Mom, I'm fine."

Mike said, "Okay, let's get loaded and on the road. We want to get there in time to practice."

They loaded the trailer. Betty and Dave rode with Barry's parents. Cat, Ben, and Barry rode with Mike. The parking lot was over half full when they got there and was filling up fast.

After Mike parked the truck, Cat got out and said, "Wow, sure are a lot of shooters here!"

Mike said, "Put $750,000 up for a prize…what do you expect?"

"Yeah, I guess you're right."

"Now, don't get nervous. Just concentrate on putting holes in the X-ring."

Ben said, "Make sure it's your target."

Cat replied, "Not funny, Ben."

Mike said, "I'm gonna sign you in for practice. You guys get the equipment out."

Cat replied, "Okay."

Ben and Cat got the rifles and the rest of the equipment out of the trailer.

Mike came back and said, "Okay, we can practice on lane 7. Cat, you need to go up and draw for the first relay at nine o'clock."

"Okay."

After Cat was done practicing and waiting for the match to start, Mike walked up.

Cat looked at him. "Any suggestions?"

"Keep them all in the 10-ring with most of them in the X, and make yourself the one to beat."

"Same question, same answer."

"Go get 'em, girl."

Mike went back and took his seat to wait for the match to start. Ben would be spotting for Cat this relay.

Ben looked up at Cat. "You ready?"

Cat looked at the cartridges on her bench, "As ready as I'll ever be."

"I've checked the range. It's a thousand yards."

Cat gave him a puzzled look. "Well, it is a thousand-yard match."

"Yeah, I know, but I'm not taking any chances. I read over the rules, especially the fine print. The paragraph on distance reads, '*Distance: one thousand yards*,' under it in fine print is, '*Give or take a few yards*.'"

"They're covering their butts."

"Yep, have to be careful especially with what's printed on the first page in bold print: *Boon and Crocket's Match, Boon and Crocket's Rules*."

*****

While Barry was getting set up for lunch, his dad came up and asked, "How far are the targets?"

"This match is one thousand yards."

"I don't see the point. It'd be a lot easier to get closer."

"It's the challenge, like me trying to develop an apple to taste like a peach. Just to see if it can be done."

"I guess I see the point. The math involved in shooting that far would be challenging."

"It is. I've really enjoyed perfecting programs to account for wind and bullet drop."

"What are those flags on the range for?"

"Those are wind flags. They let the shooter know the direction and the speed of the wind. Some matches they're not used. That makes it a real challenge."

"Why don't they just use a laser wind indicator?"

"Probably because they're too big and expensive."

"Maybe I should work on that. I need a new hobby."

"I'm sure it'll sell."

"There sure seems to be an interest in shooting."

"It's getting more popular all the time."

"It's pretty expensive, ain't it?"

"It can be."

"Can you win any money at it?"

"Not really, if there are prizes, they're usually pretty small. That is till two guys named Boon and Crocket came along and decided to put on a match with a $750,000 first prize."

"Where did they get all the money?"

"I heard that they made a killing in the Dot Com stocks and wanted to do something that had never been done. So they decided to open a theme park for shooters. They're even building an old west town complete with old-time saloons, hotels, and restaurants. The thousand-yard match is the draw. It is limited to 500 shooters, 490 from the qualification matches and ten from contests sponsored by the firearms industry."

"I bet there will be a lot of people try."

"Yeah, they're coming from all over the world. There's been nothing like this. They have come up with their own rules. They ain't bound by any association. In fact, in their newsletter, it states: *Boon and Crocket's Range, Boon and Crocket's Rules.*"

"You think they'll be fair?"

"Yeah, they hired a panel of seven shooters to oversee the contest from the qualifications to the Big Shoot. Boon and Crocket look over their suggestions before implementing any. The panel will have the final word on any scoring disputes."

"You know, I may have to take vacation time so I can go to the Big Shoot."

"Really? I thought you'd think this was boring."

"It has piqued my interest. The calculations are what interest me the most."

"When we get home, I can show you the program I designed for Cat."

*****

Cat finished her first relay then walked over to the picnic area to get a bite to eat.

Mike came up to her and asked, "How did you do?"

"I kept all my shots on my target."

"That's good, one cross fire and we might as well pack it up and go home."

"Yeah, I know, the scores are going to be tight."

Cat went and shot her second relay then came back to the picnic area to eat lunch and rest. It would be two hours before the third relay. Ben and his parents cleaned up the area and put what they could back into the trailer.

After Cat finished shooting, she went to the range office to get a copy of her score and compare it with her score card. She signed the card. It was put in an envelope, sealed, and put in a locked box. The boxes would be sent to a secured location, and when the qualifications were completed, they would be sent to the B&C range to be tallied. The scores were also entered into a secured website. The shooters would not know where they were placing until the end. It had been a long day. Cat slept most of the way home.

*****

Cat was at the range practicing when Mike came up. "I want you to shoot the rest of the day without using the flags."

"No flags? But it's pretty windy today."

"I know, but you don't know what they might change when you are at the Big Shoot. Use the senses you have. Be aware of your surroundings. Sounds and odors move with the wind. I want you to use the flags less and less."

"Okay, I hope I don't have to shoot without the flags."

Cat shot the rest of the day without using the flags. She was exhausted by the time they got home.

As she walked into the house, Betty said, "Supper will be ready soon. How are you feeling today?"

"I'm fine, just a little tired. I think I'll take a shower and go to bed."

"You've been tired quite a bit the last couple of weeks. I'm gonna make you an appointment with the doctor."

"But, Mom…"

"No buts, I don't want you to get too worn out. You are more prone to sickness with your spleen removed."

"Oh, all right, I ain't gonna win this one."

"No, you're not."

The next morning Betty made an appointment for Cat that afternoon. Cat wasn't too happy but thought she might as well get it over with.

On the way to the doctor's office, Cat asked, "Mom, do you think there's something wrong with me?"

"Oh, I've always thought there was something wrong with you."

Cat smiled, "Now you're sounding like Dad."

"At least I got you to smile. As young as you are, you shouldn't be tired all the time."

Betty and Cat walked into the waiting room. Betty went to the desk to sign in. Cat went over to see if there was a magazine she'd be interested in. There wasn't much to her liking. Then the receptionist said, "Cat, here's something you might like."

Cat walked up to the window. The receptionist handed her a copy of *Long Range Rifles & Optics.*

"This is more like it."

"The doctor thought you'd like it. He got a free subscription for a year."

Cat sat down and started reading it. There was an article about the B&C Shooting Range and the Big Shoot. She was just getting into the article when the nurse called her. Cat and Betty walked into the examining room. The nurse took Cat's vitals then said, "The doctor will be with you pretty soon."

It wasn't too long when the doctor came in and asked, "So, Cat, what brings you here?"

"Mom."

"So you have a drug problem."

Cat gave a puzzled look. "Drug problem?"

"Yeah, your mom drug you here."

Cat smiled as Betty said, "She's just been so tired lately."

"Cat, you been getting plenty of sleep?'

"Yes, but I'm still tired. I've been staying active."

"Well, let me take a look at you." He took her blood pressure, pulse, then listened to her heart and breathing. "Everything sounds good. I can tell you've been staying active."

"Then why am I so tired?"

"There could be several reasons. I want you to go to the lab tomorrow morning after a twelve-hour fast and get a blood test. Then I'll see you next week after I get the results."

"I have to go twelve hours without eating?"

Betty said, "I'm sure you won't starve."

*****

The night before Cat was to go back to the doctor, she was kneeling by her bed, getting ready to pray. Betty was walked past as Cat began to pray. Betty stopped and listened. Dave walked up.

"What are you doing?"

"Listen to this."

Cat folded her hands and started praying. "Okay, Lord, what's up? How much longer till this test is over? I know it probably ain't a test but that you are preparing me for something in the future. I still don't get it. I know you are with me always. Like when I was younger with the broken arm and sprained ankle that took forever to heal, the broken leg and the migraine I thought would never end. I thought things were going pretty good when we moved down here. Then we ran into those guys at the rest area on the way to Camp Perry. I ain't gonna lie. I was scared. Things were going pretty smooth for a while. Well, except when I tried to out drink the local boys. That wasn't my smartest move."

Cat looked around her room then continued, "Then me and Mike get beat up at the ice cream shop, with me getting the worst of it. Not that I wanted Mike to get hurt instead. Oh, you know what I mean. I did appreciate it that you sent Big John to help us out. Sorry, I fibbed when they asked me if I knew him. I just didn't want him to get into trouble. And then I had to take a bunch of blood tests. I get to hear the results tomorrow. Of course, you already know what they are. I hope it ain't serious, and if it is, you'll help me through it. It'd sure be a lot easier for me if you'd just meet me for a cup of coffee and let me know what I'm supposed to do for the week. I know, then you wouldn't be letting me use my free will."

Cat paused and again looked around the room then continued, "I know the Good Book says that you won't give a person more than they can handle. Just to let you know, you're getting pretty close. I ain't no *Job*. Well, I'll let you go. I know you are probably pretty busy with the third rock from the sun. I'll let you get back to blessing those that need blessed and cursing those that need cursed. Talk to you later. Oh, one more thing, I'd sure appreciate it if you'd help me keep it in the 10-ring. I'll work on putting them in the X-ring. Amen." Cat climbed into bed.

Dave said to Betty, "Amazing, she talks to her Heavenly Father the same way she talks to us."

"Do you think that's right?"

"I don't know. Ask the Lord. You already know what Cat's gonna tell you."

"I guess that girl never ceases to surprise me."

"Thank you, Captain Obvious!"

"Good night, dear."

*****

Cat and Betty were sitting in the waiting room reading magazines when the nurse called Cat. Cat and Betty went into the exam room.

As the nurse took Cat's vitals, she asked, "How are you doing today?"

"I've been better."

"Your pulse and blood pressure is good. The doctor will be with you shortly."

"Okay."

The doctor walked in and asked, "How have you been feeling?"

"Still feeling tired."

"Well, I have some good news."

"I'm not gonna die?"

Betty exclaimed, "Cat!"

The doctor laughed a little and said, "No, not for a long while, as long as you don't run into any more carjackers. It looks as though you're just a little low on iron."

Betty sat there shaking her head. She could not understand how people could joke about death the way Cat did, and then the doctor just joined in. *No wonder my hair is turning gray.*

Cat replied, "That's all, I'm low on iron?"

"Yes, I think that's all. The only thing that showed on your blood work was that you're low on iron."

"So what do I have to do?"

"I'm gonna write you a prescription for iron. You should start feeling better soon. Do you take any vitamins?"

"No, I figure I get enough from the food I eat."

Betty said, "You don't exactly eat a balanced diet."

The doctor laughed. "I'd like you to start taking a multivitamin. I have a list of the ones I recommend. Get one that is formulated for active young women. I'll order another blood test in four weeks, and we'll go from there."

"Thanks."

"You like that magazine?"

"Yeah, I do."

"I thought you would. Take it with you. I'll have another issue when you come back."

"Thanks, Doc."

As they walked out of the doctor's office, Betty asked Cat, "You want to stop and get something to eat?"

"Is that a trick question?"

"I'll take that as a yes."

Betty pulled into the parking lot of a family restaurant.

Cat asked, "A sit-down restaurant, not a fast-food joint?"

"Yeah, I figure we can sit and talk while we eat."

"A mother-daughter talk?"

"Well, it's been a while since we've been able to just sit and talk. We've all been pretty busy."

They walked into the restaurant. As the hostess seated them, she asked, "May I get you something to drink?"

Cat answered, "Coffee, black."

Betty said, "I'll have orange juice and a glass of water."

"I'll have a glass of water too."

The hostess brought their drinks and said, "Your server will be with you in a minute."

The waitress came to the table and took their order.

While they were waiting on the food, Cat said, "Okay, Mom, I can tell there's something on your mind. I haven't gotten any more tattoos, haven't been drinking, and I'm not having sex. So now that we have that out of the way, is there something else that you want to talk to me about?"

"Those subjects weren't even on my mind."

"I didn't figure they were, so it should be easier to bring up what you wanted to talk about."

"I was outside your room the other night when you were praying. I didn't mean to, but I eavesdropped."

"Why didn't you knock and come in? We could've prayed together."

"I didn't want to interrupt you. I probably should've just walked by."

"You didn't want to interrupt me, but you hung around to listen? Why, was there something wrong with my prayer?"

"Well, it was just that you asked for help in keeping it in the 10-ring and that you'd work on putting it in the X-ring."

"Well, yeah, I don't expect Him to do it all. What would be the reason to do anything at all if I wanted the Lord to do it all? It would be the same if I expected you and Dad to do everything for me. How would I grow and fend for myself?"

"I know, but praying to be a good shot?"

"Why not? It is a skill I was blessed with. I ask the Lord for most everything. He answers every prayer with no, yes, or not now."

"All right, but blessing those that need it and curse those that need it…"

"What's wrong with that? Jesus cursed the fig tree because it was not bearing fruit. So I figure the Lord can bless or curse anyone or anything he wants to. He has that authority. If I follow his rules, I may be blessed."

"Do you think when bad things happen you are being punished?"

"No, not exactly, sometimes it's to prepare me for trials in the future. It could be because I took a wrong turn somewhere and it's a wakeup call and I had better listen. He is with me no matter what. Sometimes he helps you when you don't even realize it. Like the believer that was caught in the flood. The water started rising. He cried out, 'Lord save me.' A boat came by. He said, 'No, thank you, the Lord will save me.' The water kept rising. Another boat came by, same thing, 'The Lord will save me.' A chopper dropped a ladder. He waved it off. He drowned and went to heaven. He asked the Lord, 'Why did you forsake me?' The Lord answered, 'Forsake you? I sent you two boats and a chopper. What more did you want?'"

"No wonder the chaplain said that I had an interesting daughter."

"Feel better now?"

"Yeah, you do put a different light on things."

21

The end of summer was fast approaching, as was Cat's final qualification match being held at the B&C. Cat would get into the routine of driving around the area outside the range and take notes of what was there. This helped her rely less on the wind flags. The wind would carry odors as strong as a hog or dairy farm or as pleasing as newly mowed hay.

Dave and Betty went to as many of the matches as they could. Cat was amazed at the support the town was giving her. The newspaper had a weekly column on her progress and when and where she would be shooting next. The downside of being a small-town celebrity was the pressure she was putting upon herself. She did not want to let her supporters down. Plans were made that Betty would fly out to visit with Liz before the Big Shoot. Dave, Cat, and Ben would drive to Liz's, then the whole family would go to the Big Shoot.

*****

Cat was lying in bed trying to fall asleep. She had been having trouble sleeping lately.

Betty knocked on Cat's door. "May I come in?"

"Might as well, I can't sleep anyways."

"You're worried about the last match?"

"I guess so. I have a couple scores that ain't that great. I wish I knew where I'm at in the scoring. Boon and Crocket sure ain't making this easy."

"You wouldn't like it easy. You've always liked a challenge."

"I know, but this will make it or break it. Still, I've never been this nervous before."

"Cat, think back. What did you do when you were nervous about a test or special project that was coming due in school? It always helped you."

Cat smiled, went to the kitchen, filled her canteen with water, and grabbed a package of cookies. She went back to her room and picked up her sketchpad and some pencils and put everything in her backpack, went over, and opened her window and started to climb out.

Betty said, "You can just use the door."

"It wouldn't be the same."

Betty laughed. "Okay, I'll see you at breakfast."

Cat finished climbing out the window and hiked to her favorite spot to relax, clear her head, and pray. She sat down between a rock and tree on top of the ridge overlooking the valley. It was a perfect night. Stars sparkled like diamonds in the sky. A couple of does stood in the moonlight munching on grass. The quietness of the night was broken only by a hoot owl and the howling of coyotes in the distance. This would make the does ears perk up. When they satisfied the threat was far enough away, they would go back to eating.

Cat took a drink out of her canteen and ate a couple of cookies. She started drawing a sketch of the deer. *It is so peaceful out here.* This was a place she could get away from everything. She had become so wrapped up in getting to the Big Shoot that she had almost forgotten how to relax. And it was her mom's subtle way that reminded her.

It was morning by the time the deer left. Cat put her stuff back into her backpack and started hiking back home. It was a success. She was feeling much better. When she got home, she climbed back through the window, took a shower, and then walked into the kitchen.

Betty asked, "Feel better?"

"Yes, I do. I don't know what it is, but I always feel better when I've spent some quite time in the woods."

"Probably 'cause that's where you feel most comfortable."

324

"You're probably right. All I know is that now I'm ready for the last match."

"Good. Coffee's ready. Breakfast will be ready in a few minutes."

Cat poured herself a cup of coffee. "How long have you known that I was sneaking out?"

"I had an idea that you weren't staying in your room all night, the morning you came to the breakfast table with pine needles in your hair confirmed it."

"Yeah, I was running late that morning. Why didn't you say anything?"

"You were doing well in school, and I couldn't see fixing something that wasn't broke."

"Thanks, Mom, it really does help me."

"Your dad said that it was cheaper than a psychiatrist."

"That sounds like Dad."

"After breakfast, I have to go to the diner. What are you going to do today?"

"I'm going over to Mike's to practice."

*****

Mike pulled his truck and trailer into Cat's driveway and parked it. Cat and Ben came out to meet him. Mike got out of his truck.

"Ready to go?"

Cat replied, "Yep, soon as we get our stuff loaded."

Ben joined in, "We have to wait on Barry."

Mike asked, "Your mom and dad going?"

"Yeah, Dad wants to check out the old west town. They're going to follow us in the van."

"That's something I want to see. According to the newsletter, it will be ready for the Big Shoot."

Mike and Dave loaded the trailer while they waited on Barry. Barry showed up just as they were finishing up. Dave and Betty got in the van. The rest of them piled into Mike's truck and headed to the B&C.

*****

Mike found a place to park his truck and trailer. Dave parked his van beside Mike's truck. Dave walked up to Mike.

"Well, we've made it."

"If we have time before Cat shoots, let's check out the old west town."

"I'll take Cat to confirm her registration and find out when she shoots."

The B&C looked like a small city with stores, hotels, and gas stations. A tree line separated the modern world from the old west town. The only way to the old west town was by stagecoach. It was like riding back into history.

Mike and Cat came back to the truck.

Ben asked, "How long before she shoots?"

Mike answered, "We have three hours before we can set up."

Dave said, "That should give us some time to check out the town."

"That's what I figure. The stagecoach leaves in fifteen minutes."

"Riding back into history, anybody else wanna go?"

Ben and Barry responded, "Yeah!"

Cat said to Betty, "Mom, you want to go with me? I want to walk around the firing line and see where I'll be shooting."

"You don't want to go to the old west town?"

"Not now. I have to concentrate on getting a good score. I need to know what's around the area and what might affect my shooting."

"Sure, I'll go with you."

"Thanks, if we have time after I shoot, maybe we can go then. I'd like to take a ride on the stagecoach."

It had been a long but good day for Cat. One could not have asked for a better day to shoot. Today's score was her best yet. She knew she had moved up on the list. The question would be, *Was it far enough?* Now would come the waiting. This would be the longest four weeks of her life.

*****

Cat woke up around noon and went over to Mike's. She knocked on the door.

Mike, in his usual manner, said, "Come on in."

Cat walked in. "Hi, Mike."

"Hi, how you feeling?"

"Not too bad."

"Yesterday was a long day."

"You think I'm still in the running?"

"I think so. I've been going over your scores."

"I hope so."

"It won't be long till we find out. You gonna shoot any today?"

"Nah, I think I'll take a break. I thought I'd clean the rifles and help you with the brass."

"At least we'll have time to get caught up on reloading. I have some new loads I'd like you to try out. They're supposed to be accurate to over a mile."

"It's a little late for trying out new loads, ain't it?"

"Yeah, but we don't know what to expect. If there is a shoot-off, they might stretch the distance out. They do have a lane a mile and a half."

"You never know with Boon and Crocket."

"I'll load a few and see how they do. It sure is handy to have all the details in the computer."

"Yeah, as long as it's backed up."

"Don't worry. I have a hard copy, and I'm sure Ben and Barry have copies."

"Yeah, it's on both of their computers, plus an external hard drive."

*****

Cat did her best to keep busy so that she wouldn't dwell on whether or not she qualified. When she wasn't shooting or helping Mike reload, she would be jogging or riding her bike. One afternoon while she was sitting on the porch, the phone rang. She got up and answered, "Hello?"

"Hi, Cat. This is Mike."

"Hi, Mike."

"Hey, I got a letter today from the B&C."

"What's it say? Did I make it?"

"I didn't open it. I'll wait till you come over."

"I'll be right there."

"Okay, see ya in a bit."

Cat hung up the phone and yelled, "Mike got a letter from the B&C. I'm going over to his place now."

Ben said, "Hang on! I'll go with you."

"Hurry up! I ain't waitin'."

They jumped in the van and drove over to Mike's. Cat parked the van and ran toward Mike's house. She knocked on the door, walked into the house, and said, "Where's the letter?"

Mike replied, "Now where did I put that?"

"Come on, Mike."

Mike laughed and handed Cat the letter. She tore the letter open and sat down to read it. Mike watched the excitement and color drain from her face. She laid the letter down on the table and sat there staring at the wall. She could not hide the tear rolling down her face.

Mike picked up the letter. "I take it you didn't make it."

"No, I came in 491st I was beat by one X-ring. It ain't fair. Ten people get to compete in the Big Shoot by writing an essay on shooting. Just because you can write about it don't make you a good shot."

Mike read the letter. "Don't give up yet. It says here that if I wait on the refund till the day of the shoot, you would be next in line if somebody drops out."

"Like that'll happen."

"It ain't over till the fat lady sings."

"Huh?"

"You know, opera."

"What?"

"Never mind. What I mean is, it's not over till it's over."

"Well, I say that it's over. I have two chances to compete now, slim and none."

"You can't give up now while there's still a chance, no matter how slim."

"Oh, all right, I'm going home, see you tomorrow."

"I'll see you tomorrow."

As Cat and Ben walked toward the van, Cat said, "You drive."

"You must be feeling bad letting me drive."

"Just shut up and get me home."

"Okay."

Ben pulled into the driveway. As the van stopped, Cat got out and went into the house. She walked right past her dad and mom, straight to her room, and slammed her door.

As Ben walked into the house, Dave said, "I take it she didn't make it."

"No, she came in 491st."

"That sucks."

"To say the least."

Betty asked, "So she has no chance now?"

"There is a slight chance. If someone drops out, she'd be next in line."

Betty went to Cat's room, knocked on her door, and asked, "Cat, may I come in?"

"Just go away. I don't want to talk to anybody."

"Now, honey, it's not the end of the world."

"Just go away."

"Come on, honey, you'll feel better if you talk about it."

"I don't want to talk."

Dave walked up to Betty. "We have to leave her alone. She'll talk when she's ready."

"But I feel so bad for her."

"Now you know how bullheaded she is. Just let her be."

"But she'll make herself sick."

*****

Mike waited a couple of days then went over to Cat's. He knocked on the door.

Betty answered. "Hi, Mike. Come in."

"Hi. How's Cat doing?"

"She's still in her room…only comes out to eat and go to the bathroom."

"She hasn't left her room?"

"Nope, she said she don't want to talk to anyone."

"I was afraid she'd take it pretty hard."

"It's too bad. She worked so hard."

"Mind if I talk to her?"

"No, go right ahead, if you think it'll do any good."

Mike walked to Cat's door and knocked. "Cat, you gonna stay in your room and wallow in self-pity the rest of your life?"

"Just leave me alone."

"Not a chance, now open the door."

Cat opened the door. "Why don't everybody just leave me alone?"

"'Cause we care about you. Now get ready! You're going to the range!"

"What's the use?"

"The Big Shoot isn't the only dance in town. Now get ready."

"It's the biggest."

"You need to keep practicing. You'll really feel like an idiot if a spot comes open."

"But I've let everyone down. I don't want to show my face in town."

"You want to give up?"

"What's the use?"

Mike walked over to Cat's practice rifle, picked it up, and started walking out.

Cat asked, "What are you doing?"

"If you're gonna give up, I might as well give this to someone that isn't a quitter. I'll take the rifles and equipment to Crazy Jane's and see if she'll sell them for me. I might as well cut my losses. I misjudged you."

Mike's words cut like a knife.

She looked at Mike. "You do have a way with getting my attention. Is there still time to change my mind?"

Mike chuckled, "That's a woman's prerogative."

Cat smiled, "Give me an hour and I'll be ready."

Mike replied, "I'll be back around noon."

Betty asked Mike, "Did I hear right? She's gonna practice today?"

"Yep, I'm gonna be back to pick her up around noon."

"How did you talk her into that?"

"There are two things to get Cat's attention. One is to threaten to take away her rifles…"

"The other?"

"Take away her bacon sandwich."

Betty laughed, "I take it you only had to threaten to take her rifles away."

"Oh yeah, that got her undivided attention!"

"Thanks, Mike."

"You're more than welcome. I don't know what I'd do if she quits shooting."

"Probably go back to being grumpy."

Mike smiled, "Yeah, probably. I'll be back around noon."

Cat was ready and waiting when Mike pulled into the driveway. After Mike parked his truck, Cat walked up and asked, "Not taking the trailer?"

"Nah, thought we'd travel light. I've got your rifle and spotting scope. Thought it'd be good to just shoot for fun today. I called Don and reserved an hour at the range."

Cat climbed into the truck and asked, "Do you think a spot will come open for me at the Big Shoot?"

"Don't know, but there are some lesser competitions coming up after the Big Shoot if you're interested."

"Might as well, as you said, 'the Big Shoot ain't the only dance in town.'"

"That's my girl. I loaded up those rounds that are supposed to be accurate up to a mile and a half. I want you to give them a try."

"So do you want me to continue shooting for me or for you?"

Mike smiled, "You know the answer."

Mike parked his truck and followed Cat to the office. As they walked in, Don said, "Hi, just you two today?"

Mike answered, "Yeah, want to try out some new loads."

"I kind of figured that when you reserved the mile-and-a-half range."

"I'm glad it's finished."

"Well, it's not complete yet, but you can use it."

"Sure, appreciate it."

Don looked at Cat and said, "Sorry to hear you didn't make the Big Shoot."

"Yeah, that was a disappointment, but that isn't the only dance in town."

"You're taking it pretty good."

Mike smiled, "Yeah, she is."

"We are holding a competition here a week after the Big Shoot if you're interested. It's opened to anyone that tried out for the Big Shoot and didn't qualify. It'll be first come, first serve. You're welcome to sign up today."

Mike looked at Cat.

Cat said, "Well, yeah."

Mike and Cat shot for better than an hour. As Mike spotted for Cat, he kept notes of the hits. The rounds performed well at that range.

When they were done, Cat said, "That was fun. I can't believe I was gonna give up."

"You did good. I'll have Barry enter the results in his computer. You never know. You may get a chance to shoot that far."

"I'm glad you talked me out of my slump."

Cat put the rifle and spotting scope in the truck while Mike went to the office and signed out. Mike dropped Cat off at her place and went home.

Cat walked into the house Betty asked, "Have fun?"

"Yes, I did. It was great!"

"I'm glad to see you back to your old self."

"Yeah, me too. I'm gonna take a shower and go to bed."

"Okay, good night, love you."

"Night, love you too."

*****

Mike went to the mailbox; there was a notice that he had to go to town to pick up a letter that needed his signature. *Great, I wonder what this is about.* He got into his truck and drove to the post office. He walked in and showed the notice to the postal worker.

The postal worker said, "Just a minute, Mike. I'll get it for you."

He came back, had Mike sign the receipt, and handed the letter to Mike. Mike opened the letter and read it.

He put it back into the envelope and exclaimed, "I'll be damned!"

The postal worker asked, "Is everything all right?"

"Couldn't be better."

Mike left the post office and went to the diner. He sat up at the counter.

Betty walked up. "Hi, Mike, coffee?"

"Hi, glad you're here. Yeah, I'll take a coffee."

Betty went to get Mike a cup of coffee then said, "You look happy."

"Yep, is Cat home?"

"She's coming to the diner. I told her I'd buy her lunch, well, late lunch. She should be here soon. Why?"

"I have some good news."

"What's that?"

Mike handed the letter to Betty. After Betty read it and handed it back, she said, "Oh, this will make her day!"

Mike was on his third cup of coffee when Cat walked into the diner. She walked up to the counter. "Hi, Mom." Then she sat down beside Mike. "What are you doing here?"

"Oh, I had to stop by the post office, so I thought I'd stop in and get a cup of coffee."

"You think we can go shooting tomorrow?"

"I think we'd better." Mike handed her the letter.

"What's this?"

"Read it."

Cat took the letter out of the envelope and read it. Mike could see her eyes light up the more she read. After she was done, she jumped up, gave Mike a hug, ran around the counter, and gave her mom a hug and exclaimed, "I'm going to the Big Shoot!"

Mike asked, "So you want me to call them and let them know that you'll take that spot?"

"I'd bet that you've already called them."

Mike chuckled, "You think you know me pretty good, don't you? You're right. I've already confirmed it."

"I can't wait to tell Dad, Ben, and Barry."

Betty brought Cat a cup of coffee and refilled Mike's. Cat couldn't believe her luck. She was actually going.

She looked at Mike. "Was there anything in the letter about why and who dropped out?"

"It was on the second page."

"I didn't get past the part that I could compete."

"A Marine that got called back to Iraq to provide sniper support for military convoys." Mike reread the letter then continued, "I didn't notice this before. The Marine is Billy."

"You mean the bully that Barry knocked on his ass?"

"Yep, one and the same. The Marines said that they would let him wait till after the competition. He said no. He didn't want it on his conscience if a fellow Marine was killed while he was competing."

Cat started to feel bad for Billy. She knew that had to be a big disappointment for him. She hadn't heard anything about him since he graduated and went to boot camp. His dad would still come to town every week but mostly kept to himself.

Cat looked at Mike. "I feel kinda bad for Billy."

"Hey, it was his choice, and as a Marine, I know he made the right decision. I would've done the same thing. Now, we had better start practicing."

"I'm gonna win this."

Mike finished his coffee. As he left, he said to Cat, "Tell Ben and Barry I'll be over at eight in the morning to pick you guys up."

"Okay, I will."

Betty said, "I'll call Liz and let her know."

"Okay, we still on for lunch?"

"Yeah, I'll be done here in a few minutes, then we can go."

"I'll take another cup of coffee while I wait."

*****

Cat spent the remaining time before they left for the Big Shoot practicing. Betty flew out to visit with Liz. Mike brought the trailer over to Dave's and helped him hook it up to the van. Dave, Cat, and Ben were going to leave a few days early to pick up Betty and Liz. Mike and Barry would meet them at the B&C. The judge chartered a bus for some of the town's people that were interested in going but didn't want to drive.

The morning Dave, Cat, and Ben were getting ready to leave Mike came over to see them off. Mike walked up to the trailer as Cat was loading the last suitcase.

"Ready to take off?"

"About as ready as I'll ever be. You think I have a chance to win?"

Mike gave Cat a stern look. "Young lady, get rid of that self-doubt, or you won't get past the first relay!"

"Yeah, I guess you're right."

"You guess?"

Cat smiled, "You're right."

Dave, already in the van, said, "You two ready to go?"

Ben and Cat got into the van and replied, "Yep."

Mike waved. "Barry and I will see ya in a few days."

As Dave pulled out of the driveway, he said, "I can't believe we're getting started this early."

Cat replied, "Well, you said you wanted to leave before the sun rose."

"I told you that because I wanted to get out of here before noon. We'll have time to stop for breakfast."

"That sounds good to me."

Dave drove for about an hour then stopped at a restaurant. They all walked in and sat down. The waitress took their order and brought back their coffee. They took their time eating, talking about what lay ahead. Cat was getting excited. The fact that a lot of people from the town were going to be there to watch her made her a little nervous. She was grateful for all the support she was getting from everyone. She had to get rid of the fear that she might let them down.

As Cat was getting her second refill on her coffee, Dave said, "Better take it easy on the coffee."

"It's still a few days till I compete. Besides, this is some good coffee!"

Dave smiled. "Yeah, you're right. I might as well have another cup."

"Can we stop at that rest area I was telling you about?"

"Sure, it'll be a little early for lunch, but we can stop and look around."

After they were back on the road for a couple of hours, he took the exit that went past the dam. He asked Cat, "Is this the road the rest area is on?"

"Yeah, it's not too far. It is on the left side. That way traffic going both ways can use it."

It wasn't very long until Dave saw the exit sign for the rest area. He took the exit behind a truck and car. They were just on the exit ramp when the ground started to shake. The truck ahead of the car stopped suddenly. The car ran into the truck. Dave managed to stop the van before hitting the car. They got out of the van and started walking toward the car. The ground started to shake again. Rocks were falling onto the highway making huge clouds of dust.

Cat asked, "I wonder what that is, an earthquake?"

Dave replied, "Hard telling, but that would be my guess."

Cat and Ben walked up to the car to check on the driver. The airbag had already deflated.

Cat asked the driver, "Are you okay?"

The driver got out of the car and straightened his cowboy hat. As he was fixing his jacket, Cat and Ben noticed his US marshal badge and his handgun. He was a big man. He stood about six feet two and had to weigh at least 260 pounds.

He looked at Cat and Ben and replied, "Just great, the first day of my vacation, I run into the back of a truck, the airbag made me swallow the rest of my cigar, and my brand-new Stetson gets smashed!"

There was another rumble, then a dust cloud. He continued, "Now, it looks like the highway is being blocked by either an earth-quake or explosives, more like explosives."

Dave walked up to Cat, Ben, and the marshal when a phone started ringing. They looked around and saw an emergency phone.

Dave said, "I didn't think those phones had ringers. I thought they were for *call out only.*"

The marshal said, "Not only that, why is it this close to the rest area?"

Cat said, "You might as well answer it. I didn't order pizza."

The marshal walked over, picked up the phone, and said, "Hello."

After listening for a few seconds, the marshal lost all expressions in his face. He started looking around the area, especially the top of the ridges.

Cat said to Ben, "I don't think it's an earthquake."

Dave said, "Me either."

22

Previously at the US marshal's office, the boss opened his office door and yelled, "Skip, get in here."

Skip walked into the office, "What's up?"

"I've been here only six months and am convinced the only reason Noah took that job with Homeland Security was to get away from you."

"What, you don't like my job performance?"

"Do you ever go by *standing operating procedures*?"

"I lost a good partner 'cause he was following the agency's SOPs. I ain't gonna make that mistake. My life, my coworker's life, and the life of innocent people are more important than any regulations."

"You can't just make up your own rules as you go along."

"I don't. I just skip a few."

"Like that suspect you shot at that fast-food restaurant? You shot before you announced that you were law enforcement."

"That's how my partner was killed."

"How did you know he was robbing the place?"

"Oh, I don't know. Maybe cause the girl behind the counter had a scared look on her face and was putting money in a paper bag. I didn't see a McMoney breakfast burrito on the menu."

"Why did you shoot him three times in the chest?"

"Because I couldn't get a clear head shot."

"You have an answer for everything."

"I try to."

"That isn't why I called you in here."

"There's more?"

"Yeah, I have a job for you. You need to pick up some new secure radio and deliver it to one of the Homeland Security offices."

"Why me? I'm starting vacation next week."

"It's a new top-secret portable prototype they want to test. It was designed by some nerdy high school kid. The base radio has been installed for a while. I think it's a lot of science fiction. Supposedly, if anybody comes across the frequency, they will hear country music."

"What's next, flying unicorns doing reconnaissance?"

The boss ignored the comment and handed Skip a copy of the orders. Skip looked at the address of where he was to deliver the radio. "Isn't this where my former boss went?"

"Yep, he requested that you deliver it."

"Why me?"

"That's what I asked. He replied, 'I know he'll get it delivered.'"

"I guess I ain't got a choice."

"No, you don't. Now get out of here. I'm looking forward to you going on vacation."

"Not as much as I am."

Skip walked back to his desk and put a couple cigars into the inside pocket of his jacket and put on his Stetson. As he walked out the door, he said to one of his coworkers, "Anything important, forward them to my cell phone."

After Skip left, a rookie officer asked another officer, "Dan, why is he called Skip?"

Dan laughed and said, "Kevin, it's like this. He has been an US marshal for nearly twenty-five years and has never been one to follow procedures. When he was asked if he read a suspect their rights or announced that he was law enforcement, he would always answer, 'I kinda skipped that part.' So Noah, our former boss, started calling him Skip, and it stuck."

"Noah, was that *his* real name?"

"No, that name was given to him by Skip, and *it* stuck."

"Why Noah?"

"He had to have two of everything. He'd buy a new truck, he'd get two...a new gun, he'd get two."

"Was he married?"

"Yeah, rumor had it that he had a girlfriend also. I know he owned two houses."

"Wow, how could he afford that?"

"The story is that while most young guys spent their money drinking and chasing girls, he bought stock in a computer company. All his friends said he was crazy."

"He may be crazy, but crazy rich."

"Back to Skip. How did he keep from getting fired?"

"Short answer. Criminals hate him and the public love him. Plus, he can get more information from the street than anyone else. He can talk to anyone from the homeless guy and streetwalker to a bank's CEO. He says you just have to speak in a language they understand."

"Did he ever get suspended?"

"More than once, I think he holds the record in the office for having the most suspensions and still have his job. He also has the most awards, commendations, and medals."

"How can he have both?"

"Every time he'd get reprimanded or suspended, the public would support him."

"Sounds like someone I'd like to have on my side."

"If you have time after work, we can stop and have a beer, and I will tell you about a case he and I worked together on about six years ago."

"Sure, I haven't anything planned tonight."

*****

After work Dan and Kevin met at Wings & Suds. They walked in and sat down at a table. The waitress walked up, "Hi, may I get you something to drink?"

Dan replied, "A pitcher and two mugs."

"Anything to eat?"

"Yeah, we'll take the medium wing wheel."

"Sauce?"

Dan, looking at the list of sauces, said, "Let's try the middle five. Oh, and we'll take some ranch and blue cheese."

"Okay, be right back with your beer."

Kevin asked, "What's the wing wheel?"

Dan replied, "It comes out on a platter set up like a wagon wheel. The spokes divide the different wings, and the dressings are in the hub."

"Sounds good."

The waitress brought their beer. As Dan poured the beer, he said, "I worked with Skip on a case involving a serial killer a little over six years ago."

"Was that the one where he would kill the parents and kidnap the daughter?"

"Yeah, that's the one."

"I remember reading about that. That was before I moved here."

"It was on national news."

"The killer would seek out parents that only had one child, a female. He would kill the parents and kidnap the daughter. He would molest, rape, torture, and kill her. After he was done, he would cut the body up and place the pieces around the city."

"I bet that put people on edge."

"Oh, you bet! Defense classes, handgun, and alarm sales went through the roof."

"Was it you and Skip that caught him?"

"We were there. The killer had struck again. Skip was determined to catch him and save the girl this time. The suspect's van had been spotted. The girl had been missing for twenty-four hours. We knew that if the killer kept his schedule, body parts would start showing up in another eighteen."

Kevin filled the beer mugs and said, "There must be something wrong with us if we can drink beer and eat while talking about this."

"No, it's just we've become numb. It's the body's defense mechanism."

"I guess."

Dan took another drink of beer and continued his story…

*****

Noah came out of his office, "Skip, the suspect's van been spotted."

Skip asked, "Where?"

"That abandoned warehouse on the north side of the city. Here's the address. City officers are already there. You and Dan meet them. I've already called the judge for a warrant."

Skip and I met the city officers outside the fence of the warehouse. One of the officers said, "It looks like he drove through a hole he cut in the fence on the back side. A couple teenagers reported it."

"You sure that's the van?"

"Yes, it fits the description right down to the damage to the front right quarter panel."

Skip said, "Okay, let's go."

"You have the warrant?"

"It's on the way. I ain't letting this girl die."

Skip and I then went in the front while the rest of the officers went through the back and side entrances. There was no way anybody could be prepared for what was seen next. The girl was tied to a high-back chair. Her head was duct-taped to the back, her eyes were taped open so that she was unable to move her head or close her eyes. In front of her was a television playing a tape of her best friend getting tortured and raped while he was telling her that she would be next.

Skip threw the suspect face-first against the wall and cuffed him. Skip then turned him around and slammed his back against the wall. In the meantime, I freed the girl. As I was walking her to the door, the girl grabbed a revolver from the holster of a police officer as we were walking past him. She turned toward the suspect, pointed the gun at him, and said, "My turn, *dirt bag.*"

Skip turned around and backed away from the suspect. The weapons that had been pointed at the suspect now were trained on the young girl. The last thing he wanted was this girl getting shot protecting this scum.

Skip said, "All right, everyone, calm down."

He told the officers to stand down. He could tell by the way she was holding the revolver that she had experience in shooting.

He knew she wasn't going to miss. He also knew that if she shot the suspect, it would make a bad situation worse.

Skip walked up to the girl. "Okay, let's think this through."

"I'm gonna kill him."

"I ain't gonna give you any bullshit that you don't want to do that. I know you do. Hell, I'd love to put a bullet between his eyes myself. Will you give me ten minutes?"

"I'm gonna send this scumbag to hell and hope the demons have their way with him." She pulled the hammer back.

Skip knew he had better come up with something pretty quick. He didn't care about the suspect, but he didn't want her to ruin the rest of her life. He did have a fleeting thought of shooting the suspect himself.

The girl said, "Okay, ten minutes."

A little relieved, Skip reached into the inside pocket of his jacket, pulled out a cigar, and bit the end off of it. He pulled out his Zippo to light it. The rest of the officers looked at him in disbelief, as though he had lost his mind. He looked at them and said, "It helps me think. Don't like the smoke, leave." He lit the cigar then said to the girl, "You know, if you send him to hell, you won't see him punished."

The girl started to turn her head, "You have a better idea?"

Skip, as though talking to a new recruit, said, "Never take your eye off your target."

The girl turned her head back toward the suspect.

The suspect, almost crying, asked, "What are you doing?"

Skip looked at him. "Shut up, or I'll put a bullet between your eyes myself."

The girl, not moving her head, asked, "What's your idea?"

"Just hold on a second." Skip walked over to one of the officers. "May I borrow your Taser?"

The officer, wondering what Skip was up to, replied, "Sure."

Skip, with the Taser in hand, walked back to the girl and asked, "You right-handed or left?"

"Right, but I can shoot either hand."

"All right, so that you know that I ain't trying to trick you, I want you to hold the revolver in your left hand and take this Taser in your right."

The girl followed instructions. Skip took the revolver, released the hammer, and put it in his belt. *So far, so good.*

The girl asked, "Now what?"

"This won't kill him, but he'll wish he was dead. It fires like a pistol. Aim for center of mass."

The suspect started to protest, but it did no good. With an evil grin, the girl pulled the trigger. The barbs of the wires struck the suspect in the chest. The suspect fell on the ground, jerking around in uncontrollable spasms.

"Take that, scumbag!"

The suspect quit moving. Skip said to the girl, "If you pull the trigger again, he'll get another shock."

"Oh really?" She pulled the trigger again.

The suspect flopped around on the ground like a fish out of water. After the suspect quit moving, she asked, "One more time?"

"No, better not."

"Oh, okay." She handed the Taser back to Skip.

Skip pulled the wires out of the suspect and handed the Taser back to the police officer. He walked back to the girl, handed the revolver to her, and said, "Give this back to the officer you took it from."

The officers were looking at Skip in disbelief. The girl took the revolver to the officer, handed it back to him, and said, "Sorry."

Skip said to the girl, "We have to take you to the hospital. You want to go in the ambulance, or you want me to take you."

"I'd rather ride with you."

"Dan, take her out to my car and wait for me."

As I walked the girl out of the building, Skip walked up to the officer that the girl had taken the revolver from and handed him six cartridges.

The officer said, "You had me going for a minute."

"I ain't that crazy. I just wanted to see if she would still try to kill him anyway."

"I guess you found out."

The girl and I were standing by Skip's car when he came outside. Skip walked up to me.

"See if you can catch a ride back to the office, and I'll take Sally Jean to the hospital."

The girl replied, "That ain't my name."

Skip ignored her.

I asked, "You want me to write up the report?"

"You do such a good job," he answered.

Then I told him, "I might as well, 'cause I'd have to rewrite yours. The last time you turned one in, HR was all over us."

"I can't help it if they can't handle the truth, to hell with that politically correct shit."

"You know, you're gonna have to get into the twenty-first century."

"No, I don't… Think I'll get suspended?"

"According to the office pool, the odds are two weeks."

"They already have a pool started?"

"It started as soon as you lit your cigar."

"Oh well, I didn't want to burn my vacation time on that fishing trip anyway."

At that, I told him to get the girl to the hospital and I'd see him back at the office.

As I was getting in my car, I heard him say to the girl, "Okay, Sally Jean, get in the car."

As she was getting in Skip's car, she said, "That ain't my name."

Skip didn't say anything. He got in the car and drove to the hospital.

*****

Kevin sat listening intently as Dan relayed the rest of the story as told to him later by Skip.

*****

Skip parked his car in front of the emergency entrance, got out, opened the passenger door, and helped the girl out. As he and the girl walked into the hospital, one of the staff said to Skip, "Hey, you can't leave your car parked there."

"The keys are in it. Move it. Lock the doors and bring me the keys."

The staff member, knowing it would be easier and faster to move the car than to argue with Skip, got in the car and moved it.

Skip took the girl up to the emergency room desk and explained to the receptionist what had happened. While the girl was taken to the ER, Skip walked over to the desk of the nurse who was doing some paperwork.

She looked up, and Skip said, "Hey, good-looking, you busy?"

"Skip, you had better get some glasses."

"Nah, I like women with a little meat on their bones."

"It's more fat than meat."

"Maybe, but it's in all the right places."

"I never have to wonder what's on your mind. What brings you here today?"

"Found that girl that was kidnapped."

"That was her going into the ER?"

"Yep."

"Perp at the morgue?"

"No, he's in lockup."

"Oh well, at least you got him. She looks pretty calm for what she went through."

"Yeah, she's pretty tough. Hey, is my favorite shrink here?"

"He's here. You didn't learn much in your sensitivity class, did ya?"

"Ain't nothing to learn."

"I'll call him and let him know you're here."

"I'll be in the break room getting a cup of what they call coffee."

As Skip was drinking his coffee, the psychiatrist walked in and said, "Hi, Skip."

Skip turned around. "Hey, my favorite head doctor."

"How have you been?"

"Getting by."

"How may I help you?"

Skip explained what had happened and that he wanted him to talk to the girl. Skip liked this doctor even though he didn't care much for psychiatrists. He figured they were just fortune-tellers with a fancy degree. The two had met after Skip's partner was killed. Skip didn't want to go, but it was mandatory. He went to the minimum number of appointments. The only other contact they had with each other was in cases such as this, where Skip thought somebody could use the doctor's help.

After listening to Skip, the psychiatrist said, "That was some interesting therapy. Think you'll get any time off for that?"

"Yeah, probably, since I told her to give him a second jolt."

"I'll talk to her and let you know."

As they were walking toward the examining room, the psychiatrist asked Skip, "Do you think she's suicidal?"

"I don't know." Skip opened up the curtain and asked, "Sally Jean, you don't plan on killing yourself, do ya?"

"Nope, I'm gonna stay around long enough to see that scumbag get what he deserves, and long enough for you to learn my name."

Skip looked at the psychiatrist, "Nah, I don't think so."

"Sometimes I wish all my patients were as forward as you."

"Then you'd be out of a job."

"If you want you can wait in the break room. I'll tell you what I think after I've talked to her." He looked at Skip and said, "You're still running, aren't you?"

"I've told you, I'll handle it my own way."

"Very well, I'll see you in the break room after I've talked to her."

After talking to the girl, the psychiatrist went to the break room and said to Skip, "She's a remarkable girl. Since she wasn't able to close her eyes, she used anger to block the effects of the video. She had only one thing on her mind, and that was to kill her attacker. Since she didn't break down as soon as planned, she was able to delay the inevitable till you got there."

"You think she'll be all right?"

"She should be. She'll never be able to forget what happened to her parents or her. She will be able to deal with it and move on. I am sure she would've shot him if you hadn't intervened. Although unorthodox, your *therapy session* helped her more in a few minutes than I could have done in six months. She was able to release most all her anger at once, without ruining the rest of her life."

"I could see it in her eyes that she was determined to kill him. I couldn't really blame her."

"She told me her name. Do you want to know?"

"Nope."

"You can't keep running. You need to talk about it."

"No, I don't."

"All right, but if you change your mind, call me no matter what time it is."

"There is one more thing."

"Yes, I'll testify at your hearing."

"Read my mind."

"One of the hazards of my job."

"Thanks, Doc, see ya at the hearing."

"Take care."

Skip went back to the office...

*****

As he poured another beer, Kevin asked, "Did Skip get in any trouble?"

Dan replied, "He was suspended right away. They were getting ready to fire him."

"What changed their minds?"

"During the hearing, the psychiatrist for the hospital testified on Skip's behalf. Two court-appointed psychiatrists testified that Skip had helped the girl release her anger and rage without committing murder. It may have been unorthodox, but very effective. Also, the people were behind Skip, and it was an election year."

"Yeah, that wouldn't be a good political move to fire a guy that saved a girl's life."

"Of course, they couldn't let Skip off scot-free, so they gave him a thirty-day suspension. After that, he was given a citation from the city for saving the girl's life."

"What happened to the girl?"

"Skip visited her at the hospital every day while she was there. The court was trying to find a foster home for her. Skip offered to keep her till a home was found. Skip and his wife wanted children but weren't able to have any on their own. They had talked about adoption but never pursued it."

"Did the court let her stay with Skip and his wife?"

"Yes, they did. You could see a change in Skip. He canceled his fishing trip to Canada to spend time with her. During his suspension, he would bring her to the office and let her visit with the other officers. He would even sneak her down to the gun range."

"Sounds like they got along pretty well."

"Oh, they did. Skip's wife got along with her great."

"How long did she stay with them?"

"I think it was a little over three months."

"Skip and his wife fixed up their spare room for her. Skip found her an estate lawyer and a financial adviser to set up a trust fund that the court would approve. There weren't any close next of kin."

"So she was basically alone."

"Yeah, Skip and his wife decided to try and adopt her."

"I take it the adoption fell through."

"Yes, it did."

"What happened?"

"Everything was moving along pretty good. Then one day Skip had taken her to the grocery to pick up a few items. She asked Skip if she could get some snacks. He told her she could. She went over and grabbed six candy bars. Skip looked at her and said, 'Easy, girl. You eat that much candy, it'll make you fat, rot your teeth, and cause your face to break out. You can have two candy bars. You can get a bag of trail mix, and we can get a bag of apples or other fruit.' The girl said in a disappointed tone, 'Oh, all right.'"

Dan poured another beer and continued, "A woman overheard him and said, 'You shouldn't talk to her like that. She'll get an inferiority complex.' Skip answered, 'No, she won't, and besides that, how's she gonna learn if someone don't tell her? Furthermore, it's none of your business.' The woman snapped back, 'I can make it my business.' To which Skip replied, 'Don't make any idle threats. If somebody would've told you this when you were younger, maybe you wouldn't need so much makeup now.' She shouted back, 'You can't talk to me that way.' Skip continued, 'I just did! Now, how about you go to the corner of *Walk* and *Don't Walk* and pound-sand up your high-class ass?' As the woman walked away, she said, 'You haven't heard the last of me.'"

Kevin ordered another pitcher and said, "I take it the woman caused some problems."

"Oh yeah, the woman was from Child Protective Services. She filed an order to get the adoption stopped. Skip talked to a judge friend of his to see what he could do."

"There wasn't anything that could be done?"

"He could have gone to court, but he didn't want to drag her through a hearing. He said she had been through enough. After it was all said and done, Skip wasn't to have any contact with her till she was eighteen."

"What happened to the girl?"

"I don't know for sure. I was there when he brought her to the office to say goodbye to all of us. His wife came by to take her to her new foster home. Skip walked her over to his wife, gave Sally Jean a kiss on the cheek, and said, 'Sally Jean, don't let them liberal ninnies brainwash you. Be all you can be.' She looked up at him with a tear in her eye, 'Okay, I won't, and I'll be the best I can be.' She gave Skip a hug and continued, 'Thank you, I'll never forget you.' Skip looked at her, holding back tears of his own, and said, 'Quit your crying, and get out of here.' Skip turned around and went back to his desk."

"Sounds like Skip took it pretty hard."

"Yeah, and to add insult to injury, his wife divorced him. After that, he buried himself in his work."

"Did his wife blame him for the adoption falling through?"

"That's what we all thought. He didn't say, and we didn't ask."

"I guess that would be a sore subject."

"Yeah, he kept burying himself deeper in his work, hardly taking any time off work. Oh, he might do some Cowboy Action Shooting on a weekend. Other than that, he was either at home or the office. It kind of surprises me that he is taking a two-week vacation. He hasn't done that since the divorce."

Dan and Kevin finished their beer.

Kevin said, "Thanks for the beer and wings. I'll see you tomorrow."

*****

The boss walked out of his office and asked Dan, "Where's Skip?"

"I think he's out by the back door."

"Probably smoking those stinky cigars."

"Don't really know."

Skip was standing by the back door smoking a cigar and drinking a cup of coffee.

His boss walked up. "We don't pay you to drink coffee, smoke cigars, and look at the skirts walking down the alley."

Skip took a sip of coffee, looked at his boss, and said, "You did yesterday."

"Well, when you get done, get to my office. I have that address and orders for that radio. After you get them, I don't want to see your ass till your vacation is over."

"But I still have two days before I'm to leave."

"You can start early. I think I'm gonna enjoy your vacation more than you will."

"Doubt it."

Skip finished his coffee and cigar then went to the office to pick up the orders.

His boss said, "Now get out of here! I don't want to see you a second before your vacation is over."

"No problem." Skip walked out the door.

After picking up the radio, he went home to pack. Two extra days—couldn't beat that.

*****

Skip woke up the next morning and put on a pot of coffee. After he took a shower and got dressed, he fixed himself some breakfast. He went to the door, picked up the paper, and looked at the headline: "*NEW TERROR THREAT.*" Skip took the paper and threw it in the trash without reading any more of it.

I'm on vacation. I ain't got time for this shit.

He sat down and ate his breakfast. He went to the closet, took out his brand-new Stetson, and put it on. After making sure the house was secure, he went to the garage, got in his car, pulled out of the garage, and closed the door. He was finally on his way. It was a long time coming. Nothing was going to spoil it.

Skip drove through town then turned onto the interstate. He set his cruise control on 70 and then took a sip from his coffee mug. He sat his mug back in the cupholder, reached into his inside jacket pocket, pulled out a cigar, and bit the end off. He pulled out his Zippo, lit his cigar, took a puff, and thought, *Won't be long. I'll be in cowboy heaven.*

A couple of years ago, Skip had read about a new shooting range. When he found out that there was also going to be Cowboy Action Shooting, he knew he had to make plans to go when it opened. All his cowboy gear was in the trunk. He was looking forward to sitting at the poker table with a bottle of whiskey, a glass, and a chubby saloon girl standing beside him. He had $10,000 saved up for this occasion.

Skip stopped at a motel for the night. The next morning he drove toward the dam. While he was driving, his thoughts drifted to what it must have been like in the old days. When a man had his horse, saddle, and gun and could work a cattle drive for a few months. Then get paid and spend it all in the town on whiskey, gambling, and saloon girls. *What a life!*

His thoughts were interrupted by a commentator on the radio saying that we needed to understand the terrorists and find out why they hated America. We needed to talk to them and get them to understand our way of life and that we wanted to live in peace.

Skip yelled at the radio, "You moron! I don't give a rat's ass why they hate us! They don't want peace! There should be a price put on their heads! The ones brought in alive should be hung! You can't reason with them idiots!"

Skip turned off the radio, calmed down a little, then thought, *I'm not gonna let any of this spoil my vacation. I'm not gonna think of anything except, cowboy shooting, poker, saloon girls, and drinking whiskey for the next two and a half weeks.*

Skip took the exit to go by the dam. If all went well, he could drop the radio off and still get to the range a few days early. He decided to stop at the rest area and stretch his legs. He took the exit for the rest area. His mind again wandered back to the old west days. A little rumble in the road brought Skip back to reality. He looked over and saw dust rising up where the sides of the mountains were falling onto the highway.

"What the hell?"

By the time he looked ahead, it was too late. A truck had stopped in front of him. He ran into the back of the truck. The airbag deployed, smashing his new Stetson, shoving his cigar halfway down his throat.

A boy and girl came up, opened the door, and said, "Are you okay."

Skip got out of the car, "My cigar got shoved halfway down my throat and my brand-new Stetson is smashed." He straightened out his hat and jacket and continued, "Yeah, I'm just *great*."

23

As the marshal listened to the voice on the phone, he started looking around. Then he said into the phone, "You'd better hope I'm dead, or I will hunt you down and put a bullet in your head." He listened a little more. "You don't want to fuck with me! I'm a direct descendant of Rooster Cogburn, US marshal. I'll hunt you and the rest of your camel breath buddies down and bury you with pig guts!"

After he hung up the phone, Dave, Ben, and Cat looked at the marshal.

Finally, Cat asked, "What was that all about?"

"Some rag head telling me I had better follow his instructions or we'll all drown."

"Where's he at?"

"Probably on top of the mountain somewhere. He told me I have to call him back in three minutes to get instructions, or he'll blow that big pine tree across the road."

Ben asked, "What was that *Rooster Cogburn* comment about."

"Camel breath said Americans always threaten, but always wuss out. They're about to find out."

Cat asked, "What do we do now?"

"Come up with a plan."

"You gonna call them back? It's been close to three minutes."

"Not yet, *always* call a bluff in the firsthand."

There was an explosion. They all turned around and looked back toward the highway. A huge pine tree fell across the highway on top of some cars.

Cat commented, "I guess they ain't bluffing."

"No, guess not. I thought they were talking about that other tree." Skip went to the phone, picked it up, and said, "Hey, camel breath, what the hell you doing? You said three minutes."

"It's been four."

"Just like a goat breeder, can't read a clock."

Cat and Ben moved a little closer so that they could hear the other side of the conversation.

Skip continued, "All right, you got my attention, what's next?"

"Go to the pavilion. Pick up the phone that has an 'out of order' sign on it. I will give you further instructions when you get there."

"How much time you giving me?"

"I give you one hour. We are monitoring all frequencies on radio. Try and talk to Homeland Security, you will drown. You should know by now I am not bluffing."

Skip slammed the phone on the hooks.

Ben asked, "What do we do now?"

Skip replied, "Camel dung says we need to get to the pavilion."

They all looked at the cars and trucks blocking the road, wondering how they were going to get there by not walking. Skip walked up to the truck that he had hit and asked, "Where's the driver?"

Cat replied, "I think that's him talking to the driver of the car ahead of the truck."

Skip walked up to the man. "You the driver of this truck?"

"Yes."

"What's in it?"

"Medical supplies going to the hospital."

"Make yourself useful and see if any of the EMTs can use anything you have. I'm sure there's a need where the rocks fell on the highway."

"I can't open the door. It's locked and sealed. The manifest has to be signed before I open the door."

"Get the manifest, I'll be right back." As the driver went to get the manifest, Skip went to his car and retrieved a pair of bolt cutters. He cut the lock and seal. The door opened. The driver handed him the manifest. Skip took the manifest and wrote on it, "*Opened by US Marshal Skip.*" He handed it back to him and said, "Now, get busy!"

"But I'm blocked in."

Skip shook his head, "Do I have to do everything?"

Skip walked to the cars ahead of the truck and then told everyone to get out and get away from their vehicles. After everyone was cleared out, he got in the truck, pushed the cars out of the way, turned the truck around, and got out, "Think you can handle it from here?"

"Yeah."

Skip walked over to Dave, Ben, and Cat and said, "Now to the pavilion."

Dave replied, "Okay, we'll follow you."

Skip tried to start his car, but it wouldn't start. He yelled, "Now what?"

Ben said, "Might be a safety device, you have the owner's manual?"

"Damn safety devices!" Skip got the manual and handed it to Ben.

Ben looked through the manual, "Here it is, a fuel safety switch in the trunk."

Ben showed it to Skip. Skip opened the trunk moved some of his stuff out of the way and reset the switch. The car started this time.

Skip yelled out his window, "Follow me."

Dave, Ben, and Cat got in the van and followed Skip to the pavilion. It was an eventful trip. Skip pushed a couple of compact cars out of the way. Other times they had to go off the road, but they made it. Dave parked the van and trailer beside the marshal's car. Skip got out and walked over to Dave.

"Didn't have much time for introductions. I'm Skip, US marshal."

"I'm Dave, and these are two of my children, Ben and Cat."

"Well, I had better go into the pavilion and give them rag heads a call. It's been fifty-seven minutes."

"Okay, we'll just wait out here."

Skip walked into the building and found the phone with the *"out of order"* sign on it. He picked up the receiver and said, "Hello."

"Well, rooster, I see you made it on time."

"Yeah, camel breath, now what?"

"Behind the vending machine, you will find a list of our demands. After you read them over, call me back. I will be monitoring the radios, so don't try to talk to any government agency. I will let you know when to talk to them and what to say."

"How much time?"

"You guess." Then the phone went dead.

Skip went over to the vending machine and found an envelope with the list of demands. He opened it and started to read them.

All foreign troops must leave Iraq, Afghanistan, and the rest of the Middle East. Israel must release all Arab prisoners.

*****

While Skip was reading over the demands, Cat went to the trailer and got her spotting scope. While she was setting it up, Ben started scanning the top of the mountains with his binoculars. He noticed something out of place by a group of trees. He looked at Cat.

"Cat, check that spot under that group of trees left of that big rock straight ahead of you."

Cat looked through her spotting scope then exclaimed, "Ben, get my notebook and pencil!"

"What is it?"

"Just get it and hurry up!"

"Okay, okay." Ben went to the trailer, retrieved Cat's notebook and pencil, brought it back.

Cat would look through her spotting scope then write in her notebook. Ben kept asking questions, but Cat just ignored him. Ben tried to see what he could through his binoculars. When Cat was done taking notes, she said to Ben, "We are in a little trouble. I'm gonna take these notes over to the marshal."

Ben looked through the spotting scope. *Uh, more than a little.*

Cat walked up to Skip, who was rummaging through his trunk mumbling to himself and asked, "Looking for something?"

"Trying to find my binoculars, I know I put them in here."

"No need." She handed her notes to Skip.

Skip looked at them and asked, "You sure about this?"

"Yep, you're welcome to look through my spotting scope and see for yourself."

"You a shooter?"

"I like to shoot once in a while."

Skip walked over and looked through Cat's spotting scope. She was right. Through the scope he saw three men of Arab descent and supplies to last for quite a while. There was a generator, computers, and cases of ground to air missiles. They probably controlled the detonation of the explosives from the computers. The whole area had camouflage netting on top so that they would be hidden from the air. Another advantage the terrorists had was that the sides of the mountains were almost straight up, making it difficult to climb.

Skip, Ben, and Cat sat down at a picnic table. Skip showed them the list of demands. "Here's what they want. If they don't get it, they will blow the dam. Who the hell do they think they're trying to fool? They're gonna blow the dam anyhow!"

Cat asked, "So what do we do?"

"I'm gonna need your help. They think they have the winning hand, but they don't know about my hole cards."

"Hole cards?"

"Yeah, you two, I'm sure you've played *smoke the camel jockey* or *drilling for radioactive oil through glass.*"

Cat looked at Ben and said, "Are there games like that?"

"I've never heard of them. When we get out of this mess, I'm talking to Barry about designing some. I'm sure it'll be a great seller."

Skip looked at Ben and Cat. "It doesn't look like I have much choice. Would you two help this old marshal stop these rag heads?"

Ben asked, "Why us? I'm sure there's some law enforcement around here that will help you."

"Yes, I'm sure there is. I'm gonna talk to them to see if they can help keep the people calm. I need you two 'cause you ain't gonna worry about ruining your career. I need somebody that can think outside the box."

Cat said, "Sure, we'll help. How come you keep calling them names? Won't that make them madder?"

"I hope so. It's hard to keep your mind on a plan if you're upset and mad."

"Just let us know what we can do."

"Let's go back over to my car and see if there is anything we can use."

They all walked over to the car. Skip opened the trunk and started moving things around. Cat noticed the cowboy stuff in his trunk and asked, "You into *Cowboy Action Shooting*?"

"Yep, that's where I was headed when this shit started. If they were closer, I'd put a .44-40 slug between their eyes."

"Well, they're not, so you'll have to come up with plan B."

Ben asked, "What's in the box?"

"Some kind of new top-secret radio that's supposed to be impossible to monitor." Skip paused a minute, remembering what the terrorists said about listening to the radios. "You know, I could probably get a hold of Homeland Security, and they wouldn't know. It's probably got some special code."

Cat said, "Ben could probably figure it out."

Skip looked at Ben and said, "I take it you're the geek and she's the shooter."

"Yep, now back to the radio. Did it just come from the manufacturer?"

"I guess, I just followed orders and picked it up."

"We can take it over to the picnic table side of the building, and I can look at it."

"Good idea, don't want them to see what we're doing."

Skip took the box and set it on the table. Ben looked at it.

"What about the lock, seal, and warning stickers?"

"Hang on, I'll be right back with the key." He went to his car, got his bolt cutters, came back, and cut the lock and seal. "See what you can do."

"If they haven't put the access code in yet, it'll be easy."

*****

While Ben was working on the radio, Dave went to the trailer. He sorted out the equipment that he knew that Cat and Ben would need should Skip call on her shooting skills. He put the rifle, range finder, computer, and ammo just inside the trailer door. After that, he started looking around for a place that would be hidden not only from the terrorist but also from the people in the area. The less people knew what was being planned, the better.

Fifty yards from the building was an area where state workers had been cutting down some trees. There were stacks of firewood and two downed trees. The firewood would hide them from the people in the area while the downed trees would hide them from the terrorists. Dave looked the area over. *This should work, at least it would in the movies.*

Skip walked across the median and found a state police officer, "Are there many injuries?"

"Not too bad in this area, further down the highway there are a few more. It's keeping the EMTs busy."

"If you would, see if you can call a few of the officers up here. Be careful what you say on the radio. The terrorists are monitoring them."

"It is terrorists, and you are?"

"Oh yeah, I'm US Marshal Skip."

"I'll see what I can do."

"Okay, I'll be back in ten minutes."

Skip walked around trying to come up with a plan. Was it smart to depend on two teenagers to help him out? Maybe not, but there was something about those two he liked. He walked back to where the state policeman had gathered some other law enforcement together. Skip said to the group, "Hello, I'm US Marshal Skip. In case you're wondering who put me in charge, I did. We have no time for protocol. If someone else wants to take the responsibility, let me know."

The state policeman replied, "Fine with me, just tell us what we're to do."

"Chaos would be an understatement. There are three terrorists on top of the mountain. I have located them, but they don't know it. If the United States doesn't cave to their demands, they will blow the dam and drown everyone. Then they'll blow the side of the mountains to finish us off."

One of the officers asked, "So we shouldn't try and get the people to higher ground?"

"No, not yet. Let's just try and keep them calm. After the situation is evaluated a little more, we'll decide then. What I'd like you all to do is set up some teams and have one of them report to Officer Joe, and he can report to me."

"That's not my name."

Skip ignored him and continued, "I'm gonna trust your judgment on the best way to handle the crowd. The radios are being monitored so watch what you say on them. Keep your eyes open. I'll be back for an update. Do not mention terrorists. I don't want a panic if we can help it. To the leaders of the teams, follow your gut. We don't have time for you to get permission for everything. So don't bother me or Officer Joe with what you can handle yourselves. Although be sure to report anything that is suspicious. I'll be back in thirty minutes."

The group of police officers went to set up teams, and Skip walked back to the pavilion. He walked up to Ben and asked, "Any luck with the radio?"

"Yeah, it was so simple that Dad could've figured it out. There was even a power cord that we can hook up to the car battery."

"Good, I wanna talk to someone on the outside before I call camel dung back."

"Just punch in 1, 2, 3, and 4 on the keypad twice and you're good to go."

Skip put on the headphones, punched in the numbers, and pressed the mic key. "Anybody monitoring this channel?" He didn't hear anything, so he yelled, "Anybody out there?"

Ben walked over. "You might want to plug in the headset."

Skip looked at Ben and plugged in the headset. Ben walked away shaking his head.

Skip keyed the mic again. "Anybody monitoring this channel?"

A voice came back and said, "Sir, this channel is for authorized use only. Please give me your security code."

"Ain't got none. Is this Homeland Security?"

"Sir, I need your code, or you must get off this channel."

"I told you, I ain't got none."

"You must cease talking on this channel."

"Hey, bonehead, is there anybody on that end that has any authority or just a bunch of college-educated idiots that don't understand when I say I ain't got no security code? Now let me talk to someone above your pay grade, or I'll reach through this radio, grab you by the throat, and shut off your air!"

Another voice came over the radio. "Skip, is that you?"

"Yeah, is this Noah? Maybe you'll listen."

"I take a job to get away from you, and you keep showing up like a bad cold."

"Don't blame me. You requested I deliver this radio."

"Deliver it, not use it. Didn't you see the warning stickers?"

"Yeah, but I skipped reading them."

"Well, I have bigger problem. An explosion has blocked the highway below the dam."

"No shit, I'm right in the middle of it."

"Should have known where there's trouble, you're in the middle of it. Why didn't you just use your radio?'

"'Cause three rag-heads are on the mountaintop and have all the radio channels bugged."

"I see you skipped your sensitivity training again."

"Oh, I went, but I didn't listen to them idiots. I really don't care if I hurt people's feelings. They'll have to get over it. This is the real world!"

"Well, since you're there, what's going on?"

Skip told Noah everything he knew and what he expected to happen.

Noah replied, "I expected as much. We've been picking up some radio chatter lately. I'm gonna order a drone to fly over and take some pictures."

"Can't you get some from the satellite?"

"Now, you know we can't use them on US soil. We couldn't see anything out of the ordinary."

"They have camouflage netting over the area."

"It must be good for the satellite to miss it, but they can't hide from infrared."

"Okay, I'll get back with you after I call camel dung and find out when I'm supposed to tell you their demands."

"Still using your piss-off-your-opponent technique?"

"Ain't failed me yet."

"Maybe not, but it makes me nervous. How did the terrorists contact you?"

"You wouldn't believe me if I told you." About that time, a news helicopter started flying around the area. "Hey, there's a news chopper in the area! Why didn't you send out a no-fly order?"

"I did, but the powers to be canceled it because they didn't want the public to think this could be an attack."

Skip looked up in time to see a rocket trail, and then the helicopter blew up. "Well, the public won't have any doubts now. The rag heads just blew up the chopper!"

"I just received word there has been a no-fly order issued."

"Close the barn door after the horse gets out! I have to go. Camel dung is waiting on me."

"Keep me informed."

"If I have time."

"Skip?"

Skip turned off the radio and walked into the pavilion. He picked up the receiver of the phone and said, "What the hell was that, goat breath?"

"Just to let you know who's in charge. Did you read over our demands?"

"Yeah, you must be drinking goat piss. Ain't no way they're gonna agree to that."

"Well, you had better convince them."

"Like they won't figure out where that rocket came from?"

"You think we're stupid enough to fire from our position. Now go tell your superiors what we want, and you had better be convincing. Remember, I can hear the whole conversation.

Skip thought for a second, *That's right. It didn't come from the mountaintop, it means there's another terrorist down here somewhere. This is going to be a challenge. The good news, they don't know we have them located.* As he walked toward his car to call Homeland Security to relay the demands, he passed Ben and said, "There's terrorist down here too. I need to talk to you and that girl when I get back."

"You mean my sister?"

Skip didn't answer as he continued to the car. After he was done relaying the message to Homeland Security, he went over to Ben and Cat and said, "Let's go sit at the table."

As they did so, Dave came up and asked, "Did that chopper get blown out of the sky?"

Skip replied, "Yes, that means there's at least one more terrorist down here. I need to go talk to Officer Joe and tell him. I think it came from somewhere on the opposite side. While I'm gone, glass the area and see if you can see anything suspicious. My guess is, it'll be a big car or a truck, something large enough to hide handheld rockets."

Cat replied, "Is there anything else we can do?"

Skip sarcastically replied, "Yeah, come up with a plan to put camel breath and company out of commission."

"Okay."

Ben stood up, thinking, *I hope the marshal is prepared for our plan.*

*****

Back at Mike's place, Mike and Barry were looking over Cat's scores and going over the computer programs.

Barry asked Mike, "Think Cat has a chance to win?"

"Just as good a chance as the other 499 shooters."

"Can't wait to get there."

"It won't be long. We'll be leaving the day after tomorrow."

"I hope my dad and mom can make it for at least part of the match."

Their attention was drawn to the TV when they heard, "We interrupt this program to report an explosion on Falling Rock Ridge. Now this is from our eye in the sky."

Mike and Barry watched the video. There were wrecked cars and trucks along the road. The sides of the mountains had fallen onto the highway. It was blocked by debris of the explosion. The low end of the highway was filled in; nothing would be able to get through for quite a while. Then the screen went blank.

The announcer came back on and said, "This is just devastating news. It is being reported that our chopper has crashed."

Mike said to Barry, "Crashed my ass, it was shot down."

"You sure?"

"Yes, I'm sure, and they're right in the middle of it."

"If they didn't stop to eat, they should have been through before it happened."

Mike gave Barry one of his looks. "Cat, not stopping to eat?"

"You're right, ain't no way. What do you think, a terrorist attack?"

"More than likely. That's what happens when you don't finish a job. Iraq and Afghanistan shouldn't even be on the map now. Just like Nam, politicians trying to run a war when it should be left to the generals. We wouldn't have half our problems if we'd fight to win, but no, we have to think of their feelings."

"You think Cat will be all right?"

"You know her as well as I do. If there's a way out, she'll find it."

"Ain't much that can stop her?"

"Except maybe an all you can eat buffet."

They both started to laugh then they came back to reality.

Mike said, "Go home and pack, we'll leave tomorrow."

"Okay."

Barry went home to pack. Mike sat in his chair, hoping and praying that Cat and her family would make it out alive.

*****

Cat and Ben went to the trailer to sort out the equipment they would need. As Cat walked around to the rear door, she said "Dad, what are you doing?"

"Well, I didn't have much to do so, I thought I'd get your shooting stuff set out."

"Did the marshal talk to you?"

"No."

Ben said, "Skip told us to come up with a plan to put those guys out of business."

"He probably has no idea what he asked."

"I know he didn't."

Cat commented, "Marshal *Skip* is going to be surprised."

Ben said, "I'll take the laptop and range finder."

"We already have the spotting scope, but we're gonna need a better place to hide."

Dave responded, "I found a place fifty yards south of the pavilion. There are two fallen trees to hide you from the terrorist and stacks of firewood to hide you from the people down here."

"Speaking of people, there aren't many around this end of the park."

"The marshal put this pavilion off limits. He has two guards telling them they have to use the other pavilions."

Ben said to Cat, "Okay, have the laptop and range finder, get your rifle and ammo."

Cat picked up her rifle, looked at the ammo, then said, "I don't know which ammo to use. I've always known where I was going to shoot. Sometimes I have days to plan. Plus, it has always been on level ground."

"Dad, bring a box of each. After we get set up, I'll figure out the range and angle. I'll punch the numbers in the laptop and see what I come up with."

Ben could see that Cat still had a worried look on her face. He looked at her and said, "Don't worry, the program Barry designed takes everything into account, including the temperature, humidity, altitude, and even the rotation of the earth."

"How you gonna find the altitude?"

"He loaded a TOPO map in the laptop. You worry about your trigger squeeze. Me and the laptop will take care of the rest."

"Okay, if you say so."

*****

Cat and Ben followed Dave to the place he had found for them to set up. Dave and Ben rolled two eighteen-inch-diameter-by-sixteen-inch-long pieces of wood over to the trees and set them upright. It made a solid shooting table. Cat broke off some of the branches to be able to get a clear line of sight and put her shooting pad on the wood. She took her rifle out of the case and attached the bipod. Ben sat up the range finder and spotting scope. Cat put the rifle on the shooting pad. As she looked through the scope, she thought *I could use a couple of sandbags.* She turned around, and Dave handed her two sand bags.

Cat smiled, "You read my mind."

"No, I've just been around you long enough to know what you need."

She smiled, "Thanks, Dad."

Ben asked, "You set up?"

"Just about."

Ben looked through the spotting scope and said, "They're out."

Cat looked through her scope. It really looked different seeing a human in the crosshairs. She had shot plenty of animals and targets, but this was going to be different. She stepped back, looked at the rifle, and sat down on a log. *Will I be able to do this?* Her thoughts were interrupted when Ben said, "It shouldn't take too long to figure this out. Barry may go overboard with his programs, but it's sure coming in handy now."

Ben looked at Cat. "What's wrong?"

"I don't know if I can do this. I've shot plenty of animals, but lining up a human in the crosshairs, I've never done that before. The closest I've ever been was when I saved the warden. That was different. The decision had to be made quick. This time it is being planned, more like a murder than defense."

Ben realized that Cat would have to turn stone cold. This would be very foreign to Cat, who was always one to help people. Ben looked Cat in the eye. "Cat, you will be defending more than yourself. Think of all the people who don't know it but are depending on you. Now, you can do this."

"I still don't know. What if I fail?"

"You have to try. What do you always do when you have big problems?"

Cat's expression changed. She smiled a little. "Ben, go get my life manual."

"Life manual, which one is that?"

"My Bible."

"Oh, that one, okay."

Ben went to the van, retrieved Cat's Bible, and brought it back to her. As he handed it to her, he asked, "What do you want me to do?"

"While I'm talking to the Man upstairs, you watch them and write down their routine and movements."

"All right, I'll do that."

Cat took her Bible and sat down by a tree. She opened her Bible then looked up and said, "Okay, Lord, you know you are getting pretty close to what I can't handle. I don't get it. You sent Billy over to Iraq. He should be the one here. He's trained to do this."

Cat started reading about when young David went up against Goliath with no more than a sling and five smooth stones. She read about other battles where the Israelites were outnumbered. As long as they trusted the Lord and followed his instructions, they were victorious. One thing bothering Cat was that she was becoming angry at the terrorists. She feared this might not sit too well with the Lord. She recalled the verse: "*Vengeance is mine says the Lord.*" She looked in the New Testament and found where the Lord said, "*Be angry, but sin not.*"

Cat closed her eyes and thought about that verse for a moment. She opened her eyes. *I guess the Lord was angry when he turned the money changers tables over in the Temple.*

Cat walked over to her rifle, looked at it, and said, "All right, Lord, I'll do this. As I've said before, I can get them in the 10-ring. I'm gonna need a little help getting them in the X-ring. All three shots have to be perfect. You know, you're really pushing the envelope."

Ben walked over to Cat, "You got it figured out?"

"Yeah, I have to do this if I'm asked."

"Okay, I've written down the calculations. Here's the ammo you'll need."

368

"I haven't shot that ammo much."

"You haven't shot at these ranges much either. According to the laptop, this is our best chance."

"All right, you have my snap cap?"

"It's in the ammo box. You need it?"

"Yes, I have to get my timing down."

Ben got the snap cap and handed it to Cat. Cat put it in the rifle and closed the bolt. She lined the crosshairs on one of the terrorists and squeezed the trigger. She looked at Ben and said, "While I'm practicing and praying, go ahead and tell the marshal our plan."

"Okay."

*****

Skip walked up to Officer *Joe* and said, "Anything to report?"

"Yes, there is. I'll let the deputy tell you."

Skip looked at the deputy. "What do you have?"

"I was checking vehicles to see if anyone needed help. I walked up to a truck. The driver just sat there. I tried to wake him but couldn't. I checked him out, he was dead. His neck had been broken. I put his hat back on him and took a look at the cargo. There were a few cases of medical supplies in the back. I moved some of them and saw a big bomb in front. I found the detonator. It had a green light on."

"Anything else?"

"Yes, I found a fired handheld rocket launcher under the truck."

"Have you told anyone about this?"

"The only other person that knows is my partner. He is keeping people away from it."

"Looks like camel breath and company have a backup plan. The question is, did he get killed by his own or do we have someone helping us?"

"What do you want us to do?"

"Keep an eye on the truck. See if you can get some big trucks to park next to it. That should help contain the blast. Keep an eye on that detonator. The green light means it's armed. Did you see a timer?"

"Yes, it was reading three minutes."

"When the red light comes on, the timer will probably start. I don't suppose there's a bomb tech anywhere close."

"I'll check around."

"Okay, I'll talk to you later."

*****

As Skip was walking back to the pavilion, he thought, *I ran into a truck loaded with a bomb. What a vacation!* He saw Ben and asked him, "Well, did you two come up with a plan?"

"Yeah, we have. Cat has her rifle set up over there by the firewood behind those downed trees. It is a good hide. I have the spotting scope, range finder, and my laptop next to the rifle. It'll be a difficult shot. The distance is a 1,740-yard line of sight. The horizontal distance is 1,570 yards.

Skip stared as Ben continued, "I have been watching their movements. They do have a routine. About every thirty minutes, all three of them will stand together, and the one in the middle has binoculars, and they all look this way. There is a phone on some kind of stand beside them. It is probably the one they use to talk to you. The next time you talk to them, I want to watch them and see if they all stand still. The way I have it figured, if you can get them to stand long enough, Cat can take out the one on the left, then the one on the right. Hopefully, the one in the center will be confused long enough for the third bullet to hit its mark."

Skip stood there stunned for a moment, not expecting anything like this from someone so young. After trying to process everything that was told to him, he said, "You telling me that young girl has the skill and ability to take out all three rag heads at that distance?"

"Yes, she has."

"What kind of rifle does she have?"

"A Surgeon chambered in .338 Lapua with a SN-3 T-Pal scope."

Skip took out a cigar, bit the end off, and lit it with his Zippo, and said, "That's an AT&T rifle."

"AT&T rifle?"

"Yeah, one that will reach out and touch someone."

"Yeah, it will."

"You think she can hit all three of them?"

"I know she can."

"Okay then, what do we do next?"

Cat walked up in time to hear the end of the conversation. Ben started to answer, but Cat interrupted him.

"David was only a young boy when he sent Goliath to the other side and was ready to send his brothers along. What do you mean what are we going to do next? You put yourself in charge. We did what you asked. It's up to you to do the rest of the planning, *Marshal*, or do you just play one on TV?"

"Well, *girly*, I'll have to think about this."

"Girly? Don't take too much time, *Marshal*, or we'll all be dead, and I plan on winning that competition when we get out of here."

Dave came up, put his hand on Cat's shoulder, moved her to the side, and said, "Easy Cat, he's on our side. You need to hold your temper."

"I know, but he called me girly."

"I know. I'm glad you didn't punch him."

Cat laughed, "You're right, Dad."

Skip asked Ben, "You think she can pull this off?"

"With the computer program we have, I'd rather be down here than up on the mountain, much safer."

Cat walked up to Skip. "Sorry, I lost my temper. I'm going back to my rifle to practice dry-firing to get my timing right and pray. Just let me know what you want me to do."

"Praying, you think that helps?"

"I wouldn't waste my time if it didn't help."

*****

Skip sat down and thought, *At least my vacation isn't boring. Now, do I follow my gut and let that girl shoot them rag heads? How do I explain this to Noah?*

Skip's thoughts were interrupted when Ben walked up to him and asked, "How soon are you gonna call them back?"

"I'm getting ready to do that now."

"Give me time to get to the hide. I want to see what they do while you're talking to them."

"Okay."

Skip waited a couple of minutes then went inside the building, picked up the phone, and said, "Goat breath, the government is working on your demands."

"I know, we are listening to your conversations."

"Yeah, yeah, how do you plan on drowning us?"

"How do you think? We are going to blow the dam, and all you infidels will die."

"It ain't over yet."

"It will be if our demands are not met soon."

The phone went dead. Skip looked at the phone. "That goat-breeding bastard hung up on me."

Ben walked toward the pavilion and met Skip. "That was great. While you were talking to them, they all just stood there looking toward us. Another good thing is, they put up an Al-Qaeda flag. The flag and that big oak tree seven hundred yards out will help us judge the wind. All you have to do is keep them busy long enough for Cat to take them out."

"I should be able to do that. I have to give Noah a call."

"Okay, I'm gonna go back and watch them some more."

Skip walked back to the radio. He sat down thinking about what he was going to tell Noah.

Dave walked up and said, "Find out anything?"

"Yeah, they plan on blowing the dam and drowning us. They must have someone working at the dam."

"So if Cat shoots those three, we still have to worry about the dam anyway?"

"Yeah, I'll have to tell Noah to see if he can find out anything. Say, you think your daughter can really take them three out?"

"I'd rather be behind her than in front of her."

"That's what your boy said."

"He would know. She shot his new hunting knife off his belt once."

"What'd he do to piss her off?"

"Put a piece of black tape over her scope so he could get the first squirrel."

"Sounds like someone I want on my side."

"Not a good idea to cross her. She punched a boy for calling her a four-eyed girly-girl."

"Well, I had better give Noah a call."

"All right, I'll go check on the kids."

Dave went to the hideout while Skip went to the radio, picked up the mic, and said, "Noah, you there?"

"Still ain't learned proper protocol?"

"What for? I ain't even supposed to be using this radio. Have any news for me?"

"News for you? I was hoping you could tell me something."

"It's pretty simple, some Middle Eastern rag head group plan on blowing the dam. I'm working on a plan. I'll let you know when I have it done. I need to know if anything is going on at the dam."

"Should have known…" Noah was handed a paper. He looked at it then continued, "Skip, I'll get back to you." The radio went dead.

Skip looked at the radio. "What the hell is this? 'Hang Up on Skip' Day?"

Ben walked up. "How's it going?"

"Like clockwork, a broken clock. First camel dung hangs up on me, then Noah cuts me off in midsentence. How's it going with you two?"

"I've been watching them, and Cat has been practicing. She has her timing down pretty good. She has the elevation set on her scope. All we will have to do is adjust the windage. Just give us the green light, and she'll send them to meet their virgins."

"All right, keep up the good work. I still have to find out how they plan on blowing the dam. If they plan on detonating the explosives from the mountaintop, I'm sure they have a backup plan."

"Hey, there's a red light on the radio."

Skip walked to the radio, keyed the mic, and said, "You want to tell me what was so important that you cut me off?"

"I just got some info that should have been here weeks ago."

"What's that?"

"You were right. They do, or did, have someone inside the power plant."

"A lady came into the sheriff's office to ID her nephew, who was found in a truck at the bottom of the lake. She gave them a box of papers, pictures, and a flash drive. The idiots put it on top of a box that the guy's girlfriend brought in two days after he went missing. They never even opened the box. A cleaning crew found them yesterday. The boxes have the same information in them."

"They have someone at the dam?"

"Yeah, this guy was on to something according to the pictures and notes. The dam has explosives in an old maintenance tunnel. Both sides of the highway are lined with explosives."

"We found a truck bomb on the east side of the highway with the driver's neck broken. Don't know if any more terrorists are down here."

"Someone helping us, or did they kill their own?"

"The deputy that told me about it said it looked like the work of someone with military training."

"Hope it was our side."

"I have a plan to take out the three on the mountaintop."

"I don't want to know the details. Don't do anything till I get back with you. I want to get a team in the power plant in case they have a fail-safe plan. I've already sent an agent to the phone company to ride with a repair vehicle to see if there are any unusual phone lines around the power plant."

"All right, let me know when you're ready."

Dave walked up to Skip. "The kids seem to be doing okay. Have you found out anything else?"

"Yes, I did." Skip told Dave what Noah had told him.

"Sounds like it was well planned."

"Yeah, I have to wait on Noah to get back with me."

*****

The light on the radio came on. Skip picked up the mic and said, "Yeah, Noah?"

"I just got word back from the agent from the power plant. They found wires coming from the maintenance tunnel to the poles that carry power across the mountain. They do have a hard wire to the explosives, so blocking radio frequencies won't work."

"Can you just cut the wires?"

"Can't do that 'cause that will let them know we're on to their plan. I still think there's a suicide bomber in the plant. If need be, are you sure you have the ability to neutralize the three on the mountain?"

Skip thought for a second. "Yes."

"Okay, I'll get back with you."

Noah was looking over the information coming in from the sheriff's office and the agent from the power plant. With that information and what Skip was telling him, he knew he had no choice. He looked up and said, "Lieutenant, activate the Team."

"The Team? The only difference between them and a bunch of outlaws is they're on our side."

Noah didn't say a word. He just gave the lieutenant an *"I'm in charge"* look.

The lieutenant said, "Yes, sir."

24

Jack was sitting on his porch smoking a cigar and sipping some 80-proof. He looked over at his pet bear. "Jake, this is the life, out here in the middle of nowhere. There's nothing like having a smoke and a drink after a breakfast of venison steak and eggs."

Jake looked up from his half eaten catfish and nodded.

Jack had been working on his cabin for a few years. It was finally finished. He planned to retire in six months. He had been divorced for ten years. Jack loved his wife and their twin boys, probably more than anyone knew, but his wife couldn't handle Jack going on missions, all the time worrying if he'd come back alive. The excitement of fighting the enemy under the radar kept pulling him away from his family. He had fought enemies in places that people never heard of. He always told himself that he was doing it to make the country safer for future generations, but now he was ready to retire. His investments would provide him a monthly income to live on. Jake would keep him company.

Jack found Jake one night when he was a cub, along a highway, lying beside his dead mother who had gotten hit by a vehicle. Jack walked up to the cub, and the cub looked up at him with those "*Help me*" eyes. Jack was always a sucker for kids and animals.

Jack said to the cub as though he could understand English, "Look, kid, your mother's dead. You might as well stay with me a day or two."

The cub followed Jack back to his pickup. Jack opened up the door, and the cub jumped in and sat in the seat as a person would. The bear had been with Jack ever since.

Jack took another sip of his bourbon, and his secure cell phone rang. He answered it, "No."

"You ain't retired yet."

"What's up? Someone need killing, where and what country?"

"It's a domestic job."

"I ain't doing a job on US soil. Not after the FBI made me their scapegoat after that failed mission. It wouldn't have failed if I'd done it my way."

"Jack, we need the power plant and dam secured, or terrorists are going to blow the dam and drown several innocent people. There are no rules of engagement. I told them you would do it, no other way."

"I guess I have no choice."

"Get your team together. The details are on the way to your secure fax."

"All right, you know how to ruin my day."

"You weren't doing anything besides drinking bourbon and talking to that fur ball."

"See ya."

Jack sent a code to his men of where to meet. Then he went inside to his fax machine and waited for the orders and details. After he looked them over, he went to his file cabinet, pulled out three folders, and sat them on his desk. Jake sat on the floor beside him. Jack said, "They think I'm pretty quick coming up with plans. They don't know that I have all kinds of plans ready, and I just pull one off the shelf."

Jake just nodded.

Jack picked up his phone and dialed. When it was answered, he said, "Max, I need a ride... I'll let you know where when you get here. Oh, and I'll need you to take care of Jake... Just what I need. All right, on my way."

While Jack was waiting on Max, he gathered his gear together. He tried to remember what it was that drew him to this line of work. Was it some idea in his young mind that he was going to save the world? He didn't know. As he walked to the porch, he stopped and read a quote he had hung on his wall from Hemingway: *There is no hunting like the hunting of man, and those who have hunted armed men long enough and liked it, never care for anything else thereafter.* He turned around and said to Jake, "I guess ole' Ernest was right. I do like hunting and stalking the enemy, but I don't like hostage rescue or securing some building. Too many things can go wrong."

Jake shook his head and followed Jack out to the porch. Max drove up. Jack put his gear in the bed of Max's pickup. Before Jack got in. Jake stood up on his hind legs and gave Jack a hug.

"I don't know about theses bear hugs. Take care of the place, and no wild parties."

Jake shook his head, growled a little, and went back to the porch.

As Jack climbed into Max's truck, Max asked, "Where to?"

"Take a right at the end of the road, then a left on the second crossroad, and I will tell you when to stop."

Max followed directions, then Jack said, "This will do."

Max stopped. "There ain't nothing here except a big rock and two trees."

Jack got out of the truck, grabbed his bag, walked over to the driver's side, handed Max $200, and said, "I know. Remember how to get here. I'll send you word when I need to be picked up."

"I probably don't want to know where you're going."

"Nope."

"Well, you keep giving me these C-notes, and I'll drop you off anywhere you want."

"If you don't hear from me, you have a copy of my will. Take it to my lawyer."

"You better make it back. That fur ball of yours don't like me."

"Yeah, he does, or you'd be dead. See ya when I get back."

"Later."

Max turned his truck around, and Jack was gone. *How does he do that?*

*****

Jack met his team at an abandoned feed mill and grain elevator. He walked into the planning room.

"Everyone here?"

One of the men said, "Everyone except Dead Eye."

Dead Eye walked into the room. "I was the first one here."

"Okay, here's the orders. A chopper will pick us up in twenty."

Jack and his men went over the plan. They were going to go into the power plant as maintenance workers and secure it. This mission was like all others. If all went well, the FBI would get the credit for a job well done. If the mission failed, it would be reported that rogue agents disobeyed orders. Jack's team did not exist.

Jack's team entered the plant wearing uniforms of a generator repair company. They carried their weapons and gear in their tool boxes. The FBI had already replaced the guards with their own personnel. Jack and two others walked into the control room to look for anyone and anything suspicious. The plan was to secure the control room, take the personnel to the break room, and question them. One problem that could arise is that the plant personnel would think this was a terrorist plot.

Jack went out to the van and sent Noah a coded message that they were ready to go. The time was set.

*****

Cat had picked out three cartridges and laid them on the pad by her rifle. Ben had been monitoring the wind.

Dave came up. "How's it going?"

Ben replied, "As good as it can. The flag on the mountaintop and the oak tree seven hundred yards out will help me judge the wind. I wish I had something a little closer."

"I'm sure it'll work out."

Dave walked back to the trailer. Skip walked up. "I just got done talking to Noah. It's a go. He has a team in the power plant. He wants this done on the hour. I'm gonna tell the girl. Want to come along?"

"No, I have something to do."

Skip went to the hideout. "We have a go. Noah wants you to start on the hour. Let's synchronize our watches. Are you ready?"

Cat replied, "As ready as I'll ever be."

"I'm going back to the pavilion. I'll call them thirty seconds before the hour. That should give them time to get in position."

"Where's Dad?"

"He said he had something to do. I'm sure he'll be back."

Cat said, "Ben, I'm getting nervous."

"Do what you always do, pray."

"Good idea. Lord, calm my nerves and give me the strength I need." Cat tried to calm down as the minutes crept by like hours.

It was less than ten minutes to the hour. Cat said, "I thought Dad would be here with us. I wonder what he's doing."

Ben looked through the tree limbs and saw smoke. He looked to the left, and there was his dad with the grill burning something that smelled like hamburger. The smoke was going up and drifting to the north.

"Hey, Cat, I know where Dad is."

"Where?"

"He's cooking."

"What?"

"Yeah, he got us a wind gauge."

Cat looked out. "I guess that'll work."

One minute to go. The smoke was moving to the north, as were the leaves on the oak tree. Ben looked at the flag. It was pointing to the north also. Cat had to shoot into the sun. She was glad that Mike had bought a sunshade for her scope. Ben entered some numbers into his laptop and was ready to give Cat the corrections. Thirty seconds to go, then all of a sudden, a cloud blocked the sun. The smoke rose straight up, the limbs on the oak tree stopped moving, and the flag fell motionlessly against its pole. Cat and Ben looked at each other in surprise.

Ben said, "Cat, I think you have a direct line to the Man upstairs."

Cat smiled, "This ain't no coincidence."

*****

Skip picked up the phone and said, "As you've heard, they are working on your demands."

"Yes, Rooster, I heard. Soon as I hear the announcement on TV, you can start clearing the road. Who's the idiot with the fire?"

"Some clueless, homeless guy."

"Better hope I hear that you infidels are leaving Iraq soon."

*****

Ben was watching through the spotting scope. The terrorists did as always. All stood in line, looking toward them as though they had nothing to fear.

Cat looked at the three cartridges she had picked out, thinking how it must have been for David when he went up against Goliath. She looked over at Ben. He nodded and started counting down the seconds.

Cat loaded a cartridge in the chamber and closed the bolt. She slowed her heart rate down the best she could, wishing she had not had that last cup of coffee earlier that morning. When Ben got to two seconds, she put herself in a bubble. Nothing would stop these sequences of events now. The first domino was about to fall.

Ben said, "One."

As Cat slowly squeezed the trigger, she said, "Good night, camel dung." She opened the bolt, put a fresh cartridge in the chamber, closed the bolt, squeezed the trigger the second time, and said, "Good night, rag head." Cat opened the bolt, put the last cartridge in the chamber, closed the bolt, squeezed the trigger the third time, and said, "And goat breath."

Ben was watching through the spotting scope. Right after the second report of Cat's rifle, the first bullet hit the terrorist who was standing on the left, just above the nose. The top of his head came off, splattering blood on the other two. They just stood there. Ben heard the report of the rifle for the third time. Before the terrorist could move, Cat's second bullet hit the terrorist standing on the right in the throat. He started flopping around on the ground like a headless chicken. The one in the middle froze, which gave time for Cat's third and final bullet to take off the right side of his head.

*****

Jack and his men in the control room pulled out their weapons.

Jack said, "Everybody put their hands on their head and go to the break room single file."

The boss asked, "What is this about?"

"It'll be explained in the break room. Don't try anything stupid."

Everyone was following directions except for a brunette. She was working her way slowly over to the side of the control panel. Dead Eye noticed her. He pointed his weapon at her and said, "Stop! Put your hands on your head and get back in line!" She ignored the order and reached up on the side of the panel. A single 9 mm bullet from Dead Eye's MP5 hit the woman in the forehead. People started screaming.

Jack yelled, "The rest of you, keep your hands on your head and go to the break room, and no one else will get hurt!"

Jack always backed his men's decisions, and this time would be no different. He trusted Dead Eye. After everyone was in the break room, Jack and Dead Eye went back to the control room.

Jack asked him, "Okay, what was she doing when you shot her?"

"She was reaching up on the side of the control panel."

Jack took his flashlight and looked on the side. He found an unmarked switch painted the same color as the panel. He looked at Dead Eye. "Go get the boss, and tell the FBI we need to run prints on the woman."

Dead Eye brought the boss back to the control room.

The boss asked, "Why was she shot?"

Jack replied, "That's what we are going to find out. Do you know what this switch is for?"

"No, I've never noticed it before. It's not even marked. It could have been done when an outside company did inspections on the panels."

"Do you know who the woman was?"

382

"I thought she was from Corporate making sure we were following regulations, but some said she was from the Department of Energy."

"What was on her ID?"

"She was issued one here as an employee."

While Jack was talking to the boss, the FBI agent taking the fingerprints said to Jack, "This woman isn't who she said she was."

"How so?"

"She has a covering on her fingers with new prints."

"Peel it off and run the prints."

Jack asked, "You have an electrician that can check out these panels?"

"I have two on duty."

"Dead Eye, take him to the break room and bring back the one that has been here the longest."

While Dead Eye and the boss went to the break room, the FBI agent said to Jack, "We got an ID on the woman."

"That was quick. Who is it?"

"Modern technology. She's an international terrorist that's been off the radar for over a year."

The boss and Dead Eye came back with the electrician.

The electrician took the panel off and exclaimed, "Oh shit!"

This is not what Jack wanted to hear. "What?"

"These wires bypass the safety switches for the generators, and another one goes to a transmitter behind the panel."

"A bomb?"

"I don't know. May I leave now?"

"Yeah, go back to the break room. Dead Eye, get the bomb tech in here!"

The bomb tech came in and looked everything over. The transmitter would send a signal to the detonator in the tunnel. Also, when the switch was turned, it would cause the generators to overheat. After the explosives were disarmed in the tunnel, they disconnected the transmitter in the control room. The power plant had been saved.

Jack asked Dead Eye, "How did you know?"

"I didn't like what she was saying with her eyes."

"What was that?"

"Her eyes told me that I didn't have the balls to pull the trigger."

"No wonder you never got married."

"We ready to get out of here?"

"Yep, we'll let the FBI deal with the press."

Jack and his team put their weapons and gear back into the toolboxes and went back to the van and disappeared.

*****

Ben looked over toward Cat and yelled, "Cat, you did it!"

Cat was already taking her rifle off the bipod and putting it in the case. She said to Ben, "Come on! Let's get this stuff in the trailer!"

"But, Cat, you pulled it off."

"I know, you gonna help me or not?"

Ben and Cat took everything back to the trailer and put the firewood back where it was. They waited at the trailer. Dave came up with the grill. "Good job, Cat."

Cat, in a low tone, replied, "Thanks."

Ben said, "That was some shooting, wasn't it, Dad?"

"Go see if Skip found out anything about the power plant."

"Okay."

Dave said to Cat, "Let's go over and sit down."

"Okay."

They went and sat down. Cat looked at Dave. There was a tear rolling down her cheek.

"I know I did the right thing. So why do I feel so terrible?"

"It's just not in you to hurt someone. I have no idea how you feel. The one to talk to would be Mike."

"I hope the news doesn't find out who killed those guys. I don't feel like a hero."

"I'll talk to Skip and see if he can keep it quiet. I'm sure he can make something up to please the news. Now just think about the competition. We should still be able to make it. I had better call your mom and let her know we are okay."

"Thanks, Dad, love you."

"Love you too."

Ben found Skip by the radio talking to Noah. After Skip put the mic down, Ben asked, "Did they save the dam?"

"Yep, it's all secure. A chopper is dropping men on the mountaintop now. That girl can shoot. I want to go thank her."

Ben and Skip walked over to the trailer, and Skip said to Cat, "Girly, you saved the day! That was some shooting! You can have my back any day!"

Cat smiled a little, "Thank you."

Skip pulled out two cigars, bit the end off one, and handed the other to Dave. He pulled out his Zippo, lit his then Dave's, and said, "Damn, I ain't never seen shooting like that."

"Yeah, she can shoot. I have a favor to ask you."

"Sure, what is it?"

They walked to the side of the trailer, and Dave said, "Cat doesn't feel like a hero now. Is there any way you'll be able to keep her out of the news?"

"Yeah, I had planned to do that anyways, for y'all's safety. I don't want them rag heads putting a price on her head. I heard on the radio that the northbound lanes should start moving pretty soon. When you're loaded up and ready, I'll get you in the traffic flow. I'll tell the officers that you have priority and need to get to the hospital or something."

"Thanks."

"No! Thank *you*!"

Dave walked up to Ben and Cat and said, "Ready to get out of here?"

Ben replied, "Is that a trick question?"

"Let's get loaded up."

"How we gonna get through the traffic?"

"Skip's gonna help."

After the trailer was loaded, Skip got them into the traffic flow. It wasn't long until they were in the restricted lane. As they drove by, the officers waved at them.

Cat asked, "I wonder what Skip told them that they are letting us drive in this lane."

Dave replied, "I don't know, but it's working."

Ben said, "I bet it was a whopper."

They would have to take the long way around the mountains, but at least they were safe and on their way. When they stopped for gas, Dave called Betty and let her know that they were fine and would be there later than expected. Betty kept asking questions. Dave told her he would explain when they got there.

*****

Skip met up with Officer *Joe* and asked, "Did you have any luck finding a bomb tech for that truck bomb?"

"Yes, we did. The strange thing is that it had already been disarmed."

"We must have more friends than we thought."

"I heard on the radio that the threat has been neutralized."

"Yes, it has."

"I thought I heard some rifle fire by that pavilion where you were hanging out."

"You know, I thought I heard some too. I think it was a little south of me. Echoes in these mountains will play tricks on your hearing. You and your guys did an outstanding job. Now let's see if we can get these people out of here. The only way out now is north. It's gonna take a while for them to clear the road. You might as well turn the southbound lanes into northbound."

"Okay."

*****

Not wanting to lose any more time Dave, Ben, and Cat traded off driving. There was still time to pick up Betty and Liz and make it to the B&C a day before the competition started. About the only thing on the radio was the news of the attack.

Dave pulled up in front of the house where Liz was living. They all got out of the van. Betty and Liz ran to them and gave them all hugs.

Betty said, "I was so scared when I heard on the news that an explosion blocked the highway. I am so glad you all are okay."

Dave replied, "We were lucky. We hadn't made it down where the bombs were set."

"There are so many conflicting reports. Some say it was terrorists and that the dam was the target. That's what I heard on the radio. There was also a report that three of them on the mountaintop were shot by a sniper."

"All I know is, I'm glad we were able to get out of there."

"I'm glad too."

Liz said, "My roommate is gone for the week. Dad, you and mom can take her room. Cat, you can sleep in my room, and, Ben, you can have the couch."

After resting up for a day, they got in the van and headed for the B&C. Cat was doing her best to concentrate on the competition. She was having a hard time sleeping. Every time she'd close her eyes, she would see the faces of the terrorists. It would only be a matter of time before Mom would find out what happened. The news was reporting that it was a private citizen that shot the men on the mountaintop. Others reported that it was someone from the Special Forces that happened to be on a training exercise.

Some government officials didn't like the idea of a private citizen doing their job, even if it did save the day. They wanted to know who it was, not to thank them but to keep an eye on them. Talk of banning long-range rifles was being brought up again.

A senator from California was interviewed and said, "We can't have ordinary people taking the law into their own hands. No one will be safe."

Dave could tell the news on the radio was bothering Cat, so he turned the radio off and put a CD in the player.

*****

Dave pulled into the parking lot of the B&C. There were already a lot of people there. It looked like a town of its own.

Cat asked, "I wonder if Mike and Barry are here yet?"

Ben replied, "I'll try and get a hold of Barry on his cell."

They all got out of the van and walked around. Ben walked up and said, "They're here. Barry said wait here and they'll meet us."

Liz asked, "How do they know where we are?"

Ben pointed to the number on the light pole and said, "I told them we were by this pole."

Mike and Barry walked up to the van.

"Hi, all," said Mike.

Dave asked, "Been here long?"

"We got here day before yesterday. We left a little early when I heard about the trouble on the highway. I see you made it through okay."

"Yeah, we had to take the long way around, but we made it."

"They hauled in some cabins to rent out. One good thing about getting here early, I was able to rent us a duplex. There's enough room to park by it. We won't have to work out of the trailer."

Barry said, "Yeah, it's great. There's Internet. I have my laptop set up."

"We might as well head over there. I'll even cook lunch."

They got in the van, and Dave drove over and parked it by the cabin. After they moved their stuff into the cabin, Dave said to Mike, "This is great, I sure appreciate it."

"No problem, I thought this would be nicer than a hotel room. The boys can stay with me, and you, Betty, Liz, and Cat can stay in the other side."

"Looks like we'll have more room too."

"Yeah, Barry has already got his laptop set up. He's been looking at the other shooters' scores. Cat has her work cut out for her."

Ben asked Barry, "Do you have a hard drive with the shooting program on it?"

"Yeah, I loaded two extra in case something happened. Why?"

"It has everything set up for this range?"

"Yes."

"Don't ask any questions. Just put a new one in my laptop."

"Okay, but what happened?"

"I'll tell you later. I changed a few things and don't know if I can get it back to the way it was. I'll tell you about it later. Hide the old one, and don't let anyone have it. It doesn't exist."

"Did you download something your mom wouldn't like?"

"Just do it. I'll tell you about it later."

Mike called, "Food's ready."

They all sat down to eat.

Cat said, "This looks good."

Ben said, "Who cares about looks? I just want it to taste good."

Mike said, "After we eat, we can go and get Cat registered. Then we can look the place over."

"Have you been over to the Old West Town yet?"

"Yeah, Barry and I went over there yesterday. It is something else. Looks like you go back to the 1800s. The saloons are booming."

After they finished eating, Mike took Cat to register. The rest of them looked around. When Cat was done, they got on the stage-coach and took a trip back over 150 years. As they were walking down the street past one of the saloons, Mike said to Dave, "Let's go in here. I'll buy you a drink."

Dave said, "Sounds good." Then he said to Betty and the kids, "I'm going in here with Mike. We'll catch up with you later."

Betty replied, "Yeah, probably much later. We'll just see you guys back at the cabin."

Mike and Dave went inside the saloon and walked up to the bar.

Mike said to the bartender, "Two whiskeys."

"Two shots or a bottle with two glasses?"

Mike looked at Dave. "I think I'll like this place." Mike looked back to the bartender. "Bottle, two glasses."

Mike grabbed the bottle and glasses. They sat down at a table. Dave asked Mike, "You think this is the way it was?"

As Mike poured the whiskey, he looked around at all the saloon girls and the men playing poker at the other tables. "Don't know for sure, and don't really care."

Dave looked over at one of the poker games and saw a big guy in a Stetson, biting the end off a cigar, sitting with a stack of cash in front of him. He thought to himself, *Can't be*. The guy looked up, and sure enough, it was Skip sitting there playing poker. Skip recognized Dave, though he didn't let on.

Mike poured another shot. "Betty was right. It'll probably be a while before we get out of here."

"Yeah, good thing we didn't drive."

Skip picked up his money from the table, walked over to Mike and Dave's table, and said, "There's a seat open at the table. I'm gonna call it a night."

Mike said, "Thanks, but I think I'll pass."

"Probably keep more of your money that way." Skip put his hand out and said, "Hi, I'm Skip. This is some place."

Mike and Dave shook his hand and introduced themselves. Then Mike asked, "Care to sit down and help us finish this bottle?"

Skip sat down. "Don't mind if I do. Here for the Cowboy shoot?"

Dave replied, "No, my daughter is competing in the Big Shoot."

"She must be pretty good to qualify for that."

Mike said, "Yes, she is. I taught her."

Dave said, "I take it you're here for the Cowboy shoot."

Skip took a puff from his cigar. "Yep, I started saving money when I read that this place was going to be built."

Mike asked, "What do you do for a living?"

"I'm a US marshal. How about you?"

"I'm retired from the Marine Corp."

Skip poured the last of the whiskey into his glass, drank it, and said, "Thanks for the drink. I'll see you guys around."

Mike replied, "Yeah, we had better get going. It's practice day tomorrow."

*****

The next morning Mike was sitting at his table drinking a cup of coffee. The boys were still sleeping. Cat walked in.

Mike said, "Good morning. Want a cup of coffee?"

"Yes, thanks."

"You ready to get started?"

"Yeah, I think so. I have something to ask you."

"Sure, what's that?"

"Did it bother you the first time you killed a man?"

Mike got a serious look on his face; he had an idea of why she asked.

"Why do you ask?"

"Oh, I was just wondering."

Mike looked at her. "That wasn't a government sniper that took out those terrorists, was it?"

"No."

"I suspected, especially when I read that there were reports of two young kids carrying equipment from a trailer to a stack of firewood."

Cat told Mike the whole story of what happened that day. Mike said, "I think we met that marshal last night at the saloon. He's a big guy."

"He's here?"

"Yeah, he did a good job of not letting on that he knew your dad."

"He said something about going to a Cowboy shoot."

"Back to your question, yes, it did. Every once in a while, I can still see the face of the first guy I killed. It just didn't seem right, me being five hundred yards. It was either him or my fellow Marines."

"When I close my eyes I can see the three of them standing on the mountaintop, not having any idea of what's gonna happen next."

"It's hard to do, but try and think of all the people you saved, including yourself and your family."

"I guess you're right."

"Ready to go practice?"

"Yeah, I plan on winning this."

"That's a girl."

Mike and the kids gathered up their equipment and went to practice. This would be the last time Cat would be able to practice before the competition started. Mike signed out a lane for Cat. There were shooters from all over the world—men, women, young, and old. After a day of practicing, they went back to the cabin.

Barry got on his laptop and said, "They have a list of all the shooters and where they're from. They also have their qualification scores."

Cat walked over and looked at the list. She knew this was going to be a challenge. She was 490th on the list. The only good thing was that the scores for the bottom hundred were close.

The next morning, Cat woke up and walked into Mike's room. Mike was sitting at the table drinking a cup of coffee.

Mike asked, "You want a cup?"

"Yeah, I know I can have only one."

"I have your breakfast ready."

Cat ate her breakfast and nursed her cup of coffee, knowing that that would be the last cup till the next morning.

Ben and Barry woke up.

Mike said, "About time you two woke up, breakfast is ready."

Ben replied, "Good, I'm hungry!"

"Barry, will you check the web page and see when Cat shoots?"

"Sure."

Barry got on his laptop, looked it up, then said, "Nine o'clock, Savage range, lane 5."

Cat made it through the first day of competition. She had a hard time putting what had happened a few days ago in the back of her mind and concentrate on her shooting. When they got back to the cabin, Barry got on the web page and said to Cat, "Well, you made it through the first day. You haven't been eliminated."

"Is that all, just not eliminated?"

"No, actually, you did pretty good. There's a girl around your age that is ahead of you."

"Let me see." Cat looked at the scores, then had Barry look up the bio on her.

Cat read over the bio then said, "The only way she got here is by writing some fancy essay. Winchester supplied her equipment and training. She didn't even have to work for it, and look at her picture. Does she think she can win it by her looks?"

Mike was taken aback by what Cat had just said. This was a side of Cat he had never seen. Cat had always respected other shooters. Was jealously creeping in?

Mike looked at Cat and asked, "What's wrong, Cat? She may have gotten here by writing, but she had to work hard to compete."

"Why are you sticking up for her? Her parents were probably rich, and everything was probably handed to her. Look at her picture the way she smiles, like she's better than anyone else."

"I don't see that. I see a girl that is happy to be here. You had better get rid of envy, or you won't have a chance to win."

"Whatever, I'm gonna go run now then go to bed. I'll see you in the morning." Cat walked out the door.

Ben asked Mike, "What's up with Cat?"

"I don't know, but she had better get over it soon, or we might as well leave now. Do you have her shooting time for tomorrow?"

"Yes, she's scheduled for the Winchester range, lane 5 at ten o'clock... Oh..."

"Now what?"

"That girl is shooting on lane 4."

"Great."

The next morning Cat and Barry were setting up their equipment on the firing line. Cat looked over toward lane 4 and said, "What's she doing there?"

Barry replied, "Probably shooting."

"Smart-ass."

"What's wrong with you, Cat?"

"Nothing, I'm fine."

The girl looked over at them and smiled. Barry smiled and waved back.

Cat saw this. "Maybe you'd rather spot for her."

"You're not fine."

Mike, overhearing the conversation, walked up to Cat and whispered in her ear firmly, "Cat, see that target in your lane. That is the only thing you need to be thinking about. Get your emotions under control *now*, or we may as well pack up and go home. I didn't come all this way to see you throw away a chance of a lifetime over a little jealousy."

"But…"

"No buts. Get your head out of your ass, and concentrate on putting bullets in the X-ring!"

"Yes, Mike."

Cat didn't do as well as she had the first day, but she held her own. Fortunately, the girl wasn't shooting next to Cat on the following relays. After five days, there were twenty shooters left. Mike was confident that Cat could win.

*****

Skip was sitting at the poker table with a stack of cash and a half-full whiskey bottle in front of him. After the cards were dealt, he looked at them. He had been dealt two pair, aces and eights, all black. He looked at them and thought. *Oh, this is just great, and my back is toward the door. What else could go wrong?* Just then, he felt a finger tap him on the shoulder.

He turned around and said, "Boss, Noah, what are you guys doing here?"

Noah replied, "We need to talk to you."

"I'm on vacation, and I'm busy. Can't this wait?"

"No, it can't."

"I'll lose my seat, and Lady Luck is on my side."

Boss said, "Skip, now!"

"Oh, all right." Skip looked over toward three saloon girls standing by the bar and yelled, "Hey, chubby, come here." The three just looked at one another. Skip continued, "You with the big boobs."

The saloon girl walked over toward the table and asked, "Need another bottle?"

"No." Skip took $500 and stuffed it into her cleavage and continued, "I need you to save my seat. Just ante and fold. This shouldn't take too long."

"What if I have a good hand?"

Skip looked at her, grabbed another $1,000, stuffed it with the $500, and said, "Use that."

The saloon girl sat down, looked at the cards, and said to Skip, "Great, you leave me with a dead man's hand and my back toward the door."

"Nothing like giving away your hand. I'd try and draw to a full house if I were you."

Skip grabbed his bottle and glass and then followed his boss and Noah to an empty table.

Skip asked, "Care for a drink?"

Noah replied, "No, we're on duty."

Skip poured himself a drink and said, "I'm not. So what's so damn important that you took me away from the game?"

"We need to know what happened on the highway."

Skip bit the end off of his cigar, lit it, and said, "I turned in my report to both of you."

"Yeah, some guy in camo that just happened to be there training asked if you needed help."

"Well, what can I say? Sometimes luck just follows me."

"We've had reports that civilians, more importantly *teenagers*, were seen setting up by the pavilion by you."

Skip took a puff from his cigar and replied, "Really?"

Skip's boss said, "Come on, Skip, we're getting pressure from the Justice Department. We need to find out who it was."

"What do they care? The threat was neutralized."

"They don't like the idea that civilians are running around with that kind of skill."

"They getting a little scared of 'We the People?'"

"They just don't like the idea."

"Well, it's a good thing they ain't here. They'd shit their pants."

"You're not gonna tell us, are you?"

"I don't want the radicals putting a price on anybody's head. I stand by my report. I'll take a polygraph."

Noah replied, "Like that'll do any good. The last time you took one, when asked if you worked for any other law enforcement agency, you replied, 'Yes, for Wyatt Earp in Dodge City, arresting drunken cowboys.' That just proves that you can beat a polygraph."

"Or I was telling the truth."

"Well, we'll find out who it was with or without your help."

"I was wondering why all the undercover feds were around. You should have them change their dress code. They stick out like a Holstein in a herd of Black Angus. Maybe if you'd concentrate on getting the bad guys instead of picking on innocent people, we wouldn't have the problems we have."

"We'll see you around."

Skip's boss and Noah left the saloon. Skip went back to the poker table. The saloon girl had a stack of cash in front of her. She looked up and said, "Oh, you're back. I only used the money you gave me." She got up, taking her money with her. As he sat down, Skip said, "You might as well bring me another bottle of whiskey."

Skip played a couple more hands then decided to call it a night. He called over to the saloon girl and said, "Hey, chubby, I'm calling it a night. You can have this seat if you want."

She walked over and said, "Don't mind if I do. If you change your mind later, come back and I'll buy you a drink."

"With my money?"

"Was your money."

"I'll have to take a rain check."

Skip walked over to Mike's cabin and knocked on the door. Mike opened the door and said, "Skip?"

"Yeah, you got a minute?"

"Yeah, sure, hang on."

"I'll wait out here."

Mike put on his boots, grabbed his hat, and went outside. He asked Skip, "What's up?"

Skip pulled two cigars out of his jacket pocket, handed one to Mike, and then bit the end off of the other. After he lit the cigars, he said, "There might be a problem."

"What's that?"

"I was just questioned by my boss and the head of Homeland Security. They're bound and determined to find out who took those terrorists out. I'm not sure, but I think they recovered a bullet from one of them."

"I was wondering. I noticed a few feds in the crowd."

"You noticed them too?"

"Hard to miss when you've had experience with them."

"They're pretty sure who they're looking for is in this crowd. I'm sticking to my story that a sniper on a training exercise happened to be there."

"Thanks for letting me know."

"No problem, I'll let you know if I hear anything else."

"Thanks."

Skip left and Mike went back inside. Mike poured himself a glass of whiskey and sat down. Should he tell Cat? She was having a hard enough time concentrating without the added worry. Mike finished his drink. He decided that he would just keep this information to himself.

*****

Cat woke up and went over to Mike's cabin to have her morning coffee, which had become routine. After breakfast, they all went to the competition area. The day would start as all others with the raising of the American flag and the singing of the national anthem. After everyone sat down, Boon and Crocket walked out in front of the crowd.

Boon spoke into the microphone, "Well, everyone, I think the Big Shoot is a real success. There are twenty of you left. We're gonna make it a little more interesting. You'll still be shooting at a thousand yards, but the target will be replaced with a two-hundred-yard target."

Crocket interrupted, "Uh, Boon, you had better look at your notes again."

"Oh, yeah, it's getting replaced with an eight-hundred-yard target. Hope I didn't scare anybody."

"I think we had better take a break and let the shooters change their pants."

The crowd started laughing. Boon said, "Well, let's get started…
see if we can get it whittled down to ten shooters for tomorrow."

The day's shooting was completed early in the afternoon. Cat
made it for another day, as did the girl that Cat didn't like. Everyone
except Mike took the rest of the afternoon and looked around. Mike
went back to the cabin.

*****

Mike was sitting at his table going over Cat's scores. Cat had
come a long way since the first contest she shot. Mike knew that the
home stretch would be the roughest. There was a knock at the door.

Mike said, "Come in, it's open."

The door opened, and Mike looked up. In front of him stood
a Marine in dress blues. His uniform was impeccable, boots shiny
and you could cut yourself on the creases in uniform. The clus-
ter of ribbons looked like a platter of fruit salad on his chest. He
stood there with his cover in his right hand. Mike read his name tag:
Weatherspoon.

The Marine asked, "Sergeant Dixon?"

It had been decades since Mike had been addressed as such. He
said, "Yes."

"I am Sergeant Weatherspoon."

"Mark's son?"

"Sort of, he and his wife raised me."

"Sit down. Want a cup of coffee?"

"Yes, thank you."

"I hope I'm not bothering you. I have had mixed feeling about
looking you up. I heard that you got to see Dad before he passed."

"Yes, I did. Mary didn't mention that she had a brother."

"That was to protect me."

"Protect you?"

The Marine took out his wallet and pulled out an old photo-
graph and handed it to Mike. Mike looked at the photo. It was the
same as the one that was in the briefcase that Mary had given him.
Mike looked up and asked, "That was your mother?"

"Yes."

"I didn't know there were any survivors."

"My aunt took me to the river and hid us there until the VC left."

"How did you end up over here?"

"When Dad stole away on the cargo plane, he hid me, along with a small oxygen tank, in a duffel bag. He had a medic give me a sedative. He put an oxygen mask on me and wrapped me in part of a parachute to keep me warm. Then he put me and the tank in the duffel bag. He knew he was taking a chance, but he also knew there was no future there for me."

"Mark and his wife raised you?"

"Yes, and when I was sixteen, Mary told me the story of where I came from. Mary's grandfather was able to get all the documents to make me an US citizen."

"How did you happen to join the Marines?"

"When I turned eighteen, I had to make a choice, either work for the family or go out on my own. It was a hard choice; I had been well treated. After Mark told me about you and how hard you worked to get my mom and me to the United States, the choice was easier. On my eighteenth birthday, I said goodbye and joined the Marines."

"How did they take it?"

"Mary's grandfather said he knew what choice I would make and wished me the best. To protect me, they cut off all contact with me. The only ones I had any contact with was Mark, his wife, and Mary."

"Am I the reason you came to the contest?"

"That and I wanted to see what kind of shooters were here. I am stationed at the Marine Scout and Sniper School."

"Looking for a few good shooters?"

"Yes, there are some young shooters that have a lot of potential to be a Marine sniper."

"Yes, there's a lot of talent here."

"I'm impressed with two of the young female shooters."

"You gonna try and recruit them?"

"I'll give them the information and let them make up their minds. I have already talked to a few of the others."

"Anyone seem interested?"

"A couple."

Sergeant Weatherspoon received a message on his phone. After he read it, he said to Mike, "I am glad I found you. I have to get going. Maybe we can meet up later."

"I'd like that. Wait a minute." Mike got a pen and paper, wrote his address and phone number down, handed it to Sergeant Weatherspoon, and continued, "If you're in the area, stop by."

Sergeant Weatherspoon looked at the address and said, "I will do that. Hey, by the way, would you happen to know a man that goes by Big John who lives around there?"

"Yes, I do."

"Do you think he's here?"

"Don't know, haven't seen him. His son was supposed to compete, but he was called back to Iraq. He could have delayed it, but he put duty first. Did you know him?"

"Yes, he served under me in Iraq a year ago. That was just before I received orders to teach at Scout Sniper School. Well, I have to go."

They shook hands. Sergeant Weatherspoon said, "I am glad I met you, Dad."

"I'm glad you looked me up, son. You take time to visit me."

"I will do that. See you later."

After Sergeant Weatherspoon left, Mike sat down, thinking about what had just happened. All these years he had a son in the States and didn't know it. Mike was curious why Sergeant Weatherspoon asked about Big John. There was an uncomfortable feeling in his gut. His gut was seldom wrong. Mike poured himself a glass of whiskey, read the local newspaper, and went to bed, wondering what tomorrow had in store for him.

25

Everyone stood as the American flag was raised before the shooting began. The flag was raised to the top, but it came back down to half-mast. You could hear the sighs in the crowd.

Boon spoke over the loudspeaker, "I have some sad news this morning. We just received word that Marine William Smith was killed in Iraq. He had qualified to compete in this shoot but was called back to his unit to protect convoys. He was offered a delay in his deployment but turned it down."

Cat turned to Mike and asked, "Why?"

"I don't have the answer."

"But I wouldn't be here if he hadn't gone."

"You can't blame yourself. None of this is your fault."

"Still, I feel bad."

"Billy did what he had to do."

Boon continued, "After talking it over with Crocket, we're going to postpone the shoot till tomorrow morning."

Cat said to Mike, "Good. I would have a hard time concentrating today."

"Okay, let's get this stuff back to the cabin."

After they returned to the cabin, Cat and her parents sat down at the table. Betty made a pot of coffee. Betty asked Cat, "Would you like a cup?"

"Yes, thank you."

No matter what Dave and Betty said to Cat it didn't seem to help. There was a knot in her stomach. She remembered back to when she hit Billy in the nose with the chalkboard eraser. She smiled a little when she thought about the day when Barry had enough of Billy's bullying. Billy had really changed after that day. It just didn't seem right that she was here competing when it should have been Billy. Cat finished her cup of coffee then said to her parents, "I think I'll go find a quiet place and pray. I will be back for supper."

Betty stood up, gave Cat a hug, and said, "All right, honey, we'll see you then."

*****

As Mike was going over the scores of the previous days, his stomach started growling. Now would be a good time to get some bratwurst steamed in beer. He had walked past that food tent every day but never took the time to stop. This would be a good day to see if the food tasted as good as it smelled.

Mike placed his order then went to sit down. As he walked toward an empty table, he saw Sergeant Weatherspoon talking to Big John.

He walked over to the table, extended his hand to Big John, and said, "John, sorry to hear about your son."

John stood up and shook Mike's hand. "Thank you."

"Let me know if there's anything I can do."

"There is one thing you can do."

"Name it."

"I could use some help with making arrangements."

"I'd be more than happy to."

"Thank you. I will see you guys later."

After John left, Mike asked Sergeant Weatherspoon, "Was that the message you received on your phone?"

"Yes, I had been looking for John to tell him his son was in the hospital after hitting a roadside bomb. I couldn't get ahold of him on the phone, so I went to his house. He wasn't home. His neighbor told me he was here. While I was at your cabin, I was notified that his son had died. I couldn't tell you anything since I hadn't notified his dad yet."

"I understand. How did you find him?"

"He walked up to me and asked if I knew his son."

"Oh."

"Yeah, that wasn't easy. He asked me to meet him today and tell him about what happened."

"You leaving soon?"

"Yes, this afternoon. I'm flying to Iraq to escort the body home."

"Tough job."

"Yes, it is."

"I'll see you at the funeral."

They shook hands. Sergeant Weatherspoon left. He asked for a bag and took his food back to the cabin.

*****

Mike, as well as everyone else, could tell that the pressure was starting to get to Cat. She wasn't her usual happy "*I can do it*" self. The incident on the highway and now Billy having been killed were definitely taking a toll on Cat.

Cat and Barry sat at the bench and waited to see if there would be any rule changes this morning. You never knew at this place. Sure enough, there were. They would be shooting at a thousand yards, but it would be a six-hundred-yard target and no flags.

Cat looked at Barry, "I'm glad they ain't trying to make this too tough."

"Yeah, what do we do now?"

"Plan B."

"Plan B?"

"Yeah, notice any odors?"

"It smells like horse shit."

"Barry!"

"Well, it does."

Cat laughed/ "They keep the horses on the south side of the range. See anybody smoking?"

"Yeah, some guy over there with a big cigar."

"See which way the smoke is blowing."

"I guess this will work."

"It has to."

The first relay went well; Cat was back on her game. The start of the second relay, it started raining. Cat looked at Barry. "I wonder what's next."

"I don't know. It's a pain to try to read the laptop through a plastic bag."

"Just shut the laptop off. We've been here long enough. Use your head, and just tell me the corrections."

"If you say so."

Before the start of the third relay, the rain stopped, and the sun came out. Cat looked over to Barry, "If I didn't know better, I'd say Boon and Crocket ordered this."

"I'm sure they did."

"First the rain, now I have to put up with the mirage. I don't know which is worse.

"At least when it's raining, you only see one target."

After they were done, they went back to the cabin before the scores were announced. Cat wanted to take a shower, put on some dry clothes, and clean her rifle. She was hoping she had scored high enough to get into the finals. While Cat was cleaning her rifle, Ben looked up the scores on his laptop.

"Well, you get to shoot tomorrow. You made it to the top five. This will be make it or break it."

"Did that blond make it?"

"Yeah, why don't you like her?"

"I just don't."

"You don't even know her name or anything about her."

"So?"

*****

Cat and Barry sat at the bench wondering what surprises would be coming. It wasn't long till they found out that no spotters or computers would be allowed. Shooters would be allowed to use their spotting scope. Barry looked at Cat as he closed his laptop.

"You're on your own."

Cat replied, "Yep."

After Barry left the bench, Cat looked through her spotting scope and adjusted it. *Only three more relays and I'm done.* Or so she thought.

Barry went back to sit with Ben. Ben asked, "You think she'll do okay?"

"I think so. At least the other girl is sitting to her right."

The weather was cooperating. One could not ask for a better day. All five shooters were doing well. It was a real test of skill. After the third relay, Boon came on the loud speaker and announced, "I thought this would be the last relay, but we have a tie for first place. We will have a tiebreaker at nine o'clock tomorrow morning. One thing for sure—the champion will be a woman."

Cat turned to Mike, "Great. How can somebody as good-looking as her shoot so good?"

"You had better chill, or you'll be taking home second-place prize."

"Ain't gonna happen."

*****

As Cat carried her rifle to the bench, the girl walked up and put her hand out. "Hi, I'm Beth."

Cat shook her hand. "Hi, I'm Cat."

"Cat?"

"Short for Catharine."

"Ain't this great? I didn't think I'd get this far. This is the greatest thing that has ever happened to me."

Cat, doing her best to be polite, replied, "Yeah, this is fun."

"Well, good luck."

"Thank you."

Cat walked to her spot wondering why Beth would wish her luck.

Boon spoke into the loudspeaker, "You will shoot three relays. If it's still a tie, you will shoot one relay at a time till there is a winner."

Ben said to Mike, "This could be a long day."

"Yeah, I should've brought my lunch."

After the third relay, the scores came back tied.

You could hear Boon over the loudspeaker, "Looks like there will be another relay. It will start in fifteen minutes."

Ben said to Mike, "I think you're right. Should have brought our lunch."

"One of them has to outshoot the other sometime."

After the next relay, Boon spoke to the crowd, "It will be a few minutes; the targets need to be looked at by another official. They may have to go to the board for final scoring."

As they waited, Cat was getting anxious.

Mike said to her, "You might as well calm down."

"I know, but I'm so close."

Boon's voice came over the loudspeaker, "We have a winner. Would all the finalists please come forward?"

Cat was relieved that it was finally over, but she was nervous whether she won or not. She stood there as they called the names of the fifth- through third-place shooters. Now the time had come.

Boon spoke, "I want to congratulate all that participated in the first annual Big Shoot. You all have made it a success beyond of what either Crockett or I was expecting. With the interest this high, we will have one every year till either the participation goes down or it is outlawed. With that said, there can only be one winner. That's why we keep score."

Cat was thinking, *Come on, quit dragging this out. Did I win or not?*

Boon continued, "The first place winner is Beth. The second place is Cat."

The color drained from Cat's face. Mike could feel the disappointment.

Beth and Cat walked over to claim their prizes. Boon handed Cat her ribbon, shook her hand, and congratulated her.

He walked and handed Beth her trophy, congratulated her, then asked, "Is there anything you'd like to say?"

"Yes, there is."

Cat thought, *Oh, bother.*

Beth continued, "There are so many people that I want to thank for this opportunity. I will keep it to the two most important people in my life. A few years ago my parents were killed in a home invasion. I was kidnapped and tortured. I'm sure some of you read about it in the paper. I won't go into details. A marshal saved me. He and his wife were going to adopt me, but an agency thought he would not be a good parent for me. The adoption fell through, or sort of. This marshal talked to the court, and they offered him a deal."

Beth started tearing up. She continued, "If they would divorce and she would move out of state they would let his wife adopt me. He couldn't have contact with me till I turned eighteen. I know the court wasn't expecting him and his wife to agree with that. The marshal is a little bullheaded, so he and his wife accepted the offer. I remember the last day I saw him. He said to me in his stern but kind voice, 'You be the best you can be. Now, stop your crying and get out of here.' Well, I've rambled on long enough. I know that he is here. He wouldn't miss this for the world. I'm sure he took time from the poker table to watch me. I hope my shooting times didn't change your luck. I want to let you know I'm eighteen now, and I would like to see you. Oh, and I really don't care if you call me Sally Jean. In fact, that name has become special to me. Thank you, all… Hope to be back next year."

Boon asked Cat, "Is there anything you'd like to say?"

Cat replied, "I would just like to thank all my family and friends that helped me get here."

Boon said, "The contestants may pick up their prize money in the morning."

There was a round of applause as the contestants left the stage.

After Cat got back with her family, Mike added insult to injury, "I bet you feel lower than a snake's ass in a wagon wheel rut. You know, that's what happens when you make an opinion about someone when you don't know the whole story."

"Let's just go."

Boon's voice came over the loudspeaker again. "Since the top five shooters worked so hard, we decided to have a contest for you five only. It will be over at the mile range at ten o'clock tomorrow morning. Only three shots at three terrorist targets, distance—1,600 yards. The winner gets $10,000. You can sign up now."

Cat's eyes lit up. She looked at Mike, "I can win that!"

Mike, knowing this was a trap, said, "Better not. I think we had better head home."

"Ain't no way!"

Before Mike could say anything, Skip came up, "It's a trap. When you shoot, miss."

Cat asked, "A trap?"

Skip explained that they were trying to find out who shot the terrorists on the mountain.

Mike replied, "I guess she has to shoot, or it'll make her look more suspicious. Okay, Cat. Shoot, but miss."

"What about the $10,000?"

"Cat, it ain't worth it."

After they all got back to the cabin, Cat said to Mike, "I think I'll go to the practice range."

"Why?"

"Oh, to let off some steam, and I had better practice to miss."

Mike laughed. "Okay, I guess you're taking this pretty good."

"I'll see you later."

*****

Nine thirty the next morning, Cat and Ben were sitting at the bench waiting for the contest to start. Ben checked the range and said to Cat, "The range is 1,650 yards. The wind so far is calm. I bet this is going to be hard for you to miss on purpose."

"Who says I'm gonna miss?"

"Uh, Cat, you heard what Mike and Skip told you."

"Trust me."

"Okay, I hope you know what you're doing."

There was some time for the shooters to fire some practice rounds. After Cat was done, she pulled three cartridges from her pocket.

Over the loudspeaker, Boon said, "Okay, shooters, this is a timed event from your first shot to your last, accuracy and speed count. The targets may move after the first shot."

Ben said to Cat, "This does sound like a setup."

"Yep."

Boon spoke over the loudspeaker again, "Shooters, you may start anytime."

Cat said to Ben, "Watch the other shooters, and see if their targets move."

Ben watched the lane next to him. "When that guy shot them left to right, the third target moved."

"Just what I thought."

"You gonna shoot?"

"Yep." Cat loaded her rifle, shot the one on the left, then the right. Her last shot hit the middle target.

Ben asked, "What are you doing?"

"I ain't passing up $10,000!" Cat put her rifle in its case along with the spent brass. Then she sat her backup rifle with a box of half-shot ammo on the bench.

Barry walked up.

Cat said, "Barry, take this rifle and put it in Mike's trunk, and keep your mouth shut."

"But why?"

"Just do it."

Barry hesitated.

Cat looked at him. "Do it now, or I'll post on Facebook that you tried to kiss me in the computer lab."

"I didn't try to kiss you!"

Cat gave him a stare.

Barry said, "Okay, okay. I'll do it." Barry grabbed Cat's rifle and headed toward Mike's car.

Mike saw him. "What are you doing?"

"I think Cat has lost it. She told me to put her rifle in your trunk and not say anything, and if I didn't, she'd post on Facebook that I tried to kiss her in the computer lab. She's gone bonkers."

"You tried to kiss Cat?"

"No!"

"Come on, Barry, you sly dog."

"Hey, there ain't no way I'm gonna have a girlfriend that can shoot my heart out at a thousand yards!"

Mike noticed the agents approaching Cat and Ben. He said to Barry, "Here's my keys. Put the rifle in my trunk and cover it up, not a word to anybody."

"Okay, okay."

Barry walked to Mike's car, mumbling all the way, "What have these people been smoking?"

Mike got to Ben and Cat just as the agents got there.

Agent One said to Cat, "That was some pretty good shooting."

"Did I win?"

"You were the only one that hit all three targets."

"So I won."

"Not quite."

"What's that mean?"

"We think you are the one that did our job taking out those terrorists on the highway."

"What makes you think that?"

"The sequence in which you shot these targets. We're gonna confiscate this rifle. We recovered a bullet from one of the terrorists, and after we match it up with one from this rifle, you'll be arrested for interfering with law enforcement."

Mike said, "You can't do that."

"Yes, we can, the Patriot Act."

Cat asked, "Do I get my money?"

"I guess we should let them give it to you so you can hire a lawyer."

Mike said, "You gonna give her a receipt for that rifle?"

"Yes, we have to."

Ben started closing his laptop. The agent said, "Oh, and we'll take that too."

Cat asked, "Can I go now?"

"Yeah, but don't try and go too far from your home. We will be seeing you again."

"Yeah, to give my rifle back."

The agents just laughed and walked away.

After the agents were gone, Skip walked up to Cat, "What were you thinking? When they match up them slugs, there's no way I can help you. Plus, they have the laptop."

Cat replied, "They ain't gonna get a match."

"How so?"

"They took my backup rifle. Sorry, Mike, I know you went to a lot of trouble building that for me."

"They're gonna be suspicious since it hadn't been fired."

"Oh, it was fired. I used it for my practice shots. I shot it last night so that there would be enough empty brass."

Mike said, "Let me get this straight. You practiced with one rifle and shot with the other."

"Well, yeah, it was dead-on yesterday."

Skip asked, "What about the laptop?"

Ben answered, "I had Barry put in another hard drive as soon as we got here."

"I'd sure like to be there when they don't get a match."

Cat said, "Yeah, me too. Skip, do you think I'll get my rifle back?"

"I'll see to it. I still have friends in high places."

"Thanks."

Beth and a woman walked up.

Skip said, "I think you all know Sally Jean."

Beth laughed, "Still don't want to call me by my name."

"And this woman is my ex-wife."

The woman said, "Beth is eighteen now, so if you're done playing poker and chasing those chubby saloon girls, we could change that."

"I wasn't sure you'd want to get back together."

"I'd rather be with the devil I know than a new one I don't."

"I was hoping you'd want to get back together. We wouldn't need two houses."

"Three, if you count that one you bought so we could sneak off and meet once a month."

"Okay, I'm game."

"Your place or mine?"

Skip pulled out a cigar, bit the end off of it, and lit it with his Zippo. He looked at her. "If you're gonna argue about it, maybe we should just forget it."

The woman smiled. "You ain't changed a bit. Why don't we find a new place to live?"

Skip took a puff from his cigar, "Yeah, I could retire, and then we could find a small town to move to."

"You retire?"

"Yeah, then after we've been there for a while, I could run for sheriff."

"Only you would call being a sheriff retiring."

"It would be for me."

"I suppose you'd want to come back here next year."

"Well, yeah, I'm sure Sally Jean will want to shoot next year. After all, the top three are qualified for next year."

"And you'll want to play poker. How did you do this year?"

"Great! Every time Sally Jean was up to shoot, I was ahead, so I had an excuse to leave the table with my winnings."

"Sometimes I wonder what I see in you."

"The best man you've ever met."

"I guess."

Skip turned to Mike, Cat, and Ben. He said, "See you all next year."

Mike said, "Lord willing and the creek don't rise, we'll be here."

Skip, Beth, and the woman left. Mike, Cat, and Ben went back to the cabin.

*****

Cat, Ben, and Barry loaded the van and trailer while Betty and Liz straightened up the cabin. Dave helped Mike load his car. When they were done, Mike walked through the cabin one more time to make sure they had everything. He walked to the vehicles.

"We might as well stop and get something to eat. I'll buy."

Dave replied, "You get no argument from me."

"There's a little place about fifty miles from here. The building ain't much, but the food's good."

Cat replied, "As long as they have good coffee… Finally, I can drink more than one cup."

Mike laughed, "Follow me."

Barry got in the car with Mike. The rest of them loaded into the van. An adventure was over. They were heading back home. Liz would visit for a few days before flying back to her place.

Dave followed Mike as he pulled into the parking lot of the restaurant. It was an old place. The parking lot was made of gravel.

As they got out of the car, Betty said, "Looks like time passed this place by."

Dave replied, "Don't judge a book by its cover."

"Yeah, I know, should have thought of that when I said 'I do.'"

Cat said, "Come on. I'm hungry."

To which Ben replied, "What a surprise!"

They all went inside and sat down at a table. The waitress walked over to the table, handed out menus, then greeted them. "Hi, may I get you something to drink?"

Cat replied, "Coffee, black."

The rest of them gave their drink order.

"I'll be back with your drinks."

Barry said, "Look at that old TV up there, and it still works."

Before anybody could say anything, an announcement came over the TV.

"We interrupt this program to bring you a special report. Now here is our correspondent Tom, live with Officer Stillman."

"Hi, Ann, I'm here with Officer Stillman." He turned to Officer Stillman. "I understand that you have a lead on who shot the terrorist on the mountain."

"Yes, we have. We don't have anybody in custody yet, but we did confiscate the rifle we believe that was used."

"You haven't made any arrests yet?"

"No, but after we test the rifle, we will issue an arrest warrant."

"What if that isn't the rifle?"

"That's very unlikely, but if that is the case, we will still talk to that person and see if there is another rifle."

"Where did you confiscate the rifle you have now?"

"At the Big Shoot."

"There were five hundred shooters there that could have made that shot. What makes you think you have the right one?"

"We had agents watching the shooters, and this one stood out."

"So in other words, you profiled?"

"We don't like that term."

"I'm wondering, why are you worried about who shot them? I mean, they were bad guys."

"We can't let this go. This person or persons might decide that it's okay to just start shooting bad guys."

"Don't you think that's overreacting? I'm sure they just wanted to help."

"We cannot have civilians doing law enforcements job."

"Are you confident that law enforcement could have stopped the attack?"

"I'm sure we could have, but that doesn't matter. Whoever did this could have caused a lot of people to lose their lives."

"Thank you for the information. Back to you, Ann."

"Thanks, Tom. I for one am glad the attack was stopped. I don't care who did it. My mother was trapped on that highway. So if you are listening, you have my heartfelt thanks. Now, back to our regularly scheduled program."

The waitress brought their drinks and took their order. Barry took a drink from his glass then started putting two and two together. He thought about the rifle and hard drive that was in Mike's trunk. He looked up at Ben and Cat and asked, "Do I want to know why I had to hide the hard drive and rifle in Mike's trunk?"

Cat replied, "It'd probably be better that you didn't, but you already know."

Mike said, "I'd better stop at Crazy Jane's and order another barrel for the Surgeon."

Ben said, "And destroy the old one along with the hard drive?"

"Yeah, that's the plan."

Barry said, "There are some things I wish I didn't know."

Betty asked Dave, "Do you think they'll ever figure it out?"

Dave hiding his concern, "No, I don't think so."

Mike took a drink and said to Cat, "At least you won't have to shoot the qualification matches next year."

"Why not?"

"They're gonna let the top three from this year enter next year. Just have to pay entrance fee."

"I'm not sure if I want to come back or not."

"What! Why not?"

"I think I'll try and do something else."

"What would that be?"

"I'm gonna have to decide what I'm gonna do since I've finished high school. I either have to go on to school, get a job, or both."

"You have a little time to decide. The second-place prize money wasn't bad."

"I've been thinking about maybe get into creative writing."

"You write a book?"

"Yeah, that way the ending can come out the way I want it to."

"What kind of story would you write?"

"I was thinking about writing about the life of a well-mannered girl who always listens to her parents and never gets into trouble. She always has to bail her brother and sister out of trouble."

Mike laughed and said, "Oh, I thought you'd write a story about yourself."

Cat smiled.

After they finished their meal, they got back into their vehicles and headed for home. During the ride home, Cat pulled the second-place ribbon out of her pocket and looked at it. Her thoughts drifted to Billy's funeral. It still bothered her that he had been killed and that if he hadn't been called back, she would not have had the chance to compete. She wished there was something she could do. As she put the ribbon back into her pocket, a thought came to her. It wouldn't be much, but she would place the ribbon in the coffin with Billy. Her only regret was that it wasn't the first-place trophy. It had truly been an eventful summer.

THE END

About the Author

Ronald C. Hilty is a longtime resident of Fort Wayne, Indiana. He spent the majority of his young life working on the farm he grew up on. He left farming to join the US Air Force and upon his discharge returned home and back to farming for a few years. During that time, he married and moved across the road from his family farm. Due to a growing family of his own, he left the family farm and began work at a factory, where he stayed until they closed twenty-one years later. He woke up one morning about ten years ago and thought, "I think I'll try writing a book!" That's exactly what he did! Once completed, he made every effort to find a publisher, but to no avail, and set it aside for a later time. Roughly eight years later, he saw an ad on television that triggered him to try again and was successful. He still resides in Fort Wayne, is divorced, and has three adult children and a grandson he can't get enough of.

CPSIA information can be obtained
at www.ICGtesting.com
Printed in the USA
FSHW010834021020
74301FS